PRAISE FOR BRIAN FREEMAN

"If there is a way to say 'higher' than 'highly recommended,' I wish I knew it. Because this is one of those thrillers that go above and beyond."
—*Suspense Magazine* on *Goodbye to the Dead*

"Deftly plotted . . . a standout."
—*Publishers Weekly* on *Goodbye to the Dead* (Starred Review)

"Freeman skillfully weaves together diverse story lines . . . with twists that build suspense, in this fine, character-driven addition to a strong series."
—*Booklist* on *Goodbye to the Dead* (Starred Review)

"*Goodbye to the Dead* is a superior psychological thriller that adroitly weaves obsession, sex and revenge into a page-turning mystery. At the end there is the Freeman hallmark: a shocker of a plot twist that turns everything that's gone before upside down."
—Open Letters Monthly

"Thriller fiction doesn't get much better than *The Cold Nowhere*."
—Bookreporter

"[*In the Dark* is] Freeman's most ambitious—and accomplished—work to date . . . Powered by darkly poetic atmospherics and deep character development, this harrowing and heartrending novel will leave readers guessing until the very last pages."
—*Publishers Weekly* (Starred Review)

"Brian Freeman is a first-rate storyteller. *Stalked* is scary, fast-paced, and refreshingly well written. The characters are so sharply drawn and interesting, we can't wait to meet the next one in the story."

—Nelson DeMille, #1 *New York Times* bestselling author

THE
NIGHT
BIRD

ALSO BY BRIAN FREEMAN

The Jonathan Stride Series

Immoral

Stripped

Stalked

In the Dark

The Burying Place

Spitting Devil (e-short story)

Turn to Stone (e-novella)

The Cold Nowhere

Goodbye to the Dead

The Cab Bolton Series

The Bone House

Season of Fear

Stand-Alone Novels

Spilled Blood

The Agency (as Ally O'Brien)

West 57 (as B.N. Freeman)

THE
NIGHT
BIRD

BRIAN
FREEMAN

THOMAS & MERCER

Published by Thomas & Mercer, Seattle

www.apub.com

Amazon, the Amazon logo, and Thomas & Mercer are trademarks of Amazon.com, Inc., or its affiliates.

ISBN-13: 9781503943568 (hardcover)
ISBN-10: 1503943569 (hardcover)

ISBN-13: 9781503941892 (paperback)
ISBN-10: 1503941892 (paperback)

Cover design by Rex Bonomelli

Printed in the United States of America

First edition

For Marcia
and in loving memory of
Thomas Freeman

A thousand fantasies
Begin to throng into my memory.

—John Milton

When I was younger I could remember anything,
whether it happened or not;
but I am getting old, and soon I shall remember
only the latter.

—Mark Twain

1

Like a shiny Christmas display, red brake lights flashed to life across the five westbound lanes of the San Francisco–Oakland Bay Bridge. Two hundred feet above the frigid waters off Yerba Buena Island, the car horns, bangs, and skids of a chain-reaction fender bender transformed the traffic into a parking lot. Hundreds of gridlock-weary Bay Area travelers knew they were going nowhere fast. They turned off their engines, grabbed their smartphones, and settled in to wait.

Trapped in the rightmost lane, Lucy Hagen began to panic. Her fists squeezed closed; her nails dug into her palms. "Oh, damn, damn, damn," she murmured, shutting her eyes. "Not up here."

Her friend Brynn, who was behind the wheel of the top-down Camaro convertible, patted Lucy's leg. "Hey, it'll be okay."

But it was not okay.

Lucy hated bridges. If she could have never driven across another bridge in her life, she would have happily done so, but Lucy lived in San Francisco. There was water, water everywhere, and going anywhere meant crossing a bridge. The Richmond Bridge. The Bay Bridge. The San Mateo Bridge. The Dumbarton Bridge. The Golden Gate Bridge. She took BART under the bay whenever she could, but too often, she had no choice but to venture across the tall spans to get where she was going. Bridges were her enemy.

"Can you get us out of this lane?" Lucy asked Brynn.

"And go where?" Brynn sighed.

They were boxed in. The parked cars around them filled every space. Brynn switched off the motor of the Camaro, but she left the radio playing. Steely Dan sang "Do It Again," and Brynn tapped her thumbs on the wheel with the beat of the music. She was utterly unaffected by their situation, but Lucy was living her worst nightmare—frozen on the bridge, inches away from the railing and the terrifying drop to the water.

It was night. Eleven o'clock. Tendrils of fog laced through the darkness like ghosts spiriting between the bridge cables. The giant suspender climbed above the car, outlined by white lights, with rows of taller and taller cables leaning toward the main tower. A cold, ferocious wind whirled and sang. Lucy sensed the almost-imperceptible sway of the bridge deck under the car, reminding her that she was trapped in midair. Clammy sweat bloomed on her skin. Involuntarily, her body twitched, as if she'd been shocked by electricity.

"Maintenance people have to *walk* up there to replace the lights," Brynn said, pointing at the sharp slope of the suspension cable. "Now that's freaky. Think about having a job like that."

"Shut up, Brynn."

Her friend giggled. "I guess this would be a bad time for the Big One to hit."

"I said, shut up. Please. It's not funny."

"I'm sorry," Brynn told her, reaching over to squeeze Lucy's hand. "This is really bad for you, huh?"

"Awful."

"You should talk to my shrink."

"That won't help. Nothing helps."

"Hey, she's pretty good. She helped me with my thing. What do you think is going to happen, anyway? Do you think the bridge is going to fall down or something?"

"No," Lucy said.

"Then what?"

"Brynn, I don't want to talk about this, okay?"

Her friend held up her hands in surrender. "Okay. Just relax. We'll get out of here soon. I'll turn up the music."

Brynn did. The radio blared an Elton John song. "Bennie and the Jets." Elton thumped through the speakers, and the music fought with the roar of the wind.

Lucy knew that bridges didn't bother most people. Here they were, all of them imprisoned on a strip of steel and concrete high above the bay, and nobody else cared. She looked around at the other cars. A man in a Lexus beside them barked into a cell phone; he was simply annoyed by the delay. Several people texted; she saw thumbs flying. A DVD played on the dashboard screen in a minivan. She recognized the movie. *Inside Out.*

It was just one more California traffic jam.

Then Lucy's mouth went dry. With her head craned to look behind her, she spotted a black Cutlass with smoked windows three lanes over and one car length behind them. The Cutlass was dented and dirty. She only noticed it because at the moment she looked, the passenger window rolled halfway down. The window was dark, the night was dark, and the car was dark. Even so, for a single moment, she saw a face behind the glass, deep inside the car.

Not a face. A mask.

The mask was bone white, with a grotesquely oversized smile, framed by cherry-red lips. The rounded eyeholes were chambered, like the eyes of a fly. The chin made a sharp V, and the white forehead had deep, exaggerated bones that stretched halfway up the skullcap. Ropes of black hair—a wig—hung down on both sides of the mask. It grinned at her.

"Holy shit!" Lucy exclaimed.

Brynn glanced at her. "What is it?"

"That guy! Look!"

Brynn peered over her shoulder. "I don't see anything."

The window of the Cutlass was closed now. They couldn't see inside. Lucy wondered if it had ever been open. Maybe she was hallucinating. The terror of the bridge was making her imagine things that weren't there.

"What did you see?" Brynn asked.

"Nothing. I'm sorry."

"You're still really scared?"

"Yes."

"Look, all you have to do is sit and wait," Brynn said. "Nothing's going to happen."

"I know, but I'm afraid I'm going to freak out."

"Close your eyes. Breathe slowly in and out. My shrink said it was called self-soothing."

Lucy shut her eyes and tried to measure out her deep breathing. In through the nose, out through the mouth. Twice, three times. It helped at first, but then a gust of wind rocked Brynn's Camaro, and Lucy's eyes shot open. She screamed and wrapped her arms around herself. Beside her, Brynn simply savored the fresh air blowing off the water. Even in her lace shift, which bared her legs up to her thighs, Brynn didn't look cold. Her expression was dreamy.

Lucy envied Brynn because her friend was so damn put together. They both worked counter jobs at Macy's. They shared a Haight-Fillmore studio apartment. If you weren't a lawyer or banker or tech guru and you wanted to live in the city, you had to cram bodies into tiny rooms. Brynn was one of those tall blondes who sucked up all the male energy wherever she went. Great hair, great body, long legs, electric smile. That was annoying, but hanging with Brynn meant getting into the best clubs and the best parties. Lucy liked her. Brynn was pretty, but she wasn't a mean girl who rubbed her advantages in your face.

You couldn't be around Brynn and not feel her happiness. She had the magic touch. Looks. Sexy new boyfriend. Parents with money for when times got tight. Lucy wished she could trade places with her. Even for a day, it would be nice to know what it felt like to be inside her head and inside her body. To be confident and unafraid. Lucy felt anxious in the city every day.

"Come on, Lucy, let's dance it up," Brynn told her.

As Elton John crooned the chorus, Brynn sang about Buh-Buh-Buh Bennie and the Jets in an off-key voice. She swayed; she drummed on the dashboard. She shook her loose blond hair. Lucy gave in and sang, too. Nearby, other drivers saluted them with a toot of their horns. For a moment, Lucy forgot about the bridge and felt a timid smile creep onto her face. Seeing it, Brynn beamed at her and flashed a thumbs-up.

"That's it! Show 'em, girlfriend!"

Lucy laughed. She danced faster and sang louder. Her chestnut hair flew.

"You're crazy!" Lucy shouted at Brynn, but crazy was what she needed right now. Brynn was weird, wonderful, and keen, just like Bennie.

When the song finally ended, Lucy flopped her head onto the seat rest. She stared at the hypnotic lights over their heads as another, quieter song began on the radio, something by Carole King. She listened to the wind and felt the sway. For the first time, being trapped up here felt beautiful and not scary at all.

"Thanks," she said. "That helped."

When her friend didn't answer, Lucy looked over at her. "Brynn?"

Brynn had both hands clamped like a vise around the wheel. Her knuckles were white. Beads of sweat formed like raindrops on her forehead, below the silk of her blond hair. Her mouth hung slack and open. Her blue eyes were huge. Something was wrong.

"Brynn, if this is a joke, it's not funny," Lucy said. "Cut it out."

A scream bubbled up from Brynn's chest between desperate breaths. She peeled her fingers off the wheel. Her hands shook like palm leaves. She clawed with long nails at her forearms, making scarlet streaks, and then she ripped at the skin of her face, scratching until blood smeared across her mouth and spattered her golden hair.

"Brynn!" Lucy cried.

The people in the other cars noticed what was happening. Some called out. Lucy heard car doors opening.

Brynn lurched up in the front seat of the convertible. Wind swirled her hair and tore at her purple dress. She scrambled over the windshield and rolled clumsily down the hood of the Camaro to the bridge deck. Other drivers were out of their cars now. Brynn kept screaming. She covered her face as if birds were picking at her eyes.

"Brynn, what *is* it?" Lucy shouted at her. "What's wrong? Brynn, it's me, it's okay."

Lucy unbuckled her seat belt. She pushed open the door, but when she tried to climb outside, she saw the blackness of the water beyond the railing. Her legs became lead. Spasms rippled through her, knocking her knees together. All she could think about was the height. The wind. The water. The fall. She couldn't go out there.

Brynn bolted in her lavender high heels to the railing. No words dribbled from her mouth, only screams. She climbed the concrete barrier and clung with both arms to one of the ascending cables high above the bay. Her skimpy dress hugged her body. The wind threw her back and forth like a toy.

"Brynn! No!"

Lucy slid from the car, but she crumpled to the bridge deck. She couldn't stand up. The sensation of being outside, on the bridge, vulnerable, overwhelmed her. The world spun. The concrete was ice-cold.

She crawled, twitching, and stretched out a hand to Brynn, who wasn't even ten feet away.

"Come here! Come down!"

Brynn climbed away from her in a weird, unsteady crawl, like a crab scuttling through the sand. She wrapped her legs around the cable, and her blood-slippery fingers clung to the steel. She pulled herself two feet above the railing. And then three feet. Four feet.

Lucy curled into a ball, staring at her. "Brynn, what are you doing?"

Brynn took a hand from the cable and slapped at the wind as if mayflies had swarmed around her face. One high heel came off her bare foot and spun away like a maple seed pod. Her foot scraped for traction. The rough wire bit her knees. Her fingers pawed, pulling herself higher inch by inch. She looked down and wailed, because whatever she saw was following her. Climbing after her. She kicked at an invisible enemy, and her leg dangled and twirled.

"Brynn!"

A man on the bridge deck thrust up his arms toward her, but she was too high for him to reach. He beckoned her. Smiled at her. "Hey, it's okay, honey. Just slide down. I've got you."

Brynn didn't see him or hear him.

She didn't see or hear Lucy shouting her name.

Brynn shut her eyes. Her bloody hand slipped from the wire. So did her legs. With nothing to hold her, she was free, flailing and falling. The roar of the air swallowed her screams. Lucy buried her face in her palms as Brynn dropped past her and disappeared to the bay far below.

2

Frost Easton of the San Francisco Police leaned between the cables of the Bay Bridge and stared down. In the water, Coast Guard searchlights crisscrossed the waves. They'd been there for an hour, but the body of Brynn Lansing remained hidden among the frothy whitecaps. Eventually, he knew, she would make landfall. Jumpers from the Golden Gate sometimes washed into the Pacific and were never found, but the more inland Bay Bridge usually returned its victims.

He knew hydrologists at the state college who analyzed the bay currents and made wagers on when and where the bodies would turn up. It was never smart to bet against them.

Frost got up on the tips of his shoes. The wind buffeted his body, making him unsteady. His short, slicked-back hair, which was a messy mix of gold and dark brown, loosened into tufts on his high forehead. He frowned as he thought about the young woman, falling, and the black water sucking her in. Five seconds was all it took to end a life.

"Could you not do that?"

He looked down at the voice below him. His lean, tall body was still halfway over the bay. The witness to the incident sat in Brynn

Lansing's Camaro convertible. She stared straight ahead, her body rigid with fear.

"What?" Frost asked.

"Could you please not do that? Lean over the edge like that? It makes me want to throw up."

Frost climbed down to the bridge deck. He strolled to the passenger door of the Camaro ten feet away. His dark blazer flapped like a cape in the wind, and his tie blew over his shoulder. He knelt beside the door and balanced his bearded chin on his hands. The girl had a sweet face behind her tears and terror.

"I'm sorry," he said. "I know this must be terrible for you."

"I thought she was teasing me."

"What do you mean?" Frost asked.

"Brynn. I thought she was just making fun of me because I was so afraid to be stuck up here. I was freaking out."

Frost nodded. "What is it that scares you? The height?"

"It's the bridge, actually."

"I've heard of that. Gephyrophobia, isn't that what they call it? Fear of bridges?"

"Yes. You're right." She looked surprised that he knew what it was called.

"I guess everybody has something like that," Frost told her. "With me, it's frogs. Those slimy little things just scare the crap out of me."

He smiled at her. He had a warm, slightly off-balance smile, and his blue eyes were lasers that never left her face. His thick blond-flecked eyebrows matched his trimmed beard. He stared at the girl until her head inched to the right, and she stared back with an empty expression. She was traumatized, like a robot with the power switched off.

"It's Lucy, right?" he asked her.

"Yes."

"Lucy what?"

"Lucy Hagen."

9

"Okay, Lucy, I'm Frost. I'm with the police. And I'm going to get you off this bridge just as soon as I possibly can, but I have to ask you some questions about what happened."

"Okay."

Frost pointed at a black SFPD Chevy Suburban parked on an angle between a police squad car and an ambulance. "Would you mind if we talked in my car? I've got forensics people who need to get evidence in the Camaro, and we can't really do that with you in it, see what I mean?"

Lucy stared at her lap. "Well, I'd love to get out of this car, except for one thing."

"What's that?"

"I can't move," she said.

Frost stood up and rubbed a hand over his beard. "You can't move at all?"

"No. I can turn my head, but my arms and legs don't work."

Frost gestured to one of the uniformed ambulance workers. Lucy shook her head as she saw a paramedic coming closer.

"There's nothing physically wrong with me," she told him. "This has happened before. I'll be fine as soon as I'm off the bridge. Sometimes the fear just overwhelms me, and my body shuts down."

"We'll take you to the hospital and get you checked out," Frost said.

"I don't need to go to the hospital. I just need to get off the bridge."

"Well, unless you start moving soon, you're going to the hospital, Lucy. It's kind of a rule we have. Last time I left a woman paralyzed in the middle of the Bay Bridge, my lieutenant got really pissed at me."

He smiled again. His cheeks and eyes had deep laugh lines. This time, Lucy's mouth twitched upward into a shy smile of her own, and a blush deepened on her face.

"Please just get me out of this car," she said. "I dragged myself back here after Brynn went over the side, and then I couldn't move. It's been an hour. I'm really cold."

"I can carry you if you'd like. Or I could ask one of the EMTs to do it."

"Do whatever you have to do," Lucy said. "As long as I don't have to watch. I can't look over the edge."

Frost opened the passenger door of the Camaro. Lucy Hagen was small, maybe five foot three. Her shoulder-length brunette hair had been mussed into tangles by the wind. She wore a long-sleeve gray shirt untucked over black tights, with calf-high boots. He guessed that she was no more than twenty-five years old. Life was about perspective; to Frost, at thirty-four, twenty-five sounded young. Her skin was creamy, her large brown eyes sunken by darker moons underneath. She had lips that pushed out from her mouth in a permanent pucker, and her lipstick was deep red. Her rounded nose was slightly too large for her face, but she was pretty.

Lucy closed her eyes. Frost leaned down to her waist and lifted her effortlessly. She was as limp as a sack of Chinatown rice. He hoisted her so that her torso nudged over his shoulder and carried her the short distance to his Suburban. With one hand, he opened the passenger door, and then he gently draped her inside. When he went around to the other side of the truck and got behind the wheel, her big eyes were open, and she was staring at him.

"Thank you."

"No problem," Frost said. He turned on the engine. Heat surged from the vents. "How are you feeling?"

"It's better inside. The convertible makes the bridge thing worse."

"That makes sense." He tugged the knot to tighten his tie and smoothed his hair down as much as he could. It was still messy as it swept back high on his forehead, but messy worked for him. His hair was buzzed short on the sides of his head, emphasizing his small ears. "Can you move yet?"

"No, but I'm sure the feeling will come back soon."

"Okay. Can you tell me what happened out there?"

"Brynn went nuts," Lucy said. "That's what happened."

"Nuts how?"

"We were stuck in traffic. I was scared because of the bridge, but Brynn was fine. Joking, singing. Totally normal. And then she turned psycho. It came out of nowhere. She was screaming, going crazy, clawing at herself. She tried to climb the bridge, like she was being chased, and she fell. It was horrible."

"Did she fall or did she jump?"

"I think she fell. I mean, she wasn't *trying* to kill herself. This was something else, but I don't know what it was."

"Did she say anything while this was going on?"

"No, she never said a word. She just screamed."

"Where were the two of you coming from?" Frost asked.

"A party in Alameda."

"Was Brynn drinking at the party? Did she take any drugs?"

Lucy shook her head firmly. "No drugs. That wasn't her thing. Brynn had a martini at the party, but that was it."

"Could someone have slipped something into her drink?"

"I don't know. Maybe. There are freak jobs who will do anything. But she seemed fine as we were driving home."

Frost didn't say anything for a while. He was making connections. "Do you know a woman named Monica Farr? Or do you know if Brynn did?"

"Monica Farr? I don't think so."

He slid his iPhone from his belt clip and swished through a few photos. He showed Lucy a picture of a young redhead. "Do you recognize this woman?"

"No. Who is she?"

Frost didn't answer. "How well did you know Brynn?"

"Pretty well. We've been roommates for a year. We both worked at Macy's."

"Did she seem depressed or unstable? Did you notice any other instances of erratic behavior?"

"Brynn? No way. She's Mary McCheery. Nothing gets her down. If anything, she's been even happier the past few months. She's dating a guy, and I think she felt like he might be the one, you know? Wedding bells. She's been sleeping over at his place a lot. I didn't see her the past couple of nights."

"What's the boyfriend's name?" Frost asked.

"Gabriel Tejada. He's an attorney in Sausalito."

"How'd they meet?"

"He was in Macy's, buying perfume for his girlfriend before Christmas. She became an ex-girlfriend pretty fast after Gabe met Brynn."

"Okay."

Frost paused as he heard a gravelly noise from the far back of the truck. He looked over his shoulder as a noxious cloud wafted into the front seat, making him cover his nose. "Aw, c'mon, Shack, really? Now?"

Lucy's face scrunched in confusion. Then she screamed as a tiny tuxedo cat flew over the seat and landed on the dashboard of the SUV. It had huge, curious dark eyes, a pink nose, and a black chin set against white cheeks and chest. Its stubby ears ended in white wingtips. The cat cocked its head, snaked a short tail around its paws, and analyzed her face like a psychiatrist.

"Sorry," Frost told her. "He always waits to hit the litter box until I have someone in the car."

"Your cat?"

"Yeah, sort of. Long story. This is Shack."

"Shaq? Like the basketball player?"

"No, Shack as in Ernest Shackleton. The Antarctic explorer."

"Oh," Lucy said.

"I'm sort of a history buff. Sorry, are you allergic?"

"No."

Shack took that as an invitation. He padded from the dashboard onto Lucy's lap, kneaded her thigh briefly, and stretched across her legs, exposing a black stomach with a single white stripe that looked like an Oreo cookie. The cat was barely a foot from nose to tail. Lucy lifted a hand and stroked under Shack's chin, and Frost noted the movement in her arm.

"Looks like you're not paralyzed anymore," he pointed out.

"Oh!" Lucy exclaimed. She wiggled her fingers. "You're right. I told you, it's always temporary."

"Do you want me to put Shack in the back? I have a carrier for him."

"No, he's fine," Lucy said. "Is he like a police cat? I didn't know they had such things."

"No, he's just a cat cat. He likes to ride along with me sometimes."

"I thought cats hated cars."

"Not Shack. He goes everywhere. He's got the heart of an explorer. Hence the name."

"I think that's sweet," Lucy told him. "I mean, that you take him with you."

"Yeah, homicide inspectors. We're as sweet as they come."

Lucy's eyebrows arched. "Homicide?"

"That's my department. We look at any death that's considered suspicious. Based on what you're telling me, Brynn's behavior is way out of character for her, and I'd like to know what caused it."

"Have you seen anything like this before?" Lucy asked.

Frost hesitated. "Extreme behavior usually makes me think about PCP or certain synthetics. What you're describing sounds like a severe hallucinogenic reaction."

"I'm telling you, Brynn never did drugs," Lucy insisted. "Not even a joint. She was a vegan. 'My body is a temple.' That kind of crap."

"Did she smoke?"

"No."

"And did you notice anything unusual prior to her breakdown?" Frost asked. "Did anything strange happen while you were stuck on the bridge?"

"No, nothing at all." Lucy chewed her lower lip, and her eyebrows squeezed together, making crinkled lines on her forehead. She rubbed Shack's stomach, and the cat stretched luxuriously with its front and back paws. Shack had very clear likes and dislikes among people, and he'd obviously decided that he liked Lucy Hagen.

"Nothing?" Frost asked, watching her face. "Are you sure?"

Lucy glanced at the other cars around them. A trickle of vehicles pushed westward through the one open lane the police had carved out for traffic. "There *was* the mask thing. That was odd."

"The mask thing?"

"There was a car stuck on the bridge with us, and the driver was wearing a creepy mask. At least I thought he was. His window opened and closed so fast that maybe I just imagined it. Brynn didn't see anything."

"What kind of mask was it?" Frost asked.

"Scary. Bone white. Big, weird, exaggerated smile, red lips. Fly eyes. The hair was fake, too."

"It doesn't sound like you imagined it. Do you remember the car?"

"I want to say it was a Cutlass, but I'm not sure. It had smoked windows. Black, I think."

"Could the car have been following you after you left the party?"

"I guess. I never looked back, so I don't know. It's not like the guy did or said anything while we were stuck on the bridge. He just opened the window and stared at me."

"You're sure it was a man?" Frost asked.

"I assume so, but I guess I don't really know for sure."

"Did this person get out on the bridge deck when Brynn began behaving strangely?"

Lucy shrugged. "If he did, he didn't have the mask on. I was too freaked out to notice who came out of which cars. By the time I even thought about it again, the car was gone."

"Okay."

"Do you think it means anything?" Lucy asked.

"I don't know. It's strange, but the whole thing is strange." Frost added, "You said you've never heard of a woman named Monica Farr. Are you sure about that?"

"Pretty sure. The name doesn't sound familiar."

"Have you or Brynn ever been to the San Francisco Film Centre at the Presidio?"

"No, I've never been there. I don't think Brynn has, either, at least not since I've known her. Why are you asking me these questions? What does this have to do with Brynn?" When Frost didn't answer, Lucy went on: "You know I'm just going to Google this woman when I get home."

Frost knew that was true. There were no secrets anymore.

"Okay, the fact is, Brynn's not the first person to go crazy like this," he told her. "Two months ago, a woman named Monica Farr had a similar breakdown during a wedding reception at the Film Centre. She died, too."

3

"Come on, Shack," Frost said.

He scooped a hand under the small cat's belly and tramped up the steps of the Russian Hill house where he and Shack lived. It was a two-story brown stucco home on a high dead-end spur of Green Street. Inside, it had a multi-million-dollar view of the bay. The furnishings were dark and baroque, as if the house had been decorated by an eighty-year-old woman with European tastes. Which it had.

Frost blinked with exhaustion. It was four in the morning. He didn't bother turning on a light, because the city lights through the bay window allowed him to see. He was hungry; he hadn't eaten anything since a hot dog near the Moscone Center eighteen hours earlier. When he'd left in the morning, the refrigerator had been empty, but he made his way to the kitchen and opened the fridge door anyway. He grinned, seeing four small silver trays topped with aluminum foil.

Care package.

His brother, Duane, who was five years older, was a chef. Nine months ago, Duane had opened a food truck that could usually be found at lunch or dinner in the city's SoMa district south of Market Street. Duane practically lived in his truck, but two or three times a week, he found time to park leftovers in Frost's fridge. His brother knew that, left to his own devices, Frost would subsist on Pop-Tarts and Kraft mac and cheese.

Frost peeled back the foil and found Korean kimchi, bulgogi, and two mandu dumplings. He grabbed a fork and took the meal to the massive dining room table in the next room and ate it cold. Shack hopped up on the table and rubbed against his arm until Frost gave him the chance to lick some of the bulgogi sauce from his fork.

Outside, the overnight lights of the city melted down the hill into the blackness of the bay. He'd lived in San Francisco his whole life. He'd only set foot outside California twice, and both times, he couldn't wait to get home. When you lived in paradise, going anywhere else seemed anticlimactic. It was still hard to believe that his parents had left the state for the heat of Arizona, but he knew that their move was about other things, not the city itself.

The dining room table, which sat ten, doubled as his home office. It was covered in paperwork. He had photos there, too. Family pictures. His parents. Himself and Duane. Their sister, Katie, mugging for the camera at a Giants game. That was the last picture he had of her. It made him remember that Katie's birthday was coming up soon. He and Duane usually celebrated it together.

The girl on the bridge, Lucy, reminded him a little of his sister. Lucy had the same sweet, fresh-faced look. The same single-in-the-city attitude. Their voices even sounded alike, enough that if he closed his eyes, he could picture Katie in his head. That wasn't easy to do anymore.

His MacBook Pro was open, and he booted it up as he finished his dinner. The screen glowed white in the semidarkness. He returned to the fridge and grabbed a bottle of Sierra Nevada Pale Ale and drank it as his index finger swirled the touch pad and called up the video file he wanted.

He'd seen the seven-minute video dozens of times. He'd advanced it frame by frame. It made no more sense to him now than it did the first time. Frost turned up the volume.

"Hey, Mike and Evelyn! Can you believe you're really *married?*"

The iPhone video showed an uncomfortable arm's-length close-up of a plus-sized couple with their faces smooshed together as they filmed themselves. Their cheeks were flushed from champagne. He could see up their noses and spot salad between their teeth. In the background, a DJ played a Blake Shelton bro-country stomper. Frost heard the clatter of crystal and silverware and the burble of other guests talking and laughing. He'd watched the video so many times that he'd been able to piece together most of the conversations.

As if someone in the room might have said something to explain what was about to happen.

He knew the names of the couple with the camera, because he'd interviewed them. They were Jeff and Sandy Barclay. Jeff was the groom's cousin. Neither of them knew the guest named Monica Farr. She wasn't connected to the happy couple at all; she was the last-minute date of one of the groomsmen. They'd met at a dry cleaner two weeks before the wedding, when Monica was dropping off and he was picking up. The groomsman had broken up with his long-time girlfriend the previous day. It was pure chance that he asked Monica out. That was the only reason that Monica Farr attended the wedding and reception of Michael Sloan and Evelyn Archer-Sloan. She didn't know anyone there.

"Great party, guys!" Jeff Barclay shouted into the camera.

"Love the quinoa salad!" his wife, Sandy, called.

Frost chuckled to himself. What San Francisco event would be complete without quinoa? And organic kale, of course.

"Next stop, honeymoon!" Jeff bellowed. "Aruba, mama! Sex on the beach, am I right?"

"Jeff, shhh!" his wife hissed.

"Hey, come on, it's their honeymoon. Remember ours? I didn't think that bed in Paris was going to hold up!"

"*Shhh!*" Sandy said again, but she turned and kissed her husband on the lips, and the camera bounced, losing them from the frame. When they appeared again, both of them were rumpled and smiling. Frost could hear the music changing behind them. Blake was done. The DJ went to a mellow '70s pop song. People shouted for Mike and Evelyn to take the floor, and a cheer went up from the guests as they did.

"Love you guys!" Jeff said.

"Hey, they're dancing! Quick, quick, turn the camera around."

Jeff Barclay fumbled with his iPhone. The video went in and out of focus, and Frost saw a blur of Jeff's black shoes. When the camera came up again, the picture jittered as Jeff tried and failed to hold it steady. Frost saw the Palm Room of the San Francisco Film Centre. Strings of orchids threaded around the white columns. Round tables dotted the glistening hardwood floor. Guests lingered over dessert and wine, and some, in suits and dresses, bobbed on the dance floor. He saw Michael Sloan in a gray tuxedo and, in his arms, Evelyn Archer-Sloan in an off-the-shoulder white wedding dress. They weren't great dancers, but they swayed with the beat, beaming and leaning into each other. This was their big day.

Jeff Barclay zoomed in on the couple.

Frost's mouth twitched. He knew what came next.

Off camera, he heard a woman scream. There were so many kinds of screams. Tittering, yelling, cheering, even laughing screams. This was a scream Frost had never heard before—a scream from inside a black hole, a scream where death was preferable to life. He watched Michael and Evelyn separate on the dance floor and look toward the source of the cry.

He could read Evelyn's lips: "Who's that?"

He heard Sandy Barclay: "Oh my God, what's going on?"

The screaming rose like the wail of a banshee, but the music warbled on, gentle and unaffected. The DJ was too shocked to switch off the sound system. Crystal goblets and champagne flutes shattered as guests lurched away in surprise. Chairs tipped over and clattered. The camera swung, bouncing, off-kilter, to a young redhead in a low-cut emerald dress.

Monica Farr.

Frost froze the video and stared at her face. He'd seen other photos of Monica since that night—happy, smiling pictures. Vacations. Graduations. This was something completely different. Even out of focus, caught for a brief moment, her face was as primitive as a trapped animal. Her eyes were wide and wild. According to the groomsman who'd brought her to the party, she'd been completely normal up to that moment. Her breakdown came out of nowhere. In midsentence.

Just like Brynn Lansing.

Frost started the video again. Monica grabbed her purse from the table and dug inside it, and as she did, shouts of terror arose in the ballroom. He saw something dark in her hand, and then he heard:

"Gun!"

"She has a gun!"

People dove. The phone, still filming, fell to the floor, and all Frost saw was the ceiling and track lighting of the ballroom. He heard the soundtrack to the chaos—people stampeding, tables crashing—and then the explosion of a bullet and glass breaking in the bayside windows. He heard a voice wailing louder than everyone else—it was Monica Farr again—and then, horribly, one more gunshot cut off the scream as a bullet went from under Monica's left ear, upward through the bone and brain of her skull, and exited and buried itself in the ceiling.

A body dropped with a sickening thud. He heard whispers. Crying. The devastated aftermath. The whole incident took less than thirty seconds to unfold.

Frost shut down the video and closed his laptop.

He'd talked to everyone in Monica Farr's life since her death two months ago. It made no sense to anyone. He'd found no evidence of drugs. No evidence of depression. No history of strange behavior. Monica had been an unmarried twenty-seven-year-old woman living with her parents in a townhome near Lake Merced, working as a marketing manager for a downtown accounting firm. Her parents didn't even know where or how she'd acquired a gun. The autopsy showed no abnormalities, no tumors pressing on the brain that could have caused hallucinations, no foreign substances in the blood work.

There was absolutely no explanation Frost could find for why Monica Farr had shot herself in the head at a wedding reception.

Just as there seemed to be no reason for Brynn Lansing to fall to her death from the Bay Bridge.

And yet he was convinced there was a connection.

Frost got up from the dining room table. He needed at least a couple of hours of sleep. He whistled a song idly to himself as he walked from the dining room and climbed the steps to the master bedroom. Undressing, he threw his clothes in the walk-in closet. When he turned on the bedroom light, he saw the pale-pink remnants of a bloodstain on the white carpet near the heavy walnut bedroom set. At first, he'd tried to clean it. That hadn't worked. Then, for weeks, he'd walked around it, giving it a wide berth with his bare feet. Now he didn't even care. He crossed the bloodstain like it was part of the decor.

He didn't sleep in the king-sized bed. Instead, he went back downstairs to the living room with one of his pillows and stretched out on the tweed sofa near the bay window. It didn't match the rest of the upscale decor, because it was the only piece of furniture in the house that belonged to him. His face sank into his pillow; his arm draped to the floor. Shack tiptoed up his back and curled up in the crook of his neck. Seconds later, they were both asleep.

4

Water.

Dr. Francesca Stein poured water into a glass and stared through the observation window at a patient alone in the therapy room. Her name was Jillian Clark. She was fourteen years old. She had long nut-brown hair, freckles, and a sweet smile. Her body had the gangly awkwardness of a growing teenager, but she could run like the wind on the soccer field. Jillian got straight As in school. She wanted to be an eye doctor, because her mother was an eye doctor, and Jillian idolized her mother.

Jillian lay on a white chaise in the middle of the therapy room. When Frankie pushed the intercom button, she could hear piano music playing softly inside. Jillian's eyes were open, but she was already under hypnosis. The curved wall in front of her served as a movie screen, playing a slow-motion track of flowers and plants growing. Typically, Frankie used a video of ocean waves to relax her patients—but not for Jillian.

Water was Jillian's problem.

When Frankie first met the girl a month earlier, they'd chatted in Frankie's office, which adjoined the therapy room. They talked about boys. School. Music. The ordinary parts of a teenager's life.

And then, with a glance at Jillian's mother, Frankie poured a glass of water.

The reaction was even worse than she expected.

Jillian gasped for air. A choking noise belched from her open mouth, and redness rose in her face. Her chest seized. The episode continued until Frankie poured the water out in the sink, and once the water was gone, Jillian became her typical young self almost immediately. She laughed and joked about Taylor Swift. She talked about her last vacation with her parents to Disneyland. Neither her mind nor her body showed ill effects of the trauma.

It was the most extreme case of aquaphobia that Frankie had ever seen.

"Three months ago, I took Jillian kayaking in the bay near the San Mateo Bridge," her mother had explained. "We ran into unstable currents, and her kayak flipped. She couldn't right herself. I paddled like crazy to get to her, but it was nearly a minute before I could reach her and get her out of the water. She nearly died. The doctors said there was no physiological damage, but a few days later, I noticed that—well, I noticed that Jillian was starting to smell. And I realized she hadn't showered since that trip to the bay."

"I can't stand to have water touching me," Jillian added. "As soon as I get wet, I'm back there under the bay. The whole thing comes to life for me again. It's not just that I remember it. I'm *there*."

"Since then, it's gotten worse," her mother went on. "The very sight of water can trigger an episode. We've gone to doctors and therapists, and no one has been able to help. We're desperate, Dr. Stein."

Jillian leaned across the desk and took Frankie's hand. Her young eyes had pleaded with her. "I read an article that called you the master of memory. You help people forget bad things, right? Please, can you help me forget what happened in the bay?"

Frankie squeezed the girl's hand. "I'll do everything I can to help you, but this won't be easy, Jillian. You can't change your memory without reliving it. That's how it works. So before you forget anything, what I really need you to do is *remember*."

As Frankie stared at Jillian through the window of the therapy room, she caught a glimpse of her own reflection. It was strange how you could live inside your skin and still see someone you didn't know in the mirror. For months, she'd felt like a stranger in her own life. People told her that was how it was when you lost your father. You became a shell, empty, stranded on the sand.

At least you have your memories, people told her in the sympathy cards they sent. Which, to Frankie, was a cruel joke. She of all people knew that memory was unreliable. Memories played tricks on the brain.

She was nearly forty years old. Her brown hair was short, with a few loose strands dangling past her ears. Her face and nose were long and narrow, with a sharply defined chin. She dressed more like a CEO than a psychiatrist or scientist, in dark pantsuits. She was very thin and tall, and she wore high heels to make herself even taller. Her pencil shape attracted notice. In college and medical school, she'd endured whispers of anorexia. They weren't true. She had skinny genes; her parents were tall and thin, like her. Genetics were funny, though. Her sister, Pam, had an almost identical face, despite being four years younger, but her body had luxurious curves that Frankie envied.

Men's eyes followed Pam, and she welcomed it. Frankie, who was just as pretty, had spent most of her life shutting men down. They looked at her and knew she had little time for anything or anyone outside her brain. Her cool dark eyes cut people down to size. Her husband, Jason, was the only one who'd ever stood up to her, in the lab or the bedroom, but their relationship was more a meeting of minds than a passionate love match. Frankie reserved most of her passion for helping her patients, which didn't make for a happy marriage.

In her therapy practice, she worked with kids like Jillian who'd developed crippling phobias. She worked with soldiers returning from overseas who'd seen the worst horrors of war. She worked with victims of physical and emotional abuse—and sometimes, she worked with the abusers, too. The criminals. The sociopaths. Regardless of who they were, they all had one thing in common.

They were haunted by memories, and they wanted to exorcise their ghosts.

Frankie let herself quietly into the therapy room with Jillian. This place, more than anywhere else, was her home. It was lushly carpeted to reduce extraneous noise, and sound baffles were built into the walls. She kept the temperature at a consistent seventy-two degrees, day or night. Built-in speakers allowed her to communicate from outside the room, depending on the patient—but with kids, like Jillian, she preferred to be seated next to them. The wrap-around floor-to-ceiling screen, almost like an IMAX theater, created a 4K high-definition world in which to shape what the patient's brain saw and remembered.

She customized the visuals on the screen to each person's needs. Jillian watched the video that Frankie had made for her. Flowers sprouted and blossomed. Tree leaves unfurled. What the girl didn't know was that, every few seconds, an isolated image of water appeared and disappeared on the screen too quickly for her eyes to perceive. But her brain saw it. At the very first session, Frankie had seen the girl's hands tightly clasp the arms of the chair as the water images made their way into her mind. Subliminally, her tension grew, but she didn't choke or gasp. The images of water that her brain saw were happy images. Swimmers. Surfers. Laughter on the beach. And then herself—in a pool, at the ocean, on a kayak. Safe.

"Hello, Jillian," Frankie said in a honey tone.

"Hi."

The girl's eyes were immersed in the images on the screen. She was highly susceptible to hypnosis, which was good. With many of her adult patients, Frankie used a sedative to loosen their consciousness and make them open to suggestion. She rarely did so with children.

"How do you feel?"

"Good. Good."

"Are you comfortable?"

"Yes."

"Excellent. It's time to remember now. Are you ready to remember?"

"Sure."

"You know how we do this. You're looking at your memories through your own eyes. You're telling me in detail everything you see and everything you hear. It's as if you're there, and it's happening all over again. But it's not really happening *to* you. You're just an observer. You're detached. Do you understand?"

"Yeah."

"If there's a little detail you don't get right, I'll correct it for you, because I want you to remember *exactly* how it was. And whatever I tell you is the *truth* of what happened. It's important that you remember it that way. Okay?"

"Okay."

They'd repeated this exercise multiple times in each session and in multiple sessions over the past month. With each session, Frankie slowly changed the details of what Jillian remembered from her day at the bay. People thought memories were fixed, but nothing could be further from the truth. Every time you pulled a memory off the shelf and put it back, you changed it. Therapists had a name for the process. Reconsolidation. Her husband, Jason, was a neuroscientist who could describe how it worked in terms of proteins synthesized in the brain. What it really meant was that every recalled memory was like soft clay. While it was out there, in your hands, it could be molded and shaped into something new.

"Are you ready?" Frankie asked.

"Yes."

Frankie pushed a button on the remote control, and the video screen dissolved into a new loop. She'd filmed it at the bay herself, near the San Mateo Bridge, from a kayak, using actors. It showed the water and the waves. It showed gloved hands paddling and the sleek craft slicing through the water. The day was perfect, with sun and blue sky. Music played—the same music that had been humming from the overhead speakers. The same music she'd played at every one of Jillian's sessions. Music had power over the mind.

"Tell me about that day," she told the girl.

Jillian did. She went over the details of that trip with her mother, the way she had done dozens of times before. The first time, weeks ago, she'd begun to reexperience the trauma of drowning when Frankie stopped and focused her solely on relaxing images of water. The next week, she'd let Jillian remember the accident, but she'd guided her to believe that her mother had been beside her almost immediately, righting the kayak. There was no danger.

Now she wanted to disassociate Jillian from the accident altogether. That was the last stage of the treatment she'd developed for the girl.

"I feel a current," Jillian said, her voice quavering. "Where did that come from? I'm losing control."

"Don't worry. You've got this."

"No, it's going over. I'm scared. I can't get out. Mom!"

"It's not you, Jillian," Frankie told her. "It's someone else."

"I'm going into the water!"

"No, it's not you. Look closely. There's another kayak near you. Do you see it? *She's* in trouble, but you're safe."

Frankie pointed at the video on the screen, where another kayaker paddled a few feet away. She'd reconstructed a completely different version of the accident for Jillian to see and remember. The new kayak—the fictitious one—wobbled unsteadily in the waves. The San Mateo Bridge loomed beyond them, tall and silver.

"See? It's not you, Jillian. It's someone else. You're fine. You're in control."

"She's going to tip!"

"Yes, but your mother is right there to help her."

"I see her!"

"Yes, she's right there. She's helping. Everything's okay. See, that other girl is already right-side up again."

"Yes."

"Everyone is safe now."

"Everyone's fine," Jillian said.

"You're fine, aren't you, Jillian?"

"I'm fine."

"Okay. Why don't you relax for a few minutes, and then we'll do it again."

"Sure."

Over the next hour, they repeated the entire recollection four times. By the third time, Frankie didn't need to prompt her. Jillian told the story from beginning to end, and in her telling, she didn't topple under the weight of the current. She kept control. Another kayaker fell, just for a moment, and her mother helped her get free.

That was her reality now. That was what she remembered.

The terrible irony for Frankie was that her patients forgot the past, but she kept their secrets in her own head. She could still feel Jillian's panic as she suffocated under the water. Thinking about it made her own chest heavy, and she had to struggle to breathe. The same thing happened with every patient, whether it was a soldier or a child. She heard the vibration of every bomb, saw the torn limbs of every victim, winced under the touch of every abuser. It was as if their memories became hers.

When the session was over, Frankie left Jillian in the therapy room to sleep before being brought out of hypnosis. She kept the music on and the video of flowers playing on the screen. Outside, the girl's mother was waiting. Her face was anxious, and there was a question in her eyes. Frankie smiled.

"I think we're there," she said. "We'll know soon."

Ten minutes later, Frankie used the speakers to awaken the girl and let her come back to full consciousness. Not long after, the door to the therapy room opened, and Jillian walked out on her own. She stretched her arms over her head, gave a bleary yawn, and beamed at her mother.

"Hey," the girl said. "You been waiting long?"

"No, not long at all," her mother replied. The woman got up and hugged her daughter.

"Would you like a drink, Jillian?" Frankie asked. "I poured you some water."

Frankie pointed at a glass of water on the bookshelf by the door. She could see Jillian's mother wince and hold her breath. Jillian's eyes shot to the water glass. Her head jerked once. A sharp inhalation swelled her chest, and confusion blew like a fast-moving cloud across her face.

Then she relaxed and grinned. Her freckles danced.

"Wow, yeah, thanks. I'm really thirsty."

Jillian picked up the glass and drank the whole thing.

5

"I can't believe Brynn's gone," Gabriel Tejada murmured, not for the first time.

Frost stood next to the Sausalito attorney at the end of Johnson Street, where the sailboats bobbed in the town's yacht harbor. Beyond the waters of the small inlet, he could see the brown hills of Tiburon. This little stretch of paradise north of the Golden Gate Bridge was where you lived if you had more money than God. Even God couldn't afford the views here.

"I'm very sorry for your loss," Frost told him. He hated saying that. It sounded so trite, but there was nothing else to say.

"Do Brynn's parents know?"

"Yes, I talked to them last night."

There was no worse task in the world than waking up parents in the middle of the night to tell them that their daughter was dead. Frost knew that only too well. Brynn Lansing's mother and father went to pieces, the way parents always did. He had no explanations for them. Nothing that made any sense. One moment, your daughter was fine, and the next moment, she was plummeting from the Bay Bridge.

"I was in love with her," Tejada said. "I hadn't told her that yet, but I was."

Brynn's boyfriend leaned against the wooden railing and stared into the water. Waves slurped against the pier. The mild breeze turned the boat riggings into a constant, clanging music.

Tejada was a big man. Frost wasn't small at five foot eleven, but Tejada dwarfed him by four inches. He wore a three-piece suit, which was unusual in California, even for a lawyer. His copper skin glowed under the bright sun. He had a prominent nose and jet-black brilliantine hair. His build was broad but athletic. He hadn't reacted with tears to the news of Brynn's death, but Frost could see the man's face tighten with grief.

"How long had you known Brynn?" Frost asked.

"About four months. I met her shortly before Christmas. There was an instant chemistry between us. I'd never felt anything like it before. You never know how a relationship will turn out, but I thought we had a future. I simply can't believe that Brynn committed suicide. Not her."

"This doesn't appear to be a straightforward suicide," Frost told him. "This was a psychotic breakdown of some kind."

Tejada shook his head. "That doesn't make any sense. Brynn had a zest for life. I never saw any kind of secret, deep-seated depression. You couldn't find a more level-headed woman."

"When did you last see Brynn?" Frost asked.

Tejada turned around to face the main street of the seaside town, which was crowded with tourists. He shoved his hands in his pants pockets, and his brow creased. "Four days ago. She stayed over."

"Did you talk to her after that?"

"Not for a couple days. She didn't answer her phone or reply to my texts. Actually, I thought she was shutting me out. I'd floated the idea of her moving in with me, and I was worried that she wasn't ready for a step like that. Then she texted me back yesterday and said everything was fine. We were planning to go away for the weekend."

"Did she say that anything unusual was going on in her life? Did she mention any problems?"

"No. Nothing at all."

"Her roommate, Lucy Hagen, said that she and Brynn went to a party in Alameda last night. Do you know anything about that?"

"Yes, I was supposed to be there, too. I had a client emergency. The host was a law-school classmate of mine who's an in-house counsel at Oracle." Tejada noticed Frost's smile and added, "A lawyer's party isn't as stuffy as it sounds, Inspector, when you have that kind of money. I think he flew in Iggy Azalea to perform. This was all young, pretty people. Like Brynn."

Frost didn't want to admit that he had no idea who Iggy Azalea was.

As young as he was, Frost took pride in being unhip. He knew the wild side of San Francisco, but rarely joined the crowd. He was single and had made his peace with staying that way. His brother, Duane, periodically tried to fix him up, and Frost got a lot of offers because he gave off a Justin Timberlake vibe that women found attractive. More often than not, he said no. When he went on dates, they typically didn't lead to relationships. It wasn't that he was uninterested. He simply enjoyed his solitude. If he had a free evening, he usually spent it reading history books in a hole-in-the-wall Italian restaurant two blocks down from the Russian Hill house where he lived. The owner let him bring Shack in a carrier.

"Was Brynn uncomfortable going to the party without you?" Frost asked.

"Brynn was never uncomfortable. She fit in everywhere. The one who was probably uncomfortable at the party was Lucy. She's sort of a fragile flower. If there was anyone who would go nuts and have some kind of breakdown, I would have put money on her, not Brynn."

"Your lawyer friend, does he throw parties where drugs are available?"

Tejada shrugged. "Pot? Maybe. Anything harder? Doubtful. And Brynn had no time for drugs of any kind. It wasn't her scene."

"That's what Lucy said, too. And Brynn's parents."

"Well, they're right," Tejada told him. "I can't explain what happened to her, but you can rule out drugs."

Frost wasn't so sure. People were good at keeping secrets from those close to them, whether it was about affairs, alcohol, or addictions.

"There was a similar incident a couple months ago," Frost told Tejada. "A woman had a psychotic episode at a wedding reception. She shot herself. Like Brynn, the behavior seemed to come out of nowhere. I've been trying to find some overlap in their lives, to see if they had a connection that might explain what happened to both of them. So far, I've come up empty."

Tejada nodded. "I remember that incident from the news. Brynn and I talked about it."

"What did she say?"

"Just that it was scary and bizarre. We both assumed what you did, that it must be drugs."

"And did she mention anything that might suggest a connection between the two of them?"

"I'm sorry. No."

"The thing is, Mr. Tejada, this behavior usually has an explanation, but friends and family often miss the clues. Then they look back and remember little things that seem important in the wake of what happened. Was there anything like that with Brynn?"

Tejada was silent for a long time. He crossed his arms and stared at his shoes. Lawyers didn't give flip answers. Frost knew that because he had a law degree himself. He'd also worked with a lot of lawyers in his years with the police, and if there was one thing he liked about them (among the many things he didn't), it was that they never answered a question without thinking about it.

Finally, Tejada said one word, but it was something that Frost didn't expect.

"Cats," he said.

Frost cocked his head. "What?"

"Do you like cats, Inspector?"

"I do, in fact," Frost replied.

"So do I. I have four cats."

"Okay," Frost said, not understanding.

"Brynn was scared to death of cats," Tejada went on. "When I first met her, she couldn't spend five minutes in my condo. She *hated* cats, couldn't stand being around them. People who don't grow up around cats often don't understand them, but this was a deeper phobia with Brynn. When I asked her about it, she told me that she'd had a bad experience with a feral cat as a teenager. She was bitten multiple times. She had to undergo a painful round of rabies shots."

"I don't understand the connection," Frost said.

"You wanted clues, Inspector. You wanted something unusual. This is the only unusual thing I can think of."

"That Brynn was scared of cats?"

Tejada shook his head. "No, here's the strange thing. The two of us typically met at restaurants, not at my place, because of my cats. If we wanted to be together overnight, I'd get us a hotel room. And then, last month, she showed up at my place on a Saturday afternoon. I went to open some wine for us, and when I came back, I found her sprawled on the living room floor, playing with my cats and letting them walk all over her. Since that time, she hasn't had any issues with my cats at all."

"Did you ask her about it?"

"Of course. She said she didn't want my cats to be a problem between us, so she'd been seeing a psychiatrist to help with her fears."

"Apparently, it worked," Frost said.

"Yes, I guess it did. I was glad she felt strongly enough about our relationship to do something like that. But there was one peculiar thing.

Last week, I made some kind of joking reference to the time when the feral cat had bitten her. She seemed genuinely puzzled—she said nothing like that had ever happened to her. I began rattling off the details of the story, but she got upset and said I was wrong and told me to drop it."

"Did you?"

Tejada frowned. "Sure, I did. I was glad she'd become a cat lover. But I wasn't wrong, Inspector. The cat attack really happened to her. At first, I assumed she didn't want to think about it anymore, but it was more than that. It was as if the whole episode had been completely erased from her memory."

6

Frankie kept one sympathy card on her desk from the death of her father. She'd filed away all of the others weeks ago. It wasn't even a card from a close friend, because Frankie didn't have many people that she considered friends. The woman who sent it was a colleague from a nonprofit board. Frankie kept the card because it was a reminder of how wrong people could be.

Inside, the woman had written

My father was the greatest hero in my life.
I know what you're going through.

If only that were true. People assumed that when you lost a parent, you felt nothing but pure grief. They didn't account for complex relationships. And the relationship between Marvin Stein and his daughters was nothing if not complex.

She kept a photo of her father on her desk. When she picked it up, she could hear his cold voice in her head, passionless and demanding. The photo showed him in his physics lab at UC Berkeley, in his white lab coat. Like her, he was tall and thin. He had wiry gray hair and a neat mustache. He didn't smile, and his eyes were impatient. Her father never liked to bother with emotional frills like photographs. When Frankie took the picture with her phone, he'd said, "Get on with it, get on with it."

Her mother had died of cancer when Frankie was five, just a year after her sister, Pam, was born. Since then, their family had been just the three of them. Marvin Stein, physicist, was not meant to be a single father. He dealt with numbers, theories, and formulas, not children. And definitely not girls.

It was hard enough when they were young, but it got worse during high school and college. Their father demanded perfection. Anything but straight As and top test scores was a failure. Because he was a success himself, he pushed his daughters to do more and achieve more. Nothing was ever good enough. Frankie responded by setting crazy expectations for herself that might win his praise. Pam responded by defying him altogether and throwing her failures in his face.

And now he was gone. More than three months later, he still haunted her.

"Are you thinking about Marvin again?" Jason asked.

Her husband stood in the doorway of her office. He was dressed in running clothes, and his hands were on his hips. Sweat glowed on his narrow face.

"Yes, I keep thinking about that last camping trip," she said, toying with the photograph of her father with her fingertips.

"Dwelling on it won't change what happened," Jason told her.

"Oh, I know."

Jason sat in the comfortable chair in front of her desk. He worked in the headquarters of a large pharmaceutical company a few blocks away on Post Street, but he often went running through the city midway through the afternoon and showed up at her office while she was on a break between appointments. Her own office was located on the top floor of a ten-story building on the east side of Union Square, looking out on the palm trees of the park.

"It's also not going to change what a son of a bitch Marvin was," Jason added.

Frankie's lips bent into a sad smile. "I know that, too."

"So how do you feel?" He asked it in a clinical way. They were both scientists. Sometimes it was hard to remember they were husband and wife, too. She expected him to take out a yellow pad and start taking notes while they talked.

"I feel off," she said.

"Can you be more specific?"

"Not really. Something's not right with me, Jason, but I don't know what it is."

"I think it's called grief."

He was right, but that didn't make her feel better. Another husband might have come out of his chair and hugged her, but that wasn't Jason, and that wasn't the kind of relationship they had. They weren't touchy-feely.

She'd met him seven years ago at a conference in Barcelona. He was British. They were both in their early thirties. She'd noticed when she met him that he was handsome, although their interactions were purely professional in the beginning. He had an athletic build and close-cropped black hair. His dark eyes missed nothing, and he had an expressive mouth that could shift from humor to disdain with a twitch of his lips. His face was full of sharp angles, and so was his personality. She liked that. She hated men who tried to woo her.

They'd stayed in touch after the conference because they both specialized in memory. He worked on the neurological side, focused on brain chemistry. She worked on the therapeutic side. Nine months later, he took a research position with a pharmaceutical company in San Francisco, and their meetings evolved slowly from professional to personal. A year after that, they married, to the amusement of her sister, Pam, who'd assumed that Frankie would never leave her clinical office long enough to meet a man.

She'd found a husband who was a carbon copy of herself. Smart. Demanding. Unemotional. Or maybe—she occasionally whispered to herself—she'd done what so many other women did and married her father.

"After he died, you told me you felt some closure with him," Jason reminded her.

"I know. I still do."

"Do you remember why?"

Frankie did. The camping trip snapped like a photograph into her mind. It was something that she, Pam, and their father had done annually since they were children. On New Year's Eve, they would travel to a state park around Northern California and spend two nights there. They'd stayed as close as Angel Island in the bay and traveled as far afield as Redwood National Park north of Eureka. It was a family tradition, but their father had a way of turning the outings into intellectual exercises. He selected a discussion theme. He assigned reading and quizzed them like a professor. The topics had ranged over the years from politics to science to economics. Minimum-wage policy. Extraplanetary life. Addiction. Alaskan glaciers.

This year's topic had been a strange departure. It was *risk*. Which turned out to be a tragically ironic subject in the wake of what happened to him.

"He was different with me that last evening," Frankie said. "Maybe it's because it was just the two of us this year. He relaxed. We talked about Mom. Before we went to sleep, he told me he was proud of me. I'd been waiting my whole life to hear something like that from him."

"So you got what you wanted," Jason said.

Frankie stared out her office window. She could see the crowds in Union Square ten stories below her. "Yes, he could have told me he loved me, and it wouldn't have meant as much as him being proud of me."

He heard her hesitation. "So what's wrong?"

"I don't know. I just—I don't know."

"It hasn't even been four months, Frankie. That's not long when you lose a parent. Don't rush yourself."

"You're right." Frankie shook her head and added, "Pam missed out."

"If she'd been there, it wouldn't have been the same," Jason reminded her. "Marvin treated her differently."

"I know."

"Maybe you got the closure you needed because it was just the two of you," he pointed out.

"I've thought about that, but it makes me feel guilty."

"You had no way of knowing what was going to happen."

"No."

On New Year's Day, her father had awakened early, at sunrise, which was typical. He made coffee and took a hike along the bluff trails of Point Reyes. He told Frankie to stay behind, which was a surprise. Normally, he made her and Pam get up and join him on his early walks. It didn't matter how late they'd been up the night before. He hiked north of Arch Rock where the cliffs dropped sharply to the rocks and beach. It had rained overnight. The earth of the headlands was soft and yielding.

Hours later, when he still hadn't returned, Frankie alerted the rangers. They found Marvin Stein's body at the base of the cliff.

Jason checked his watch. "I have to get back to work. Are you and Pam going to Zingari tonight?"

"Probably. Do you want us to wait for you for dinner?"

"No, I might be late."

"Okay."

Her husband got up, and his sharp eyes examined her face. "Are you still feeling off?"

"Yes, I don't know exactly what it is." She stared out the window again, and without looking at Jason, she said, "Do you think that he—?"

Jason waited, but Frankie didn't go on. He answered her question without her asking it, because she couldn't form the words.

"No, I don't think that Marvin killed himself," Jason said. "He's not the kind of man who would take his own life. It was an accident. The cliffs are dangerous. He fell."

7

Frost heard Lucy Hagen's footsteps inside as she hurried to answer the door at the apartment she shared with Brynn Lansing.

"Oh, hi, Frost," she said, her face flushing happily when she saw him. Then she corrected herself: "Sorry—Inspector."

He returned the greeting with his own friendly, crooked smile. "Frost is fine."

"Come on in."

He crossed the threshold past Lucy and eyed the apartment. There wasn't much to see. It was a studio in an old building on Haight near Octavia. A bay window overlooked the street. Three steps led up to the bathroom, where he could see a toilet and claw-foot tub. The kitchen could have been slipped into the back of his Suburban. He noticed two twin beds, one made, one unmade. Fashion posters were thumbtacked to the walls. The apartment was overstuffed with furniture and clothes.

"It's not exactly Seacliff, is it?" Lucy said. "Although it feels that way when I pay the rent."

"It's an expensive city."

"Yeah, no kidding. I don't know where people get the money. We get some of the super-rich types shopping in the jewelry department at Macy's sometimes. That must be the life, huh?"

"They can have it," Frost said. "I've seen what money does to people. It's not pretty."

"Oh, I don't know. I wouldn't mind giving it a try. Cops do okay, though, huh?"

"The union takes care of us."

"That must be nice. Nobody's signing up to take care of me. Not that you guys don't earn it. You do." Lucy shook her head. "Sorry, I'm babbling like an idiot. I don't know what I'm saying."

"Don't worry about it. How long have you lived here?"

"Two years. I need a new roommate now, or I'll have to move. I called my parents to tell them what happened, and they think I should get out of the city. They don't think it's safe here. I don't know, maybe they're right, but I'd miss the funk if I left San Fran. Know what I mean?"

"I do."

"How about you? Have you been here long?"

"All my life."

"Where do you live?"

Frost hesitated. Normally, he didn't talk about personal things. He didn't share secrets easily. Even so, Lucy was easy to talk to, in her sweet, awkward way. She was an ordinary girl with an ordinary life, which was something that Frost liked. The city's beating heart was all the people who got up and went to work and ate lunch and grabbed takeout for dinner and watched the Giants on TV and went to bed. People like Lucy.

People like Katie.

He also knew that she'd made an effort for him. She was made-up, her hair neat, her lipstick bright. She wore going-out clothes, not stay-at-home clothes. That was no accident. She wanted to make an impression.

"My situation is a little odd," he told her. "I live in a house on Russian Hill."

"Wow," Lucy remarked. "Nice."

"It's not mine. The house belongs to Shack."

Her head cocked. "Wait, isn't Shack—?"

"My cat."

"You rent from your cat?" she asked.

"Yeah. He's a pretty good landlord."

Lucy folded her arms across her chest. She wore a white sweater. Her brown curls brushed the collar. Her capris showed off the thin taper of her legs. "You're teasing me."

"Nope."

"Are you going to tell me the story? Because now I'm intrigued."

Frost grinned and shoved his hands in his pockets. "Yeah, okay. About a year ago, I was called in on a home invasion case. Rich old widow, beautiful house on Russian Hill. She'd been shot dead in her bedroom. The uniforms who responded had a problem because the woman's cat was sitting on her chest, and he wouldn't let anyone near the body. Hissed and batted at them with his claws if they came close. He was protecting her. I grew up with cats, so I figured I'd give it a try. So I just talked to him."

"You talked to the cat?"

"Yeah. I told him I was sorry that the woman was gone, that it was brave of him to want to protect her, but there was nothing he could do anymore. Eventually, he got off her body and walked over to me. He climbed up my leg, curled up on my shoulder, and wouldn't leave. Right then and there, he adopted me."

Lucy blinked back tears. Cat stories did that to women.

"The other cops wanted to take him to animal control, but I said I'd look after him while we did the investigation. Eventually, I talked to the trustee of the woman's estate and asked if there was some family member who wanted to take Shack. He said there was no family. I said, well, would it be okay if I kept the cat? The trustee got very suspicious and asked if I knew anything about the woman's estate, which was weird. I said no, all I wanted was to adopt the cat. After an hour in which I felt like *he* was the cop doing an interrogation, I found out that the estate instructions left the house in a bank trust as long as Shack was alive, and whoever took care of him could live there for a dollar a month. The old woman wanted to make sure that somebody had a hell of an incentive to look after her cat. The funny thing is, I was willing to take him for free."

"That's quite the story."

"Yeah. So here I am, the cop who rents a house from his cat."

"Is all of that true? Or have you figured out that a man with a cat is sort of a chick magnet for girls?"

"Honestly, I *have* found that out, but the story's true. I did have to change his name, though."

"Why?"

"Well, the old woman called him Señor Bubbles. That didn't seem manly enough for either one of us."

Lucy smothered a laugh. "No."

She bit her lip and played with her hair in a flirty way, but she wasn't really good at flirting. He knew she was attracted to him. He liked her, too, but for different reasons. There was something real about her, and he met a lot of people in San Francisco who weren't real at all. It didn't matter what she said; he just liked listening to her talk.

"What about you?" he asked. "What's the Lucy Hagen story?"

She blushed and looked away. "Oh, that's a boring story."

"I doubt it. Everybody's got a story. Did you grow up in the city?"

"No. Out in Modesto. I went to SF State and wanted to stick around after college. Nobody was hiring business majors, so I applied at

Macy's. I had dreams of being Jennifer Aniston on *Friends*, you know? Work my way up into the fashion business? But that's not going to happen. So I don't know. I've thought about going back to get a nursing degree, but I'm already hip-deep in debt. This economy sucks if you don't have a cat who comes with a nice house."

Frost smiled. "You don't want to follow Brynn's example? Hook up with a rich lawyer?"

Lucy rolled her eyes. He guessed that there had been a certain amount of jealousy between Lucy and Brynn.

"Yeah, she always had her eyes on the prize when it came to men. The richer the better. I don't blame her for it. She and Gabe looked good together. I'm sure they would have gotten married and had kids and had a nice house in the hills. Me, I want to figure out who I am before I get involved with somebody."

"That's not a bad plan."

"Yeah, well, I'm not making much progress on either one."

Frost walked over to Brynn's bed. There was an elegant perfume in the sheets. Everything was neatly folded and creased. The nightstand was dusted; the books on the table—all romance novels—were arranged in a perfect stack. Brynn was a precise person, and he thought Lucy was right that Brynn would have fit in well as a Sausalito wife.

He asked Lucy, "When did Brynn last sleep here?"

"Three nights ago, I guess. I told you, she was spending a lot of time at Gabe's. It was nice having the place to myself, actually."

Frost frowned. Something didn't add up. "Gabe said he hadn't seen Brynn in several days."

"What?"

"He said she stayed with him four nights ago, then she was off the grid for a couple days. She didn't respond to his calls or texts until yesterday. Did you see her during that time?"

Lucy looked unnerved. "No, she wasn't here."

"Was she at work?"

"I don't know. She's on a different floor. We usually don't see each other. We spend enough time together stuffed into this place, so we don't go out of our way to hang out during the days."

"Is there anyone else she might stay with?"

"Not that I can think of," Lucy said. "Her parents, maybe."

Frost shook his head. "They said they hadn't seen Brynn in a month."

"Well, I don't know. I'm used to her not coming home, but I just assumed she was at Gabe's."

"When did you meet up with her yesterday?" Frost asked.

"After work. She was already home when I got back."

"Did she say anything about where she'd been?"

"No."

"How was her mood?"

"Fine. Happy. Whistling. I told you, Brynn was always up. We dressed for the party, and then we headed out. She was completely normal, except for—"

"Except for what?" Frost asked. He thought about Brynn whistling, and he started to whistle, too, until he consciously made himself stop.

Lucy sat down in one of the chairs next to the matchbox kitchen table. "Well, I made some comment about thank God tomorrow's Friday. She gave me the blankest look I've ever seen. She took out her phone like she was checking the date, and then she just shrugged it off."

"Did she say what was wrong?"

"No, she just said, 'Brain fart.' That was it. We left for the party."

Frost studied Brynn's half of the studio again. "Did Brynn own a laptop?"

"Sure, she kept it under the bed."

Frost got down on hands and knees and peered under Brynn's twin bed. He slid out a Toshiba laptop and booted it up. When the screen turned on, it asked him for a password.

"It's secured. Do you happen to know her password?"

Lucy nodded. "It's BL-a-go-go."

Frost keyed it in as Lucy spelled it out for him. When the home screen loaded, he opened up the calendar application. The only appointment listed for the week, other than last night's party, was a dentist appointment for the previous day at nine in the morning. The calendar listed the dentist's name and number, and he slid out his cell phone and dialed the office.

He explained who he was to the receptionist and asked his question. Then he hung up.

"Brynn was scheduled for tooth whitening on Thursday morning," Frost said. "She never showed up."

"Weird. Brynn was fussy about her teeth."

"I'd like to know where she was that day," Frost said.

"I'm sorry, but I have no idea. She didn't say anything."

Frost didn't know if Brynn's missing time was connected to what happened to her, but he didn't like the fact that she was off the grid so soon before her unexplained breakdown. And that she was acting as if she didn't even know what day it was.

"Was Brynn seeing a shrink?" he asked Lucy. "Gabe said she went to see someone about her fear of cats."

"Yeah, that's right. Brynn was really high on her. She said I should see her for my bridge thing."

"When was this?"

"A few weeks ago. The shrink was pretty expensive. Her parents gave her a couple grand for the treatment. That's how much Gabe meant to her. She didn't want the cat thing to get in the way of their relationship."

"Gabe thought the treatment had a strange effect on her memory."

Lucy nodded. "That's right. Brynn said the goal was to make you forget whatever was causing your problem. Take away the memory, take away the fear. I guess it worked. Suddenly, Brynn loved cats."

"What was the shrink's name?" he asked. "Do you remember?"

"Sure, because it was a little creepy. Francesca Stein. You know—Frankie Stein? Frankenstein? We joked about it. I have one of her cards. Do you want it?"

"I do."

Lucy went over to her side of the apartment and rummaged through her nightstand drawers. She came back and handed him a business card. "Her office is right near Macy's, so it was pretty convenient for Brynn."

"Thank you, Lucy."

Frost headed for the door, and Lucy hesitated, as if there was more she wanted to say. He thought she wanted to ask him out, but he knew she wouldn't. It was too easy to follow the path you were on, rather than looking for cross-trails that might take you somewhere scary. He was like that, too.

"Well, say hi to Shack for me," Lucy said lamely.

"I will."

"Hey, did you ever catch the guy that killed the old woman? You know, Shack's original owner?"

"Yeah, that was easy," Frost told her with a grin. "He showed up at a hospital about two hours after the murder. Bleeding profusely. He had cat scratches all over his body."

8

Frankie waited for her sister at Zingari, which was their traditional meeting spot twice a week. She had a glass of Russian River pinot noir in front of her, along with an order of *cozze*. That was her dinner. The jazz bar was loud, with a nighttime piano and saxophone duo rising in a mellow beat over the voices of the crowd. A candle flickered on her table. She leaned back into the cushioned bench and watched the reflections of faces in the mirrored wall.

Pam was late. As usual. But it didn't matter. She sipped wine and lost herself in the noise. The garlic mussels were perfect.

She checked e-mails on her phone. Most of the messages were business related, which she could answer in a sentence or two. Follow-up on articles she'd published in scientific journals. Queries from colleagues. Conference invitations from around the world. She'd spoken on memory reconsolidation on nearly every continent over the past decade. In her field, she was widely known, but her fame had also brought controversy. Many of her peers disagreed bitterly with the ethics of her treatments, and they'd waged an academic war to discredit her.

Frankie didn't care. What mattered to her was the outcomes for her patients.

Fame as a therapist had other strange side effects, too. Every night, when she scrolled through her e-mail, she found messages from ordinary people. Some were harmless. Some were desperate. Others were hate mail she'd learned to ignore. She clicked on one as she drank her wine:

> You are playing God. You are going to Hell, and I
> am praying for your salvation.

She deleted the message, along with several others in a similar vein. She kept the e-mails from people who had read her book and wanted to share stories of how their own painful memories had taken over their lives. Many wanted help, and she could reply to those from her office in the morning.

There was one message left that she hadn't opened. The e-mail had no subject line. When she checked the date stamp, she saw that it had come into her in-box only five minutes earlier.

Frankie opened the message, which contained one line:

> Remember me?

There was nothing else. No signature. No attachment. She checked the return address of the sender and saw,

> thenightbird@gmx.com

Frankie's brow furrowed with puzzlement. Something about the message unnerved her more than the others. She wasn't sure what it was. She'd received much worse from strangers. This was nothing. And yet—

She realized what was bothering her. When she checked her name, she saw that the message had come to her personal e-mail account, not the business e-mail address from her website. Her personal address was private. She gave it out only to family and friends, and to a very small number of patients whom she considered at risk of suicide. Even when she muted her phone at night, that e-mail address was programmed to ring through and alert her to a new message.

"Fan mail?"

Frankie looked up. Her favorite waiter, Virgil, hovered over her table with a bottle of wine. He had a luxuriant wave of shock-white hair that even women envied. His dark eyes were wicked, and his lips curled into a permanent smirk. He was tall and wore a tight black shirt and black pants.

She put down her phone. The battery was low, so she removed a portable charger from her purse and connected it. "Someone's praying for my soul again."

"Well, you and me need all the help we can get," Virgil replied. "I figure I'm on the *smite* list if God gets bored. I keep looking up at the sky for a lightning bolt."

"This is California, Virgil. When the smite comes, it'll be an earthquake."

Virgil spread his long arms wide. "Did you feel that? Was that a tremor?"

Frankie laughed. Virgil could always make her laugh.

"More fruit of the vine?" he asked her.

"Definitely."

Virgil refilled her glass. His pours were generous. She was a regular, and she tipped well. The other servers at the restaurant knew that Virgil took the table whenever Frankie, Pam, and Jason came in. Frankie liked him. He was a San Francisco party child, always short of cash and crashing with gay friends. He was technically homeless, but nothing vanquished his sense of humor, which Frankie admired. He was proof that you could still live off the kindness of strangers.

"Where's your sister tonight?" he asked.

Frankie was about to answer when a voice called from behind him: "I'm here, I'm here!"

Pam threaded her way toward the table through the Friday crowd. She had a way of parting the seas as she walked. A shopping bag from Nordstrom Rack dangled from one finger. With a toss of her long bottle-blond hair, she slid into the chair opposite Frankie and gave Virgil a grin. She slid off her sunglasses.

"What should I have tonight, V?" she asked.

"Depends. Are we looking to flirt, celebrate, or get drunk?"

"All three."

"Sounds like a Bellini martini," he said.

"Done."

Virgil left, and Pam gave an exaggerated sigh as she settled herself at the table and fluffed her hair. Every motion Pam made was designed to draw attention to herself. And it worked. Around the bar, men stole glances at her. Anyone looking at the two of them could see that they were sisters, but Pam got the attention when they were together. It was partly her looks. Pam had spent some of her college money on breast implants, and she dressed to show them off. Her legs had the golden glow of time in the sun. But it was her attitude, too. Something about Pam screamed of sex.

"Where's Jason?" Pam asked.

"He had to work late."

Pam shook her head. "All work and no play. You should play with that boy more."

"Life's not all about play, Pam," Frankie said.

Her sister rolled her eyes. Frankie couldn't blame her. Whenever she was with Pam, she lectured her like a child. It had been that way their whole lives. When Pam needed rescuing, Frankie was there, and Frankie in turn made her feel like shit. They may as well have been jealous teenagers.

As they sat there, Frankie heard her phone ping. She had a new e-mail at her personal address. When she checked her phone, she saw that it was the same sender as before. This time he wrote,

I remember you.

Her sister read her frown from across the table. "What's up?"

"Nothing." Frankie put down the phone and put the message out of her mind. Someone was playing games with her. "Nothing at all."

Virgil brought Pam her martini, which had an amber glow and an orchid flower draped over the rim of the glass. Pam took a sip and licked her lips with her tongue. "Perfect, Virgil. You are my savior."

"Sorry, Frankie and I covered religion. We're all going to hell."

"Dibs on that," Pam replied.

Virgil left them alone, and Pam eyed the crowd around them, taking a survey of the male faces. When someone smiled at her, she smiled back. Frankie wanted a report on Pam's day, but she knew she'd have to drag it out of her.

"How did the job interview go?" Frankie asked.

Pam didn't look back. "Fine. Great. I'm sure I got it."

"Did you even show up?"

This time, Pam stared at her, and her look was deadly. "Excuse me?"

"Did you go, or did you blow it off?"

"Of course I went."

"If I call, is that what they'll tell me?"

"Call them," Pam said. She took a sip of her drink and added, "It's so refreshing that you trust me."

Frankie shrugged. "You're right. I'm sorry."

The truth was that Pam had never given anyone in the family a reason to trust her, but Frankie didn't bother pointing that out.

Living with a family of type-A academics, Pam had deliberately gone in the opposite direction. She dropped out of college after a year.

She bounced from job to job—dancer, waitress, model—and along the way, she developed an addiction to cocaine and went through rehab twice. Five years ago, she married a Portuguese web developer she'd met in a Mission District nightclub. He abused her. She cheated on him. When he kicked her out, she moved into Frankie's spare bedroom, and she was still there.

Pam had money now. Their father had left them a small inheritance, but the way Pam was spending her share, Frankie didn't think that the nest egg would last more than a few years in her pockets. Pam couldn't think that far into the future, but Frankie did, and she'd been maneuvering to get Pam a job. Any job. The latest interview was with a PR firm that Frankie had worked with when she testified in a litigation case. Public relations was all about looking good, and Pam fit the bill.

Frankie's phone pinged again.

Another e-mail.

She hesitated, but she picked up her phone. The message was from the same person. It read,

What's your worst memory?

This time, Frankie angrily tapped out a return e-mail with her slim fingers:

Who is this?

She sent it before she could think twice and then slapped her phone down on the table. Pam noticed.

"What's up?"

"Just a troll. Tell me about the interview."

"What's to tell?" Pam asked.

"What kind of questions did they ask?"

"I don't know. PR questions. Are you comfortable lying to a reporter's face? Would you sleep with a client to keep their business? That kind of thing."

"Funny," Frankie said.

"Come on, I'd be eye candy for them, and that's all. You know it. I know it. They know it."

Frankie didn't say anything. She sipped her wine and studied her sister's face. Pam was hiding something, but that didn't narrow it down. She always kept secrets. She always lied. The only thing she was ever honest about was her bitter resentment of her older sister's success.

"You didn't go, did you?" Frankie said.

Pam sipped her martini. "No."

"For God's sake, Pam."

"What? I'm not broke anymore. I'll find a job when I am."

"That won't take long if you keep coming home with Nordstrom bags. Do you know the strings I pulled to get you that interview?"

"Yes, thank you for taking pity on me," Pam snapped.

"I'm done with you. That's it."

"I'd like to think so, but you're never done, Frankie. Just like Dad was never done."

"I mean, you're on your own," Frankie told her.

"What, do you want me to move out of your apartment? Get my own place?"

"Is that what you want?"

Pam's face was ice. "No."

"Yes, a penthouse condo rent-free is pretty nice."

"You want me to pay rent, Frankie? I'll pay rent."

"That's not what this is about," Frankie shot back.

It happened this way over and over. They couldn't be alone without arguing. Jason was the peacekeeper between them. Without him around, the two sisters took out their knives and aimed for each other's throats. Frankie hated it, and she knew she was just as much to blame as

Pam. She'd hoped it would be different with their father gone, but they'd fallen right back into their dysfunctional routine after the accident.

Frankie let the silence drag out. Then she asked, more softly, "Pam, are you clean?"

"Excuse me?"

"Cocaine," Frankie said.

"Wow, you were done interfering for a full five seconds. That's a new record, even for you."

"I just want to know. When you've had money before, most of it went up your nose. That's the truth, Pam, whether you like it or not."

Her sister looked around to see if anyone was listening. She leaned across the table. "I go to meetings. You send Jason as my watchdog, remember? Don't worry, Frankie, I get my dose of humiliation every week."

"The meetings aren't intended to humiliate you. They're to keep you alive."

"Yeah, well, you don't have to go to them, do you? Be a good girl and stand up in front of the losers and tell them that I'm an even bigger loser. I'm sorry we can't all be world-class physicists and psychiatrists and neuroscientists. Some of us are just human beings."

Pam waved her hand, which collided with her martini glass and spilled her drink across the table. Pam swore and stood up to flag Virgil to get another. Frankie sopped up the puddle from the table with a wad of napkins. She was always cleaning up Pam's messes.

Ping.

Another e-mail. She grabbed her phone to read the message. It was the same sender:

I see you.

Frankie's head snapped up. Zingari was packed with customers shoulder to shoulder. Light was low, and she struggled to see the faces.

Her eyes shot from person to person, looking for someone in the crowd who was looking back at her. Someone she knew.

There was no one. She realized that her hand was trembling, and she could barely hold her phone.

Across the table, Pam sat down again, her face tight with anger. She wouldn't look at Frankie.

"I'm sorry," Frankie murmured.

Pam said nothing.

"Really, I mean it, Pam. I don't want to fight. I don't want to run your life. I know sometimes I act like I do."

"You're just like Dad," Pam retorted, knowing it was a low blow.

Frankie held her tongue, despite the temptation to start the argument all over again. "Okay, you're right, Dad was always on your case, and I don't want to be like that. He drove me crazy, too, just not in the same way. He was difficult."

"Difficult?" Pam said, as if the word didn't begin to describe him. Which was true.

"The thing is, Dad and I made some progress when we were at Point Reyes. Before the accident."

"How nice for you, but you didn't want me there, remember? You said all I'd do is get in the way."

Frankie hesitated. "Of course. I just mean—I'm sorry."

"Don't be. It is what it is."

Virgil leaned between them. His smirk, as always, was plastered on his face. He knew they were arguing. It wasn't the first time. He'd seen worse in the year they'd been coming here. The server carried a glass of pinot noir in his hand, and Pam frowned when she saw it.

"I wanted another martini, V."

"Don't worry, Bellini number two is on the way," he told Pam. "This drink is for Frankie. Courtesy of a gentleman at the bar."

Frankie looked up. *I see you.*

"Who?" she asked. Customers lined up three deep at the bar, and she couldn't pick out any familiar faces.

"Slicked-back brown hair. Beard. Very tasty."

Frankie studied the faces again, and this time, she spotted a man staring back at her. Virgil was right. He was attractive. He was younger than she was, but he had a weak-in-the-knees smile that was like a secret weapon. His bearded chin was squared, and his nose made a sharp V, with a pronounced ridge above his lip. He was smart, too. She could always see intelligence in the eyes.

"Take the drink back," she told Virgil, but then she grabbed the server's wrist. "Wait, no, I'll do it myself."

Frankie stood up. In her heels, she was taller than the man at the bar. She let her coldness soak into her face. She approached him, and he watched her with an amused confidence. As if women always wanted him to buy them a drink. He didn't look scary, but stalkers knew how to wear a mask. He was whistling, but he stopped as she came closer.

She stood in front of him and drilled into his face with her stare.

"Who are you, and why are you sending me e-mails? How did you get my personal address?"

His blue eyes blinked with surprise. They were attractive eyes, and they latched on to her and didn't let go. "I'm sorry, I think you have me confused with someone else. My name is Frost Easton, Dr. Stein. I'm with the San Francisco Police. I'd like to talk to you."

9

Frost sized up Francesca Stein. He'd met plenty of psychiatrists in his investigations, and they hadn't impressed him. They were happy to pretend they had all the answers, but if one of their patients shot up a movie theater, the finger of blame pointed everywhere except at themselves. He thought of them as gray little Freuds, probing for weaknesses like a child poking the stomach of a fat uncle.

Stein didn't convey arrogance, but her brown eyes were cool. She had a classy grace about her that kept people at a distance. Her body was paper thin, but she didn't look fragile. Her sister at the other table—they were obviously sisters—was the bombshell, but Frost found Frankie more interesting. She looked as if you could dig down a long way and never hit bottom.

The server with the wild white hair, Virgil, found an empty window table for them. Outside, the pedestrian traffic filled the sidewalk. It was Friday night, and despite a cool mist off the ocean, the Tenderloin regulars were out in force on Post Street in the wildest of fashions. Frost's Suburban was parked in a red zone in front of the restaurant. Shack slept on top of the steering wheel, and the drunk girls who passed the SUV stopped to coo at him through the window.

"So what did you want to talk about, Inspector?" she asked. Her voice had a surprising softness.

"Brynn Lansing," he said. "She was one of your patients."

"I'm sure you know I can't say anything about my patients," Stein replied. And then, with a flicker of concern, she said, "Was?"

"Brynn's dead."

Stein's dismay flew onto her face. It looked sincere. "I'm so sorry to hear that. What happened?"

"She tried to climb the Bay Bridge. She didn't make it."

"What?"

He explained the incident in detail, and he watched Stein's face for a reaction. He saw only confusion.

"That's a terrible thing," she said when he was done. "And baffling."

"Well, I was hoping you could unbaffle it for me," Frost said. "After all, you were her therapist."

"Even if I could, I wouldn't be able to tell you anything. The patient privilege isn't automatically canceled by death."

"I thought you might say that," Frost replied, sliding a folded piece of paper from inside his coat pocket. "That's why I had Brynn's parents sign a release form. Upon her death, they took over her power of attorney."

Stein read the form. "Fair enough. I want to help if I can. Unfortunately, in this case, I don't think there's anything useful I can share with you. I hadn't seen Brynn in several weeks. The treatment we conducted was for a fairly minor problem. She was almost embarrassed to ask me about it."

"Her fear of cats," Frost said.

"Yes, that's right."

"And you helped her *forget* about it?" Frost asked. "Is that how your treatment works?"

He'd done his homework on Francesca Stein over the course of the afternoon. He tried to keep the cynicism out of his voice, but he failed.

What he'd read made him think that Lucy was right. As pretty as she was to look at, this woman was a little like Dr. Frankenstein.

"In simple terms, it's something like that," Stein told him. "The process is called memory reconsolidation."

"And how exactly do you do that?"

Stein took her phone from her purse. It was connected to a portable battery charger. She pushed a few buttons, then extended her arm and gave the phone to Frost. "This is a video I show people at conferences. Take a look. It only lasts a few seconds."

Frost pushed the play button on the phone screen. He expected a dry academic lecture in a classroom, but instead, he saw a video of an urban street somewhere in San Francisco. There were cars parked on the opposite curb. The street was lined with retail shops. Pedestrians walked back and forth in groups on both sides. As he watched, puzzled, a dark car drove into the frame and went without stopping through the intersection, where it T-boned another car with a sharp bang. Steam erupted. Voices shouted. And then the video cut off.

"I don't understand," Frost said.

"Let's say you witnessed this actual incident," Stein said, taking back her phone. "That ten seconds would be your reality. You can't reexperience it, you can't watch it again. All you can do is remember it."

"Okay."

"In other words, reality happens once, but memory happens over and over," Stein told him. "Every time I ask you to think about the blue car that zipped through the stop sign and had an accident, your brain goes back and retrieves the memory, like a file from a cabinet. However, memories—unlike reality—aren't fixed. With every recollection, we reshape what we saw. Our memories of an event are influenced by how we want a situation to be, how we perceive our role in it, what people tell us, and even by what we hear or read about what took place. After a while, our brains can't distinguish between reality and our reconstruction of reality."

"Eyewitnesses are unreliable," Frost said. "I get it."

"Exactly. Not only are they unreliable, they can be stubborn about it, too. Witnesses are often one-hundred-percent convinced of the facts, even when they're wrong. And trauma can actually make it worse. You wouldn't think a rape victim could ever misidentify her assailant, right? And yet it happens. Innocent men have gone to prison because of it."

"Like I said, people get it wrong. How does that relate to what you do?"

Stein responded with a slight dip of her chin. She had a calmness and precision in everything she did. "My point is that people can change their own memories without even being aware that they're doing so. The danger—and the opportunity—is that memories can also be *deliberately* altered. You may have heard about a controversy back in the nineteen eighties, in which therapists helped patients recover *repressed* memories of abuse. Most of those recovered memories were discredited, but to the patient they became real. And it's not just therapists who are guilty of this kind of manipulation. Attorneys do the same thing, and so do police officers. Sometimes it's accidental, and sometimes it's intentional."

"How does that work?" Frost asked.

"Think about the video I showed you. The blue car races through the stop sign and gets into an accident. There were a variety of retail stores in the background. Which coffee shop was on the street? Do you remember? Think about it."

Frost did. Finally, he said, "I think it was Starbucks."

"Are you sure?"

"No, but I think so."

"It wasn't Seattle's Best?"

"I don't think it was. Why? Am I wrong? Was it really Seattle's Best?"

"Actually, there was no coffee shop on the street at all," Stein told him. "But if we went over this a few more times, you would swear to me that it was a Starbucks. You'd *see* it in your head. Most coffee shops are Starbucks, so if someone plants the suggestion that there was a coffee shop, people tend to leap to the conclusion that they saw a Starbucks. Even when it wasn't there at all."

"Sneaky."

"No, it's just how memory works. How fast do you think the blue car was going when it blew through the stop sign? Want to hazard a guess?"

Frost shrugged. "I'd say thirty-five miles an hour."

"It was going twenty. The control group in my studies typically guesses twenty-five. You went much higher. Do you know why?"

"I'm sure you're going to tell me," Frost said, slightly irritated.

"I've described the blue car several times as *zipping* or *racing* through the intersection. 'Blew through the stop sign.' My character-ization influences your brain. You sped up the car because of how I described the incident, *not* because of what you actually remembered." Stein leaned forward and added, "In addition, you haven't corrected me about two important details, even though I've made the same mistakes several times."

"Namely?"

"The car in the video was dark green, not blue. And there was no stop sign at the intersection. It was a yield sign."

Frost thought back to the video, and he realized to his dismay that he wasn't sure if she was telling him the truth or not. Stein smiled at him with a slight turn of her lips.

"I'm not trying to make you feel like a fool, Inspector. It's simply that this is how memory fails us. It's highly suggestible. If an attorney or police officer did what I did to an accident witness, they'd be very likely to remember a blue car going through a stop sign the next time they tried to recall the incident. And that might be in a courtroom."

"No offense, Dr. Stein, but you're not exactly making me feel good about your memory treatments. The whole process sounds dangerous. I read that some of your colleagues have tried to drum you out of the profession because of what you're doing."

"You're right," Stein admitted. "Altering memories is very risky. Because of the dangers involved, the traditional viewpoint in psychiatry is that you should never do it. You can try to sever the emotional response from the memory, but you shouldn't try to erase or replace the memory itself. Many therapists and scientists think our life is the product of our varied experiences, good and bad, and that we shouldn't mess with that."

"But you're right, and they're wrong?" Frost challenged her.

"Not necessarily. I just take a different view. I believe that a patient can decide for himself or herself how they want to be treated. It's their life, not mine, not anybody else's. The people who argue against assisted suicide aren't the ones who have to experience debilitating pain or watch a family member suffer. It's the same with painful memories. I'd rather empower the patient to live a better life, and if they want to do that by altering part of their past, that's their choice. After all, a tumor is part of your life experience, too, isn't it? But we wouldn't hesitate to surgically remove it. So I don't think memories are sacrosanct."

Frost thought about his sister, Katie. All he had left of her was what he remembered. It made him believe that memories *were* sacred, the good and the bad. Even though there were things that he wished he could forget.

The car in the parking lot at Ocean Beach.

The body in the backseat.

"And how exactly do you *alter* someone's memory?" he asked.

"If you talk to my husband, Jason—he's a neuroscientist—he'll tell you that someday soon, we'll be able to use a laser and an MRI machine to light up the synapses in your brain and zap a particular memory. I try to do the same thing therapeutically. It's a process I've spent more than fifteen years honing and perfecting. It combines hypnosis with audiovisual stimuli."

"And drugs?" Frost asked.

"For some patients, yes, I'll use drugs to increase susceptibility to hypnotic suggestion."

"Does it always work?"

"No, of course not. There are no guarantees in psychiatry. My patients sign a release before treatment, because working on the brain is not like working on a car. Sometimes it doesn't work. Some people can't let go of memories. In very rare circumstances, treatment can even make it worse—intensifying the emotion or the memory, rather than removing it."

"Enough that someone might, say, jump off a bridge?" Frost asked.

"If you're talking about Brynn Lansing, my answer is no. Her treatment was weeks ago. It went fine."

"So she couldn't suddenly wake up and imagine herself being attacked by hundreds of feral cats?"

"That's not how it works, Inspector. I don't know what caused Brynn to behave as she did, but it was nothing that happened in my treatment room. This was something else entirely. There's no connection."

"Are you sure?"

"I am," she insisted.

"Really? Then how do you explain Monica Farr?"

He saw anxiety bloom in Stein's eyes. "What?"

"Monica Farr was another of your patients, wasn't she? I checked the contacts on her phone. She had an entry for 'Frankie.' Guess whose number it was? And don't worry, I can get a signed release for her patient records, too."

"Are you saying that Monica—"

"Is dead," Frost told her. "She had a psychotic breakdown just like Brynn. She shot herself in the head."

The color vanished from Stein's face. Her lips parted in horror. "Oh my God."

Frost leaned forward across the table, and his voice was harsh. "Let's face it, Dr. Stein, that's a hell of a coincidence. Two patients come to you for treatment, and both of them wind up going crazy and killing themselves? I think you better start asking yourself what you really did inside their heads."

10

"What do you remember about Monica Farr?" Jason asked.

Frankie stood in front of the solarium windows in her penthouse condominium on O'Farrell. It was almost midnight. She watched the city, and she could feel the city watching her. The art deco building between Leavenworth and Hyde was tall, with an east view toward the bay. When the Giants played at home, she could see fireworks over the stadium. In the distance, the lights of the Bay Bridge stretched toward Oakland, and she shivered as she thought about Brynn Lansing. Heights had never bothered Frankie, but she wondered what it was like to die that way, at the mercy of gravity. Like Brynn did. Like her father did.

Jason came up next to her and handed her a new glass of red wine. She'd already drunk too much this evening, and she felt the world floating, but she wanted more.

"Monica was an emergency-room nurse from Utah," Frankie told him. "Three children arrived at the hospital after a house fire in Salt Lake. All of the kids were badly burned, and all of them died. Monica couldn't get the episode out of her head. She moved to San Fran to get away from it, but she kept having flashbacks. She couldn't do her job anymore."

"How did you deal with it?"

Frankie pictured Monica in her head. Young. Redheaded. Slightly overweight. Monica's face lit up when she talked about patients she'd helped. They had that in common. Frankie remembered the treatment strategy she'd chosen for her. The strategy was the most delicate part of therapy; that was where she had to read her patients and create a new reality that their minds would embrace.

"I didn't want her to forget that the kids had died," she said. "She dealt with loss every day. It was too much a part of who she was as a nurse. Instead, I helped her believe that she wasn't really in the room when it happened. She didn't see them die with her own eyes. I was hoping that would be enough to let her work through it. Monica wasn't fragile. Nurses are tough. This was simply one tragedy too many."

"Did the treatment work?" Jason asked.

"I thought it did. Monica called me a few weeks later. She was working as a nurse again. Graveyard-shift ER. It doesn't get harder than that. But she sounded happy. She was calling to thank me."

"So you did your job, Frankie. Don't second-guess yourself."

"Yes, but now she's dead, and so is Brynn Lansing. That's *two* of my patients showing signs of severe brain dysfunction."

Jason shook his head. "Whatever happened to them wasn't your fault."

"How do you know?" Frankie asked.

He had no answer for her. He was just trying to make her feel better. He put an arm around her waist as they stood by the windows. She liked the closeness of him. She could see his reflection in the glass—his short, gelled dark hair; his sharply angled chin; his arching eyebrows and intense stare. He wore gray dress slacks and a slim-fit forest-green shirt. Her fingertips drifted onto his thigh, making soft circles, but then she pulled away, and she could feel his disappointment.

"Is it possible?" she asked.

"What?"

"Could I have harmed these women with my memory treatment?"

Jason scowled. It was late, and he didn't want a clinical discussion. She knew what he really wanted. Sex.

"I can't say it's *impossible*," he admitted. "There aren't any absolutes in brain chemistry, you know that. People behave in unexpected ways. All I can tell you is that it's very unlikely that your treatment could have produced such an extreme reaction, particularly so long after the therapy ended. I'm not saying the possibility is zero, but the risk is low."

"Risk," Frankie murmured. She was thinking about her father again.

It was funny how everything eventually led her back to him and their last weekend together. She couldn't escape it. The theme of the discussion he'd chosen for their annual camping trip was *risk*. What chances are you willing to take to get what you want? What dangers do your choices create for other people? She could hear her father's voice in her head; it had no intonations, no ups, no downs. He lectured and posed questions the way a professor would, rather than a father with a child. He jabbed with his finger to make his points. His grizzled face didn't move.

Question. Is it acceptable to pursue your own selfish satisfaction when it causes risk to someone else?

Question. Is it okay to risk another's life or happiness simply because you really want something?

"My father thought I was playing games with people's lives," Frankie said. "He said what I was doing was immoral."

Jason reacted with impatience. "What did Marvin understand about morality? He was the least emotional person I ever knew. Forget about all of his academic posturing."

"I would, but now I wonder if he was right. Maybe Brynn and Monica are dead because of me. Maybe I'm playing with fire." Her voice turned smoky. "Remember Darren Newman?"

He didn't like hearing that name, and she couldn't blame him.

"You didn't make Darren Newman the man he is."

"Tell that to the girl who was killed," Frankie said.

"Newman manipulated you. And a lot of other people, too."

Frankie didn't say anything more. Jason was right. Darren Newman had come to her as part of a deal to stay out of prison, and she wasn't responsible for the consequences.

Except they both knew that wasn't the whole truth.

She turned and faced her husband. Between the wine and the darkness of the solarium, she felt herself getting aroused. That was a rare experience this year. Her mind and her body had been strangers to each other, but right now, she wanted an escape from everything else. From memories. From loss. From her past. Her inhibitions fell away. Her fingers played with the down on the back of his neck. She kissed his lower lip and then teased him with her tongue, and she felt him respond. Her hands undid a button on his shirt, then another, and one of her fingernails explored his chest. She didn't care if the world was watching them through the windows. It had been way too long, and she needed him urgently. He sensed it. His hand tugged at the zipper of her dress pants, and when it was down, his fingers fished inside, rubbing her through the lace of her panties. Her breath caught in her chest. Her legs slipped apart. She braced herself against him.

Then, out of the corner of her eye, she saw movement in the living room, and she froze in embarrassment.

Pam.

She'd come out of her downstairs bedroom. She wore her shorty nightgown, with a mug of tea cradled in her hands. Her blond hair was mussed. She stood there, watching them, a smirk on her lips.

Frankie stepped away. Trying to be discreet, she zipped up and smoothed her hair and blouse. Jason's face screwed up in annoyance, until he glanced over his shoulder. Pam wiggled her fingers in a sarcastic greeting, and then she returned to her bedroom and closed the door loudly. They were alone again, but the moment was broken.

When Frankie kissed him again, she didn't get the same erotic response.

"Sorry," she murmured.

He shrugged. "Bad timing."

"We could go upstairs," she suggested.

"Actually, I need to finish a project. I'll work in my office for a while."

"Should I wait up?"

"No, you're tired. Go to bed."

His voice had a cold, dismissive quality. Once he'd shut the door, it didn't open again. His rejection left her humiliated but still aroused. She kicked off her heels and picked them up in one hand. She climbed the spiral staircase in her stockinged feet to the loft, where they kept their master bedroom suite, and she slipped inside and closed the door behind her. It was dark. More windows faced the bay.

She took off all her clothes inside the walk-in closet without looking in the full-length mirror. If she stared at her naked body, she would find fault with herself. Too skinny, with her ribs and hip bones showing. Breasts too small. Right now, she wanted to think of herself as perfect. She padded nude across the lush carpet and slipped between the satin sheets of the king bed without putting on a nightgown. The coolness caressed her bare skin. Her body wanted sex, but drunkenness made the bedroom spin. She squirmed with frustrated excitement, but every time she blinked, her eyes stayed closed a little longer.

She slept.

Not for long. It felt like only a minute or two. She could have slept all night, but something disturbed her. She awoke with a start, feeling anxious. Her heart raced. She'd been dreaming about something bad, but the dream vanished in an instant, and she had no memory of it. When she checked the clock, she saw that an hour had passed. She was still alone. Jason was one of those people who needed little sleep himself, and he was always working.

What awakened her?

Frankie looked around the bedroom, and nothing felt amiss. The curtains were open, letting in the San Francisco glow. Sometimes hawks or gulls struck their high windows, so loudly she was sure the glass would shatter, but she didn't think it was one of their collisions that had jarred her awake.

She looked at her nightstand. And she knew.

Her phone.

Frankie unlocked the screen. A new e-mail waited for her. The date stamp was only seconds earlier. She saw the address of the sender, and it was the same person who had stalked her at Zingari.

thenightbird@gmx.com

Her skin rippled as if someone had stroked it with a fingertip. She shivered at the chill. Normally, hate mail didn't bother her, but this was different. These messages had a quiet menace. Just like his name suggested, he felt like a bird of prey, hiding in the darkness. Instinctively, she tugged the sheet over her bare chest, as if he were somewhere among the city lights, behind the long eye of a telescope, watching her. *I see you.*

She almost deleted the message without reading it, but she had to know. She tapped on the e-mail with her fingertip.

The message, like the others, was a single line.

I'm going to watch you die.

11

The room was white.

Shimmering white. Fluorescent white. Blinding white. As her eyes blinked open, the woman named Christie felt lost in the whiteness. She was at peace, drifting nowhere and everywhere. The atmosphere was warm and perfectly silent. She lay on her back on a chaise so soft and comfortable it practically enveloped her. Wherever she was, time had no meaning here. A minute could be an hour; an hour could be a minute. She had no sense of anything but bliss.

Her body felt oddly heavy. When she went to lift her arm, it wouldn't move. The same was true of her legs. Soft bonds held her firmly in place. She couldn't turn her head from side to side or lift her torso off the cushions. And yet it didn't matter. Her mind wandered freely, untethered from her frozen body, floating with a faint breath of air. Her mind was a bubble, lazily exploring the white, windowless world.

Nothing could ever be wrong in that world. Nothing at all. She could stay there forever.

Only one strange smudge of darkness disturbed Christie's peaceful visions. Far away, farther than her mind could see, something was *missing.* There was a memory she could no longer grasp, a blank space as white as the walls. When she reached for it, it darted away. The memory teased her with its emptiness. It was like a sailboat hovering on the far edge of an ocean horizon, dotting up and then disappearing. She could hardly be sure it had ever been there at all.

But she knew it had.

She had a sixth sense that whatever was behind that blank space was worse than anything she'd known in her life. Behind that blank space was terror. Behind it was madness. She knew—*she knew*—that if she had to stare at it again, her mind would shatter like glass. She could feel herself sprinting to get away from it. Running without looking back at whatever terrible thing was behind her. Pleading. Praying. Screaming.

No.

Right now, that seemed impossible. Nothing so empty, so far away, could frighten her. She was as warm as sunshine. The room was as white as the sand on an endless beach. She never wanted to leave.

Christie's lips folded into a smile. Her eyes sank shut again, and she slept. Beautiful dreams filled her mind, as if a voice outside her brain could tell her what to see: meadows in bloom, with a gentle wind she could feel on her face; a mountain lake, waveless and deep blue, scented by pine; a porch swing, empty, creaking, with a rumble of thunder in the distance.

Whatever the voice told her to see, she saw.

The voice. It controlled her.

Suddenly, it told her to awaken. It said her name in a high-pitched, singsong way, like a child playing a game: *"Chris-tie, Chris-tie."*

She didn't want to wake up. Her dreams were too perfect. She knew she would awaken in the white room. It had all happened before. She didn't know how many times it had happened, but this wasn't the first time.

"Chris-tie, Chris-tie."

The voice sang in her head like a nightingale, but there was nothing happy about the song. She had a memory of asking: *Who are you?*

And she had a memory of his singsong reply.

"The Night Bird . . . that's who you heard."

She was awake now, and she could feel him close to her. His breath was loud and scented with something sweet. She kept her eyes closed, because she didn't want to see him, but he plucked one eyelid between his fingers and lifted it open like he was peering under a window shade.

"Peek-a-boo, I see you!"

His face was nothing but a mask, leaning over her, inches away. The mask had a grotesque plastic smile, with bloodred lips stretching to his ears. Ghost-white skin. Huge eyes—the eyes of a bug. Not eyes at all. The mask grinned at her, and behind it, the voice sang.

"It won't be long," he warbled. "Time for the song!"

Christie wanted to shut her eyes, but he used gray sticky tape to seal her eyelid to her lash. First one, then the other. The moisture in her eyes dried immediately, and her eyeballs felt as if they would come loose and roll away. Pain grew in a circle in her sockets. She needed to blink; all she could think about was how much she needed to blink, but she couldn't. She could only stare at the bug eyes and hideous grin of the mask.

Not the song, she wanted to say. Please not the song.

She remembered now. The song opened the door. The song sent her to the devil and the darkness. She wanted to scream at him and plead with him, but something was in her mouth—cloth filling every space, shutting out air and sound. All she could do was squeal in protest through her nose, making a whimpering noise. The mask giggled at her, like a child playing with an ant.

"The song is here," he sang. "See what you fear!"

Christie screamed, not out loud, but from inside her brain. It did nothing to stop what was happening to her. The song began. The music was smooth, gentle, not scary at all, but as the lyrics played, the empty whiteness changed. Things appeared on the walls and ceiling and floor, and at first, she couldn't see what they were, but then the room seemed to shrink inch by inch, and she realized the room was lined with needles.

Thousands and thousands of needles, glinting sharp and silver. Jutting out. Three-dimensional. Sleek and long.

Oh, no. No, no, no, no, no. Anything but needles.

The walls moved. The ceiling moved. Or that was how it felt to her. The needles grew in her vision. Christie saw other things now. Eyeballs appeared and floated in the air—dozens of individual blue eyes with long lashes, just like hers—and as the walls ground closer, the needles punctured each eyeball, oozing blood and vitreous gel, gathering them up like meat on a skewer. She screamed and screamed and screamed and didn't make a sound.

A face took shape among the needles. Not a face. The mask. Its grinning mouth opened and sang the song. The music became the soundtrack to a horror film as the bloody needles zeroed in on her body. Her skin. Her face. They grew larger and larger as they came closer.

The voice sang in her ear, "Chris-tie, Chris-tie."

And then a command: *"Run."*

Over and over: "Run, run, run, run, run, run, run, run, run, run, run."

She tried. She could feel her arms pumping, her legs racing, her heart hammering in her chest as she went faster and faster, but she couldn't outrun the needles. Patiently, inexorably, they came for her. To stab her. To puncture her. To slit her through and through with a thousand wounds.

"Run, run, run, run, run, run, run, run, run, run, run."

Christie's open eyes saw the needles. Her soundless screams became an unending wail for help, but there was no help. The glistening points of the needles filled her sight, so close she could feel the metal points pushing on the damp surface of her cornea, pricking their way inside. Her entire world became nothing but needles. There was a needle for every pore on her skin.

Her mind broke.

Her mind fell through a window and shattered into pieces. She wasn't even aware of the real, tiny stab of a needle in her arm, or of the terror receding as her consciousness slipped away into blackness again.

12

Frost stared at the three wooden planks fixed to the side of a sheer cliff face, making a walkway barely eighteen inches wide. There was no railing, just swags of chain nailed to the rock like Christmas tinsel. On the open side of the planks, the cliff descended straight down into a thousand feet of air. Gnarled, wind-swept trees sprouted from its rocky crevices. Misty mountains filled the distance.

As he examined the weathered beams mounted on the rock, a five-year-old with a vanilla ice cream cone ran through the open canyon to her mother. The tourists crowded around the painting in Ghirardelli Square laughed nervously. It was just a three-dimensional sidewalk illusion, but it was so real that Lucy, with her vertigo, would have fainted.

Frost sat down next to the artist on the stone steps of the plaza's mermaid fountain. Water gurgled and splashed over brass turtles and bare breasts. The morning sun cast shadows across their faces. The iconic chocolate factory sign loomed above them, and he could smell sweetness in the air.

"Impressive, Herb," Frost said. "Please tell me that's not a real place."

"It is, actually. That's the famous plank walk on Hua Shan mountain in China."

"Have you done it?"

"I have."

Frost wasn't surprised. Herb was the kind of man who'd lived ten lifetimes in almost seventy years. "And why would anyone do something like that?" he asked.

"A Buddhist would probably say to gain enlightenment," Herb replied, "but honestly, I was stoned out of my mind."

Frost laughed. The omnipresent aroma of pot from Herb's paint-stained flannel shirt was enough to intoxicate anyone who spent too much time with him. He had leathery white skin, dark eyes, and black glasses with tiny magnifiers for close-up work. He was skinny and tall, and he limped because of the time he spent painting on his knees. Shack sat in the artist's lap, and the black-and-white cat batted at the multicolored beads strung into Herb's long gray hair.

They'd been friends for fifteen years. Even in a melting pot city like San Francisco, Herb was one of a kind. He knew everybody. Hippies. Fishermen. Gays. Radicals. Yuppies. Techies. He'd spent four terms on the city council in the '80s, but for as long as Frost could remember, he'd simply painted elaborate sidewalk illusions around the city. He'd been featured on *The Tonight Show* and *Good Morning America* and had appeared in a dozen San Francisco–based movies.

"I was at your brother's food truck a couple days ago," Herb said, tickling Shack's chin. "Looks like he's doing well."

"He is. Duane loves it. It's a big change from the brick-and-mortar kitchens."

"And your parents? How are they?"

"Enjoying Arizona. They bought a golf cart, which I find truly horrifying."

"Well, I have a pretty high threshold for horrifying." Herb chuckled. "You're talking to someone who once got a ticket for riding a Segway on 101. Anyway, it must be lonely not having them around."

"I get why they moved," Frost said. "Too many memories."

Frost thought about Francesca Stein and realized that everything in life came down to memories. The good. The bad. The real. The imagined. Put them all together, and that was the person you were. Would you ever want to change that? He wondered if his parents would choose to erase that night six years ago if they could. The night he had to tell them about Katie.

"So what's up, Frost?" Herb asked. "You don't usually brave the tourist crowds on Saturday morning. I assume that means you need my help."

"I do," Frost said.

He often consulted with Herb, because his friend had a pipeline into prominent people around the city and knew most of the street dwellers, too. Herb heard rumors and sucked up secrets like a private detective. He wrote a daily blog about San Francisco life that was required reading for journalists and politicians.

"Dr. Francesca Stein," Frost went on. "Do you know her?"

"Oh, yes. The master of memory."

"That's her."

"What do you want to know?" Herb asked. "She's lovely, but there's steel behind those eyes."

"Is she legit? The whole memory game sounds like a con to me. Can you really erase a memory from someone's head? Or create a memory of something that never happened?"

"You think it's something out of a Michael Crichton novel?"

"Honestly? Yeah."

"I don't think so, Frost. The older I get, the more I realize that memory is like one of my sidewalk illusions. It can look very real and be nothing but a fantasy. I remember things that I know are false, and I forget things that I know really happened. I talked to someone who went to Dr. Stein for her memory treatment. One of our esteemed city politicians, actually. He killed a pedestrian as a teenage driver, and it began giving him nightmares years after it happened. Dr. Stein worked with him. He still remembers that the accident *happened*, but he doesn't remember it *happening*. Is that a good thing? I don't know, but it's real. And his nightmares are gone."

"Nobody could make me forget finding Katie's body."

"You would think that's true," Herb said, "but don't be so sure. The fact that it's possible to alter memories is why so many scientists are adamant about our not doing it. They accuse Dr. Stein of opening Pandora's box. I tend to agree with them, even if I had a fairly fluid sense of reality back in the nineteen sixties."

Herb turned his attention to a child standing in front of them on the bottom step of the fountain. The boy was about six years old, with messy blond hair.

"How may I help you, young man?" Herb asked in a booming voice. He was good with kids.

"Is that *real*?" the boy asked, gesturing at the three-dimensional painting of Hua Shan mountain in the plaza.

"Does it look real?" Herb asked him.

"Yeah."

"Then I guess it is."

The boy thought about this. He looked over his shoulder at the painting. "I don't think it's real. I think it's fake."

"There's only one way to find out," Herb said. "You have to walk the plank, young man."

The boy folded his arms and marched back to the edge of the painting using big steps, but he kept eyeing Herb behind him, as if to figure out whether he was kidding. He put a foot out and drew it back, and then, with a last glance at Herb, he jumped into the center of the painting. When his feet landed on cement, he looked back with a huge grin. Herb winked at him.

"So why are you asking about this, Frost?" Herb went on. "You're not thinking of going to Dr. Stein, are you? Because of Katie?"

"No."

"Then why? Did something happen?"

"Two of Dr. Stein's patients killed themselves in odd circumstances."

Herb's face darkened. "The girl on the bridge?"

Frost nodded. He found himself whistling a song under his breath. "She was one."

"Are you trying to hold Dr. Stein criminally responsible?" Herb asked. "I wish you luck, but that's a stretch. I can't see the DA taking that case."

"I just want to find out what really happened."

"Well, I have to confess, I'm biased about Dr. Stein, and not in a good way."

"Oh? Why is that?"

"Do you remember last summer? The SF State student who was murdered in her apartment near Balboa Park? Her name was Merrilyn Somers. She was stabbed seven times."

Frost's brow wrinkled. "I remember, but Jess Salceda led that case, not me."

"How about the name Darren Newman?" Herb asked.

"Newman was a suspect in the murder, but he was never charged. Jess got a DNA match on someone else in the building, and the guy pled out. He claimed to have been so drunk he didn't remember anything that happened that night."

Herb nodded. Shack nudged the old man's hand impatiently, and when Herb didn't respond by petting him, the cat got up and relocated to Frost's shoulder. He lifted his face to smell a waft of sea air.

"You know I'm on the board for a women's antiviolence coalition, right?" Herb asked.

"Sure."

"Darren Newman has been on our radar for several years," Herb said. "Women started complaining about him shortly after he and his parents moved to the Bay Area from Colorado. Bullying. Abuse.

Assault. I met him once, just to see who this man was. He's a sociopath. Slick, charming, and absolutely amoral."

"I recall Newman having some kind of criminal record, but he'd never done time," Frost said.

"Yes, his parents are venture capital billionaires. They paid off victims. Nobody filed charges. Then about eighteen months ago, Newman dated the niece of one of our board members, and he raped her. The parents tried to buy her off, but she didn't want money. She wanted him in jail. She was willing to go to trial and take her chances persuading a jury, but the parents pulled a new maneuver. They paid a psychiatrist to offer evidence to the judge."

Frost could see where this was going. "Dr. Stein," he said.

"That's right. Stein talked about traumatic incidents in Newman's childhood and suggested treatment, rather than incarceration. Newman copped to a misdemeanor. No jail time. Court-ordered therapy with Stein. Nobody was happy."

"And Merrilyn Somers—?"

"She got stabbed three months later. She lived *two doors down* from Darren Newman. Look, Frost, I know what the DNA test showed, and I know Jess Salceda did a thorough investigation before going after that other man in the building. But I have to tell you, everyone in our coalition believed that Darren Newman was guilty. He raped and killed that girl, and he managed to pin it on someone else. What's even worse is that he never would have been on the street at all if it weren't for Dr. Francesca Stein."

13

Frankie parked by the Promenade Trail on the bay.

The Golden Gate Bridge loomed immediately to the west, but the bridge was enveloped in a ridge of fog and almost invisible. San Francisco near the Presidio was often like a different city. Even when it was sunny and warm downtown, the temperature could be twenty degrees colder close to the ocean, where a damp cloud laid its chilly fingers across the coast.

She stretched in the parking lot, finished the morning coffee she'd brought with her, and took off running toward Crissy Field and the bridge. She liked to push herself hard on her Saturday-morning work-outs. Jason ran more often than she did, but when she ran, she ran fast and easily outpaced him. It annoyed him, and as a result, they no longer ran together. She felt good running again, because she'd missed the last two weekends. She let her long legs stretch out on the dirt path, passing most of the other runners, ignoring the cold bay wind that whistled into her face. Her arms pumped. Her cheeks pinked up, and sweat gathered under her headband.

Normally, she cleared her head when she ran, but the overnight threat lingered in her brain.

I'm going to watch you die.

She'd hardly slept. She kept telling herself that the e-mail was no more than a variation on the same kind of hate mail she received every day. Sometimes the work she did made her enemies. She'd forwarded the e-mail to a private security firm she'd used in the past and asked them to look into it. End of story.

Even so, thinking about it made her shiver.

Frankie ran full speed with the beach beside her. Whitecaps broke on the surface of the bay. She tasted salt on her tongue. At Torpedo Wharf, she continued around the bluff, following the paved road all the way to Fort Point below the bridge. She could see the webbed red metal of the Golden Gate here, behind the ghosts of fog. At the fort, she stopped long enough to catch her breath. She bent over, with her hands on her knees. She always thought of Jimmy Stewart in *Vertigo* in this spot, rescuing Kim Novak from a fake suicide attempt in the frigid bay waters. She'd watched the movie over and over as a teenager, trying to understand Stewart's dangerous obsession. That was when she'd begun to think of mental health as a career.

She remembered telling her father about her plans to be a psychiatrist. He was appalled. To him, psychiatry wasn't science. It was nothing more than astrology with a prescription pad. For years, she'd endured his nasty jokes.

What's the difference between physics and psychiatry?

One's full of quarks, and the other's full of quacks.

And then he'd laughed. He had the meanest laugh of anyone she'd ever met. If he were still alive, he'd be laughing at her now. Blaming her for what happened to Brynn and Monica. "Psychiatrists are like children pushing buttons on a machine they don't understand," he would say. "And now look at what you've done. These women trusted you, and you killed them."

Except it wasn't Marvin's voice in her head, blaming her for what happened. It was her own.

Frankie started running back toward the city skyline. She ran even faster, so that the noise of her breathing blocked out other sounds. If she couldn't hear, she couldn't think, and she didn't want to think right now. She focused on the domed roof of the Palace of Fine Arts, and beyond it, the hilltop skyscrapers, including the pyramid of the Transamerica building. Beside her, the beach sand was wet and brown, and the morning was gray. She wove through the Saturday crowd, trying not to slow down.

She ran so fast that she sprinted right by the man on the bench.

Among the blur of faces, someone was watching her. By the time she passed him, she realized that his face was familiar. It took her brain a moment to catch up, and then she knew who it was. She stopped and reversed her tracks, walking back toward the bench, breathing hard. He waited for her.

Frankie put on a neutral smile. "Todd."

"Hello, Dr. Stein."

She was going to comment on what a surprise this was, but she didn't think it was a surprise. You could always run into someone you knew in San Francisco, but she saw in his face that he'd been expecting her. She felt paranoid, but it was only because of the strange e-mails she'd received. Looking at Todd, she couldn't remember now whether he was one of the patients with whom she'd shared her personal e-mail address.

Frankie sat down next to him. "It's been a while."

"Five months."

"And how are you?" she asked.

"Honestly? Not so good."

Frankie didn't say anything immediately. She let her breathing return to normal. The pedestrians came and went on the trail, ignoring them, but she spoke softly. "I'm sorry to hear that. Why don't you call and make an appointment next week, and we'll talk."

"No, I can't do that," Todd said. "I can't go to your office."

"Why not?"

"Because you take notes. You have to do that legally, right? But I don't want anything written down."

Frankie leaned forward with her hands on her knees. She stared at her sneakers. "So this isn't an accident. Did you follow me?"

"No, I—"

"Because I have to be honest with you, Todd. I don't like being stalked, and that's what this feels like."

He shook his head. "I'm sorry, Dr. Stein. I didn't follow you. I just remembered that you told me how much you liked running this trail on the weekends. And I thought I would take my chances."

Her instinct was to get up and walk away. Todd wasn't the first patient to cross the line between personal and professional. She'd had patients show up at her home, and invite her to Thanksgiving, and make clumsy passes at her. The thing to do was to shut them down calmly and politely. Even so, she didn't. There was something in Todd's voice that made her stay.

His full name was Todd Ferris. He was in his late twenties, tall and bony. He had a wistful face, with faraway eyes, a feminine mouth, and a soft-spoken way of talking that made her lean in to hear him better. A gathering of longer hairs along his chin line pretended to be a beard. He wore a navy wool cap, a gray Boomtown Casino sweatshirt, and jeans. A small loop earring hugged one ear, and a silver cross dangled on a chain around his neck.

He wasn't one of her success stories. He'd come to her months earlier, troubled by memories of bullying he'd suffered as a child. The emotional trauma had worsened since he'd taken a new job at one of the large gaming companies, with a demanding and intimidating boss. He'd been unable to sleep or work. He'd started drinking heavily.

As a patient, Todd was hard to draw out. He was vague about whether the past abuse was sexual, which made her suspect that it was. He was reluctant to share details about his family and whether anyone else knew what his cousin had done to him. He'd grown up in a Nevada small town, and it was obvious that he still carried a stigma about therapy. Many people were like that. If you went to a psychiatrist, you were crazy or weak. She'd tried several approaches with Todd, but he was resistant to hypnosis, and he'd declined drugs to improve his suggestibility.

In the end, he'd thanked her and walked away. She didn't think she'd helped him at all.

"So what's going on, Todd?"

He stared off at the dark waters of the bay. His face twitched, as if his brain and mouth were struggling with what to say. "Something really weird is happening to me."

"What is it?"

"I'm having strange memories," he told her.

"Of your cousin?" she asked. "Of what he did to you?"

"No, this is completely different. I'm remembering things that never happened. And yet it's like they did."

"I don't understand."

"Yeah, me neither. I mean, it's like waking up from a dream where you have flashbacks of what was in your head, but you can't really put them together. I see things—I remember things—but only fragments. They're disconnected. Like somebody snipped pieces out of a video. I'd swear they were dreams, but it doesn't feel that way. It feels like I'm remembering something that really happened. I can't explain it."

Frankie was silent as she processed what Todd was saying. He went on in a voice that was so soft she struggled to hear him: "I was just wondering if this could be a side effect of what we did."

"You mean the therapy?"

"Uh-huh."

"No, I'm sure this is something else, Todd."

"You mean I can't remember false things? Because online, they talk about recovered memories that aren't true. People will remember things that never actually happened to them."

"I really don't think that's what this is."

He nodded, but he looked doubtful. "Okay, whatever you say, but I'm scared. I don't like what's going on in my head."

"How long have you felt this way?"

Todd rubbed a hand across his face. He blinked and looked lost. "The first time was two months ago. And then it stopped, so I figured it was some weird one-time thing. But this week—this week it happened again—"

"What exactly do you remember?" Frankie asked him.

"Torture."

Frankie recoiled. "What?"

"That's what I remember, Dr. Stein. Horrible shit. The pictures in my head, they're graphic and violent."

Her mind was in a whirl. "Did this happen *to* you? Were you suffering some kind of physical or mental abuse?"

"No, I saw it. I was watching it. It's like I was a witness, you know?"

"Who was being tortured?" Frankie asked.

"A woman. Women, actually. It's happened more than once."

"What happened to them? Who was doing this?"

"I'm not sure I can describe it. It's all bits and pieces. There's this white room, and the woman is on a bed or chaise or something. She's like—I don't know, she looks drugged. Tied up, too, so she can't move. And I remember some guy in a creepy-ass mask. He's the one torturing her."

"A mask?"

"Yeah. Some weird grinning mask with bug eyes. Scary as shit. I mean, it's so bizarre, it can't be real, right? But I feel like it *happened*."

"Have you told anyone else about this?" Frankie asked.

"Are you kidding? No way. Like I said—no notes, right? I don't want anybody thinking I'm nuts. You can't tell anyone about this, can you? Doctor–patient privilege or whatever?"

"That's right," she said.

Todd exhaled in relief. "Good."

Frankie hesitated. This wasn't the kind of question she usually asked a patient. You didn't challenge their hallucinations. "Listen, Todd, can you tell me one other thing? You said this felt like a dream, and yet you seem convinced that it really happened. Why?"

He slid closer to her on the bench. She was uncomfortable with the lack of personal space between them. He eyed the Bay Trail to make sure that no one else was within earshot. He looked frightened now.

"When this first happened two months ago, I thought it was a dream, too," he said, "but then I realized it couldn't be."

"Why not?"

"Because the women I saw are real. I saw them on TV. That chick who threw herself off the bridge this week? She was one of the women in the white room. I mean, I don't know her, I've never met her, I don't know who she is. But *I remember her.*"

14

Frost waited for the cable car to pass, and then he crossed into Union Square. He finished a foot-long hot dog as he walked. Ketchup, pickle relish, no onions. It drove his brother crazy that Frost ate so many hot dogs. Duane was a chef, and he didn't appreciate Frost's argument that street-vendor hot dogs were better than just about any other food in the world.

The sun beat down on his neck. Entering the plaza, he passed under the palm trees. The Macy's building was across the square on his right. People swarmed the park, clustering around musicians, mimes, jugglers, and acrobats. Above the street music, he heard the chants and drums of protesters, and he could see hand-painted signs waving in the air. It was San Francisco. Someone was always protesting something.

He found the terraced steps leading down to Geary Street, and it took him a minute to spot Lucy Hagen among the hundred-or-so people eating lunch on the steps on the warm afternoon. She was small and alone, watching the world go by with a dreamy expression on her face. She wore a belted red dress with black stripes at the hem. Her knees were pressed together, and she wore red high heels. The dress showed off her pretty arms and legs. Her brown hair nestled on her shoulders.

He squeezed his way down the steps and slid to the ground beside her. He whistled a tune that had been stuck in his head all day.

"Hey, Lucy," he said.

"Oh, hey, Frost." She welcomed him with a smile.

"Sorry to interrupt your lunch break, but I had a few more questions for you."

"That's okay. I like the company."

Her lunch consisted of a couscous salad with olives and artichoke hearts. She took dainty, uninterested bites with a plastic fork. He guessed that if he'd offered to buy her a hot dog, she would have jumped at the chance.

"You look great," he said.

"Have to look good for the Macy's customers, you know." But he could tell she was pleased with the compliment.

Lucy always looked a little lost when he saw her. Some single women owned the city, and some looked overwhelmed by it. Her big, curious eyes followed the people around her. She was a watcher, not a doer. He had the feeling that she stared at other San Franciscans on the street and wondered how they could make it look so easy. The businessmen. The construction workers in bright yellow. The drag queens. Even the homeless wrapped in blankets.

She noticed him studying her face and went back to her lunch in embarrassment. Her mouth twitched into a frown. "Have they found Brynn's body yet?"

"No."

Lucy shivered. "That's awful."

"It is. I'm sorry."

"I checked with her supervisor, by the way. Brynn missed a day of work this week. She didn't show up. She didn't call."

"And you have no idea where she was?" he asked.

"No."

Frost craned his neck to study the plaza. "Did you say Dr. Stein's office is nearby?"

Lucy pointed at a tall building on Stockton on the east side of the square. "She works in there."

"Did Brynn say anything about seeing Dr. Stein lately? Is there a chance she could have gone to her for some kind of follow-up appointment?"

"I don't think so. She didn't mention it."

"Did she say anything at all about Dr. Stein recently?"

"On the bridge, when we were stuck up there, she suggested I talk to her. She said she was pretty good. That's it."

"Okay. Thanks."

Lucy closed the plastic lid on her salad, as if she weren't hungry anymore. She put her chin up, savoring the sun. "I love hanging out here, don't you? Especially on the weekends. It's so crazy. All the street performers. All the wild getups."

"There's nothing like it in the world," Frost agreed.

She played with her hair, wrapping a curl around one of her fingers. "So did you always know you wanted to be a detective? Were you one of those little boys who played cops and robbers all the time?"

Frost shook his head. "No, when I was a kid, I didn't have a clue what I wanted to do."

"That's like me. I still don't."

"Yeah, it's different for some people. My brother, Duane, knew he was going to be a chef when he was five years old. He was cooking dinner for all of us by the time he was seven."

"People like that amaze me," Lucy said. "I wish I had a dream like that, but I don't."

Frost shrugged. "I think the rest of the world is more like you and me. We just kind of find our way. Things happen, and we figure it all out as we go."

"Well, I'm still trying to figure it out," Lucy replied.

"You've got time. When I was your age, I was just getting out of USF law school. I didn't know what the hell I was going to do."

"Oh my God, you're a lawyer?" Lucy asked.

"I hope that doesn't destroy your opinion of me."

"No, it's just—why aren't you practicing law?"

"Like I said, things happen," Frost told her. "I went to SF State as an undergrad and got a dual degree in history and criminology. I was really only interested in history, but my parents said I should get some practical value out of my college education. They pushed law school on me, too. Duane was working ninety hours a week at minimum wage as a cook, and I think they figured one of the Easton boys should go make some money. It didn't work out that way."

"Why not?"

"Well, for one thing, there were no jobs for lawyers when I got out. That's okay. I would have hated it."

"So you joined the police?" Lucy asked.

"Nope."

She was confused. "What did you do?"

"I drove a taxi for two years."

Lucy laughed. She reached out and touched his shoulder and then quickly drew her hand back. "Wow, you really are full of surprises."

"I liked it," Frost said. "I got to know the ins and outs of the city, all the back roads and back routes. That still comes in pretty handy."

"Why'd you quit?"

"I got robbed too many times. I had too many people throw up in my cab. So I hooked up with a high school buddy down on the Wharf. We ran fishing charters for a year. We slept on the boat. I liked being on the water, but I smelled like fish all the time, and girls didn't really go for that."

Frost was enjoying his trip down memory lane, but he knew how it ended. He felt a tightness in his stomach. Things happen, and you figure out where you're going, but it doesn't mean what happens is good.

"Then I spent six months working on Alcatraz as a tour guide. I loved that, being a history buff. It was my favorite job."

"But only six months?" Lucy asked.

"Only six months."

"What happened? Did you get laid off?"

Frost glanced at Lucy and then glanced away. They were the same age. Lucy and Katie. Both twenty-five.

"No, my sister was murdered," Frost told her.

Lucy's big eyes flew open even wider. He heard her inhale sharply. Without a word or thought, she wrapped her arms around him and held him tightly. "Oh my God, Frost. I don't know what to say."

"Thanks. There's nothing to say."

She let him go, but she held on to his hand. "That's so terrible."

"Yeah. Katie was a sweet kid."

He was about to say *she was your age*, but he didn't. He was about to say *you remind me of her*, but he didn't.

"I found her in the backseat of her car. It was—"

He stopped. It was a scene only the devil would understand.

"There are so many ripple effects when something like that happens," he went on. "My parents separated for a while and only reconciled a couple years ago. They left the city. Moved to Tucson. They couldn't handle being here anymore. Duane and I actually grew closer. We were so different, and we'd never spent much time together, but without Katie, we were all we had."

"And you became a cop," Lucy concluded.

"Yes, I became a cop. Suddenly, the criminology degree, the law degree, seemed to make sense in the world. Up to that point, they didn't. But I guess there's a weird synchronicity to life. The puzzle pieces come together eventually."

Lucy still clung to his hand.

"Did you catch the guy?"

"Yes, we got him. My lieutenant was the detective on the case. Now he's gone away for good. Honestly, I don't always know how to deal with it. That guy completely changed my life. I'm sitting here right now because of a murderer." He shook his head and gave a silent, unhappy laugh. "Sorry, Lucy. I don't mean to drag you down with my stories."

"No, I'm glad you told me. I don't have any stories like that."

"Be glad you don't."

"I don't know. I want there to be *something*, you know. I feel like I'm not going anywhere. I think I'd rather be like you. Drive a cab, or live on a fishing boat, or work on Alcatraz, instead of selling jewelry to rich old women."

"Nothing's stopping you," Frost said.

"Except myself." Lucy checked the time on her phone. "I better go. Break's over."

"Sorry. One more question."

"Sure."

"Did Brynn tell you anything about her treatments with Dr. Stein? I'm trying to find out more about how this memory thing really works."

"No, she didn't talk about it, but she seemed fine afterward. Nothing was wrong, as far as I could tell."

"She didn't give you any details?"

"Not really, but if you want to find out more about it, I know someone who can help."

"Who?" Frost asked.

"Me."

"You? What do you mean?"

Lucy looked embarrassed. "I decided to talk to Dr. Stein about my gephyrophobia. It's stupid, living in the Bay Area and freaking out about bridges. I want to know if she thinks she can help me."

"I'm not sure that's a good idea right now," Frost said.

"Oh, I won't do any treatments yet. I probably can't even afford it. I just figured I'd do an initial consultation to find out what it's all about. That's what you want, too, isn't it?"

"Lucy, don't do this for me. Really."

"But it might help you anyway, right?"

"It might," Frost admitted.

"Well, there you go. Win-win for both of us. I have an appointment on Monday afternoon. We can talk afterward."

Lucy didn't give him a chance to object. She pushed herself off the step and smoothed her red dress. Frost got up, too, and their bodies accidentally bumped together in the hustle-bustle of the crowd. Lucy's mouth puckered, as if she had an impulse to kiss him. He defused the moment by reaching out to shake her hand. She took it, and her palm had a nervous dampness.

"Bye, Frost," she said, with a twinge of disappointment on her face.

"Good-bye, Lucy."

She turned and skipped down the steps, dodging between the crowds. He watched her until she disappeared through the revolving door at Macy's, and then he turned back to the park. As he climbed into the plaza, he nearly collided with a tall man who wore a white flowing robe and a bizarre mask that completely covered his face. The mask featured a red-lipped grin from ear to ear, long white fangs, and huge bug eyes. A black wig of dreadlocks hung down his head.

Frost was startled, but weirdness was the coin of the realm in San Francisco.

"Sorry," he said.

The mask bobbed up and down, and the man replied in a singsong falsetto.

"*Sorrrr-eeee,*" he chanted. "*Sorrrr-eeee.*"

Frost continued past the man into the square. He was fifty yards away beneath the palm trees when he remembered what Lucy had told him about the man on the bridge.

The man wearing a strange mask, two cars away from Brynn Lansing.

Frost didn't like coincidences.

He ran back to the steps of the plaza and scanned the crowd. He looked everywhere, but the man in the mask had already vanished.

15

Frankie spent the evening alone at Zingari. Jason texted that he was in his laboratory, and Pam still wasn't speaking to her after their last argument. She sat at a window table beginning at six o'clock, and by the time she got to her fourth glass of wine, darkness had taken over the neighborhood outside the restaurant. She had her Kindle with her. She started the night by rereading *The Myth of Repressed Memory* by Elizabeth Loftus, but at the halfway point in the bottle of pinot noir, she switched to *The Magus* by John Fowles.

When she heard the ping on her phone, she knew her mysterious stalker was back. She opened the e-mail and saw

She needs you.

He was baiting her to write back, but instead, she forwarded the e-mail to Pell Security, and then she called the CEO of the company to see if they'd had any luck tracing the overnight message to its source. She reached him, but he didn't have good news. The GMX account had been accessed via a generic IP address on a public Wi-Fi server and couldn't be linked to an individual.

He also confirmed that the sender had been logged in at Zingari on Friday while she was there.

The Night Bird was definitely watching her.

Frankie hung up her phone and spent a long time examining every face in the restaurant. No one looked back at her. No one looked familiar. She realized that the stranger had what he wanted. He was playing with her head.

"Everything okay?" Virgil asked as he refilled her glass, emptying the bottle. His lavish white forelock spilled down his forehead. He was dressed in the usual black uniform, which he wore a size too small to show off his physique.

"More love letters," Frankie said. She connected a charger to her phone to juice the battery.

"Well, aren't you the lucky one."

"Not so lucky. This one says he wants to watch me die."

The dark brows over Virgil's hawk-like eyes arched in surprise. His smirk froze as he tried to figure out whether she was joking. "Seriously?"

"Seriously."

"Are you going to call the cops or something?"

"They won't do anything. They'll come if he shows up waving a gun, but short of that, I'm on my own." She added, "He was in here last night, Virgil."

"The hell you say."

"My security company traced him to the Wi-Fi at the restaurant. Was anyone asking about me? Or watching me?"

"Just that tasty cop."

"Keep an eye open, okay?" Frankie asked. "If you see somebody, let me know."

"My eyes are always open," Virgil said.

Frankie went back to her wine. She picked at the plate of yellowfin tuna in front of her. She gazed at Post Street to see if anyone lingered in the arched entrances of the Marriott, but no one outside the hotel paid special attention to the windows at Zingari.

She wondered if she should call the CEO at Pell Security again and ask him to provide personal protection for a few days. She'd had to do that once before, when the Darren Newman case exploded. The knifing death of the young woman, Merrilyn Somers, had put Frankie in the headlines, and she'd received anonymous threats from people who were convinced that she'd set a killer free. Legally, she was blameless, but morally, she couldn't shake her own sense of guilt. She was relieved when Newman was cleared, but her doubts about him had never gone away.

Frankie felt surrounded by ghosts in the restaurant. Her father. Darren Newman. The Night Bird. And now Todd Ferris, too—the man at the Bay Trail with his memories of torture in a white room. She wasn't convinced that what Todd had experienced was real. Some people made up stories that put themselves at the center of current events. It made them feel important. His descriptions also had a hallucinatory quality, maybe from drugs, maybe from dreams. Even his recollection of Brynn Lansing—if it had happened at all—could be easily explained. Brynn worked near Frankie's building; he might well have seen her as he was going in or out of the Union Square office.

She'd urged Todd to schedule an appointment, but he declined. He still didn't want anything in writing. And then he'd left. That was that. She wondered if she would hear from him again.

Virgil slid into the chair opposite her. He smoothed his beautiful hair. "Want company?" he asked.

"Yes."

"Oh good, because I wasn't going to give you a choice."

"Can I ask you a question, Virgil?"

"Nine inches," he said.

"Oh, oh, oh, TMI," Frankie replied, knowing she was drunk and not particularly caring. "No, I want to know if you take drugs."

"Say it a little louder, honey," Virgil told her.

Frankie realized she was almost shouting, and she was glad the noise of the restaurant drowned her out. She lowered her voice and leaned across the table and took Virgil's hands. "Sorry. Do you?"

"Are you a cop now?"

"No."

"Well then—duh. Of course I do."

"Are you careful?"

"I'm careful about all things I allow inside my body. It pays to be cautious, no?"

"It does." She added, "What drugs do you take?"

His teeth flashed behind his plump lips. "Are you in the market? Do you need me to hook you up?"

"No. Just curious."

"Well, I don't usually share that information with people I'm not sleeping with," Virgil said, "but since you're a friend, let's just say I don't discriminate between legal and illegal pharmaceuticals."

"Have you heard anything on the street about bad drugs? Laced heroin? PCP? Bath salts? Any reports of extreme hallucinogenic reactions?"

"Only among your patients," Virgil replied.

Her face bloomed with shock and anger, and he held up his hands in surrender. "Sorry, honey, that was nasty. Pam was in here for lunch. She told me what's going on. Didn't mean to poke the porcupine."

Frankie leaned back in her chair and shook her head. "Am I an evil person, Virgil?"

"What, for messing with minds? Some minds need to be messed with."

"I change reality for people," Frankie said.

"Because they ask you to, right?"

"Yes, but maybe I have no business playing God with what's real and what's not. My father accused me of being no better than a lobotomist."

"What a charming man Marvin was," Virgil said.

"Can I tell you a secret? I don't really miss him. I can't even say I'm sorry he's dead. I've never said that to another human being. Not even Jason."

It lifted a burden for her to say the words out loud. She'd felt that way for months. Her father had been emotionally abusive to her and Pam his whole life. Making them feel small. Making them feel worthless. To have him gone was—a relief. It was horrible, but it was the truth.

"Do you feel guilty for feeling that way?" Virgil asked. In black, he looked like a priest in the confessional.

"Yes."

"Well, don't."

"He was my *father*."

"And that means what, exactly? It's biology. He donated a sperm cell. Is that some kind of noble act? Parenthood ain't the sex, honey. It's everything that comes after."

"Is your father still alive?" Frankie asked.

"I have no idea, but I suppose he is. I don't think God is too anxious to meet him. Do you know what he did when I told him at age ten that I thought another boy was cute? He shoved a broom handle into my mouth until I vomited. He said, 'No son of mine is going to be a filthy homo.'"

Frankie closed her eyes. "I'm sorry, V."

"Don't be. All I'm saying is, some parents aren't worth mourning. There's good ones, and there's bad ones. You and me, we had bad ones."

"I guess I should be grateful it wasn't worse. He never physically harmed us."

"You can get plenty of scars without ever being touched," Virgil said.

"You're right. Ever thought of changing careers? You give good shrink."

He winked. "You'll get my bill."

Virgil pushed back the chair and stood up. He bent down and kissed Frankie on top of the head, and then he disappeared into the Zingari crowd. She felt lonely being alone now. She called Jason, but the call went to voice mail. She called Pam to apologize for their fight, but her sister didn't answer, either.

And then ping.

Another e-mail.

It was almost as if her stalker were keeping her company. As if he knew she was alone and he wanted to be there for her. She studied the restaurant again, but if the Night Bird was here, he was hiding in a crowd of faces. She opened the e-mail.

> You have ten minutes to save her.

Frankie told herself, *Do not respond.* That was what the security company had said. Never respond. He will try to goad you into replying. That's what he wants. To engage you. To suck you in.

Do not respond.

She tapped out a response on her phone: "Who?"

Her finger hovered over the "Send" button. To send or not to send. She knew she was making a mistake by playing his game, and yet the darkness of his messages felt ominous.

> She needs you. You have ten minutes to save her.

No.

Frankie deleted the reply without sending it. She deleted the original message. No more games; it was time to go home. With a sigh of relief, she removed her wallet from her purse and peeled off cash to pay for her dinner and wine. She left the money on the table. She looked for Virgil in the crowd to wave good-bye, but she didn't see him.

Outside, on Post Street, the night air was cool. Trees shivered in the planter boxes. High buildings dwarfed her on all sides. She checked the street, but she felt safe among the garish throngs of Saturday-night partiers. Her condo on O'Farrell was only five blocks away.

She heard the chime of her phone again. Ping. He wasn't giving up.

Frankie hesitated. No matter how much she wanted to pull away, she found herself going deeper into this man's game. She had no choice. She opened the message:

Five minutes.

This time, there was something more to the e-mail. She saw an attachment file—a JPEG picture. He'd sent her a photograph.

Do not respond.

Never open attachments.

But she did. She clicked on the image, wondering if she'd made a mistake that would give him access to her whole electronic life, but it felt as if he knew everything about her already. Where she was. What she was doing.

Frankie stared at the photo on the small screen of her phone. It had been taken from above, like a still image captured from a ceiling-mounted webcam. The photo showed the inside of a busy cocktail lounge. People crowded shoulder to shoulder in the semidarkness. The bar glowed with red and green lights reflecting on dozens of liquor bottles stocked on mirrored shelves. She squinted and saw something else, too—three vintage pinball machines from the '80s. She knew where this place was.

It was a bar two blocks away. She and Jason had been there many times. Loud pop music. Drinks. Dancing.

Frankie checked the time. It was five minutes to midnight. Five minutes.

She didn't understand why this photograph was supposed to mean anything to her, but then she remembered: *She needs you.* With a pinch of her fingers, she enlarged the image and scrolled from face to face. No one was looking at the camera. No one knew they were being photographed. She didn't see anyone she recognized. The faces were all strangers, except—

Frankie felt the breath leave her chest.

She zoomed in on one face until the image began to lose its focus. And she realized that she knew this woman. Her name was Christie Parke. She was thirty-seven years old. She lived in Millbrae and worked as a loan officer at a branch of Wells Fargo downtown. Five years ago, while volunteering at a homeless shelter, she'd been stuck with a dirty needle and diagnosed with AIDS. The lab result turned out to be a false positive. She was fine. But the experience had left her with a deadly fear of needles.

It was a fear that Frankie had helped her erase.

Christie was one of her patients.

Frankie stared at the steep Mason Street hill that led up toward the bar. She started running.

16

Christie watched as her date, whose name was Noah, pushed the pinball flippers, firing a silver ball straight up the super-jackpot ramp and making the eyes of the Terminator's skull glow red.

"Fire at will," said the voice of Arnold Schwarzenegger from the game's display.

After a quick fist pump, Noah used a rotating gun to shoot a new ball into play. He juggled three balls up and down the machine, and Christie couldn't keep track of the action. Arrows lit up. Bumpers flashed and exploded. The machine rocked as Noah slammed it with his hips.

"Awesome," Arnold said.

"*Awesome,*" Noah imitated in a deep voice. He glanced at Christie, whose boredom must have shown on her face. Thirty-something men playing teenage games didn't thrill her, especially on a first date. With obvious reluctance, Noah took his hands off the flippers, and one by one, the silver balls rolled into the belly of the machine. He gave her an embarrassed smile.

"Sorry," he told her. "I used to play this game when I was a kid. I just wanted to see if I still had the knack."

"I guess you do," Christie said coolly, sipping her cranberry martini.

There was a line to take Noah's spot at the pinball machine. They were all men who weren't getting laid tonight, Christie figured. That included Noah. She'd decided that soon after she met him for dinner. He was nice enough, but he acted like a kid, and she wasn't interested in kids.

"I'm going to get another beer," Noah told her. "You want anything?"

"No, I'm good."

He jostled his way through the crowd, leaving her alone. She saw other guys give her the eye, wondering whether to come in for a landing. A few smiled, and she smiled back, but not enough for an invitation.

Christie liked being in demand. After her divorce last November, she'd lost twenty pounds, and she looked good in her shorty skirts again. Dating was a hassle in her thirties, but for now, she enjoyed being single. She'd hooked up a couple of times, and it was strange to be the one to say, "I'll call you," when she knew she never would. She was happy to head to work the next morning with a satisfied smile on her face. No walk of shame, just the coffee cup of freedom.

Christie liked the vibe of the Bush Street bar, despite the juvenile pinball machines. It felt like a throwback to the '90s. Most of the people were her own age, not the usual millennials. A jukebox played Aerosmith at a shattering volume. The drunk Gen Xers danced fast, as if they were still young, but she knew they'd wake up, roll out of bed, and groan at the ache in their knees.

It was warm near the bar's fireplace, and she felt heat on the back of her legs. Perfume, cologne, and hair gels clouded the air. The effect was dizzying, but she couldn't really blame the bar. She'd felt off all day. She'd awakened with an odd sense of disorientation, as if she didn't even belong in her own apartment. Since then, she'd been up and down in huge swings. One minute, she would be euphoric, and the next she'd feel a formless anxiety grip her stomach.

Her brain kept trying to remember something, but nothing was there.

Noah came back, holding a bottle of amber IPA. He wore a black sport coat over a red T-shirt and blue jeans and sneakers, which was how thirty-six-year-olds tried to shave a decade off their age. He was a few donuts shy of being overweight. He had messy red hair and a goatee, as if he'd spotted a photograph of Ed Sheeran in *People* and decided that was the way to meet girls. Christie could have told him that the Redbeard pirate look only worked for Ed Sheeran because he was Ed Sheeran.

They'd been set up on a blind date by one of her colleagues at the bank. She should have been firmer in saying no.

"You having fun?" Noah asked.

"Sure," she replied without enthusiasm. He didn't seem to notice, so she checked her watch to make her point. She wasn't looking to prolong the evening. It was almost midnight, and her date was already a pumpkin.

"You know, I thought you were going to blow me off," he said.

"Oh?"

"I texted you like four times yesterday, but you didn't answer."

"Sorry. I slept the whole day. I guess I wasn't feeling well."

"Was it a cold or something? I take a crap load of vitamin C every day, and I never get colds."

"No, I don't know what it was," Christie said. "Maybe some kind of twenty-four-hour bug. I crashed out and lost the whole day."

"Are you feeling better now?"

"A little, but I don't want to make it a late night."

Noah still didn't take the hint. The music on the jukebox changed from Aerosmith to the B-52s, and his freckled face brightened into a grin. "Hey, great song!" he said. "Come on, let's dance!"

"No, I don't really feel up to it—" she began, but he didn't take no for an answer. He took her wrist and pulled her through the crowd to the postage-stamp dance floor. Most of the dancers were drunk. Noah writhed to "Love Shack," and she was pleasantly surprised to find that he followed the beat like a pro. His supple moves made him much more attractive than he'd been a minute earlier. He knew it, and his confidence glowed in his face.

Christie loosened up as she danced with him. Some of her energy came back. She wasn't a great dancer herself, but she didn't care. She forgot about the anxiety that had dogged her all day. Noah pointed at her smile and called over the music, "See? You're having fun!"

She gave him a thumbs-up. He was right.

The B-52s became the Go-Go's, and the Go-Go's gave way to Donna Summer. He laughed as she lip-synched to "Bad Girls." When the song was over, Noah put a meaty arm around her shoulder, and she left it there. They were both breathing hard. She looked up into his blue eyes and wondered if she'd judged him too quickly. Suddenly, he did look a little like Ed Sheeran.

"I love this place," he said.

"Yeah, it's great."

"How about that next drink now?" he asked.

"Okay, sure."

"Cran-tini?"

"Yeah, thanks."

She watched him go, and he had a swagger in his step as he headed toward the bar. It was cute now. She tugged at the collar of her blouse because she was hot from dancing. She fluffed out her hair with her hands. Overhead, the music changed—something mellow this time, a Carole King song.

Somebody at the pinball machine whooped in excitement, and Arnold Schwarzenegger called out, "Awesome!"

Christie laughed.

Frankie took off her heels to run faster, but she was too late.

Midnight came and went. Half a block down the sharp hill from the cocktail lounge, she heard a scream that was more animal than human. It rose and fell, cutting through her brain like a knife. It was the scream you made when you saw hell. It was the scream you made when you were on fire.

A door slammed. Shouts overlapped. Warnings. Cries.

Ahead of her, a truck flew down Mason Street into the green light. As it did, a woman ran into the intersection, her hands over her face, not even seeing the danger. The truck's horn blared in a wild, continuous roll. Brakes screeched, and tires burned black skids onto the pavement. There was no time to stop. Frankie turned away in horror, but she heard the sickening thump of metal and body colliding. Not ten feet in front of her, the woman's broken form tumbled down the hill and lay still.

Frankie smelled the stench of hot rubber. Headlights and shadows crisscrossed the intersection. Footsteps pounded. She couldn't see the face of the woman in the road, but she already knew who it was.

The dead woman in the street was her patient, Christie Parke.

The Night Bird had killed her.

17

"The Night Bird," Frost said.

He watched Francesca Stein stare at the accident scene. The evening was cool, and she wore his sport coat draped over her shoulders. "Yes, that's right," she said. "That's the name he uses in his messages."

"And you think this person is somehow *programming* these women?"

She disconnected her cell phone from its portable charger and handed it to him. "You can see the e-mails he sent. He knew Christie was going to have her breakdown at midnight. He wanted me to see it happen."

Frost studied the messages on Stein's phone. He enlarged the photograph that had been taken inside the bar, but there was nothing in Christie Parke's face to suggest what was about to happen to her.

Just like Monica Farr. Just like Brynn Lansing.

The police had closed the intersection. The medical examiner was processing the body. The truck that had struck and killed Christie Parke was still parked in the middle of the street, with blood on its dented grille. He saw a uniformed officer taking a statement from the driver, but there was nothing the man could have done to avoid the collision. Pedestrians gawked from behind the police tape, and neighbors stood in the lit windows of the apartment buildings that overlooked the scene. The media had arrived, too. He spotted video cameras from the local news channels.

Stein's face pinched into a frown. She saw the cameras, too. Her name would be on television again. It was never good news that made the headlines.

"How is he doing this?" Frost asked. "How does it work?"

"I don't know."

Frost handed her the phone. "Can you forward these e-mails to me?"

"Of course, but I'm not sure it will help you. I asked a private security company to examine the messages, and they weren't able to trace them."

"We have our own experts," Frost said. "And if you get any more—"

"You'll be the first to know, Inspector," Stein replied.

Her face was a chaos of emotions. She was distracted. Confused. Afraid. Upset. Her eyes kept going back to the street, as if the moment of the accident were replaying in her mind. The impact. The noise. Once you saw someone die, you were never the same. A body always left its mark.

Katie had been his first.

Wind blew down the street and whisked strands of her short brown hair into her face, but she didn't seem to notice. She leaned her head back against the stone wall of the building behind her and closed her eyes. The downward turn of her lips was eloquent in its sadness.

"He's taunting you, and he's targeting your patients," Frost said. "This is obviously personal."

"Obviously," she murmured.

"Do you have any idea who could be doing this?"

Her eyes opened. She stared, not at him, but past him. She was hiding something. "I can't tell you anything. I'm sorry."

"Because you don't know anything, or because this involves your patients?"

The psychiatrist was silent.

"Privilege doesn't apply if you know a patient represents a serious risk of harm to others," Frost added.

"I'm well aware of my legal responsibilities, Inspector."

"Then can you tell me why someone would be doing this?"

"To destroy me," she replied.

"You think that's what this is about?"

Her eyes were hard. "Yes, I do."

"Has this person made any threats against you?" Frost asked.

"He said he's going to watch me die. Does that count?"

"I wish you'd told me about that when it happened," he said.

"I've been threatened before, Inspector, and the police are no help. Sorry, but that's reality. The law guards the victimizers, not the victims."

"You're preaching to the choir," Frost replied. He added, "If *you* wanted to do this to someone—make them behave in an extreme, erratic way—could you do it?"

"It would depend on the person, but yes."

"How?"

"A combination of drugs and hypnotic suggestion."

"Like in your memory practice?" he asked.

"Yes."

"So someone who went through your treatment would know how the process works."

"I suppose so," she said. Her voice was flat. Drained of intensity.

"What kind of drugs do you use?"

"That depends on the patient. A sedative like amobarbital would be a common choice. Sadly, no one would have much trouble putting their hands on it on the street."

"So the drugs loosen the brain's control, and hypnosis provides the direction?"

"Basically."

"Don't you find that scary?" Frost asked.

"Anything is scary when it's misused," she replied.

"Okay. True."

"Do you need anything else from me right now, Inspector? I'd like to go home."

"One more question. What did you treat Christie Parke for? What was her problem?"

Stein didn't answer immediately, but then she said, "Needles."

"She was afraid of needles?"

"Terrified."

Frost nodded. He watched her eye the crowds, and he said, "Let me have someone drive you home, Dr. Stein. You don't want to run the gauntlet."

"Thank you."

Stein slipped his sport coat off her shoulders and handed it back to him with a weary smile. She had a precise, elegant way about her. Her movements were graceful, and yet she kept a mysterious distance, as if she invited no one else inside. Frost often chose to be alone, but he enjoyed his solitude when he could get it. Francesca Stein's aloneness looked like melancholy.

He signaled a policewoman, who accompanied Stein to a squad car. She took a last look at the crime scene before climbing inside. Frost tried to read her mind, and he guessed that she was thinking that her life would never be the same after this night.

Murder was a before-and-after moment.

He knew what that felt like.

Christie's date, Noah, hummed incessantly. The same chorus of the same song, over and over. Frost found it distracting, but every witness had a different kind of nervous tic. The redheaded man sat on the floor of the lounge, with his back against the pinball machine and his hands wrapped around his knees. They'd already interviewed and dismissed the other patrons from the bar, but Frost wanted to talk to Noah himself.

Frost stood over him. Noah's head bobbed as he hummed, and he wore an awkward, inappropriate smile. He had a boyish face naturally, and fear made him look even younger.

"Thanks for sticking around," Frost said.

"Oh, yeah. Sure." He added, "So is she—I mean, did she—?"

"She didn't make it. Sorry."

"Wow. I mean, I didn't really know her, but still—wow. That's awful."

"So exactly what happened, Noah?"

"Hell if I know. I went to get her a drink. Cranberry martini. It was her second. When I got back, she was shaking, screaming, covering her eyes. Then she ran out into the street, and bam. That was it."

"Was she behaving strangely during the evening?"

"No. If anything, she looked bored. Most of the night, we didn't really click, you know."

He started humming again. Same song. It was like an earworm on an infinite loop.

"Did you slip her anything?" Frost asked.

His mouth fell open. "No! No, that's not my style. No way."

"What about Christie? Did she take anything? Prescription or otherwise?"

"Not that I saw," Noah said.

"Where were you before you came to the bar?" he asked.

"I took her to dinner at a Japanese place a couple blocks up Bush Street. I'm not much into sushi, but she said she liked it. Always give the lady what she wants on a first date."

"Whose idea was it to come here afterward?"

"Hers. I said, how about we get a drink, and she suggested this place."

"Had she been here before?"

Noah shrugged. "I don't know. She didn't say."

"Did Christie talk to anyone else while you guys were together? Or did anyone talk to her? Did you see anyone who seemed to be watching her?"

Noah hummed again, louder, as he thought about the evening. Then he shook his head.

"I don't think so."

"Are you sure?"

"Well, Christie was cute. Short skirt, guys go for that. I saw other dudes checking her out. I got the feeling she liked the attention, you know? Pissed me off a little. After all, I was the one paying for dinner and buying the drinks."

"Was there anyone in particular that she noticed? Or who noticed her?"

"Not that I remember. Sorry."

"Did Christie talk to you about having been in therapy?" Frost asked.

Noah grinned. "What, like seeing a shrink? No, most girls are smart enough to keep the cray-cray hidden when you start dating them. Comes out sooner or later, though."

Frost slid out a card and handed it to Noah. "I think that's all for now."

"I can get out of here?" he asked.

"Yes. If you think of anything else, my number's on the card."

Frost headed for the door of the bar, but as he did, he found that he was whistling under his breath. He was on the street and into the third replay of the chorus before he realized that Noah's earworm had gotten inside his own head. He was whistling the same song that Noah had been humming, and once a song got into your brain like that, it was impossible to get it out.

Then Frost realized something strange.

The earworm stuck in his head wasn't new. He'd been whistling a fragment of a song wherever he went for the past couple of days. It popped onto his lips and demanded to come out. Noah had been humming *the same song* that Frost had been whistling for days.

He went back inside the lounge and nearly bumped into Noah, who was on his way out of the bar.

"What are you humming?" Frost asked.

"Huh? Oh yeah, I do that. I know, it can be irritating. Most of the time, I don't even know I'm doing it. Women have to tell me to stop."

"What's the song?"

Noah listened to the tune on his lips. "I think it's a Carole King song. It was playing when Christie did her freak-out. I guess it kind of stuck with me, you know?"

Noah was right. It was a Carole King song. Frost had heard it before. Recently. Over and over.

"Which one?" he asked, even though he knew the answer.

"It's called 'Nightingale,'" Noah replied. "I always liked that one. It's a song for lonely people, you know? It's about the night bird winging his way home."

18

In her dream, Frankie hiked along the Point Reyes beach with her father beside her.

He took long, determined steps in the sand, and she had to walk fast to keep pace with him. His back was as straight as a light post. His wiry hair defied the wind. He walked the way old men did, with his hands laced behind him. He fired questions at her like an impatient professor.

"Question," Marvin said. "Is there a formula for measuring acceptable risk?"

She was practically running. "No."

"Question. Then how do you assess whether a risk is worth taking?"

"It's a judgment call," she said, panting. "You have to look at the circumstances in each case."

"Question. Is it acceptable to pursue your own selfish satisfaction when it causes risk to someone else?"

Slow down, she wanted to say. *Slow down!*

"I suppose it's a trade-off. How badly do you want something, and how big is the risk?"

"Question. So it's okay to risk another's life or happiness simply because *you* really want something?"

"That's not what I said."

"Question. Are you and Jason still sleeping together?"

Frankie stopped.

"*What?* How dare you ask me something like that? What does that have to do with anything? It's none of your business!"

Marvin kept walking, leaving her behind. He seemed taller than he was in real life.

Frankie's senses felt oddly sharp. The noise of the waves was crisp and unnaturally loud, making her want to cover her ears. The beach was littered with hundreds of dead fish, their carcasses swarmed by flies, and rotting flesh squished under her bare toes. A briny smell filled her nose. Everything in the world felt bigger, brighter, and more intense. The ocean. The huge rocky cliffs climbing to the sky. Her father striding ahead of her. It was like a movie playing in her head.

She caught up with him. His voice was softer now.

"Was I a good father?" he asked her.

She shook her head. "No."

"You're successful."

"Not because of you."

"Did I praise you enough?"

"No."

"I need you," her father said.

She cocked her head. "What?"

"You have ten minutes to save me."

"*What?*"

She blinked, and her father was suddenly gone. She stood alone on the beach. The wind and waves grew more ferocious, as if she were in the center of a storm. Dead fish washed in with each slap of the tide. Spray soaked her skin. She looked all around to find her father, and then she saw him—a silhouette high on the tall cliff, his arms spread wide. He was going to jump.

"*Stop!*"

Frankie shouted, but the noise drowned her voice. She ran, but the wet sand sucked her down. He flew. Gravity brought him shooting toward her, larger and faster with each second. She turned away in horror, but she heard the sickening thump of flesh and rock colliding. Not ten feet in front of her, when she looked again, her father's broken form cartwheeled down the beach and lay still. She stood over him. His limbs were twisted. Blood striped his face.

His eyes snapped open.

They were not human eyes under his eyelids. They were fly eyes. Bug eyes. His lips grew into a giant, red-lipped grin from ear to ear. He sang to her in a horrible falsetto.

"Fran-kieeee, Fran-kieeee."

She bolted upward in bed, screaming. Her body under her nightgown was clammy with sweat, and she threw off the covers. Warm sunlight streamed through the windows of her bedroom. She shook herself to drive the dream out of her brain, but the memory lingered, making her shiver.

She got out of bed. Below her in the condo, she smelled coffee brewing. It was Sunday morning. She refreshed herself with a long shower. The pulse of the water massaged her back, and she breathed in steam. When she was done and out of the bathroom, she'd almost forgotten the dream.

Then the creepy, falsetto voice came back.

This time, it was real, calling to her from inside her own bedroom.

"Fran-kieeee, Fran-kieeee."

She screamed and spun around, but she was alone. The voice was coming from the phone on her nightstand. Someone was calling her— but somehow, her ringtone had been changed. She ran to the phone, but she was too late to grab the incoming call. She fumbled with the buttons on the phone to check her settings, and when she found the listing of ringtones, she saw a new one:

0001—Night Bird

Frankie threw the phone against the wall, where it shattered into pieces. How? How had he done it? She always had her phone with her; she never left it anywhere. But as if to taunt her further, the phone rang again. Not the broken phone on the floor. This was another phone, using her ordinary ringtone. The noise was muffled. She looked everywhere and realized that her own phone was still in her purse. Her real phone.

Somehow, he'd slipped a *second* phone into her bag. As if to say, *I was this close to you once. I can be this close to you again.* He was worming his way into her life. Into her brain.

She remembered sitting next to Todd Ferris on the bench the previous day. Was it him?

Or had the Night Bird been among the crowd at Zingari again?

Frankie dove into her purse and answered her phone. She didn't recognize the incoming number.

"Dr. Stein?"

"Yes, who is this?"

"It's Khristeen Smith with the *San Francisco Chronicle*. I wanted to see if you had any comment about the unusual deaths of three of your patients."

Frankie's fist tightened around the phone. The news was out. Soon she'd be under siege. "No, I don't have any comment right now."

"Should your patients be worried? Do you have any idea how this could be happening?"

"I can't talk to you right now, Ms. Smith," Frankie said. She hung up the phone. Almost immediately, it rang again. She didn't answer; she knew it would be another reporter. The vultures were gathering. She powered down her phone and returned it to her purse. She felt déjà vu. This was how it had started with Darren Newman, too. Her life was spinning out of control.

Frankie went downstairs. She poured coffee from the pot and took it out to the solarium. Pam was there, reading the newspaper on her iPad, and she didn't look up as Frankie took the chair next to her. A cool distance blew between them.

"Hey," Frankie said.

"Hey yourself."

"Where's Jason?"

"Running." Pam's head swiveled. Her blond hair was casually messy. Her long bare legs were propped on a second chair. "Looks like you're famous again. It's on TV. It's in the paper."

"I know."

"Did you screw up? Give somebody the wrong meds?"

"It's not me. Someone else is doing this."

Pam sipped coffee. "What do you mean?"

"Some psycho is targeting my patients. And me."

"Are you sure?"

"I'm sure."

"I thought I heard you shout earlier. Did something happen?"

"Just a bad dream," Frankie said. After a pause, she added, "The dream was about Dad, actually."

"Sounds like a nightmare."

"It was. Remember how he used to ask us all those questions on our camping trips?"

"Oh Lord," Pam groaned. She lowered her voice to imitate their father. "Question. Does addiction constitute a brain illness or an absence of will? Question. Does the intervention of family help or hurt in an addict's trajectory of dependence? Like I didn't know he was talking about me. His questions were always designed to remind me that I was a shit-hole failure in his eyes."

Frankie knew Pam was right about that. Marvin's questions usually had a sharp edge, and the edge was always directed at Pam. "Hey, you lucked out when the topic was extraplanetary life. There wasn't much he could do with that."

"I don't know. I kept waiting for him to say, 'Question. If humans were relocated to another planet, would Pam be a minimum-wage waitress or a whore?'"

"He wasn't quite that bad."

"He was every bit that bad, Frankie," Pam replied.

Just like that, the shadow was back between them. Even from the grave, their father drove the two of them apart.

"I dreamed that I saw him on the cliff," Frankie said.

"Lucky you."

"He didn't fall. He jumped. In my dream."

"Maybe he did."

"Pam, don't say that," Frankie chided her.

"You said the rangers couldn't be sure. If he slipped, or if he jumped, what difference does it make to us? In the end, it's the same. He's gone. And you know what? I don't miss him."

Frankie hesitated. "Neither do I."

"Okay, then," Pam said. "Let's leave the bastard behind instead of talking about him every time we're together."

"Sorry. It still haunts me."

Frankie got up. She wasn't done with her coffee, but she wanted to get to the office. She always felt safe at her office. That was where her life made sense. Plus, she was sure she had messages waiting for her. Patients would be watching the news, and they'd be scared.

"Do you think I'm a bad person?" she asked.

Pam's eyes had the sharpness of knives. "I asked you that once myself. Remember? I OD'd and nearly died. I was in rehab for the second time. Dad wouldn't even come to see me. I was crying because I needed a father, and I didn't have one. I asked you if I was a bad person."

Frankie closed her eyes. "I do remember."

"You told me there was no such thing as bad people," Pam went on. "Only bad memories."

19

Frost played the song for Lucy.

She sat across from him on a bench in the SoMa market on Sunday morning. Shack licked crepe syrup from her finger through the door of his carrier. The market was loud with the roar of cars on the elevated ramp of Highway 101 behind them. The stone wall of a parking lot across the street looked like a prison. The appeal of the market was its food, not its ambience.

He increased the volume and put his phone between them. Carole King began singing. The song was "Nightingale."

"Do you recognize it?" he asked her.

"Sure, I know the song." Lucy nodded along with the music, but then her face clouded with unease as a memory came back. Her lips pressed tightly together. She closed her eyes. He could hear the raggedness of her breathing.

"Wait, that was the song on the radio that night," she said. "It was playing when Brynn . . . "

Frost nodded. "I'm sorry. I figured it was, but I needed to be sure."

"Why does that matter?" Lucy asked.

He took his phone back and found the video of the wedding where Monica Farr shot herself. He played the video for Lucy—not as far as the chaos and the shooting, but far enough to hear the screaming begin in the background.

The DJ at the wedding was playing the same song.

"Oh my God," Lucy said.

"The same thing happened in a bar in the Tenderloin last night," Frost continued. "The same song was playing. Another woman had a mental breakdown. She ran into the street and was killed."

Lucy pushed away his phone as if it had become hot to the touch. "This is creepy as hell."

"I know."

They were silent for a while, eating Duane's crepes. He could see his brother at the window of his food truck. A line of two dozen people backed up at the truck, waiting for Duane's famous Sunday morning banana-granola crepes with sweet hoisin-maple syrup. Lucy spotted Duane, too, and she held up the crepe and shouted, "This is *amazing*!"

Frost's brother took a little bow with his hands folded across the chest of his white chef's uniform. The customers around him applauded.

"You and your brother don't look much alike," Lucy said to Frost.

"You don't think so? Funny, most people pick us out as brothers right away. But I agree with you. I don't see it. After all, I'm much more handsome than he is."

Lucy grinned. "Well, you're right about that."

"Now, Katie and I, we were practically twins," Frost went on.

"Do you have a picture of her?"

Frost slid his phone across the bench to Lucy. He reached over and tapped the digits to unlock it so she could see the photo of him and Katie that he used as his screen saver. The picture showed the two of them at Alcatraz on a perfect summer day, with the city and the bay waters behind them and an endless California sky overhead. Her hair was sunny blond. Her head leaned into his shoulder.

"Wow, she was pretty," Lucy said. "And yes, you two definitely could have been twins."

"Thanks."

Shack nudged the door of the carrier with his paw, demanding more syrup, and Lucy obliged. She dabbed a little on his pink nose, and Shack used his tongue to clean it. Frost found himself staring at Lucy, and he knew she was aware of his eyes. Her cheeks blushed red. She had a shy contentment in her face, looking back at him and then looking away. He knew the signs when a relationship with a stranger was on the brink of becoming something deeper. Her glow sent him a romantic invitation: come get me.

What Frost couldn't tell her was that he felt a completely different emotion when he was with her. He missed his baby sister. Something about being with Lucy made Katie feel not so far away.

"There's a reason I wanted you to know about the song," he said.

Lucy sighed as he steered their conversation away from personal things. "To scare the crap out of me?"

"Sort of, yes. These incidents didn't happen by accident. The jukebox in the bar last night is controlled by a phone app, and someone hacked the app to play that song. I called the DJ who did the music at the wedding where Monica Farr died. He said someone in the crowd requested 'Nightingale.'"

"What about Brynn on the bridge?" Lucy asked.

"Someone posted a request for the song on the radio station's Facebook page. Take a look."

He'd saved the post on his phone, and he showed it to Lucy. Her smooth forehead crinkled as she spotted the name of the user behind the post.

"The Night Bird?" she asked.

"That's right. Does the name mean anything to you? Have you heard it before?"

"No, never. What does this mean, Frost?"

"It means that what happened to Brynn and these other women was murder. Someone targeted them."

"Now you really are scaring me," Lucy said.

"I'm sorry, but that's the point. Remember what we talked about yesterday? About you going to see Francesca Stein? I don't want you to do it. Not now. That's why I asked you to meet me. I think you should cancel your appointment."

Lucy thought about it, but then she shook her head. "It's just to find out more. I'm not going to do anything yet."

"It's too dangerous, Lucy. At least right now."

"I understand what you're saying, but you know what? I'm sick of being afraid. I'm sick of what happens to me when I try to cross a bridge. Dr. Stein helped Brynn. She really did. So I'd like to find out whether she thinks she can help me, too."

"If you do this, I want to be waiting outside the building."

Lucy giggled. "My hero."

"I'm serious. I want to make sure no one is watching you when you leave."

"Okay, fine. If that's what you want."

"It is. And keep your eyes open. If you see *anything* that looks weird, you call me right away. Got it?"

She saluted him. "Got it."

"I have to go," he told her.

"Yeah, I need to get to work, too. Thanks for breakfast."

He gestured at the food truck behind her and waved to his brother. "Thank Duane. If it were up to me, we'd be eating Cap'n Crunch."

"Well, I love Cap'n Crunch, too," Lucy said.

She stood up and reached a finger into Shack's carrier to say good-bye. The cat licked her fingertip. Frost stood up, too, and walked around the bench to be next to her.

Their faces were close. Before he could stop her, she leaned quickly toward him and grazed his lips with her own. Her mouth had the sweetness of syrup.

"I just wanted to put that out there," she said. "For what it's worth."

"Lucy . . . ," he murmured, in a tone of voice that meant disappointment for someone on the other side of a kiss.

"It's okay. You don't have to say anything."

With a fragile smile and a shake of her brown hair, she was gone. He could still taste her. No matter how wrong it was, he couldn't pretend that he didn't enjoy the kiss, but he also knew that she was looking for something that he couldn't give her. She was sweet and lonely, and she was misreading the signs from him. Or maybe he was accidentally sending the wrong signals.

Duane saw the kiss, too. From the food truck, his brother called something crude, and Frost shook his head, as if to say, *It's not what you think.* He shouted out a good-bye and grabbed Shack's carrier. He pushed through the crowd toward Eleventh Street, but he stopped when a text tone chimed on his phone. He set the carrier between his ankles and grabbed his phone from his belt.

The number was unfamiliar.

He read the message, and he realized that the game had gone to a new level.

```
Hello, Inspector Easton. What's your
worst memory?
```

20

Frankie was right about her patients. They'd seen the news, and they were scared. When she got to her office, she found messages from six patients who'd canceled all their future appointments. Ten others wanted to know whether it was safe to see her. She spent two hours on the phone, reaching out to all of them, but it was hard to offer answers when she didn't know what was going on.

Finally, she put down the phone and wandered into her treatment room, which was her oasis. One wall was devoted to books. On quiet weekend days, she would come here to read. She activated the surround-sound speakers and played the noise of a rain storm, with the plink, plink of showers and a distant turbulence of thunder. She turned on a video of Fern Canyon. It was at the end of a trail in Prairie Creek State Park that she and Jason had hiked on their honeymoon, where the narrow riverbed was lined by vertical stone walls dense with green ferns. Life had felt good then.

She stretched out in the chaise that her patients used. She tried to read more of *The Magus* by Fowles. The novel was about a young, self-centered teacher in Greece facing erotic manipulation by two sisters and a mysterious magician. She'd read it before. Some days she felt as if she were the magus herself. The manipulator, using dreams and drugs. But she was the one being manipulated now, and the plot felt too close to the reality of her world.

She put the book down. When she glanced at the doorway, she saw Jason watching her. She hadn't heard him enter the office. His thumb and forefinger stroked his chin, which was unshaved. He wasn't smiling. Fern Canyon played on the screen, and the rain fell, which it had done on that long hike together. There had been a real chemistry between them on that trip. It felt like a long time ago.

"You heard what's going on?" Frankie said.

"Yes."

"I canceled my appointments this week, at least until the police catch this guy. I'm calling everyone else to warn them to be careful."

"I suppose that's a good idea," Jason said.

He sat down next to the chaise in the chair she usually used as a therapist. It was strange having him there, as if he were the doctor and she were the patient. Somehow, it took away her power, and she didn't like it. She got up. She switched off the music and video. The treatment room, with its sound-baffled walls, was as silent as a crypt.

"Do you think the person who's doing this is one of your patients?" Jason asked.

"I don't know. The fact that he seems to be manipulating their behavior with some kind of hypnotic programming makes me think he must have seen my techniques up close, but he could have simply read up on me in the psychology journals, too. A lot of people think I'm evil. They'd love to hurt me."

"Don't exaggerate, Frankie."

"I'm not. I don't show you the mail I get."

She'd testified in many lawsuits about the unreliability of recovered memories, even among people who believed they were victims of abuse. She'd also testified in criminal court about the problems of eyewitness identification, and thanks to her, accused murderers had been acquitted.

She'd made a lot of money as an expert witness, and she'd made a lot of enemies, too. Nothing she said in court was false, but that didn't matter to people who felt robbed of justice.

"If it's a patient, you know who's got my vote," Jason said.

She did. "Darren Newman?"

"That's right."

Frankie walked to her bookshelves and ran a hand along the spines of the hardcovers. She looked back at the empty chaise. It was easy to picture Darren Newman there, talking about his Midwest childhood. Almost dying in a collapsed snow fort. Being lured into bed by his math teacher. He was singularly handsome and charming, a man who was nearly impossible to resist. She'd never met a better liar.

"Why would Darren do that?" she asked, her voice soft. "He already got what he wanted. He fooled me. He's free because of me. And Merrilyn Somers is dead."

"Why does a sociopath do anything? Look at this guy's behavior. The taunting. The secret identity. The game playing. The risk taking. That's exactly who Darren is."

He was right, but she knew there was an extra reason why Jason believed in Darren Newman's guilt. He blamed him for the state of their marriage, and he wasn't entirely wrong. The revelations about Darren Newman—and the murder of Merrilyn Somers—had shaken Frankie to her core. She'd grown distracted. Out of touch. Withdrawn. She'd become emotionally unreachable, and the emptiness had made its way into their bedroom. They'd gone months without making love.

Jason hadn't made things better. Another man might have tried to crack her shell and draw her back to him. Jason didn't. He buried himself in his lab and waited for her to fix herself. They'd never really been the same since then. There was still a canyon between them.

She'd never told Jason about the pass that Darren made at her. Patients did that from time to time. Usually, the attachment was just a side effect of therapy, and she knew how to turn it aside. Darren was different. For the first and only time, she'd been tempted, regardless of the consequences. He was smooth. Alluring. The physical effect he'd had on her was unlike anything she'd felt with another man. Even Jason. She resisted Darren, but she found herself in the grip of sexual fantasies about him for months. When he stared at her, she thought he knew exactly how she felt.

Later, she'd realized that his skillful seduction was a ploy. If they'd had an affair, he could have used it against her. She was part of his plan. And she hated him for it.

"No," she insisted. "I don't think it's Darren."

Jason looked as if he wanted to argue with her, but they'd argued enough about Darren Newman in the past. The damage was done. "Then who?"

"There's someone else," Frankie said.

He came over and stood very close to her. "Who is it?"

"A patient. I can't tell you who, and I can't tell the police, either, not unless I know something for sure."

"Why do you think it's him?"

Frankie thought about Todd Ferris on the Bay Trail. "He approached me when I was running yesterday. It made me uncomfortable, like he was stalking me. He said he didn't want to come to the office, because he didn't want anything in writing. In other words, he didn't want a trail of evidence—or at least that's how I took it."

Her husband's dark eyes looked even darker. "What did he say?"

"He was having strange memories. He claimed to remember women being tortured. He said he came to me because he recognized one of the women from the news. It was Brynn Lansing."

"This guy says he saw one of your patients being tortured?"

She nodded. "I didn't believe it when he talked to me. It sounded too wild, like someone who was making up stories just to get attention. But now—"

"If it's him, why would he come to you and admit it? Why would he play these games and then simply tell you what he's doing?"

"I don't know. He could be schizophrenic, but I didn't get that sense from him in treatment."

"Did he say that *he* was the one torturing these women?" Jason asked.

"No, he said he was a witness. He saw it."

"You should talk to the police about this."

"Don't you think I want to? I can't. Unless he says or does something that lets me break privilege, my hands are tied."

"Then what are you going to do?"

Frankie crossed the treatment room to the door that led to her office. She went behind her desk and used her keys to unlock her filing cabinet. That was where she kept all her patient records. She hunted in the second drawer and found the slim folder for Todd Ferris.

"I need to reach out to him," she said. "Meet him. Talk to him."

"Alone? No way. Take me with you."

"I already told you that I can't break privilege. I can't let you find out who he is." Jason didn't answer, and she added, "I'm sorry."

"This is the way it always is between us," he snapped.

"What do you mean?"

"It's you on your own, Frankie. It's never you and me."

"That's not true. It's not my choice."

"Of course it is. You don't need me. You don't need Pam. You don't need anybody."

"Jason—"

"Do what you want," he snapped. "I'll see you at home."

He turned around and stalked out of the office. The first door slammed, and then she heard the outer door slam, too. She was alone again.

He's wrong, she thought.

She didn't need to keep the rest of the world off her island. Or maybe she was just kidding herself. She'd learned her lessons from her father growing up. Don't ask for help. Don't need anyone else, because they won't be there for you.

Frankie opened Todd Ferris's file and found the patient information sheet that every new patient completed. Hesitating, she keyed the number of his cell phone. She tried to think about what she would tell him. When she heard the phone ringing, she held her breath.

"Hello?"

It was a woman's voice.

Frankie was silent for a moment. "I'm sorry, I was trying to reach Todd."

"Who?"

"Todd Ferris."

"You got the wrong number," the woman replied.

"Oh, I'm sorry."

Frankie rattled off the number she'd dialed, thinking she'd made a mistake, but the woman said, "That's the number, but no Todd here. Good-bye."

"Wait, sorry. Can you just tell me, did you recently acquire this phone number?"

"I've had it for six years. Now good-bye, okay?"

The woman on the other end of the line hung up. Frankie stared at the patient information form. It was handwritten, not typed. Each patient filled in the details personally.

Todd Ferris had given her a fake phone number.

21

The only evidence Frost found at Christie Parke's apartment in Millbrae was a ticket from a downtown parking ramp in the cup holder of her Honda Civic. It was stamped on Friday morning at 7:36 a.m. As far as Frost could tell, no one had seen Christie again until her date with Noah on Saturday night.

The parking ramp was on California Street, where the financial district bled into Chinatown. The ramp attendant was a dark-skinned Filipino kid with black hair that sprouted from his head like wheatgrass. Frost guessed that he was no older than nineteen. His long legs were propped on the office desk as he watched the Giants on television and ate cold *lumpia* from a plastic container. The name tag on his shirt said Arne.

Frost introduced himself, and Arne sprang to his feet.

"What can I do for you, Inspector?"

He dangled a plastic evidence bag in front of the kid's face. "This ticket came from your ramp, right?"

Arne leaned closer and studied it. "Yes, sure did."

"The date stamp shows a car entering this ramp on Friday morning. The bank where the owner worked is just a couple blocks away, but she never showed up. Is there a way to look up when she left?"

"Sure, sure, come on over."

Arne rolled his wheely chair to a flat-screen monitor and keyboard. When he nudged the mouse, the screen awakened and revealed a series of camera angles on different levels of the underground ramp. He clicked on an app that showed daily ticketing activity.

"What's the number on the end of the ticket?" Arne asked.

Frost rattled it off, and the kid's fingers flew on the keyboard.

"Here you go. In on Friday at seven thirty-six a.m., just like you said. She didn't stay long. Ticket stamped back out on Friday at seven forty-nine a.m."

"Less than fifteen minutes?" Frost asked.

"Yes, sir."

Frost frowned. Christie worked at one of the downtown branches of Wells Fargo. According to her supervisor, Christie had a client meeting scheduled in Santa Rosa on Friday afternoon, which meant driving to work that day, not taking BART as she usually did. Instead, she missed work and missed her meeting. And yet here she was, arriving at the ramp downtown on Friday morning—and then heading back out almost immediately.

"Your security cameras," Frost said. "How far back do you keep the video?"

"A month. Then the files get deleted automatically."

"Can you pull up footage from the entry and exit camera on Friday morning?"

"Sure," Arne replied. "It's all web-based now. The app saves a new file for every camera every hour."

He clicked over to the archive and selected Friday from a calendar pop-up. He chose the camera focused on the main entrance and played the video file beginning at 7:00 a.m.

"We should have her going in and out in the same file. What time did she come in? Just after seven thirty? I'll speed it up."

Frost saw a steady stream of cars entering the ramp in fast motion. When the on-screen clock approached the time at which Christie Parke entered the ramp, Arne slowed the video down to normal speed. Frost watched two more cars turn into the garage, and then, after a gap of about ninety seconds, he recognized Christie's burgundy Honda Civic and matched the license plate. The car stopped at the ticket machine, and he saw a woman's slim bare arm reach from the window to take a ticket.

"Freeze it," Frost said.

The video motion stopped.

"Can you zoom in?"

"A little, but this isn't high-def."

Arne was right. By the time he'd enlarged the video to make out the front window, the features of the driver were unrecognizable. Even so, the woman's general look was consistent with the photographs Frost had seen of Christie Parke.

"Okay, keep going," Frost said.

He watched the car disappear. There was another minute-long gap before the next vehicle entered the ramp. He waited to see a few more cars turn into the garage, and then he asked Arne to fast-forward the video to Christie's departure time. At that time of the morning, the exit lane was mostly unused. The only departing vehicle he saw was Christie's Civic, which pulled up to the payment machine at 7:49 a.m.

"Maybe she forgot something," Arne suggested. And then he whistled. "Whoa."

"Freeze it!" Frost said.

Arne wasn't fast enough, and he had to back up the video. Then he stopped the playback just as an arm reached from the window of the Civic to insert the ticket in the payment machine. It was the same car—Christie's car. But Christie wasn't driving. The arm they saw was covered by the sleeve of a black sweatshirt, and the hand with the ticket was protected by a surgical glove.

"That don't look like her," Arne muttered.

"No, it sure doesn't. What other cameras do you have in the ramp?"

"We've got a camera on each aisle on each floor."

"I need to see where she parked," Frost said.

"Yeah, sure, let's take a look."

Arne went back to the archives and selected a camera focused on the first aisle on the next level down. Only seconds after she arrived in the garage, Christie's Civic drove into view on the down ramp and passed a full slate of parked cars and disappeared. Arne tracked her back up the next aisle and down another level.

"There," Frost said.

The Civic pulled beyond an open parking space at the far end of the ramp, and Christie backed into the empty spot. He saw the car's headlights go dark as she turned off the engine. A few more seconds passed, and then he saw Christie Parke appear, purse over her shoulder, her phone in her hand. She made the long walk from one end of the ramp to the other, getting closer to the camera.

Frost waited. He knew what was going to happen; he just didn't know when. He wished he could tell her, *Don't pay attention to your phone. Pay attention to your surroundings. And walk down the* middle *of the aisle, not the side.* But she didn't. She was preoccupied, her head down. She approached one of the concrete support columns, and that was when he grabbed her. It didn't even take five seconds. An arm reached out, took hold of her neck, and pulled her out of view. There was no sound on the camera, but Frost doubted that she even had time to scream.

He kept watching. Christie never appeared again. Neither did her attacker. He watched another car arrive and park, and then one more, and then he saw the headlights of Christie's Civic go on again. The car pulled out. It was too dark and too far to see who was behind the wheel, and the angle of the camera was too sharp to see inside as the car drove closer. Then it was gone.

"I guess he was waiting for somebody to come along," Arne said.

No, he was waiting for her, Frost thought. He'd been studying Christie Parke. He knew where she parked and when she usually arrived. Frost wondered if he'd hacked her phone to keep an eye on her calendar. A meeting in Santa Rosa meant she'd be driving. There was nothing spontaneous about this abduction; it had been planned for weeks. The same was probably true of Monica Farr and Brynn Lansing. And the fact that it had happened to Christie and Brynn so close together meant that this man was now playing his game on a fast schedule.

Frost didn't think he was done.

"I'm going to give you specs for a file upload site," he told Arne. "I need you to transfer all of the camera video files for Friday morning, starting at five o'clock. Can you do that?"

"Sure thing. You trying to spot when the guy got here, huh? Thing is, he may not have parked in the ramp. He could have walked in at our pedestrian entrance off California. We don't have cameras in the stairwell."

"Understood," Frost said, but he thought the safer play for this guy was to drive a stolen car into the ramp, rather than risk being spotted by one of the security or ATM cameras out on the street. The Night Bird wasn't a fool.

"I'm going to write down a few other dates this month," Frost added, "and I need the morning files for those dates, too."

Christie had already been to this parking garage several times this month, according to the tickets he'd found in her Civic. Maybe her stalker had been right behind her one of those days, and maybe he hadn't been so careful when he was following her.

After he gave the information to Arne, Frost walked to the stairwell at the back of the ramp. He headed down two flights to the parking level where Christie had been abducted. The structure was well lit with overhead fluorescents, but it was still a parking garage. There were plenty of shadows, and every car offered hiding places.

He walked slowly. The ceiling was low, and he smelled exhaust and gasoline. He spotted the webcam mounted on the wall and guessed that Christie's stalker had scouted the positions of every camera in the ramp. To do that, he would have been visible, but he would also have been one person among thousands in the garage every day. A needle in a haystack.

Frost counted the support columns to the spot that Christie was passing when she was snatched. When he got there, he stopped. He was only ten feet from the garage wall. It would have been easy to hide, easy to wait for her. Maybe he used chloroform on a rag or a fast-acting sedative injection. Pull her back, hold her, count the seconds until she was unconscious. Then drag her along the wall back to her own car.

He followed the wall and used his flashlight to illuminate the shadows. At each parked car, he squatted and shined the light underneath. Three feet under the chassis of a white SUV, something glinted in the beam of light. He squirmed toward it and saw that it was a brass button, the kind men wore on their suit coats.

Frost slipped a plastic evidence bag from his pocket and swept the button inside it. Maybe it had come from one of the businessmen who parked here every day. Or maybe Christie had yanked it off during a struggle, and it had rolled here. There wouldn't have been time for the attacker to retrieve it.

Maybe.

He reached the spot where Christie had parked her Civic. The spot was empty now. She'd been dragged here, unconscious, and her assailant had used her keys to pop the trunk and deposit her body inside. And then he drove her—where?

Where did he operate on their minds?

Frost studied the grease-stained concrete. It didn't tell him anything more. On the wall six feet away, he spotted a metal box with a glass door and a fire extinguisher inside. He noticed something on top of the wall-mounted box and walked over to check it out. He put on gloves and removed the object, which was a compact disc of an old music album inside a jewel case.

The CD was *Wrap Around Joy* by Carole King. Frost turned the jewel case over, and he read the track list.

The first song was "Nightingale."

With his gloved hands, he opened the case and was startled as dozens of tiny silver needles spilled from inside and bounced and scattered on the floor, like metal insects. He squatted down and picked one up and rolled it between his fingers. It was shiny and sharp.

He remembered what Frankie had told him.

Needles.

That was what Christie Parke feared the most.

What's your worst memory?

22

Fog chased Frankie into the coastal hills.

She took the southbound 280 freeway out of the city, then merged west onto Highway 1, the road that hugged the California coast all the way from Santa Barbara to Crescent City. It was twilight. The deep-blue sky darkened to black minute by minute. The fog made the ocean invisible below her, and its first threads feathered across the highway as the cloud moved inland.

The address that Todd Ferris had given her was on the coast in the small town of Pacifica. She didn't know if the address was fake—like the phone number—but she needed to find Todd again and find out what else he remembered from inside that white room.

The highway cut through green hills. She saw gnarled trees that grew sideways under the assault of gusts off the Pacific. Damp chill worked its way inside her car. A few drops of rain spit on her windshield. More fog washed across the road, playing games with her eyes, and she slowed and squinted to follow the curves that wound like a snake. The trees on the hills became ghosts. Milky parkland surrounded her, appearing and disappearing.

Frankie glanced in her rearview mirror. The headlights of another car came and went in the cloud. The car hung back, keeping a steady distance behind her. She had a strange feeling about it. She liked having company on the treacherous road, and yet a paranoid voice in her head made her wonder if she was being followed.

As she neared Pacifica, the GPS advised her to turn in a quarter mile, but the road to Todd Ferris's apartment was barely an alley, and she missed it in the fog. She kept going to the next turn that led toward Rockaway Beach. Pacifica by the water was no more than a jumble of buildings and a few dead-end streets. Mist blurred the beach road, and a few gauzy lights shined in the windows of the local motel.

She glanced behind her again. No headlights. Whoever had shadowed her route was gone.

Frankie drove to within spitting distance of the ocean and then turned on a narrow road. She drove three hundred feet back to the alley she'd missed on Highway 1 and turned again toward the beach. The pavement was water stained. Trees leaned over the lane and made a tunnel. She followed the alley until it opened up at a parking lot by the water.

It was nearly dark now. As Frankie got out of her car, the wind cut through her light jacket and made her shiver. Waves thundered and broke in whitecaps, surging toward the seawall. Tide was high. Spray and foam landed on her face. She could barely see the coastal headlands silhouetted on the sky. Next to her was a drab three-story apartment building facing the water. That was where Todd said he lived.

The beach parking lot was empty. She was alone.

Or was she?

She heard something above the roar of the ocean that sounded like a car engine in the alley. She stared at the darkness, back where she'd come, and saw a momentary flash of headlights. Then they went off. So did the noise of the engine.

With her hands shoved in her jacket pockets, Frankie marched to the apartment building. There was no entrance on the beach side. She stood in front of a low wall surrounding the building that dropped into a recessed parking lot. The building itself was built on concrete stilts because of its proximity to the water. She swung her legs over the wall and jumped, landing three feet below her.

She headed for the underground entrance to the apartment building, but it was locked. There was a panel with buttons for the various apartments, and she found the button that matched the apartment number on Todd's patient information form. Number 305. She pushed the buzzer.

There was no answer.

She waited and tried again, but no one replied through the speakerphone or opened the lock to let her inside. No one was home.

She dug in her purse for pen and paper and taped a note to the door.

Todd. Call me right away. FS.

Frankie felt vulnerable here. She navigated the dark parking lot quickly, eyeing the cars around her. By the time she found the steps to the street, she was practically running, and her breathing came fast and sharp. She pushed between two overgrown spruce trees near the building door and bolted back to the mouth of the alley. On her left was the parking lot. On her right, the tiny street disappeared into the fog toward Highway 1.

That was when she heard it. The voice. High-pitched and terrifying, but no louder than a whisper above the wind.

"Fran-kie . . . Fran-kie . . ."

It came from everywhere and nowhere. She froze. Fear rippled up and down her skin. Mist blew in front of her eyes, and spiny tree branches in the alley knocked together with each cold gust. She stared into the fog and listened for the voice again. It was night, and that was when the Night Bird came out to sing.

Frankie held her breath. She heard nothing, only the wind and the hypnotic thunder of the waves. The more time passed, the more she believed that her brain had conjured the voice. It wasn't real. She clutched her purse tighter on her shoulder and headed for her car. She made a point to walk, not run, but every few steps, she glanced behind her, peering through the cloud. She was alone. When she reached her car, she got inside and immediately locked the door. Her hands were trembling.

She switched on the engine. Her headlights lit up the rocks on the seawall, and she screamed.

Todd Ferris was standing in front of her car.

Her hand jumped to the gearshift. She wanted to put the car in reverse and drive away, but she didn't. Todd stared at her through the windshield, and she stared back at him. He didn't move. There was something in his eyes that made her uncomfortable. Grief. Confusion. Anger. She realized that she didn't know him at all. Even so, he was the man she'd come to see.

Frankie shut down the car and got out. Todd stayed where he was, so she walked toward the beach. His feet were in the sand. The black water rolled in behind him. His thin brown hair was wet.

"Dr. Stein," he said, so softly that she could barely hear him. "I thought that was you."

"I rang the bell at your apartment, but there was no answer," she said.

"I was walking on the beach. What are you doing here?"

She listened to his voice before answering. She tried to decide if the strange whisper could have come from him, but it was impossible to be sure. She didn't even know if she'd really heard it.

"We need to talk, Todd."

He shrugged and wandered along the boardwalk beside the beach, and she walked beside him. He wore a sweatshirt and shorts and sneakers with no socks. He stared at the ground, with his mouth turned downward in a frown. When they reached a bench, he sat down and put his hands on his knobby knees.

Frankie sat down, too. "I tried calling," she said. "You put the wrong number on your patient form."

"What number was it?"

She checked her phone and read it off to him. He shook his head.

"No, sorry. I swapped two of the digits. I do that sometimes. It's a kind of dyslexia."

She noticed that he didn't correct the number for her, and she doubted that he'd made an innocent mistake.

"Where are you working? At the same gaming company?"

"No, I couldn't take the boss anymore. I do freelance tech work now. There's a start-up company launched by a couple SF State alums. It's kind of an Uber for nerds. I go all over the city doing tech support for various businesses. I like it. I get to set my own schedule."

"Good for you," she said.

A wave crashed against the rocks and sent up a fountain of spray that slapped both of their faces.

"So what do you want, Dr. Stein?" Todd asked.

"I want to talk about those memories you've been having."

"I thought you didn't believe me," he said.

"Things have happened."

His head swiveled. In the darkness, she couldn't make out his eyes. "I know. I saw the news. I saw what they said about you. Another woman died last night, and she was one of your patients. Like all the others." He added, after a long pause, "Like me."

She nodded. "That's right."

"Of course, this couldn't be about what you did to me. You were sure about that." His soft voice was thick with sarcasm.

"I didn't do anything to you, Todd."

"Then why is this happening to me?"

"I'm sorry. I don't know."

"Ask me the question," he said. "That's why you're here, isn't it? You want to know if I saw this latest woman. The one on the news. You want to know if I remember her, too."

"Do you?"

Todd lay his head back and stared at the sky. She could see the profile of his long nose and jutting chin. "Yes."

"What do you remember?"

"Needles," he said.

Frankie felt a little shock of electricity in her body. "What?"

"The woman was terrified of needles."

"How do you know that?"

He looked at her again. "I *remember* it."

"Tell me more. What else do you remember?"

Todd was silent. He stood up from the bench. Nervously, he looked up and down the dark boardwalk. "No, I have to go. I need to get out of here. This shit is going to get me in trouble."

She reached up and held his arm. "Please, Todd. I can't say anything to anyone about what you saw. Whatever you tell me is bound by privilege."

"Not if you think I'm dangerous."

"Are you?"

Todd didn't answer immediately. He sat down again. "I'm losing time, Dr. Stein. I'm missing days. I wake up, and I don't know where I've been or how I got there. Hours will be gone. Sometimes the whole day. It's happened twice this week. All I know is that when I wake up, I have these memories stuck in my head."

"The white room," Frankie said.

"Yes. And the women being tortured."

"When did this last happen?"

"I woke up Saturday morning. Early. It was five in the morning. I was under a blanket like some homeless guy on the steps of an industrial building in Dogpatch. I have absolutely no idea how I got there. That was when I decided to track you down. I drove to the place by the bridge where you said you liked to run, and I waited to see if you showed up."

"How much time did you miss? What's the last thing you remember?"

He closed his eyes. His face twisted into a grimace. "I was at a bar near City College on Thursday night. Really late. I was pretty drunk. I don't remember if I blacked out or what. Next thing I knew, it was Saturday. When I went back, I found my car still parked near the bar."

"And you don't remember anything in between?" Frankie asked.

"Just that woman's face. The one who died. I don't know where I was, but I'm sure I was with her."

"Had you ever seen her before?"

Todd shook his head. "No."

"Are you sure?"

He dug in his pocket and removed something small and plastic, which he rubbed between his fingers. "Yeah, I'm sure. I've been watching for these women. To see if they showed up anywhere."

"What do you mean?"

"The first time this happened was a couple months ago. The woman I saw—I knew she died. I saw it online a few days later. She went crazy at a wedding and shot herself. I didn't know her, but I remembered her, and that scared the hell out of me. I began to get paranoid. I didn't know what was happening to me. So ever since then, I've been keeping records."

"What kind of records?" she asked.

"Wherever I go, I shoot a video of the people in the room." He held up the plastic object, which was a small USB flash drive. "I figured, if this happened again, I could go back and see if I'd met this woman somewhere. You know, like at a bar or diner or wherever. I went through the videos today. As far as I can tell, I never crossed paths with *any* of these women. But somehow I know them, and they're all dead."

Frankie was silent. Then she said, "May I take the flash drive and look at it myself?"

His fist closed over it. "I don't know."

"I won't show anyone else. I won't tell the police."

He shrugged, and his fingers uncurled. She took the flash drive from his palm.

"Thank you, Todd."

"You won't find them," he said. "The women aren't in there."

"It's okay, I believe you." She added, "There's a phrase I'd like to say out loud. I want to know if it means anything to you. Or if you've heard it before."

"What is it?"

Frankie didn't know if she should go on. She wondered how he would react. "The Night Bird," she said.

He turned and stared at her. He didn't say anything. She couldn't read his eyes.

"Todd?" she continued. "Does anything pop into your head when I mention the Night Bird? Any kind of memory?"

"No," he said softly, but his voice quavered.

"Nothing at all?"

"No. Why?"

She hesitated, because she didn't think he was being honest. The Night Bird did mean something to Todd. He looked unsettled, as if he wanted to run. "I think a psychopath is deliberately killing these women. Somehow he's programming their minds for extreme, self-destructive behavior. He calls himself the Night Bird. Do you have any idea who that could be?"

He leaned closer to her. She was conscious of the fact that they were on a lonely beach with no one else around. If he wanted to do something to her, he could.

"You think it's me, don't you?" he asked. "You think I'm the Night Bird."

"I have no idea."

"Well, here's the thing, Dr. Stein. I'm scared that it's me, too."

23

What's your worst memory?

Frost didn't have to paw through his brain to find it. He knew exactly what that was. A single memory haunted him every day of his life.

Katie. In the car.

"Is there anything you'd forget if you could?" he asked Duane. "If you could wipe out something from your memory, would you do it?"

The two of them sat on opposite ends of the cushioned window seat in Frost's Russian Hill house. His brother drank fresh-squeezed carrot juice from a wine glass. Frost was on his second bottle of Sierra Nevada ale. The nighttime view looked out toward the bay, Alcatraz, and the Berkeley hills. Shack patrolled the window, tapping his black-and-white paws at moths outside the glass.

It was the kind of view that never got old. There were nights when Frost stayed awake for hours, watching the city.

"What are you talking about?" Duane asked him.

"It's this case I'm working on. The women who were killed had their memories manipulated. I think someone made their worst fears come to life."

"Well, I don't care how it bad it is, I don't want to forget anything," Duane said. "Me, I worry about not remembering."

"Me, too." Frost added after a long pause, "Sometimes I can't picture Katie's face in my head anymore, you know? Not unless I look at a photograph."

His brother nodded. "I know. It's the same for me."

"She gets farther and farther away. I hate that."

Duane waggled a finger at him. "Come on, no bad shit on her birthday. We agreed. Only good stuff."

"You're right. Sorry."

"So, who's the girl?" Duane asked.

"What girl?" Frost asked, but he knew what Duane wanted.

"The one you brought to the food truck."

"Her name's Lucy," Frost said.

"She's pretty. She's a little young for you, but that's okay."

"This from the man who sleeps with a different twenty-something sous chef every week," Frost pointed out.

Duane grinned. "'Sous chef' means 'under the chef,' so what do you want from me? Blame it on the French."

Despite being five years older than Frost, Duane was an incorrigible child at heart. Most chefs were. He had limitless, espresso-fueled energy, which he needed in order to work fourteen-hour days in his kitchen. When they were together, his brother was relaxed and casual, but Duane became a different person when he ran his restaurants. He was impatient and demanding, like a little dictator chopping off the heads of anyone who crossed him. Most of his employees didn't last long, but even a few months under Duane Easton was a calling card with other chefs around the city.

Duane was a compact package. He was only five foot six and skinny. He had chin-length black hair, parted in the middle, which was how he'd worn it since culinary school in Paris. His face made a sharp V, and his nose was drooping and narrow. He had thick dark eyebrows. Like

Frost, his eyes were laser beams, and they had a way of cutting through anyone in front of him, whether it was a chef who'd overcooked the lamb or a single woman looking for a postdinner drink. His fashion sense was eclectic. Right now, he wore a button-down white dress shirt, nylon running shorts, and pink Crocs.

"How'd you meet her?" Duane asked.

"She watched her roommate take a header off the Bay Bridge."

Duane's eyebrows rose. "Strange life you lead, bro. Is it serious?"

"I like her a lot, but we're not going out."

"Why not? I saw the kiss. She's obviously into you."

"I know, but she's a witness in this case," he said, which was the obvious excuse.

"So what? That won't last forever. I think you should go for it."

Frost hesitated and then said, "There's something else, too. When I'm with her, she reminds me of Katie. It's not fair, but I'm not sure I can get past that."

"Is it her, or is it the time of year?" Duane asked. "We all go a little crazy around Katie's birthday."

"It's probably both," Frost admitted.

"You know what Katie would say about that? She'd say you're being an ass."

"True."

"What does Shack think of Lucy?"

"Oh, it's love at first sight between them," Frost said.

"See? For you, that sounds serious."

"It is, but not in a romantic way. I just like hanging out with her. She doesn't pretend to be anyone she's not. Katie was the same way."

"Have you told her that?" Duane asked.

"No."

"Well, you probably should."

Frost didn't disagree. He finished his beer and went to the kitchen to get another. The house had a briny seafood smell. Duane had made crab mac and cheese from scratch, which included dunking two live Dungeness crabs in boiling water. Shack got fresh-cooked claw meat as a treat, which he enjoyed so much that when the plate was empty, he licked it from one side of the kitchen to the other.

Frost opened his third beer. He didn't usually drink this much, but it was a special occasion.

He returned to the living room and stretched out in the window seat again. Duane was flipping through a thousand-page biography of Harry Truman that Frost had left there. When he was alone at home, Frost liked to sit in the bay window and read. Just him, Shack, the past, and San Francisco.

"So why do you like history?" Duane asked.

"I know how it ends."

"That's funny."

"Actually, historians and detectives have a lot in common. We both love details, but it's easy to lose sight of which are important and which aren't."

Duane turned to Frost's bookmark in the biography. "So you're at the part where Harry dropped the bomb?"

"Yes."

"You think we'll see another nuke go off in our lifetime?"

"Yes."

"Spoken like a pessimist," Duane said.

"Spoken like a cop," Frost replied.

Duane's mouth was pinched in a frown. "Think about all those people who woke up that day and didn't know they'd be dead before it was over."

Frost nodded. "It happens that way a lot."

They didn't speak for a while. Frost knew what Duane was thinking, and his brother knew that Frost was thinking the same thing, but neither one of them said it out loud. Katie didn't know. She woke up that awful day, and it should have been one day of many more to come. But it wasn't. It was the last. By midnight, she'd be in the backseat of her Malibu near Ocean Beach, which was where Frost would find her.

Katie would have been thirty-one years old today.

"You call Mom and Dad?" Duane asked.

"Yeah."

"They sound okay?"

"Mom more than Dad," Frost said. "It hits him hard. But Tucson has been good for them."

Duane sipped his carrot juice and didn't say anything. His eyes shined with tears, and he stared out at the bay. Shack, who had an uncanny way of knowing when people were upset, climbed up Duane's chest and began to lick his face. His brother couldn't help but laugh. He kissed Shack's head and put the cat down on the window seat next to him.

"I better get some sleep," he said. "I've got to be back at the food truck at four. Mind if I crash here?"

"Take the master bed," Frost told him.

Duane stood up from the window seat and drained the last of the juice from his wine glass. "Any reason you don't sleep there?"

Frost shrugged. "I don't know why. I prefer the sofa. It's mine."

"Well, it's your house."

"Oh, no. It's Shack's house. I'm just a guest."

Duane smiled. "Right. I forgot."

"Thanks for dinner," Frost said.

"Any time." Duane clinked his empty wine glass against Frost's beer bottle. "Happy birthday to Katie."

"Yeah. Happy birthday."

Frost waited until Duane disappeared into the bedroom, and then he drank his beer and said to the stars outside the window, "Blow out the candles, kiddo, wherever you are."

He woke up in the middle of the night and wasn't sure why. One of the windows was cracked open, and the house was cold and dark. Shack was missing. He got up from the sofa and rubbed his palm over his beard, and his fingers pushed back his brown hair. His eyes adjusted to the darkness.

"Shack?" he called.

Usually, hearing his name, the cat came running, as if he thought he were a dog. But not now. Frost climbed the stairs to the master bedroom, where the door was ajar. He peered inside and could make out the shape of his brother, asleep on top of the covers. Shack wasn't with him. Duane always slept hard, and Frost sometimes had to wake him up to turn off his alarm.

He went back downstairs. He checked the kitchen, which still smelled of crab. He was thirsty, and his mouth had a metallic taste, so he grabbed a bottle of sparkling water from the refrigerator and drank most of it. He kept the bottle in his hand as he returned to the living room.

"Shack?" he called again.

Frost heard an odd noise from the dining room. It was the kind of low, mean growl a tiger would make. He knew it was Shack, but he'd only heard a noise like that from the cat once before. That was when he'd first found Shack on top of his owner's body, protecting her from anyone who wanted to come close.

He went into the formal dining room with its heavy table, where he kept most of his work notes. One tall window faced Green Street in front of the house. Shack was on the window ledge on the other side of the curtains. The tiny cat's angry rumble rose and fell like ocean waves.

"Hey, what's up?" Frost said.

He went to the window and swept aside the curtains. Shack didn't acknowledge him. The cat was focused on the street.

Frost looked outside, where the view faced apartment buildings on the other side of the narrow lane. He noticed an old Cutlass parked sideways in front of his garage. The driver's window of the car was open. As Frost watched, a head leaned out from inside the car.

"Son of a bitch," he said.

It wasn't a face. It was a mask. The driver wore a bone-white mask with a grin reaching to his ears and huge, chambered eyes like a giant insect would have. The man with the mask stared up at the window, and Shack began to hiss and spit.

Frost had seen that same mask in Union Square. Lucy had seen that mask, too, on the Bay Bridge, moments before Brynn Lansing fell to her death.

Frost spun around and found his holster, which he'd slung over one of the dining room chairs. He unlatched it and grabbed his service pistol and his badge from the inside pocket of his jacket. Without bothering to put on shoes, he ran for the front door of the house and threw it open. He bolted down two sets of stone steps to Green Street.

The Cutlass was still parked by the house. Its engine was off, its windows closed. He couldn't see behind the smoked glass. He leveled his gun, and he held up his badge.

"Police!" he shouted at the closed door of the car. "Roll down your window and put your hands on the wheel."

There was no response from inside the car. Frost repeated his order.

"I said, roll down your window!"

He approached the car, took hold of the door handle, and threw the door open. Inside, the car was empty. Frost swore. He backed up and made a full circle, studying the street around him. He watched the dark entrances to the apartment parking ramps across from him. The area was deserted.

Then, distantly, he heard the pound of footsteps.

Frost ran to the pedestrian steps that led down the hill to Taylor Street. He took them two at a time, and at the bottom, he sprinted into the middle of the sharply angled street. He swung back and forth with his gun in both directions. Dark buildings rose around him. Cars were parked up and down the steep hill.

No one was there.

The Night Bird was gone.

24

Frankie took the measure of the woman seated in the chair in her office. She was young. To Frankie, twenty-five years old felt like a lifetime ago, when the world was as bright and flawless as a newly minted penny. The woman—barely more than a girl—kept her hands in her lap, but her thumbs rubbed nervously together. Her brown hair fell loosely at her shoulders without any special style. She wore cropped jeans, heels, and a long-sleeve knit top with pink-and-white stripes. Makeup didn't completely cover the half-moons under her eyes, and her rounded nose was a little big for the rest of her face, but she had a freshness about her that was easy to like.

"It's Lucy, isn't it?" Frankie asked.

"Yes. Lucy Hagen. I appreciate your seeing me on such short notice, Dr. Stein."

"Please, you don't have to be so formal with me. I'm Francesca. Or Frankie. Whatever you like."

"Thanks. Frankie."

"Actually, I need to tell you that I'm not taking on new patients now. I can talk to you about what I do, but if you want to move forward, I'm going to ask you to wait a little while."

"Because of the thing in the news?" Lucy asked.

Frankie hid her frustration. The Night Bird was driving a wedge between her and the people she was trying to help.

"That's right. I don't believe that what's going on has anything to do with my treatments, but I'd rather be absolutely safe. I can give you other names if you'd like to see someone else."

"No, I want to be here. At least so I can find out whether you think you can help me."

"Okay. Well, what did you want to talk to me about, Lucy?"

The young woman squirmed in the chair. "Have you ever heard of gephyrophobia?"

"Of course. It's a fear of bridges."

"That's me," Lucy said.

"That must be very hard, living in the Bay Area."

"Oh my God. You can't imagine."

"Has it been a problem for you for a long time?"

"Years. Forever. Sometimes I think I should move. I've even looked at maps to find cities that don't have any bridges. I guess that's pretty weird."

Frankie smiled and shook her head. The first step with every patient was to make them feel normal. "It's not weird at all. Does it help to know that you're not alone? There are thousands of people living in this area with the very same condition."

"Really? I feel like a freak."

"You're not," Frankie told her. "I promise."

Lucy's face broke into a grin of relief. "Cool."

"It says on the form that you're twenty-five years old. Have you talked to anyone about your fear of bridges before now, Lucy? Another therapist or counselor? Or is this the first time?"

"This is the first time," Lucy said. "I've looked it up online, but that's it."

Frankie cocked her head a little. "So why now?"

"What?"

"It takes courage to confront a phobia, no matter what it is. Many people go for years—or even their whole lives—without dealing with it. I was just wondering if anything in your life led you to face your fears at this particular moment."

"Oh. I don't know. I guess there are lots of things."

Lucy got out of the chair. She looked uncomfortable. Frankie watched her pace back and forth and knew she was on the verge of losing her. You never knew which questions would push a patient outside their comfort zone. Something was going on with Lucy Hagen— something more than a fear of bridges. But most people's phobias had deep roots.

"Tell you what," Frankie said, grabbing her cell phone from her desk. "Would you like to see the room where we actually do the work? It's a little nicer than my office."

"You don't do it right here?" Lucy asked.

"Oh no. Come on, I'll show you."

Frankie crossed to the door that led to the therapy room and gestured for Lucy to join her. After a moment's hesitation, Lucy did. Frankie held the door open for her, and Lucy went in first. The young woman's eyes widened at the high ceiling, the huge 4K screen, the book-shelves, the watercolor paintings, and the comfortable chaise in the center of the room. The carpet was so lush that you wanted to take off your shoes and dance on it.

"Wow," Lucy said.

Frankie laughed. "Yes, it's almost like a little getaway, isn't it? I love it here. I use it myself to relax. Some patients want to vacation here."

She went to the console and programmed the screen to play high-definition video of snow falling on a flat Midwestern field. She chose a Helen Jane Long album for background music. Lucy sat on the side of the chaise and soaked up the feel of the space.

"I want people to feel that this is the safest place they've ever been," Frankie told her. "There's no fear in here. There are definitely no bridges."

"Wow," Lucy said again. "I love it."

"Good."

"You're right, by the way," Lucy went on. "I do feel like I'm at some kind of turning point. I'm not sure I can describe it."

"Just go ahead and talk. It doesn't have to make sense."

"Well, these past few days, a lot of things have happened. I lost someone. A friend of mine died. And then at the same time, I met someone. I like him. So I just feel like—I don't know, like a girl who's scared to death of bridges isn't the person I want to be. That must sound crazy."

"Not at all, Lucy."

"Bridges make me feel like I'm going to freak out and throw myself off. I don't want to feel that way anymore."

"I understand," Frankie said.

Lucy's voice was low. "Can you tell me how it works? I mean, I know that you erase people's memories. Would you try to make me forget that I'm afraid of bridges?"

"No, it's not quite like that. For some people, their trauma began with a triggering event—some crisis in their past. Is there anything like that with you and bridges? Did you have a bad experience?"

"Not that I remember. They just scare the crap out of me."

"Okay. Well, if you decide to become a patient in the future, what we would do is talk a lot about your fears—and about everything else in your life, too. The more I know about you, the more I can help you find a way forward. And then we might decide to help you remember better things about bridges. Not scary things. Good things. Maybe one time you were staring over the edge of a high bridge, and then a butterfly came and landed on your hand. It was the most amazing thing.

You felt as if the butterfly had chosen *you*. That it saw something special in you. It was liberating."

"I could really *remember* something like that?"

"Maybe it already happened, and you forgot," Frankie said, smiling.

"Would I be hypnotized?"

"Yes. Have you ever been hypnotized before?"

"In a college class once. The professor said I was very susceptible, whatever that means."

"It means you respond well to hypnotic suggestion. That's good. It helps the treatment work."

"What about drugs?" Lucy asked.

"There are drugs that can help facilitate what we do, but you're the one who says yes or no."

Lucy was quiet. She stared around the room again. "And could something go wrong? I mean, could I wind up like those other women—"

Frankie wanted to say no. *It wasn't me! It wasn't my fault!*

But she couldn't say that. She wasn't even sure if she believed it anymore. They were all inside her head. Monica. Brynn. Christie. Their fears were her own now. Somehow, she'd failed them.

"The mind is a powerful thing, Lucy," she said quietly. "A surgeon can't give you any guarantees, and neither can I. But I can promise you one thing. If you want to take the first step—if you want to cross the bridge—you won't be alone. I'll be with you the whole way."

Frost waited near the doors of Saks Fifth Avenue while Lucy went inside Francesca Stein's office building. Behind his sunglasses, his eyes went from face to face in the Union Square crowd to see if anyone was watching Lucy. When he was satisfied that no one was, he crossed the street and did a circuit of the street performers and the homeless who haunted the plaza. He'd learned over the years that they made the best spies.

He'd found a photograph online that was similar to the mask he'd seen overnight. Half a dozen people recognized it. The mask was hard to forget. Even so, no one had seen the man behind the mask, and no one had seen him come or go in the square. The Night Bird was careful.

His forensic team hadn't given him good news. The compact disc that Frost had found in the parking garage had been wiped clean of fingerprints. The same was true of the Cutlass that had been left outside his building. The car had been stolen a week earlier, and the license plates had been swapped. The electronic tracing on the man's texts, e-mails, and online posts had ended in an anonymous account.

Every clue turned out to be a dead end.

Frost bought a hot dog and waited for Lucy. The cable cars came and went on Powell Street. It was a sunny Monday afternoon, warm and still. He checked his watch over and over, because he was impatient for Lucy to be out of Francesca Stein's office. He didn't want her in there at all.

An hour passed before he saw Lucy emerge from the building lobby. He waved to her, and she waved back. She cut across the street traffic to meet him, and she was a little breathless.

"Are you okay?" he asked.

"Yeah! Fine!" She saw his worried face and said, "Really, Frost, I'm fine."

"How'd it go?"

"I like her. I think I might go ahead with it."

"Lucy, let me solve this case first," he said. "Give it some time."

"I will. She wanted me to wait, too. Are you worried about me?"

"Yes."

"Good," she said. "Are you busy? Do you want to go somewhere? You can debrief me. Isn't that what secret agents do?"

"I've got to talk to Dr. Stein myself," Frost said. "How about we meet up a little later?"

"Yeah, definitely." She was in a very good mood.

"Alembic? Ten o'clock?"

"Perfect."

Lucy turned away, but Frost stopped her with a gentle hand on her wrist. "Lucy? Be careful, okay? I asked you to keep your eyes open, and I mean it. If you see anything that looks suspicious, call me."

"If I spot any creepy masks, I will scream."

"I'm serious," he told her.

"I know you are. I like that you want to protect me."

25

Ten minutes later, Frost showed the photograph of the mask that the Night Bird had been wearing to Dr. Stein.

"Do you recognize it? Have you seen a mask like this before? Or does it have any special meaning for you?"

The psychiatrist stared at it and couldn't seem to look away. He could see that the mask struck a chord in her memory. She knew it from somewhere.

"Dr. Stein?"

She broke out of her trance and handed him the photo. "No. I've never seen it."

"Are you sure? You reacted as if you had."

"No, I'm sorry. Why are you showing me this?"

"A witness spotted a man in a mask like this at the scene where Brynn Lansing went off the bridge. I saw him, too."

Stein looked surprised. "You did? You saw him yourself?"

"Yes, I saw a man wearing this mask in Union Square, and I saw him again last night outside my house."

She frowned. "I don't like that at all."

"Why?"

"He's making you part of his game, Inspector. It's personal now. If I were you, I'd be very careful. Are you any closer to finding him?"

Frost shook his head. "Not so far. As you say, he's playing games with us. He's leaving clues, but the clues haven't led us anywhere. We don't have any DNA or fingerprints. He hasn't shown up on any surveillance cameras. Whoever is doing this is tech savvy, too."

"Tech savvy?" Stein asked. Her forehead wrinkled with concern.

"Yes, he knows how to cover his electronic tracks, and he seems adept at hacking remote apps. Why, does that mean something to you?"

"No."

But he thought it did. She was deliberately keeping him in the dark.

Frost retrieved another evidence bag from his pocket. It contained the brass button he'd found in the parking ramp where Christie Parke had been abducted. "Do you recall seeing anyone wearing a suit coat with buttons like this? Or someone with a coat that had a missing button?"

Stein shook her head. "Sorry. It looks pretty ordinary."

"Unfortunately, it is. I'm not even sure it's connected to our suspect."

"I wish I could help, Inspector. I want this person found as much as you do. Probably more."

"Do you?" Frost asked.

She stared at him. "Excuse me?"

"Do you want him found, Dr. Stein, or are you protecting him? Because I think you're holding out on me."

Stein got up from her office chair. She went to a Keurig coffeemaker on the credenza against the wall and made herself a cup of coffee. She gestured to offer him one, but he shook his head. While the mug filled, she didn't talk. She took the coffee back to her desk and sat down again. She studied him over the lip of the mug as she drank.

"I've told you everything I can tell you right now," she said, as if she were choosing her words carefully.

"I'm a lawyer as well as a cop, Dr. Stein. I know a lawyerly response when I hear one."

"I'm not trying to be difficult, Inspector. The instant anything happens to free my hands, you'll be my first call. Until then, I can't betray my patients. I'm sorry."

"Does that mean you think this man is one of your patients?"

"I didn't say that at all."

Frost sighed in frustration and shifted the focus of his questions. He removed his phone from his pocket and put it on the desk between them.

"Do you ever use music in your therapy?" he asked her.

"Of course. Music is very powerful for activating emotions and memories. I select music carefully for each patient."

He pushed a button on his phone, and Carole King began to sing.

"Do you know this song?" he asked.

Stein gave him a puzzled look, but she nodded. Her eyebrows rose as she heard the reference to the night bird in the first verse.

"Is this a song you've ever used?" he asked. "Have you played it in therapy with any of your patients?"

"No."

"Well, it seems to mean something to the Night Bird. He used this song with each of the women who died. This seems to be what triggered their breakdowns. In every case, the song started playing, and that was when they had a psychotic reaction. Is that possible?"

Stein listened to the song. He could guess what she was thinking. It was strange to think of this pretty song as a murder weapon. The psychiatrist nodded. "Yes, music can be a trigger for behavior, based on hypnotic suggestions. Sometimes I'll encourage patients to play a certain song as a soothing technique for their anxiety."

"Can you interpret anything from his choice of this particular song?" Frost asked. "Does it mean anything to you?"

She shook her head. "No, it doesn't."

He needed to get through to her—to make her talk—but he didn't know how.

"You said you thought this person was trying to destroy you," Frost reminded her. "Do you still believe that?"

Stein gave him a thin smile. "The media is hounding me. I've basically suspended my practice. I'm sure somewhere along the line, I'm going to get sued over this. So yes, I believe the Night Bird wants to destroy me, and you know what? He may well succeed."

Frost saw a glimmer of emotion in her face. She didn't show much emotion at all, but right now, she wavered between anger and tears. "Someone who would go to that much trouble to hurt you isn't likely to be a stranger," he told her.

"You're probably right."

"So who hates you, Dr. Stein?"

He saw sadness creep into her face. She got up, taking her coffee in one hand and her cell phone and portable charger in the other. The door to the adjoining room was open, and she wandered inside. Frost followed her. He realized that this was the room where she treated her patients. It had the feel of a shrine, like the temple of memory. He knew some people would probably feel comfortable here, but he didn't like it at all. She used this room to get inside people's heads, and he didn't trust anyone who did that.

She was watching him closely. "You don't like me, do you, Inspector?"

"I don't know you."

"Well then, you don't like what I do for a living."

He shrugged. "You're right about that."

"I'm not an ice queen," Stein told him. "I know I may seem that way. I grew up with an emotionless father. He was a demanding academic. I learned to keep my own feelings locked away, but I hate to see other people in pain. I've devoted my life to helping patients do what I never seem to do myself. Let their emotions out. Deal with their fears. Get past the hurt."

"I'm not judging you," Frost said.

"No? Then you'd be the first. There's been a long line of people telling me what to do my whole life."

Frost took a step closer. He wanted to make her uncomfortable with his physical proximity, but she let him get within inches of her without any reaction. She wasn't easily intimidated.

"I don't have time for true confessions, Dr. Stein. All I want to know is who hates you enough to ruin your life. And who would be smart enough and ruthless enough to kill innocent women as part of his plan. I don't care how many enemies you have. That has to be a short list. So why don't you stop hiding behind your ethics and tell me what you know?"

Her eyes were cool. They were always cool. "I've already told you what I can. I wish there was something more I could say."

"So you can live with yourself if this happens again?"

"*I'm* not the one who's doing this. I'm a victim, along with these women."

Frost wanted to curse, but he swallowed it down. "Good-bye, Dr. Stein."

He walked away, but he stopped when she called after him. "Wait."

"What is it?"

Her face weighed what she could say and what she couldn't say. Then she murmured, "Lost time."

Frost's eyes narrowed. "What?"

"Did any of the women experience lost time? Periods of time they didn't remember?"

"Yes. Christie Parke was abducted from a parking lot. A day later, she went out on a date as if she had no recollection of what had happened to her. Brynn Lansing missed work and missed an appointment without any explanation shortly before the incident on the bridge."

"That's when he did it," Stein said. "That's when he programmed them."

"I guessed that, but would a missing day give him enough time?"

"Depending on the person, yes. Some people are extremely suggestible."

"Would you describe Monica Farr, Brynn Lansing, and Christie Parke that way?"

"Yes. All three were unusually responsive to treatment."

Frost walked back to her. "How would he know that?"

"Excuse me?"

"How would he know that these women were highly susceptible? It can't be an accident that he picked them."

"I have no idea."

"Is there anyone else who has access to your patient records?"

"No."

"Not even your assistant?" Frost asked.

"No, she has access to a contact database for appointments, but I keep my patient records myself. And they're all in writing. I refuse to put psychiatric records online or even in a computer. So he'd have to break into my office to read them, and this building has excellent security."

Frost thought about it. He went from wall to wall on the lush carpet of Dr. Stein's treatment room. This room had secrets. Patients talked about their deepest fears here. They shared things that they didn't share with anyone else in their lives. Only the patients knew. Dr. Stein knew.

And the room knew, too. If the walls could talk, they could spill everything.

He froze.

Maybe the walls could talk.

He stared at Dr. Stein's phone, which was connected to a portable battery charger. "Could you turn off your phone?"

"What?"

"Please. Just for a minute."

Her brow furrowed in confusion, but she pushed the button to switch off her phone and returned it to her desk.

"Do you typically keep your phone with you during treatment sessions?" he asked.

"Yes. It's muted, of course, but I have to be reachable in the event of emergencies."

"Every time I've seen you, your phone has been connected to a portable battery charger. Why is that?"

She rolled her eyes. "I've been getting terrible battery life. It drives me crazy. I should get a new phone, but I haven't had time."

"Have you received any unusual text messages?"

"Unusual?" she asked.

"Letters, numbers, garbage that doesn't make sense."

Stein frowned. "Actually, yes, I have received a few messages like that. I just figured it was weird spam. Why?"

"How long has that been happening?"

"About four or five months, I guess. What does it mean?"

"Get your phone checked," Frost told her. "Or replace it right away. It's possible someone has hacked it and loaded spyware on the phone. You'd probably never see the footprints, but he could be eavesdropping on your whole life."

Stein stared at him in horror. "Do you mean someone could be listening to my calls? Seeing all my contacts and e-mails?"

Frost nodded. "Yes, but not just that. Some spyware programs have ambient listening features. They can turn on the microphone of your phone without you knowing it and without leaving any record. He could be right here in the room with your patients during your sessions, Dr. Stein. He could hear everything they tell you. He'd have a roadmap for how to play with their minds."

26

Lucy squeezed a heavy garbage bag through the doorway of her apartment. It was filled with a year's worth of old magazines and leftovers from the refrigerator that had grown a layer of green mold. She'd already split open one bag and stuffed everything into a second bag. She could barely lift it, so the plastic dragged along the ground.

She navigated the bag down the stairwell. The plaster on the walls was cracked, and the stone floors had been worn by decades of foot traffic. The stairwell had an ammonia smell. The front and rear doors were gated, but homeless people still found their way inside, and there were mornings where she had to step over pools of bodily fluids on her way to the street.

Halfway down the stairs, her phone rang, startling her. The garbage bag slipped from her hand and tumbled end over end to the next landing. She swore, hoping it didn't break again. She grabbed her phone from her pocket. "Hello?"

"Lucy, it's Frost."

"Oh, hey." She stayed calm, but she felt a rush of adrenaline, hearing his voice. She jogged down the steps and reclaimed her bag. "What's up? You don't have to cancel, do you?"

"No. Ten o'clock at Alembic. I'll be there."

"You better be."

"I wanted to make sure you were okay," Frost said.

"I'm great. Why?"

"Did you see anything unusual while you were out?"

"This is San Francisco, Frost. When do you *not* see something unusual?"

"You know what I mean."

"I do," she replied, "and no. I kept looking over my shoulder. Nobody was watching me. You've got me paranoid."

"Paranoid is good. What are you doing now?"

"Taking out the garbage. I have to get the place cleaned up. I need to find another roommate if I'm going to stay in the city. Brynn's parents are supposed to come by this weekend and pick up her things."

"Okay."

She could hear his hesitation. "Anything wrong, Frost?"

"Not really. I'm being overly cautious."

"About what?"

"There's a chance that Dr. Stein's office isn't secure. Someone might be listening to her conversations with patients."

"Do you think that's how he found Brynn?"

"Maybe. It also means there's a chance he overheard you."

"Oh."

Lucy didn't say anything more. She listened to the silence of the stairwell. She lived in the city, so she was no stranger to voyeurs. Someone was always listening. Someone was always watching. But she hadn't said anything to Frankie Stein that would really be a secret.

"Lucy?" Frost asked.

"I'm here. I'll be careful."

"That's all I ask. See you later."

"Bye, Frost."

He hung up. She felt a twinge of loneliness, no longer hearing his voice. He made her feel good. She always saw an ordinary girl when she looked in the mirror, but something about the way Frost looked at her made her see a different side of herself. Someone special. Someone unique. She liked that feeling.

She hoisted the garbage bag as high as she could and struggled to the ground floor of the building. The marble hallway led to a metal back door with a crash bar. She nudged it with her hip and pushed outside to the street, yanking the garbage bag behind her.

The alley was crowded with evening shadows. Grease stains and tar patches made splotches on the pavement. The cool air gave her a chill. In both directions, garages lined the street, and utility wires dangled overhead like spiderwebs. Cars and motorcycles filled the opposite curb. The nearest car, a white Taurus, had its trunk open, but the owner was nowhere to be seen.

Lucy looked up and down the street from Laguna on one end to Octavia on the other. She was alone, except for Dante, the homeless man sleeping off a day of drinking in front of the garage. She recognized the tattered red quilt he used. He was harmless. He didn't try to get inside their building at night, and in return, the tenants filled his shopping cart with extra food whenever they could.

"Hey, Dante," she called. She didn't expect a reply, and she didn't get one.

She dragged her bag to the black trash bin ten feet away. When she swung open the lid, flies swarmed. The bin was mostly full. She tried to lift the bag over the lip, but the asphalt had scraped the plastic, and as she shoved it into the bin, the bottom tore, and garbage spilled at her feet.

Lucy dumped what she could into the bin, then got on her hands and knees to gather up magazines, spoiled food, and the remnants of two boxes of tissues she'd cried into after Brynn died. She was annoyed, and she wasn't thinking about anything else.

Up the block, she heard the rusted squeak of wheels on the far end of the alley, near Laguna. The noise was familiar, but something about it bothered her. Looking up, she glimpsed a man pushing a shopping cart across the intersection, and she recognized Dante, with his copper skin and pronounced limp. Her brain stuttered, trying to make sense of it. Just as she realized that something was wrong—that Dante couldn't be in two places at once—footsteps hammered behind her.

Lucy turned. Her body twisted.

She saw a man looming over her; she saw the hideous mask grinning at her. She had time for one scream that filled the alley. *"Help!"*

His arm clamped around her throat, choking off her cry. He jerked her off the ground as her body flailed. She kicked viciously backward, but his arm held her tight. His other fist shoved her head sideways in his grip, and she thought her neck would snap. A sharp prick punctured her skin. A beautiful kind of warmth flowed through her brain like a river and washed over her limbs. She went limp with a strange, formless joy. She realized she could breathe again. He'd let go. She was standing, but she was weightless. She saw the garbage at her feet and the empty street, and she knew she was free. She spun around as if to run, but she lost her balance. The terrible mask swam in circles in her face, as if a hundred masks were laughing at her. She tried to follow them, but the gyrations made her dizzy.

Lucy collapsed forward, and he caught her as she fell.

She was only vaguely aware of being lifted into the air. She could see the sky above her. The clouds looked like islands on an indigo sea that rose and fell with the waves in her mind.

They were moving. He carried her across the alley toward the parked Taurus with the open trunk. Fear suddenly made her twitch. It was like staring into an open mouth that would clamp shut and swallow her down. Weakly, she fought, and protests whimpered from her tongue, but he simply rolled her into the maw of the shark. Then her world was dark, and she drifted down until she was far away.

27

Everyone in Todd Ferris's videos had cell phones.

That was the first thing that Frankie noticed. It didn't matter where he went—Golden Gate Park, a bar, the BART train, a diner, a bus—he took videos of the people around him, and they clung to their phones like umbilical cords connecting them to the rest of the world.

Frankie stared at her own phone on the coffee table in front of her. It felt like the enemy now. Her security consultant had confirmed Frost's suspicions. She'd been hacked. For months, her phone had been a two-way street, exposing her entire life to the Night Bird. She had a new phone now, but that didn't change the horror she felt. The violation.

He knew everything about her. Every person she'd met. Every e-mail or message she'd sent or received. He'd been listening as she took every patient down into their deepest fears and then back up into the sunlight. He'd been a spy on the most private conversations anyone could have.

How could she tell them?

She burned with shame. He'd spied on her personal life, as well as her professional life. She thought about the time in February when she and Jason had reconnected after months of remoteness. Pam had been away. The apartment was theirs. He'd made love to her with a ferocity they hadn't experienced in years, and she'd found herself losing control in his arms. The connection hadn't lasted. They were like strangers again, but they still had that one intimate night together.

Except now, she knew, it hadn't been just the two of them in the bedroom. *He'd* been there, too. He'd heard the fights. The arguments. The confessions. The grief. The loneliness. Nothing had been private.

Frankie tried to put it out of her head. She couldn't think about it now. She concentrated on the videos that Todd had given her. Everywhere he'd gone, he'd captured the faces. She'd watched two hours already, and she still had hours more to review. He'd told her that he hadn't seen any of the women who'd died. Their paths hadn't crossed. And yet Frankie had other reasons to watch.

Todd was missing time. Just like Christie Parke and Brynn Lansing. He claimed to have had visions of torture and then to have awakened on the streets in the industrial area known as Dogpatch. The most likely explanation was that he'd been abducted and drugged, like the women. If that was true, then somewhere in his travels around the city, Todd must have met the Night Bird.

Unless he was the Night Bird himself.

On her television screen, Todd ate late-night breakfast at a diner. It was a favorite spot; the same restaurant had shown up in his videos at least three other times. He sat at a window table, and he kept his phone near his lap as he recorded the comings and goings. The diner looked like a vintage greasy spoon, with red upholstery in the booths and a counter filled by overnight regulars who traded jokes with a long-bearded waiter. She caught a glimpse out the window of a MUNI bus stop, a Chevron station, and a wide avenue that looked like Market Street. Todd's camera went from face to face, and she saw giggling teenagers, middle-aged nurses in scrubs, coffee-swilling businessmen, and flamboyant gays who looked like refugees from *Beach Blanket Babylon*. Every coffee shop was a microcosm of San Francisco.

But the people were all strangers to her.

She pressed "Pause" and took her wine glass from the table. She refilled it from the bottle, and she drank. When she started the video again, she found herself in a performance space, watching young people singing, like an episode of *Glee*. It was some kind of choral competition, and the arena was crowded. Todd zeroed in on each face around him and each of the young vocalists.

Strangers.

The front door to the apartment rattled, and Pam and Jason came inside. Monday night was meeting night for Pam's drug rehab. She took off her long leather jacket and hung it up in the closet, and Jason did the same with his suede coat. Frankie felt him in the room like cold air blowing off ice. They hadn't spoken since their argument in her office the previous day. He ignored her and took the stairs up to their bedroom.

Pam joined her in the living room. She was dressed in jeans and an untucked purple silk blouse. She looked good, as she usually did, and her hair was mussed. She picked up the wine bottle, which was mostly empty, and rolled her eyes.

"Maybe *you* should go to meetings," Pam said.

"I really don't need sarcasm right now."

"I wasn't being sarcastic."

Pam kicked off her heels and sat down. Frankie started the video again. The venue shifted to the grassy hills of Lafayette Park. Todd lay on a blanket, with a laptop in front of him, and she could see southwest toward Sutro Tower in the distance. It was obviously a weekend afternoon. The park was busy, but Todd used his phone to zoom in on each group, close enough that she could see their faces.

One by one.

All strangers.

"Is this some kind of odd foreign film?" Pam asked. "Most people watch Jennifer Lawrence or Eddie Redmayne or something like that."

"A patient took this video," Frankie explained. "I'm looking for someone."

"Who?"

"The person who's killing my patients."

Pam stared at her. "And what makes you think he'd be somewhere in this video?"

"I can't say anything about that."

"Of course not," Pam said.

"I'm not hiding things," Frankie told her. "It's privileged."

"Would it matter if it wasn't? You don't want help from anyone else. Frankie's island has a population of one."

"Don't start with me," Frankie snapped. "I get enough of that from Jason. He says I cut him out of my life. That I don't need him."

"You don't."

"That's not true. Of course I do."

"Like you need me?" Pam asked.

Frankie put down her wine glass. "I need you, too. Really."

"Come on, don't bother putting on an act. We're way past that. You don't really know either one of us, and I'm not sure it's worth your time to find out. Maybe the ship has sailed, Sis."

Frankie didn't say anything. She felt slapped.

Pam didn't have a glass, so she took the wine bottle and tilted it to her lips. "You know, when we were growing up, I always wanted it to be two against one. You and me against Dad. I thought maybe then I would stand a chance. But you were always out for yourself. Frankie protected Frankie, and I was on my own."

She wanted to argue, but Pam was right.

"I didn't want it to be that way," Frankie said, "but let's face it, you weren't on my side, either."

Pam nodded. "No, I wasn't."

"Don't blame me. Blame Dad."

"I blame both of you," Pam said. She stood up and headed for her bedroom, but then she stopped. She came back to the sofa. "So what did Dad tell you?"

"What are you talking about?" Frankie asked.

"That last weekend. Before you two went away, Dad called. He said I should come along. He said there was something urgent he needed to talk to us about. I told him you wanted it to be just the two of you on this trip. So what did he say?"

Frankie squeezed her eyes shut. She'd blocked out so much of that weekend. What was left was just pictures in her head. "He didn't tell me anything."

"Come on, Frankie." Her sister leaned down close to her ear. *"What was it?"*

"I already told you. Nothing. He did his usual irritating Q and A. He grilled me about taking risks. He asked about me and Jason. And then he got up and took a hike, and he never came back. Okay?"

Pam stood up and shrugged. Her lips folded into a smile. "Fine. I believe you. I just don't want there to be any secrets between the two of us."

She sauntered to her bedroom, and Frankie was left unsettled. Wine was the only answer to her problems. She poured what was left of the bottle into her glass, and she drank it down like beer until it was empty.

She went to the kitchen with an unsteady walk. She rinsed out her wine glass and washed it with soap, but as she dried it, the glass slipped from her hand and shattered on the marble countertop. Glass sprayed like the burst of a fountain. Looking down, she saw blood running from two cuts on her fingers. She put her hand under cold water, but the blood didn't stop. As the water ran, as the blood ran, she realized she was crying. It had been years since she cried. There had been no tears when her father died, but she cried now, feeling the threads of her entire life split open. Her work. Her marriage. Her family.

She shut off the faucet. She wiped her face with a damp towel, and then she cleaned the glass from the counter. She bandaged her fingers. There was nothing else to do but keep moving forward.

Frankie returned to the living room, noting the two closed doors. Pam's bedroom door down the hall was closed. So was her own in the loft. Pam and Jason had both shut themselves away from her.

She sat down and started Todd Ferris's video again.

This time, she found herself in the crowded clutches of a nighttime bar. She didn't know where it was. Wiz Khalifa played at a shattering volume, and strobe lights flashed on and off, casting a rainbow across the undulating pack on the dance floor. She saw bare skin, white teeth, and swirling hair. Lovers, smokers, and druggies slipped out through the bar door into the darkness. Others took their place.

She could see a can of craft beer in Todd's hand as he swiveled his camera around the bar. The picture wobbled; he was a little drunk. Most of the faces came and went on the screen too quickly for her to see them. They were all pretty. Young. Dressed to kill. Todd pushed into the crowd, bumping against shoulders and getting wild close-ups of the people around him. She wondered why he was still filming. Maybe it had become his habit by now.

Todd broke free of the pack. He was in a corridor where the music was muffled. Band posters lined the walls. He wobbled, heading to the men's room door. Frankie winced, wondering if he planned to keep filming in the bathroom. She reached for the remote to fast-forward just as Todd pushed open the door, revealing a lineup of three men at urinals. Todd waited behind them.

Frankie sped up the video.

And then she stopped and backed up. She realized that she couldn't breathe. She played it again. And again. Each time, she stopped as one of the men at the urinals turned and bumped heavily into Todd as they squeezed past each other and traded places. His smiling face filled the phone camera.

It was the last face she wanted to see, but it didn't surprise her at all.

"Jason!" Frankie called. When the bedroom door over her head stayed closed, she called again impatiently. "Jason!"

Finally, her husband opened the door and came to the loft railing, which he grabbed with both hands. He was still dressed. His face was angry, but his anger dissolved as he looked past Frankie to the familiar face frozen on the fifty-five-inch television screen.

"What is that?" he asked. "What are you doing?"

"I found him," Frankie replied. "It's Darren Newman. You were right. He's part of whatever's going on."

28

Frost checked his watch for what felt like the hundredth time. By ten thirty, Lucy still hadn't arrived at Alembic.

He kept an eye on the front window, where he could see the night lights of Haight Street. His phone was on the bar in front of him, and every time it lit up, he expected a text or call from Lucy, but she was off the grid. He heard from Duane. Herb. Jess. But nothing from Lucy.

A finger of worry stroked his neck. He texted her again. It's Frost. I'm at Alembic. Everything okay?

The message didn't get delivered. When he dialed her number, the call went to voice mail. Her phone was off. He left another message and then drummed his palm on the bar impatiently. He peered through the crowd, expecting to see her face. She'd see him, she'd smile, she'd wave. Everything would be fine.

But it wasn't fine.

At ten forty-five, he left. He walked two blocks back to where he'd parked his Suburban. When he got inside, he headed east on Haight. Lucy's apartment was twenty blocks away, and he cut across the city, past the wild neighborhoods of Tibetan craft shops, piercing salons, and drag fashion boutiques. He parked in front of a vacant lot opposite her apartment building. Traffic was heavy, and he ducked across the street between cars. At the gated security door, he pushed the buzzer for Lucy's apartment. No one answered. She wasn't home.

He noticed lights in the apartment above his head, so he pushed the bell to get their attention. An older woman in a paisley dress and slippers stepped out onto the balcony above him. He held up his badge, and she buzzed him through the gate into the building. Inside, the stairwell was musty. He jogged four flights to Lucy's door, and when he knocked hard, the door eased inward with a quiet click. It wasn't latched.

The apartment was dark, except for the streetlights from the window overlooking Haight.

He called out. "Lucy?"

He switched on the overhead light. The studio apartment was just as he remembered. Nothing looked disturbed. The room smelled of pine cleaner, and most of the clutter from the floor was gone. He saw a magenta dress stretched neatly across Lucy's bed, and next to it was a matching pair of two-inch heels. That was what she'd planned to wear to Alembic, but she never put it on.

Frost spotted Lucy's purse on the kitchen table. When he checked it, he found her wallet inside and her apartment keys. He felt a pounding in his head, but he pushed it aside to concentrate on what was in front of him. This was no time for emotion. Work the case.

He remembered their last conversation.

What are you doing now?

Taking out the garbage.

She'd had her phone with her, but he didn't see her phone inside the apartment. She never came back. He took her purse and locked the door behind him as he left. He took the steps back to the ground floor and followed the hallway to a locked door at the back of the building. Outside, he found himself in a narrow alley.

A streetlight halfway down the block cast a dim glow. The cold wind blew into his face. He saw a black garbage bag hanging down the side of a trash bin ten feet away. Debris littered the pavement near his shoes. The pages of an old copy of *Cosmopolitan* magazine flapped in the breeze, and Frost bent down and picked it up.

He checked the mailing label. The magazine was addressed to Brynn Lansing.

Frost slammed his fist against the stone wall of the apartment building so hard that he thought he broke a bone. He knew exactly what had happened.

The Night Bird had taken her.

"Luuuucy. Luuuucy."

Lucy heard the voice calling her back to the bridge, but she didn't want to go. Wherever she was now, she could simply drift along in dreams. Frost was there, and they were kissing. She could taste him on her lips as if it were real. They were in a park, alone on the green grass, and the sun beat down, warming them. She smelled honeysuckle and heard the rumble of ocean waves.

"Luuuucy."

She didn't want to go back, but the voice was irresistible. It chased away her dreams. The fog of her memory cleared, and she knew what to expect next. The music. When the music began, she went to the bridge. As much as she tried to hold it back, as much as she wanted to stay away, the music carried her, like a hawk snatching a bird out of the sky.

The voice taunted her. *"The ground, the ground, it's so far down."*

"Please, no," she murmured in her head, but she made no actual sound. She stared into whiteness around her. She heard only her own breathing, coming faster as she waited for the music. Her skin was damp with sweat.

"Better not fall, better not fall!"

"Oh, no, no, no, not that. Not again."

She stood frozen in place, alone among nothingness. She couldn't go back to the bridge, but she had no choice. The music exploded like fireworks in her brain. It filled the room, filled her mind—loud and wild. The beat of the song thumped so heavily in her chest that she could barely take a breath. The whiteness of the room dissolved from her eyes.

She saw the bridge. She was *on* the bridge.

"No . . . stop it . . . make it stop . . ."

Thin cables spanned two cliff tops, sinking into a nearly bottomless gorge. She stood on wooden boards, riveted with gaps so that she could see the earth falling away below her. The footbridge was no more than two feet wide. The cables sank down and down and down under their own weight. The other end of the bridge looked tiny in the distance, clinging to a snow-patched mountain like a breath of wind would unhinge it. And the wind blew. The wind howled. It made the bridge sway, dizzying her, threatening to pitch her into the abyss.

"Better not fall, better not fall!" the voice sang in her ear.

The music wailed, discordant and out of place in the outdoors. It should have been silent here except for the roaring wind, but the song went on and on, deafening her. Synthesizer. Guitars. Drums. No words, no voices—just the unrelenting music.

Lucy was paralyzed. Crippled by fear. Back and forth went the bridge. Hundreds of feet down, a green glacial lake fed a river. The glacier itself wriggled through the mountain pass. Craggy gray cliffs rose above her head. She wanted to grab the cables to steady herself, but her arms hung at her side, leaden, unmoving. She wanted to close her eyes, but her eyelids were taped open so that all she could do was see. Her legs could barely hold her. Her body shook, buffeted by the wind. She stood alone over the chasm.

"Can you fly? Can you fly? Will you die? Will you die?"

She wanted to throw herself into the gorge. Anything to make the fear stop. Anything so that it would be over. Her limbs disintegrated into shivers. Her brain rebelled and escaped. Make it stop, make it stop, make it stop.

"Listen to me, do you want to be free?"

"Yes, yes, yes, make it stop," she tried to say, but she was voiceless, and she cried dry tears. Her heart rocketed as if it would beat its way through her chest to get away. "Let me jump, let me die, I can't take anymore, I can't, I can't."

"It's up to you, you know what to do."

Something appeared in front of her. Like a hologram, spinning. It was shiny, it was bright. It was a dagger, with a black handle. The edges were honed to razor-sharp blades, and it ended with a cutting point. All she had to do was reach out and grab it. She knew that was what the voice wanted. She had to take it in her grasp, but she couldn't.

"Luuuucy. Luuuucy. It's up to you, you know what to do."

The knife twirled and glinted in the light, as if suspended on a thread that danced in the wind. She could take one step, she could reach out her hand, and she would have it. The knife made the bridge go away, but once she had it, she knew what the voice wanted her to do.

The wind got louder, fighting with the music.

She didn't want to take the knife, but she couldn't stay here, not one second longer. The blade dangled only inches away. Sharp and deadly. As if it were already dripping blood.

Lucy screamed soundlessly; then she leaped for the knife and curled the handle in her fist. She clenched it so tightly she would never let go. Immediately, the panorama around her dissolved. The bridge disappeared. The mountains and the glacier faded to whiteness. She was in a dazzling white room. Her feet were on solid ground. But the music kept playing, and the knife was in her hand now. There was only one way to stop the music once and for all. One way to keep the bridge from coming back.

The voice whispered in her ear.

"The knife is the key. Set yourself free."

29

Darren Newman.

Frankie hated that what she remembered most about Newman was his looks. He was ridiculously handsome, and he knew it. He was tall, with the sleek, strong build of a tennis player. He had LA-blond hair, short and layered, with tight curls above his forehead. His eyebrows angled sharply, and his dark eyes seemed to be laughing at a joke inside his head. He didn't show teeth when he smiled; his lips simply nudged upward. He dressed to impress, always in a suit, with pastel-colored shirts and wild Jerry Garcia ties. He was young—only in his late twenties. She never should have been attracted to someone like that, but she was.

He first came into Frankie's life a year ago because of his mother. Alana Newman came to Frankie after her son had been arrested for rape, and she offered a lot of money for her to talk to him. Her instinct, seeing that many zeroes on a check, was to say no. She wasn't a hired gun. But Alana was as smooth as her son. She told a good story, and she cried the right amount of tears. She didn't claim that Darren was guiltless in his life, but she claimed that he was a victim of his past. He'd been abused in school. He'd never learned how to respect women. He'd made mistakes, but he wasn't a rapist. The case was a he-said, she-said between her son and an SF State senior he'd met at a party. The prosecutors were trying to make an example of him.

If Frankie could have gone back in time, she would have torn the check in half. Instead, she agreed to meet Darren. To talk. To judge him for herself, face-to-face. That was her mistake. She had enough arrogance as a therapist to believe that no man could manipulate her, but she hadn't counted on a man like Darren Newman.

He knew that the best lies started with the truth. The first story he told her was a true story from his childhood. He'd spent his first eighteen years in Wisconsin, in a small town outside Green Bay. At age seven, he'd built a snow fort in his front yard during a Thanksgiving Day blizzard. He'd burrowed into its tunnels and stayed there while the family was inside, but as the snow continued to fall, the fort collapsed on top of him.

It was half an hour before anyone noticed. He spent that time trapped in a cave of white, slowly suffocating, his air leaching away breath by breath. He couldn't move or free himself. All he could do was stare at the white snow from inside his tomb. By the time they dug him out, he was unconscious, and the doctors said another five minutes would have killed him.

He still had vivid flashbacks of that near-death experience, he told her. He didn't cry about it, though. He softened his voice and stared into space, as if the trapped child were still inside the man. He looked at her with those magnetic eyes, which said, *I need you to help me.*

She was hooked.

It was also the last true story Darren told her.

He described losing his virginity to a ninth-grade math teacher, whose after-school tutoring sessions became evening seductions at her home. Looking embarrassed, he explained in explicit physical detail what she did to him and what she made him do to her. How she made him dominate her. Humiliate her. Live out her submissive fantasies. He had this way of shaking his head, as if he couldn't really believe any of it himself. *That was how I learned about women, Frankie. Is it any wonder I turned out the way I did?*

Months later, she found out that Darren's ninth-grade math teacher was a fifty-six-year-old married man, not a woman at all. There was no relationship. No virgin seduction. He'd fabricated everything. By then, it was too late.

Frankie had already given him what he wanted. She submitted an affidavit to the court that in her professional opinion, Darren would be better served by treatment for his childhood issues rather than imprisonment. The prosecution, already on shaky ground on the rape charge, accepted a plea of misdemeanor assault, rather than risk an outright loss in court. Darren did community service at a local homeless shelter, and he began therapy sessions with Frankie every week.

She blamed herself for letting him twist her around his finger. She was slow to realize that he had an answer for everything. An excuse. A reason. An explanation. His parents moved to Colorado when he was eighteen, and he went to college in Boulder. Frankie grilled him about two accusations of rape in the college dorms, and he dismissed them as the result of alcohol and morning-after regrets. She asked about cases of stalking and revenge porn, and he put the blame on his roommate. No matter what happened, he found someone else to take the fall, some way to deflect guilt away from himself. That should have been a red flag.

Despite everything he told her, despite the lies she discovered as the months wore on, she also found herself intensely attracted to him. She dressed differently on days when she knew he'd be with her. She obsessed over every detail of his face. She let herself fantasize about him. Once, in therapy, he put a hand high on her thigh, and she left it there and didn't break away until it was obvious they were about to cross a physical line from which there was no going back.

He knew exactly the effect he had on her, and he played her accordingly.

Then came Merrilyn Somers.

Smart, pretty, nerdy, artsy Merrilyn Somers.

She was an SF State junior, originally from Reno, where she'd been her high school valedictorian and a singer in the state champion choir. She was a computer science major and gamer and had already done two summer internships in Silicon Valley. Sony and Samsung were competing to recruit her after graduation. She was engaged to her high school sweetheart, and her academic scholarships meant she was debt-free. She had her whole future lined up like a row of dominoes.

Merrilyn lived with three college girlfriends in a Balboa Park apartment. Her neighbor two doors down was Darren Newman.

Frankie had seen Merrilyn's picture in the newspaper. She was black, with straight dark hair parted in the middle and arresting, luminous blue eyes. You could see intelligence in a person's face, and Merrilyn was smart. Her confident smile didn't need to prove anything to anyone, regardless of her young age. Her left arm sported a Jesus tattoo, and she wore a cross around her neck. Her body was slim and tall.

Nine months ago, on a Friday night when her roommates went to a party in Menlo Park an hour away, Merrilyn stayed home to code a gaming app she'd built from scratch. When her friends arrived back at their apartment at four in the morning, they found Merrilyn naked on her bed, gagged, tied, dead of multiple stab wounds. The coroner confirmed sexual assault. The perpetrator used a condom, but he'd made a mistake in removing it, because the CSI team found a small amount of semen on the bed sheet near Merrilyn's body.

Suspicion landed immediately on Darren Newman. He asserted his innocence to Frankie, the police, and the media—but the evidence pointed his way from the first day of the investigation. Merrilyn's roommates told police that Darren had stalked her for months. That she'd fended off passes from him since she moved into the building. His history of assault and date-rape charges made the headlines. So did Frankie's affidavit that had kept Darren out of jail.

Everyone knew he was guilty. The police and prosecutors were simply waiting for the DNA results to come back to prove it.

Except, when the results did come back, the DNA found at the murder scene of Merrilyn Somers didn't match Darren Newman. Instead, it matched another man living in the same apartment building. Leon Willis's DNA was in the California state database because of a felony conviction for mail fraud four years earlier, for which he'd served six months in prison. He had no alibi for the night of Merrilyn's murder and no memory of the night at all. He claimed that he'd been drinking and passed out.

Faced with the DNA evidence, Leon Willis took a plea. He was serving the first year of a twenty-year sentence. Darren Newman received a public exoneration and an apology from the San Francisco Police.

Frankie remembered seeing Darren not long after he was vindicated. She expected him to be angry about his ordeal. Instead, she saw a twisted triumph hiding in his smile. She knew the truth. He was guilty. He'd raped and murdered Merrilyn Somers. And somehow, he'd gotten away with it by framing another man.

She didn't tell him what she thought, but he had a way of reading her mind.

"You still think I did it, don't you?" Darren asked as he was leaving her office that last time. "That's just crazy, Frankie. I mean, think about it. For me to be guilty, you'd have to assume that I *knew* that Leon's DNA was in the state database. Not much point planting evidence on a guy who will never be found, right? Of course, maybe the guy who owns the apartment building is a college buddy of mine. So I guess I could have scoped out the background checks on new tenants and found somebody with a criminal record. Then I'd need to make sure that whoever it was didn't have an alibi on the night of the murder. That's even tougher. Well, unless I stopped by for a drink with Leon that night and spiked his beer with Rohypnol. I guess I could have poured out a couple dozen cans while he was sleeping it off, so he'd come out of his blackout thinking he drank himself into a coma. Do you think that would work? Maybe it would. But wow, Frankie, the semen they found on Merrilyn's bed. No way I could pull that off. I mean, what are you suggesting? That I paid a hooker to come on to him and give him a hand job in the men's room at some bar? And then she gave me a sample of his swimmers that I could plant near Merrilyn's body? You must think I'm some kind of evil genius to do something like that. Besides, do you think I wouldn't freak out knowing that this hooker might spot my face in the paper and go to the cops? I'd probably have to get rid of her, too, Frankie. Of course, that would be the easiest part of the plan. Nobody misses hookers."

He laughed. His face had the look of the devil.

"Anyway, that's what you'd have to believe to think I'm really guilty, Frankie. See how crazy that sounds?"

She knew that Darren was right.

It *was* crazy.

What chilled Frankie to the bone was knowing that he had told her exactly what he'd really done.

30

Frost found Herb painting on his hands and knees on a sidewalk at the base of Coit Tower. Twenty people crowded behind him, watching his three-dimensional portrait take shape. A grizzly bear with wet, matted fur rose out of the flat ground. The animal, its mouth open and teeth bared, stood at the top of a surging waterfall as Herb put the final touches on a spawning salmon that was about to become the bear's lunch.

His friend rocked back on his knees. The beads in his long gray hair knocked together like an abacus. He flipped up the magnifying lenses he wore and reached for his coffee urn. As he drank, he spotted Frost among the crowd.

"Taking a little break here, folks," Herb announced. "Don't get too close to the bear. He's hungry."

He emptied the top hat where he kept his tips and shoved the money into the pockets of his blue-jean coveralls, which were smeared with a rainbow of paint. He limped over to Frost, who held Shack in the crook of one arm. The two men walked around the perimeter of the parking lot, with the city and the bay spread out in the valley. They stopped in the shadow of the tower, across from a statue of Christopher Columbus.

"I got your message," Herb said. "You said a girl is missing? Another one of Dr. Stein's patients?"

"There's a connection, yes."

Herb took Shack from Frost's arms. He dangled a rope of his gray hair, and Shack swiped at it. "I was disturbed to hear that someone is abducting and brainwashing these women."

"He calls himself the Night Bird," Frost said.

"Do you have any idea what that means?"

"Not yet."

"If it's someone with a grudge against Dr. Stein, then he's part of a long list," Herb said.

"I know that."

"What about the girl? How long has she been gone?"

"Since last night. Jess and I interviewed the neighbors. One of them heard a scream but didn't report it."

"Do you have any leads?" Herb asked.

"Nothing that will help us find her. Lucy's phone is off, so we can't get any pings. No one saw a car in the alley where she was taken."

"What about the person who's doing this?"

Frost showed Herb the photograph of the mask he'd found online. "I talked to a homeless man who hangs out near Lucy's building. Someone wearing a mask like this gave him fifty bucks to clear out for the day. The same thing happened the previous week. I think that's when this guy took Lucy's roommate."

"Didn't the man think this was odd? Money from some stranger in a mask?"

"For fifty bucks, I don't think he asked a lot of questions. He couldn't give us any kind of useful description. Tall. Lean. That's it." Frost added, "What about you, Herb? Have you spotted anyone hanging around in a mask like this among your crowds?"

"No, but why would I?"

"Because of me," Frost said. "He knows I'm the one investigating the case, and he seems to be making it personal."

Herb put Shack on the ground, and the cat sprawled on the sidewalk between them. "How can I help?"

Frost took his phone out of his pocket and clicked over to his photos. "This is a photo of Lucy," he said, showing the picture to Herb. "This guy had to get her from her apartment to wherever he's hiding. Maybe someone saw them."

"You want me to put the word out to my network?" Herb asked.

"Exactly."

Herb had fingers in nearly every corner of San Francisco, thanks to his years on the city council. Five years earlier, he'd also pioneered a nonprofit initiative to get donated smartphones in the hands of every homeless person in San Francisco. The phones had become a lifeline for jobs, housing opportunities, food, and city services—and they'd also become ground zero for a social media network that could get news around the Bay Area almost instantaneously. Among Herb's twenty-seven thousand Twitter followers were more than five thousand homeless people who were 24-7 eyewitnesses to city life. They didn't always trust the police, but they trusted Herb.

"What would you like me to tell them?"

"I'll text you Lucy's photo," Frost said. "I'll send photos of the other three women, too. I'm hoping someone spotted them going in or out of this guy's hiding place."

"Consider it done. I'll get something out immediately."

"There's one other thing. A song. 'Nightingale' by Carole King. Do you know it?"

"Of course," Herb said. "Carole cowrote it with David Palmer. He was lead singer for a few of the songs on Steely Dan's first album. That's your music trivia for the day."

Frost smiled. There was very little trivia from the '60s and '70s that Herb didn't know. He'd grown up in San Francisco during the days of flower power and the Summer of Love.

"'Nightingale' was used as a trigger with the women who died. This isn't a Taylor Swift song that gets played thousands of times a day. If anybody heard that song recently, I'd like to know where."

"I'll put out the word, but once I do, the press is likely to get hold of the story. They follow whatever I post on Twitter, and I get calls. Is that okay?"

"That's fine. Jess wants to make it all public. The Night Bird. The song. If anybody calls, send them my way."

"The song's an odd choice, isn't it?"

"It is, which makes me think 'Nightingale' has some kind of special meaning for him. If we get the news out there about it, maybe someone will make a connection." Frost bent down and scooped Shack off the ground. "I have to go."

"If I hear anything, I'll be in touch," Herb said. "What does Dr. Stein say about all this?"

"She's not saying much. I think she's hiding something."

"What's your take on her? You know I'm not much of a fan after the Darren Newman episode."

Frost hesitated. "She's a tough one to read. She's smart, obviously. And attractive in a keep-your-distance sort of way. She comes across as a loner, like me."

"Well, be careful with her," Herb told him.

"Why is that?"

His friend smiled. "You know what they say about psychiatrists, Frost. They only go into the business to find someone crazier than they are."

31

Darren Newman's business address led Frankie to the industrial piers butting up to the bay in the southeastern part of the city. She parked next to an unmarked warehouse within sight of the water. Beyond the barbed wire fence at the end of the road, she could see gantry cranes hoisting dozens of rust-red containers off a Chinese freighter.

When she got out of her car, she was alone. She heard the thunder of metal tonnage lifted and dropped, but she didn't see another human being. Smog clung to the horizon like a brown cloud, obscuring the hills of the East Bay. Dirt blew off the concrete. She walked to the eight-foot fence and peered through the mesh. Above the security booth, she saw a list of shipping companies that operated here.

The fourth company listed was Newman Imports.

She studied the flat, open concrete around her. To her left, the road ended in a gravel lot filled with unhooked truck trailers. On her right was a beige two-story office building. It was late afternoon underneath the haze. Most of the businesses had already shut down for the day, and the workers had gone home.

Frankie headed for the office building. She climbed the steps to the glass doors and let herself inside. No one was there to greet her. A corridor stretched to the back of the building, and she walked the length of the corridor and found a door with Darren Newman's name on it, but the door was closed and locked.

"Can I help you?"

She turned around and found herself face-to-face with a young woman in a gray business suit. They were the same height. The woman's canary-yellow hair covered her head in short, gelled spikes. Her narrowed eyes were cold. She had her arms folded across her chest.

"I was looking for Darren Newman," Frankie said.

"I haven't seen Darren today," the woman replied, "and I'm about to lock up the building for the night. Do you have an appointment?"

"No, but I called him earlier and left a message. Do you have any idea where he might be?"

"What do you want with Darren?"

The woman asked the question with a personal interest in her voice. She was in her twenties and attractive, but her lips turned downward with a hardness that gave her a bad case of resting bitch face.

"I just really need to talk to him," Frankie replied, offering a smile that wasn't returned.

"Try the warehouse across the street. He might be over there."

Frankie brushed past the woman, who followed her to the building door. When Frankie was outside, the woman locked it behind her. She crossed the street to the windowless warehouse, which occupied the entire block. Its walls were drab tan. Garage doors and loading docks faced the street. One door, toward the far end of the building, was open by three or four feet.

She walked the length of the warehouse and bent down to slip under the open door. Inside, her eyes adjusted to the semidarkness. Thousands of crates, many stamped with Chinese characters, filled the space almost to the ceiling. Gaps large enough for a forklift interrupted the wall of storage every twenty feet. Lightbulbs, dangling on cords from the ceiling, did little to illuminate the closed space. The interior was cold. She saw dust and spiderwebs.

As she followed the corridor, she passed a crate on the floor near one of the loading docks, and its lid had been pried off with a crowbar that leaned against the coffin-shaped box. She peered inside and saw vacuum-sealed electronics components. Looking to the ceiling, and in both directions, she figured the contents of the warehouse could be valued in the millions of dollars.

Where the corridor ended, she faced a stone wall with a single metal door leading in or out. A Lexus sedan was parked by the wall near one of the large garage entrances. As she stood in front of the metal door, it opened. Darren Newman stood in the shadows immediately in front of her. He closed the door behind him before she could look inside, and his lips creased into a smile.

"Dr. Stein," he said. "It's been a long time. How are you?"

"Hello, Darren."

"Simona called and said a woman was looking for me. When she described her, I knew it was you. I was surprised."

"Really?"

"Well, as I said, it's been a long time. Of course, I got your message that you wanted to talk. I spotted your name on the news, too. Patients going crazy can't be good for business."

"Having a patient stab a girl to death wasn't good for business, either," she told him.

"Except that was all a mistake. Remember?"

Darren made sure the door behind him was locked. He stepped toward her, and his closeness made her back up and bump against the Lexus. Her face flushed. Despite everything she knew about him, she felt his sexual aura like warm fingertips on her skin. He looked the same, with his blond hair and hawk-like eyes. He wore a navy sport coat over blue jeans, a peach-colored shirt, and a psychedelic tie. His black boots were shined.

"So what do you want with me, Frankie?" he asked.

He reached out a hand to touch her face, and she jerked away.

"What's behind that door?" she asked him.

"I'm an importer. Some goods are more sensitive than others."

"Illegal?"

"Not at all. Just sensitive."

"Why don't you show me?" she asked.

"Because then I'd have to kill you," Darren replied. He saw her flinch, and he added with a wink, "That's a joke, Frankie. You never did appreciate my sense of humor."

She wondered what was really behind the locked door. More cartons of electronics. Or guns. Or drugs.

Or a white room.

"You still haven't told me what you want," Darren said.

"I want the truth. Someone's trying to destroy me. I think it's you."

He smiled at her with no humor. "Why would I want to destroy you? You were such a big help to me."

"I don't know, but then again, I never understood how sick you really were. You kept it well hidden."

"That must be ironic for you. After all, it was your job to get inside my head. So what is it you think I'm doing, Frankie?"

"You're abducting my patients. You're using my own treatment methods to play on their fears. If you want to go after someone, then go after me. Leave my patients alone."

Darren struck like a snake, coiling his arms around her body and pinning her against the car. She struggled to free herself, but he held her tight, unable to get away. His sweet breath was in her face. His lips were an inch away from her own. "Oh, if you want me to go after *you*, then I will. Just say the word."

"Let me go!"

He pushed his lips against her mouth, and she swung her head violently away. He whispered in her ear. "You don't want me to let go. You want me to take you right here, don't you? That's what you've dreamed about."

"Get your hands off me!" she said. "Jason knows I'm here. He's expecting me to call back."

"I think you're lying. I don't think you'd tell your husband you were coming to see *me*."

"I'm not lying." Frankie squirmed in his grasp, and finally, she shoved his chest hard and ripped herself away from him. "You bastard! I know what you're doing. I'm on to you and your games. You're not going to get away with it this time. It won't be like Merrilyn Somers."

"Oh, come on, Frankie. I told you once before. You're talking crazy."

"You're trying to do the same thing this time, aren't you? You're setting up someone else to take the fall."

She saw the faintest nervousness in his eyes, as if she knew something she wasn't supposed to know. She knew about Todd.

"I'm going to tell the police about you," she added, even though they both knew it was a hollow threat. No matter how much she wanted to call Frost Easton and give him Darren's name, she didn't have enough evidence to say a word.

"You won't do that. I know how it works. Your lips are sealed."

"Don't be so sure."

"No? Well, go ahead, tell them whatever you want, and when my lawyers get done with you, I'll own that nice top-floor Tenderloin condo of yours."

Frankie paled.

"Yes, I know where you live," Darren went on. "I make it a point to know everything about the people in my life. And the thing is, I always *liked* you, Frankie. I really did. We made such a good team, you and me."

"We were never a team."

"Too bad, I always thought of us that way. I bet you've had a tough year without me around. How are things with Jason? God, it must be awful when all you can think about is *me*."

She stared at him, openmouthed. She felt naked in front of him, as if he could see all her secrets.

"And then to lose your father, too," Darren went on. "I saw his obituary."

"Shut up," she finally said.

"But you don't really miss him, do you? I remember how you talked about him. You're glad he's dead."

"Shut up."

"How exactly did it happen, Frankie? The accident sounded so odd and tragic."

She knew that he wanted her to boil over. He was manipulating her. Playing with her head. Nothing had changed. She took a deep breath, closed her eyes, and let coldness flow through her again.

"Where do you take them, Darren?" she asked. She pointed at the locked door behind him. "Is it there? Is that where you torture them?"

"Do you want to see?"

"Yes."

He dug keys out of his pocket, then beckoned Frankie closer with one finger. She kept a safe distance. He shoved the key in the lock and twisted, and he pushed the door inward.

"Go on," he told her, standing in the doorway. "Take a look."

"Get away from the door."

Darren laughed. He strolled toward his car and waved her to the hidden space. Frankie kept an eye on him as she approached the doorway, and then she took a quick glance inside. Beyond the wall, the warehouse looked no different from the rest of the space. More containers. More Chinese characters stamped on the wood. There was no white room. No torture chamber.

"Satisfied?" Darren whispered.

He was right behind her, his hands on her waist. She slapped them off.

"This doesn't change anything," she told him. "If it's not here, then you have a space somewhere else. I know you're the Night Bird."

"I have a special name, too? Nice touch. That's so Edgar Allan Poe."

"You won't win," Frankie said.

"I've already won. You're here."

He fixed her with another smile; then he tightened the knot on his Jerry Garcia tie and tugged his peach shirt cuffs an inch beyond the sleeves of his sport coat. He smoothed the lapels.

"It was great seeing you, Frankie," he told her, "but unless you want to admit what you really want from me, you should go. I have work to do, and then I have a special evening planned."

"Special?"

"*Crazy* special," Darren said.

He pushed a button on the wall, and the garage door beside them cranked open on its tracks. Light from outside flooded the space. "No need to walk all the way back. Warehouses are dangerous places. I wouldn't want anything to happen to you."

Frankie started toward the sloped driveway that led to the street, but as she squeezed past Darren, she noticed the shiny glint of buttons on his sport coat. They were brass buttons, just like Frost had showed her. And one of them was missing.

32

Twenty-four hours.

Lucy had been gone for an entire day, and Frost was no closer to finding her. The frustration of the search left him angry, and he focused his anger on Francesca Stein. He was certain she knew more than she was telling him, but he couldn't reach her to demand answers. He'd already called her home phone. Her cell phone. Her office. She didn't call back.

Frost stood in Union Square, wrestling with himself over what to do next. He was about to cross a line. He knew plenty of cops who bent rules and broke rules, but he'd never been one of them. Jess Salceda called him a Boy Scout and told him real cops couldn't be Boy Scouts if they wanted to solve a case. He'd never believed her.

Until now. He didn't care about the consequences.

He crossed the street to the dark office building and went through the revolving door. He left his sunglasses on. Inside the lobby, he spotted the building security guard, who was in his fifties and sat behind a check-in desk near the elevators. The large man had his suit jacket draped on a chair behind him and drank Diet Coke straight out of the can. He had the *Chronicle* puzzle page open on the desk, with half the crossword completed in pencil.

Frost put his badge in front of the man's face and introduced himself.

"Is there a problem, Inspector?"

Frost showed him a photograph of Lucy. "Have you seen this woman? She's missing and at risk. We need to find her."

The man squinted at the picture through his reading glasses. "I don't think so. Not while I've been here."

"One of the street performers in the square told me he saw this woman enter the building," Frost snapped. He used his cop's don't-screw-with-me tone of voice. "He was dead sure it was her, and she never came out."

"Well, I don't know. I guess I could be wrong."

"The woman is a patient of Dr. Francesca Stein," Frost said.

"Oh. Sure. Her office is on the top floor."

"Then let's get up there. Now."

The guard eyed the phone in front of him. "I should probably call somebody."

"Call whoever you want after you let me in there. This woman is in imminent danger."

Frost marched to the elevator bank without waiting for an answer. He heard the guard's chair scraping on the marble floor and then the tap, tap of the man's leather shoes as he ran to catch up to him. The guard breathed heavily and stabbed the elevator button. The two of them got inside the car and rode in silence. When the doors opened at the top of the building, he let the man lead the way to the far end of the hallway. Double wooden doors led to Francesca Stein's office, and her name was on a brass plate on the wall.

The guard swiped a passkey against the lock. As he reached for the door handle, Frost stepped in front of him.

"You can go back downstairs now," Frost said.

"The rules say I need to go in with you."

"I can't be responsible for your safety."

The guard studied Frost's eyes, which were hidden behind sunglasses. He looked as if he might gin up the courage to question him, but Frost slid his service pistol from the holster inside his jacket as he inched the door open. Seeing the gun, the man beat a quick retreat back to the elevators.

Frost slipped inside and closed the office door. He reholstered his gun. He found the light switch for the office suite and turned on the lights in the waiting room. The door to Dr. Stein's private office was directly in front of him, and he headed quickly across the carpet and let himself inside.

Like most scientists, Stein was obsessively organized. That was unfortunate. When he'd been here before, she'd kept patient files on her large oak desk, but she'd refiled them in two locked cabinets on the wall. He sat down in her chair and booted up her computer, but the hard drive required a password to access her files. He shut it down again and frowned.

Stein kept a yellow manila pad on the desk for notes, but the pages were blank. He turned on her desk light and held the pad near the bulb to see if there were visible indentations of the notes she'd made. He found nothing. Then he pulled a garbage can from under her desk and saw two wadded balls of paper inside. He removed them and flattened them on the surface of the desk.

On one page, he saw a handwritten address. The location was near the city's container ship piers. That was one advantage of his past life as a taxi driver; he knew every street location around San Francisco. He folded the page and shoved it in his pocket.

He checked the other note. Stein had written,

White room. Where? Near Dogpatch?

Owns warehouses.

TF. Fall guy. Same as before.

And then a little lower on the page,

Something not right! What?

Frost tried to make sense of the notes, but he didn't have enough information. He reached forward and pulled the office phone closer to him. He navigated the menu to the list of recent calls, and he punched redial on the last call she'd made, which was several hours earlier.

The phone rang six times, and then a male voice answered. "So what is it now, Frankie? Can't stay away from me?"

Frost waited. He let the silence draw out without speaking.

"Frankie?" the man went on, his voice colored with suspicion. "Don't be shy. We both know what you want."

Finally, when Frost let the dead air continue, the man hung up.

Frost grabbed his own phone to call for a reverse directory on the number, but the listing came back with no identification. Whoever Stein had called was using a pay-as-you-go burner phone.

He didn't have much, but he had an address near the pier.

Frost stood up to leave, but then he heard another male voice. This one was in the room with him.

"Who the hell are you?"

A man stood in the doorway of Stein's office, with a gun lodged tightly in his fist, pointed across the room. Frost put his hands in the air slowly and carefully. He studied the man's face and recognized him. It was Dr. Stein's husband.

"Take it easy and put the gun down," Frost said. "I'm with the police. You're Jason, aren't you?"

"Let me see your badge."

Frost peeled back the flap of his coat with his fingertips and removed his badge with his other hand. He held it up so Jason could see. "I've been in contact with your wife about the Night Bird case. My name is Frost Easton."

"What are you doing in here?"

Frost could have lied. He could have used the same story he gave to the guard, but he didn't bother covering up his intentions. "Your wife is hiding something from me. I need to know what it is."

"You don't have a warrant. I could have you fired."

"Yes, you probably could, but a young woman is missing, and her life is at stake. She's connected to your wife, just like three other women who are dead now. I think Dr. Stein knows something that could help me find this woman. If you know what's going on, you need to tell me."

Jason's grip on the gun loosened. He dropped it into a pocket. "I only know what Frankie shares with me, which isn't much."

"What did she tell you?"

Jason came and stood in front of Frankie's desk. "A former patient tracked her down this week. He said he was having fugues—losing time—and waking up with memories that didn't make any sense. He had visions of being in a white room where he saw women being tortured. They were the women who died. Frankie's patients."

White room. Where?

Something not right!

"What's this man's name?" Frost asked.

Jason shook his head. "She won't tell me. It's privileged. This guy is convinced that *he's* the Night Bird, but Frankie now thinks it's possible that he's being set up by someone else. Framed to take the fall for what's happening to these women."

TF. Fall guy.

"Why does she think that?"

"Because of this," Jason said.

Frankie's husband went to a flat-screen television on the rear wall of the office. He found a remote control and switched on the screen. He changed the input to the television's USB port and launched a video, and then he froze the screen on a shot inside a crowded men's room.

"Do you recognize this man?" Jason asked.

Frost stood next to Jason and studied the face. "That's Darren Newman. What does he have to do with this?"

"Frankie's patient took this video. He was paranoid about what was happening to him, so he started recording the people he met. Frankie found Newman in this video. She didn't think it was a coincidence, and neither do I. Newman's involved."

"This address she wrote down near the piers. Is it Newman's?"

"His office," Jason said.

"Where is she? Have you heard from her?"

"Yes, she talked to him this evening," Jason said. "She says he's planning something tonight. She's going to follow him and see where he goes."

33

Darren Newman finally left the warehouse after dark.

Two blocks away, Frankie spotted the lights of the candy-red Lexus as it backed into the empty street. The car shot toward her, and she ducked down into the passenger seat as its headlights swept across her windshield. When he was gone, she turned on her engine, did a U-turn, and followed him away from the pier.

He made a right turn, heading north. She struggled to keep a fix on his taillights in traffic. He drove for several blocks and then pulled into a Shell station. She parked across the street near an auto parts store and watched him from her window. The MUNI tracks divided the street between them. When he was done filling his gas tank, Darren wandered over to a beat-up Malibu parked on the cross street. The passenger window slid down, and Darren leaned inside. Frankie couldn't see who was in the car, but Darren grabbed his wallet from a back pocket and peeled off several bills. He passed them to someone in the car and received a package in his palm that he quickly secreted in his pocket. He eyed the street and returned to his Lexus.

Drugs.

Frankie wondered what he'd purchased. Marijuana. Pills. Cocaine. Heroin. Or something that could be injected into a woman in a white room.

She pulled behind him as Darren left the gas station. Several blocks later, without a signal, he turned toward the water again. As she followed, she noticed a bar across the street named the Dogpatch Saloon. This was the downscale industrial neighborhood that was quickly being reborn as a hip arts community with yuppie condos.

It was also the neighborhood where Todd Ferris had twice awakened on the streets after his lost time.

Darren headed for the bay past a deserted construction site. Weeds grew out of the cracked street. Just ahead, the road narrowed and veered sharply to the right beside a ten-foot concrete retaining wall. She switched off her headlights, and her wheels rolled forward slowly. Where the street ended, the land near the bay opened up around her. A ruined factory loomed to her left. She saw broken windows punched out like missing teeth and metal walls dripping with rust. Directly ahead, she saw a field of boxy self-storage units protected by a tall fence.

The gate leading through the fence was open. There were no other vehicles around. Darren had to be inside.

Frankie parked near the old factory. She got out, and cold bay air wormed inside her clothes. Wind rattled the factory's metal walls and whistled through the broken windows. She shoved her hands in her pockets and marched quickly through the open gate. The storage units inside were green and no larger than trailers, dropped down in long rows. Wisps of fog swirled around her. The wind felt as if someone were breathing on her neck. Listening, she heard a bang of metal not far away as a garage door opened and closed. When she hurried to the corner, she spotted Darren's Lexus backed up against a storage unit. A crack of light glowed from under the door.

She crept closer, feeling exposed. She waited for him in the cold, but time went by slowly, and she heard no noise from inside. Her fingers grew numb, and her cheeks felt raw. When she checked her watch, fifteen minutes had passed, and she wondered how much longer he planned to stay. Then, without warning, the garage door slid up from the ground. Not all the way. Just a few feet. From inside, Darren's shadow moved like a monster. The lights went off, and she saw Darren squeeze under the open door and lock it behind him.

Frankie dove into the recessed doorway of another storage unit. Darren climbed into his car and headed toward her, throwing light across the wall inches from where Frankie hid. He passed her, driving fast. She ran to follow him, but his car was already gone by the time she reached the open gate. Behind her, she heard a guard shout from the doorway of a small security shack, but she didn't stop running. When she got to her car, she backed up into an out-of-control three-point turn. The guard, outside the gate, sprinted toward her, but she swerved around him, her lights off. She swung into the narrow street but didn't turn fast enough, and the stone wall ripped off her side mirror and gouged her door with a sickening scrape. She accelerated, taking the curve in the dark and switching her lights on. She braked hard, turned the wheel again, and found herself back on the street.

Two blocks ahead of her, she spotted taillights.

A light turned red, but she sped through it. Darren's car turned left on Third Street, heading south, backtracking on his original route. He was in no hurry now, making it easy to stay in his wake. At the gas station, he turned right and then merged onto the northbound 280 freeway. At this time of night, traffic moved freely. She matched his speed and stayed behind him. He drove two miles and exited at Sixth, heading back into the city streets.

When he turned again at Bryant, she guessed where he was going. A block later, he took the elevated highway that led toward the Bay Bridge. He was heading across the water.

They soon left the city behind as the bridge climbed over the bay. Darren stayed in the left lane. The eastbound lanes were claustrophobic on the lower level of the double-decker span, but when they passed Yerba Buena Island, they emerged into the open air under the white lights of the new bridge tower. She slowed, her eyes drawn to the westbound lanes, where Brynn Lansing had taken a fatal dive to the water. Then she hit her brakes hard, because Darren had slowed, too, in the same spot.

As if he were remembering.

She followed him to the end of the bridge. A mile later, he headed north on Highway 24. The Lexus climbed into the Berkeley hills and then disappeared into the mouth of the Caldecott Tunnel leading toward the towns of the East Bay. Beyond the tunnel, he exited immediately, and she almost missed the turn. Then he curled up the twisting mountain road with Frankie behind him.

Fog sank down the steep hillside through the trees. His taillights came and went. She was conscious of breathtaking drops falling away into darkness on the right shoulder, where she could see the faraway city lights in the valley. Houses clung precariously to the sharp slope. There had been a fire in this neighborhood years before, burning through the dry grass and reducing dozens of houses to ash, because the roads were too narrow and steep for fire trucks to traverse.

Darren pulled ahead of her, driving confidently, as if he'd navigated this route many times. She didn't dare go any faster herself. When she inched around a hairpin turn, she saw that his lights had vanished, and they didn't reappear. She was on the downslope of the mountain now, on a road barely wider than her car. Houses loomed among soaring pine trees on both sides. If he'd come this far, she assumed that he'd turned into one of the steep driveways, but she didn't know which one.

Frankie drifted to a stop. She spotted a house with no lights and a foreclosure sign posted outside. She pulled off the road in front of the house and turned off her car. Getting out, she waited in the darkness as a large SUV crept down the narrow road past her. When it was gone, she marched uphill in the middle of the street. The air was cold and damp. Most of the expensive houses were hidden behind walls of trees and vines. She stopped to examine each house, looking for Darren's Lexus. Her presence alerted a dog that barked madly from behind a gate.

She passed a car parked on a bed of pine needles, across from a Mediterranean-style home on the other side of the street. It was a blue Nissan, and the hood was warm to the touch. She couldn't see the interior, but she spotted a security decal on the Nissan's windshield from the San Francisco pier near Darren's office. That couldn't be a coincidence. She crossed to the house, which had a sharp driveway curving upward to her left. The garage wasn't visible from the street. She climbed the driveway, her heels slipping on wet leaves. Beyond a hedge wall, she spotted a brightly lit ranch home, built on the precipice of the canyon. Its garage was in front of her, and the door was open.

Darren's Lexus was parked inside.

The courtyard of the house was protected by a low wrought-iron fence. Stone steps led up to a patio, lit by mushroom lights hugging the ground. Wind chimes rang like church bells. A fig tree hung over the path, and terraced hyacinths climbed the slope. She didn't see a lock on the gate.

Frankie undid the latch and let herself inside, wincing at the groan of the metal hinges. She left it open behind her. She climbed the wet steps carefully, and when she reached the top, she found herself in a brick courtyard, bordered by flowered vines draped over a wooden trellis. A stone table was placed in the middle of the arbor for entertaining, and she saw a half-full wine glass that had been left behind. On the far side of the courtyard, the warm lights of a bay window glowed against the darkness of the cliff. The house's walls were peach stucco, and a massive double front door guarded the entrance, with narrow stained glass windows on both sides.

She crossed the courtyard and took note of the wine glass, which had lipstick on the rim. The interior of the living room was visible. She saw Native American pottery. Frontier oil paintings. Hand-blown glass art. The walls were painted in vibrant color, and the carpet was a garish pink. She didn't see anyone moving inside.

And then she heard it. Loudly, surrounding her in the courtyard from hidden speakers. As if she'd triggered it herself.

Music.

Her heart froze in her chest. She recognized the singer and the song. Carole King's mellow voice lilted from the trellises, crooning about the night bird making its way home. It was the song that had driven three women—three people who had trusted Frankie with their deepest fears—to madness.

"Nightingale."

She had to get inside the house.

Frankie started to run forward, but as she did, a hand slapped over her mouth from behind, and she felt her entire body being dragged backward.

34

"Don't say a word," Frost whispered in Dr. Stein's ear.

He peeled his hand away from her mouth and turned her around so she could see him. Despite his warning, she opened her mouth to talk, and he put a finger to her lips. He glanced at the house, then grabbed her elbow and dragged her down the stone steps. He walked her all the way back to the street.

"How did you find me?" she asked, confronting him with her hands on her hips.

"You followed him. I followed you. I picked you up when you ran the red light near Dogpatch. What the hell do you think you're doing, Dr. Stein?"

"You heard the song. The Night Bird is inside that house."

"Darren Newman?" Frost said. He saw her flinch with surprise. "Yes, I know about Newman. I talked to your husband. If you suspected someone, you should have called me, not gone after him yourself."

"Don't you think I *wanted* to call you? That's not how doctor–patient privilege works."

"Well, now you've tipped Newman off, and you could have gotten yourself killed in the process. The best thing you can do right now is get out of here. Go home."

"I'm sorry, but you need me. If he has a woman in there—if he's using my methods to torture her—then I need to be there to help."

Frost had no time to argue with her or to wait for the Berkeley police to knock politely on Newman's front door. He could hear the song playing in the garden above him. If a woman really was being tortured in the house, he knew who that woman was. Lucy.

"Wait for me in your car," he snapped. "*Don't* get out until I come back."

He turned to the driveway, but Dr. Stein held his arm. "Inspector, listen to me. I'm not wrong about this. That button you showed me? I saw Darren's sport coat. It's missing a button just like that one."

"I said, go back to your car, Dr. Stein."

He watched her walk away unhappily, with her head down and her hands in her pockets. When she disappeared, he jogged up the slick driveway to the patio gate and let himself inside. He climbed the steps, listening to the music, which came from everywhere, in multiple speakers hidden inside the arbor. The song ended and then repeated from the beginning. The Night Bird kept singing. Taunting him.

A flagstone walkway led from the courtyard to the house. At the living room window, he peered inside. He could see all the way to the open back windows, overlooking the canyon. A pass-through connected the room to the kitchen, which was dark. He could see a hallway leading to the bedrooms, but he didn't see anyone inside.

Then, through the speakers, a woman screamed.

It sounded as if she were next to him. Behind him. Above him. Her odd, strangled cry got louder until it drowned out the music, and then, with a gasp, it fell silent. He didn't recognize the distorted voice; he didn't know if it was Lucy.

Frost drew his gun. He bolted to the double front doors and pounded on them with his fist. "Police! Open the door!"

No one answered.

He twisted the knob with his hand, and it turned. The door was open. He shoved it with his shoulder and spilled inside. Cool, clifftop air whipped through the house from the rear windows. Fresh orchids scented the foyer. Down the dark hallway, a dog barked wildly at the unexpected intruder, scratching to claw its way through a closed door. He shouted again.

"Police!"

Carole King stopped singing. A door at the end of the hallway opened, letting out a triangle of light. Frost aimed his gun at the doorway and balanced his wrist with his other hand. "Come out slowly, and put your hands in the air."

He saw a bare foot nudge the door wider. A man stood in the doorway, his hands up, his body lost in shadows. He wore only loose-fitting boxers. "Come closer," Frost demanded. "Slowly."

The man approached him step by step. The light of the foyer splashed over his face, and Frost recognized Darren Newman. Newman's mouth was creased into a smile. He didn't show fear or surprise at a confrontation with an armed policeman inside his house. The dog kept barking from the other bedroom, but Newman silenced it with a snap of his fingers.

"Is there a problem?" Newman asked.

Frost didn't lower his gun. "Who else is in this house?"

"My secretary."

"I heard a woman scream," Frost said.

"What can I say? Simona is loud when we're having sex."

"Get her out here," Frost snapped.

Newman rolled his eyes and called over his shoulder. "Simona, there's someone who wants to meet you. The cops want to make sure I'm not strangling you or something."

Frost kept an eye on the doorway. The bedroom door opened all the way, revealing the rumpled end of a king-sized bed and walls covered in a metallic wallpaper made up of different stripes of blue. A young woman wandered toward him, unconcerned by his gun. She had severely short blond hair, and she wore a peach-colored man's dress shirt, unbuttoned down the front to reveal her stomach and the half-moons of her breasts. A black towel was wrapped around her waist.

"Is this one of your jokes, Darren?" she asked. "Is this guy a stripper or something?"

"No, he's really a cop."

Frost reholstered his gun. "Are you all right, miss?"

"Other than being interrupted in the middle of a good banging, I'm fine," she told him.

"Are you here voluntarily? Were you coerced in any way to have sex this evening?"

"Coerced? Hardly."

"Have you taken any drugs or consumed any alcohol?"

"That's none of your business," Simona fired back. "And if you're planning to tell me about Darren's past, don't be boring. I know all about it. You people should leave him alone."

"Do you remember how you got here tonight?" Frost asked.

"Do I *remember*?" the woman asked. "What kind of question is that?"

Newman flicked his fingers like a magician readying an illusion. "He thinks I put you in a trance to have sex with me. You're hypnotized, didn't you realize? Haven't you seen the news today? When I play the song 'Nightingale,' you will get on your back, and you won't remember a thing in the morning."

"Oh, I'll remember," Simona told Frost. "Believe me. I'm all stretched out."

Newman winked. "Well, are you satisfied, Officer?"

"For now," Frost replied.

"Then get out of the house. Leave me your card, too. I bet your superiors will be interested to hear you about you breaking in here with your gun in hand. Of course, I was really hoping it would be Frankie. I was looking forward to taking out a restraining order against her."

Frost began to appreciate Newman's talent for manipulation. He could see in the man's reptilian eyes exactly what he was. A ruthless, calculating predator.

"You knew Dr. Stein was following you?"

"Sure, I spotted her behind me on the bridge. She's scary. You should keep an eye on her. No telling what she might do."

"Darren's right," Simona added. "I met that bitch. You could tell she was hot for him. I think she's obsessed."

Newman gave the woman's bare ass a playful slap. "Go back to bed, love. I'll be there in a minute."

Simona walked down the hallway with an exaggerated sway in her hips. Frost was careful to keep his eyes on Newman's face and not on the barely dressed girl. Newman grabbed a pack of cigarettes from a bowl near the open front door and strolled with Frost out to the courtyard. He lit a cigarette and blew smoke into the cold air.

"Is this your house?" Frost asked him.

"My parents own it. They're in Zurich now. They travel a lot."

"Your parents have been very good to you. They get you out of a lot of trouble."

"That's what parents do," Newman replied.

"What about the dog? Does he belong to them, too?"

"No, that's Simona's. Pissant yipper dog never shuts up. I may have to kill it."

He made the threat so casually that it took Frost's breath away. There was not a shred of doubt in his mind that Newman was serious. It made him want to go back inside and tell the young girl that she was in danger, even if she didn't believe him.

"A lot of people think you killed Merrilyn Somers, too," Frost told him.

"Sooner or later, every bitch needs to be put down," Newman said with a smirk.

"None of this is funny."

"No? You're just like Frankie. You don't appreciate my sense of humor."

Frost leaned in close to the man, but Darren Newman didn't look easily intimidated. He was too cocky. Too sure of himself.

"Where is she?" Frost asked.

"Who?"

"Lucy Hagen."

"I have no idea who that is," Newman replied.

"I want her back. I want her back right now."

"Is this another one of Frankie's unfortunate patients? Too bad. I wonder what this one will do when the music starts playing. Drive her car off a cliff. Swallow a bottle of pills. Slit her wrists. Whoever this Night Bird is, you have to admire his imagination."

Frost didn't like being baited. And this man was good at it.

"You made a mistake this time, Mr. Newman. You screwed up."

"Did I? How so?" He took another casual drag on his cigarette.

"You've been setting someone up. A man you wanted to frame, just like you framed Leon Willis. The thing is, this man caught you on videotape in a bar. We can put the two of you together. That's going to make it hard to sell him as the one behind the game. It won't be like Merrilyn Somers."

In the semidarkness of the courtyard, Frost saw a darker shadow flit across Darren Newman's face. He'd struck a nerve. Newman didn't know about the video. Even so, the man's smile quickly returned.

"I have no idea what you're talking about," he replied. "But a video of me in a bar? Is that the best you can do? I go to a lot of bars. I'm a party animal. Simona will tell you that. I think you better take a long, hard look at the lies that Frankie has been spreading about me. I'm beginning to wonder whether Frankie is doing this herself. The woman isn't stable. She lost her father recently, did you know that? Tragedies like that can push people over the edge."

Frost turned away, but Newman called after him.

"Don't forget to leave me your card."

Frost dug in his wallet and extracted a card, which he placed in Newman's hand. The man studied it in the dim light of the garden. "Inspector Frost Easton," he said. "Who's your boss in the department, Frost?"

"Jess Salceda."

"Oh, sure, I know Jess. I'm sure she remembers me, too. I'll call her tomorrow and tell her about your visit this evening. I think she'll tell you and Frankie to stay away from me. The last thing the San Francisco Police need is another harassment lawsuit."

The light inside the car cast shadows under Francesca Stein's eyes. She brushed back a few loose strands of her brown hair and faked a smile, but Frost could see that she was broken down. Her face, which was always thin, looked fragile. She had her hands in her lap. Her back was arrow straight. Hot air blew from the vents, making the interior warm.

"He knew I was following him," she said.

"Yes."

"He played me. He lured me here, and he knew I'd make a fool of myself. No one will believe a thing I say about him now."

"For what it's worth, I think you're right about him," Frost told her, "but my own credibility isn't going to be too high after tonight, either."

Stein turned to face him. Something about her vulnerability made him conscious of how attractive she was. "I'm sorry that I put you in that position," she said.

"Newman's good at what he does," Frost said.

"Yes, he is." She leaned back against the headrest. He could see the slope of her neck. "Can I confess something to you, Frost? I'm not sure why. I just feel the need to say it out loud."

He noticed that she'd used his first name, which she'd never done before. "Say whatever you like."

"I was attracted to Darren Newman when I met him," she said. "I hate it, I'm not proud of it, but it was chemical. I'm sure that makes no sense to you."

"I'm a man. I'm never on safe ground trying to figure out what women want."

"Well, you'd think I'd be smarter than that, but I'm not. I'm married. I'm older than he is. I'm a scientist. I still found him difficult to resist."

"Did you sleep with him?"

She hesitated long enough to make him wonder what she was going to say. "No."

"Then it sounds like you have nothing to regret," he replied, but he wondered if she was lying.

"Oh, I have plenty of regrets when it comes to Darren," Stein said.

The shadows made her face difficult to read. He wished that he understood her better, but this woman lived in a separate world, where he couldn't reach her. "You're wrong about something, you know."

"What's that?"

"You said I didn't like you. I do. I didn't think I would, but that's just because I don't have a great history with therapists. You're smart, tough, and you care about your patients. I respect that."

"Thank you."

"I also need your help," he said. "Another woman disappeared yesterday. We both know the danger she's in. I need to find her. Every minute counts."

Stein closed her eyes. "One of my patients?"

"She came to your office this week. Her name is Lucy Hagen."

"What do you want? What can I do?"

"Tell me about TF," Frost said.

He could feel her freeze. "What?"

"You wrote a note. 'TF. Fall guy.'"

"How do you know about that?" she asked.

"I was in your office. I found the note in your garbage can."

"You searched my office?" Stein asked. "I can't believe you did that."

"You didn't give me any choice."

"Did you look at my patient files?"

"No, I didn't violate anyone's privacy."

"Except mine." She shook her head in dismay.

"I don't care if you're angry. The only thing I care about is stopping this man before he hurts anyone else, and you're standing in my way. I'm not the enemy, Frankie. You've got to tell me the truth. You have a patient with the initials T. F., and he knows something about the Night Bird. I need to talk to him."

"I'm sorry, he's adamant. No police. I can't give him up just because you want me to. That's not how it works."

"Then talk to him," Frost said. "Persuade him."

"I'll try, but I can't promise you anything."

"I need whatever he can tell me." Frost opened the door of the car, letting in cool air and the noise of the wind in the pines. He hesitated. "Darren told me you lost your father recently. Is that true?"

"Yes, it is."

"I'm sorry."

She didn't seem to care about gestures of sympathy. "What did Darren say about it?"

"It's not important."

"I want to know. Please."

"He said tragedies like that can push someone over the edge," Frost said.

Stein reached out and took hold of the steering wheel with clenched fists. "That bastard."

"Does that mean something to you?"

"My father went off the edge of a cliff in Point Reyes while he was hiking," Stein said.

"I'm sorry," he said again. "I haven't lost a parent, but I can imagine how difficult it must be."

"It was a complicated relationship," Stein said. "We weren't close."

"Even so."

Stein stared through the windshield. "Driving here, over the hills, I kept looking over the edge of the cliff. I thought about what it must be like to fall. How your body accelerates. How the ground rushes toward you. What do you have time to think about? What goes through your head? I wonder about his last moments—"

"You shouldn't do this to yourself," Frost said, but he wasn't sure that she was even aware that he was still in the car with her.

"I keep feeling like I'm missing something . . . ," she began.

Her voice trailed away. Her mouth was open.

He thought, *What's your worst memory?*

"Frankie?"

A tremble shuddered in her lower lip. A single glassy tear slipped down her face like melting snow. Her brown eyes were fixed in the darkness. Then, out of nowhere, her entire body convulsed. A spasm jolted her like the touch of a live wire, and she grabbed hold of herself and caved inward.

"Frankie!"

Her body twitched violently; her knees slammed up against the steering wheel. He grabbed one flying wrist. Then the other. He held her as she wriggled in his grasp, and she screamed out one word, drawing it out long and loud: *"Stop!"*

Seconds later, as quickly as it had come, the seizure washed away. Her body calmed. Her breathing quieted, and her face reddened with embarrassment. "I'm so sorry," she murmured.

"Are you okay? What was that?"

226

"Grief," she said. "A panic attack. That's all. Everything in the world caught up with me for a moment."

"Come to my car. I'll drive you to the hospital."

She shook her head. "I'm fine now."

"You shouldn't drive."

She put a hand on top of his. Her skin was moist. "It would help if you could not be a cop for a minute, Frost."

"I'm not being a cop. Just a human being."

"Then trust me when I tell you I'll be fine. It came. It went. It's not coming back."

"Do you have some kind of illness? Is it epilepsy?"

"No, there's nothing like that. Really. You don't have to worry about me. I'm a big girl. I don't need anyone to rescue me."

"I'll follow you back to the city," Frost said. "I want to make sure you don't have any problems."

"If you like."

Reluctantly, Frost got out of the car. He hiked down the narrow street toward his Suburban, but he kept looking back over his shoulder. Dr. Stein started the engine of her own car, but she waited for him instead of driving away. He climbed into his SUV and put the truck into drive, and both of their vehicles headed back into the Berkeley hills.

He thought about Francesca Stein as he followed her. She was strange, complicated, and beautiful, like a puzzle box for which there was no key. He liked her, but he didn't particularly like the way she made him feel. She was out of his league.

35

Frankie parked in the underground garage of her building in the Tenderloin. It was late, and she was alone. She walked to the elevator with her head down and her hands tightly gripping her elbows, as if she could hold herself up that way. When she got home, her condominium was dark. She uncorked an open bottle of wine in the refrigerator and poured herself a glass, which she carried up the stairs to their bedroom. Jason was asleep. She stood at the end of the bed and drank her wine and stared at her husband. When the wine was gone, which didn't take long, she cupped the glass in her palm.

Eventually, as he shifted, he became aware of her presence. He pushed himself up in bed. "Frankie?"

"Yes."

Silence lingered between them.

"Are you coming to bed?" he asked.

She didn't answer, and he leaned over to turn on the lamp on his nightstand. A yellow glow illuminated them.

"What's wrong?" he asked.

Frankie turned away and went to the windows. She put the toe of her heels against the wall and rested her forehead and palms on the glass. It was like flying. The long fall to the street stretched out below her. "Something happened to me tonight," she said.

Jason got out of bed. "What is it? Was it Newman? Did he do something to you?"

"No, it's not that," she said.

"Then what?"

"I had what I'm pretty sure was a psychogenic seizure."

Jason folded his arms on his chest. He looked clinical. "How bad?"

"Bad enough. Muscle spasms. Panic. Sweating."

"Has this ever happened to you before? Have there been previous episodes?"

"No, this was the first."

He sat back down on the bed. "We should have you tested to make sure there wasn't a physical cause."

"That's not necessary," Frankie replied. "I know what this was."

They stared at each other. She could see the truth in his face. He knew where this conversation was going. She should have guessed it much earlier, but she'd written off the mental clues to stress and grief. Doctors made the worst patients.

She turned around and leaned back against the window. Part of her hoped it would give way and let her fall.

"We *both* know what caused this, don't we?" she asked him.

"I have no idea what you're talking about."

"Do you remember the patient I told you about three years ago?" Frankie asked. "He was involved in an attempted mugging in Los Angeles. He had a concealed handgun, which he used to shoot the assailant. Then he tried to give CPR, but the mugger died of the gunshot wound. The man was tormented by what he'd done, regardless of the justification. He came to me because he wanted his memory of the event completely erased."

"I remember," Jason said.

"Two months after our treatment, he began to have seizures. The doctors thought it was epilepsy, but there were no abnormalities in his EEG. They sent him back to me, and I realized his brain was rebelling against what we'd done. The actual memory of the event was gone, but the underlying trauma was still there. It took a much longer series of traditional treatments to work his way through it."

Jason didn't ask why she was telling him this.

"Heights have never bothered me before," she went on, "but do you know what I see when I look down now?"

"What?"

"I see my father at the base of the cliff. That's strange because I wasn't there. I was at our campsite when he went hiking. I never saw my father's body. I was never on the cliff, and I never looked over the edge. The rangers found him. And yet I can *see* it in my head, Jason. I can see him lying there."

"What do you want me to say?" her husband asked.

"I want you to admit what you did to me. You changed my memory of that weekend, didn't you? All along, I thought that I'd blocked it out. All I could see were images. Snapshots. But they were images you planted there, right? You erased what really happened. You erased what I saw."

Jason stood in front of her, his face a mask. "Yes, I did."

"Why?"

"Because you asked me to," he said.

Frankie closed her eyes. He wasn't lying. She'd already realized what the truth had to be. This was something she'd *chosen*.

"Was any of it real?" she asked.

"What do you mean?"

"You know what I mean. Did he really say he was proud of me?"

Jason didn't answer immediately. Then he said, "Why go down this road, Frankie? There's a reason you wanted to forget it."

"I want to know," she snapped. "Tell me."

"No, your father never said that."

"You lied to me. You planted a lie in my head."

"A lie? Get over yourself. It's no different than what you do with patients every day. You take away bad memories, and you replace them with better memories. Don't blame me if you don't like your own medicine."

He was right about that, too. She looked into a mirror, and she didn't like what she saw. What Jason had done to her was exactly what she did to her own patients. She left her fingerprints inside their brains. She played God. Now, for the first time, she knew what it felt like to be on the receiving end. She wondered how many of the people she'd tried to help found themselves riddled with doubts after it was over. How many of them felt as if they were staring into a well where they couldn't see the bottom? How many wished they could know the truth again, after the truth had been swept away?

"What really happened out there?" she asked quietly.

He shook his head. "It's wrong for me to tell you. You didn't *want* to remember."

"Look, if you don't tell me, I'll just go downstairs and ask Pam. She knows what you did, right?"

"Yes."

"So tell me," Frankie said.

"What do you remember?" Jason asked.

"Nothing. I remember nothing. Just the image of him where he fell. How his body looked. His blood on the rocks." She stopped, because the image began to get clearer in her brain. The blood was a new detail. She hadn't seen it before in her flashbacks.

"If I tell you, it might make it worse," he pointed out. "Sometimes the memories come back more intensely and more painful than before."

"I'll take that risk. Right now, I have to know."

Jason laced his fingers on top of his head, and he grimaced, as if he were on a jury, deciding someone's guilt or innocence. "Your father didn't fall. He jumped."

Frankie's knees quivered. She felt dizzy, and she pitched forward, and Jason caught her. He helped her to the bed, and then he went to the bathroom and prepared a warm, damp towel, which he dabbed against her face. He sat down next to her, their legs touching.

"I saw it?" she asked.

"You went hiking with him that morning, the way you usually did. He was ahead of you on the cliff trail. You saw what he was about to do, and you shouted for him to stop, but he simply fell. And then you ran to the edge and saw him on the beach below. You couldn't deal with it. You went back to the campsite. You stayed in your tent for hours, and then finally, you went to find the rangers, and you told them your father was missing."

She shook her head in disbelief. "For God's sake, why did he do it? Did I say something? Did we argue?"

"You know he had bouts of depression. He'd talked about suicide before."

"Yes, but he was the supreme narcissist. It was just talk. I can't believe he actually did it."

"Sometimes people act in a split second," Jason said. "One moment he's on the cliff, and an impulse takes him, and he's in the air. At that point, it's too late to go back and stop."

Frankie closed her eyes. She tried to summon tears, but she couldn't.

"Do you remember it now?" Jason asked finally.

She stared into her brain and tried to draw a picture of that last morning. Even knowing what had happened, she saw nothing, and thinking harder didn't change anything. She dipped a brush into paint, but with each stroke she applied, the canvas stayed blank. Everything Jason had told her was no more real to her than a story that had happened to someone else.

It made her think of the theme her father had chosen for their discussions that last weekend. *Risk.*

She'd taken a risk. Just like the patients who came to her took a risk. You can take away your pain, but once it's done, it's done. You're in the air. It's too late to go back and stop.

Their memories—those little proteins that made up a life—were gone.

"No," she said. "I don't remember anything at all."

Frost awoke to music. He shifted on the sofa, which disturbed Shack, who hopped down to the carpet. Disoriented, he realized that the music was a Jefferson Airplane song. "White Rabbit." He lay on his back, listening to Grace Slick's angry, erotic voice before he realized that the music was coming from his phone.

He'd chosen "White Rabbit" as the ringtone for Herb, who'd partied with the San Francisco group as a nineteen-year-old in 1967. He'd seen a photo of Herb with Grace Slick and Marty Balin at the Monterey festival that June. Sometimes, his friend told stories from that summer, and Frost realized that, even back then, Herb was at the center of everything that went on in the city.

Frost rolled off the sofa and stumbled to the dining room table, where he'd left his phone. "Herb, what time is it?"

"Almost two. I'm sorry to wake you up."

"Don't worry about it. What's going on?"

"Street Twitter came through."

Frost was instantly awake. "What did you find out? Did someone see Lucy?"

"No, but a guy wearing that creepy mask gave twenty bucks to a homeless vet to pass along a message."

"What message?" Frost asked.

His friend hesitated, didn't answer.

"Herb? Come on, what was the message?"

"It may be nothing. This guy may just be playing games with you."

"Tell me."

"He said if you want to find what you're looking for, ask Katie."

Frost's fist clenched. He breathed in and out. "I have to go," he told Herb.

"Listen to me. He's just getting inside your head. That's what he's *trying* to do."

"I have to go," Frost repeated. "Thanks, Herb. Really."

He hung up the phone, and he stood in the nighttime chill of the house. If the Night Bird wanted to get inside Frost's head, he'd succeeded. Frost knew exactly where to look for Lucy.

She was in the backseat of a car near Ocean Beach.

That was where he'd found his sister's body.

36

Near Ocean Beach, the thunder of the waves was unrelenting. Frost got out of his SUV and felt salty spray on his face. The long stretch of the Great Highway down the hill from Cliff House was deserted, but Frost could feel the Night Bird watching him. Somewhere in the darkness of the beach, or on the rocky trails of Sutro Heights above him, the man had binoculars to spy on his prey.

The stretch of sand here was wide, flat, and seemingly endless, like a cold imitation of Santa Monica. He shivered as the damp chill got inside his bones. Across the street, he spotted one lonely car in the beachfront parking lot. It was an imperial-blue Chevy Malibu. This was no accident; the Night Bird had done his research. Katie had driven the same kind of car.

He ran the vehicle plate. The car had been stolen three days ago. It was all part of the plan.

Frost called for backup, but he didn't wait for the sirens. He had to know. Ocean wind screeched in his ears, and a headache pounded behind his eyes. He crossed the street toward the Malibu, just like he'd done once before, when a mysterious phone call took him here. In the middle of the night. Six years ago.

Are you looking for Katie?

Yes, I am. How did you—

She said she's waiting for you at Ocean Beach.

What? Who is this?

A cloud of sand rose off the beach and blew grit into his face. White surf undulated from the water. His chest felt heavy. Time drew out, making each step a journey against an invisible tide. He didn't want to get there. He didn't want to see what was waiting for him.

Streaks of mud crusted over the car's blue paint. He saw a single sentence scrawled in the dirt of the rear window. The same awful question.

What's your worst memory?

Frost remembered everything about that night. Every sensation was tattooed on his brain. The blue-and-green wool of the blanket in the backseat, covering Katie. The cool metal of the door handle. Her torso spilling out, head nearly severed, blood everywhere, like a red ocean. The wail of his own screams.

He pulled open the rear door of the Malibu, and his heart seized. Again, again, again. A blanket covered Lucy's body. Blue-and-green wool in the same diamond design. He knelt down, using both hands to peel back the blanket to reveal her face, and there she was. Eyes closed. Perfect and peaceful. He put two fingers on the soft skin of her neck, and he found—

A heartbeat. She was alive.

Frost yanked the blanket from her body. She wore the same outfit as when he'd last seen her. Cropped jeans. Striped top. Gently, he lifted her torso and climbed into the back of the car beside her. He rustled her shoulders and whispered her name.

"Lucy . . . it's Frost. Lucy, wake up."

Her eyes blinked open and closed. And open again. She tried to focus, but her gaze wandered, as if she were following the buzz of a fly. Her limbs squirmed. A groan rumbled from her throat.

"*Lucy.* It's me."

She shook off the fog. Her fingers rubbed her face and left pink impressions on her skin. Through dry lips, she said, "Frost?"

"Yeah."

"I don't—where are we?"

"Long story. Do you remember anything? What's the last thing you remember?"

Her eyes blinked again. "I don't even know."

"That's okay. Hang on. I'm getting you out of here."

Frost climbed out of the car and listened for the wail of an ambulance, but he heard nothing. He leaned in again and put his arms under Lucy's knees and around her back. Instinctively, she clung to his neck and let him carry her out of the car. He kicked the door shut with his foot and half ran across the Great Highway back to his Suburban. Part of him wanted to scream at the Night Bird, knowing the man was watching him.

Why are you doing this?

At his truck, he eased Lucy into the front seat, just as he'd done once before, atop the Bay Bridge. He called in an update and threw his phone on the seat between them. He headed east, driving fast and using his siren to cruise uphill through the stop signs. The nearest hospital was on the other side of Golden Gate Park, three miles away. Lucy stared vacantly through the windshield as the city flashed by on both sides. He kept looking at her as he drove, but she didn't look back at him. Pieces of a puzzle worked their way through her brain.

Finally, she said, "He took me?"

Frost nodded. "Yes."

Lucy was silent again as he sped through two more intersections, and then she went on: "How long?"

"More than twenty-four hours."

"An entire day," she murmured. "I don't remember any of it."

"What do you remember?"

"I—I remember picking out a dress. To meet you. I draped it across the bed. After that, nothing."

He glanced at the expression on her face, which was intense, as if thinking hard would bring everything back.

"Where are you taking me?" she asked.

"The hospital. I want you checked out."

Frost kept driving through the residential neighborhoods, which were empty of traffic. The up-and-down hills made a roller coaster, and the Suburban nearly left the ground as he shot over each peak. He made good time. He was already turning toward the emergency room on the east end of the park when Lucy suddenly grabbed his arm and said in an urgent voice, "Frost, stop!"

He swung the SUV sharply to the curb opposite the University of San Francisco campus. "What is it? Are you okay?"

Lucy unhooked her safety belt and scrambled across the seat. She threw her arms around him and leaned into his neck. He could feel the heat of her skin. Her body shivered, and her breathing was crazy fast. "Frost, I'm scared. What did he do to me? What did he put in my head?"

"You tell me. Is there anything? Any memories? Any feelings?"

"No! It's all blank! I need to know what he did. We can't wait. Whatever it is, we need to *get it out*."

"I can call Dr. Stein and ask her to meet us there. She's the expert."

Her reaction was volcanic. "*No!* No, not her, not her, I never want to see her again, *ever*. Ever. Don't make me see her again, Frost. Please, I never want to look at her face."

She burrowed closer to him and held him tight, as if she were hanging from a bridge and he could keep her from falling. Her fingernails dug deeply into his flesh.

"You don't have to see her," Frost said. "Don't worry. We'll talk to someone else."

"Take me home," Lucy said. "Not the hospital. Just take me home."

"Your apartment isn't safe."

"Then take me to your place. Please?"

"I'm sorry, Lucy, the rule is, you see a doctor first. We don't know what he did to you. We need to make sure you're okay."

Lucy slid back to her seat with a wild look of despair. Panicked tears rolled down her cheeks. She shook her head over and over, and she wrung her sweaty hands together. Blood smeared her mouth where she'd bitten through her lip. She was disintegrating before his eyes, and he wanted her with a doctor *now*. He put the Suburban into gear, but as the truck lurched forward, she took him completely by surprise. Without warning, she punched open the passenger door of the SUV. She practically fell into the street as he jammed the brakes, and then she took off at a sprint across the intersection.

Frost recovered from his shock and threw open his own door. "Lucy!"

He reached for his phone, but he realized that she'd grabbed it from the seat.

"Lucy! Stop!"

She was already twenty yards away, passing under the streetlight and charging up the Lone Mountain hillside toward the USF campus. The silhouette of the university tower loomed at the summit behind the tall trees. Frost jumped from the Suburban and laid chase. He ran for the slope and climbed after her through wet dirt and grass, but the darkness masked her trail. He followed blindly, shouting her name.

"Lucy!"

She didn't answer, and he didn't see her. The fir trees dotting the hillside kept her hidden. He stopped to listen for the noise of her footsteps as she moved higher toward the tower, but he didn't hear her. Instead, in the quiet, he heard something else. Music. Sweet, horrifying music. Somewhere close by, among the trees, he heard the gentle notes of a piano solo. He recognized the song.

It was a killing song.

"Lucy, *don't!*" he called.

He ran toward the sound, hearing it get louder, but he was too late to stop the music. The piano solo gave way to Carole King's perfect voice trilling about the night bird, about the sailor seeking rest, about the nightingale singing out the theme to a stranger's lonely life. His eyes tried to find Lucy among the trees, and all the while, he expected to hear her scream, like the others. Scream. Run. Die.

A pinpoint glow shined thirty feet away. It was the white light of a phone screen. His phone.

He skidded across the slope from tree to tree and found her with her back against one of the evergreens. In the glow of the phone, her brown eyes were scared. Her hair was messy. He closed the distance between them in a second and gathered her up in his arms, and she buried herself against him. He could feel the pounding up-and-down swell of her chest. He tried to pull the phone from her hand, but she struggled, and the song kept playing, tinny and loud. It was deep into the second verse before he realized something.

Nothing was happening to her.

Carole King sang, and the piano played, and Lucy's mind didn't break into little pieces. Not like Monica Farr. Or Brynn Lansing. Or Christie Parke.

Lucy realized it, too, and her eyes opened wide with relief.

"It didn't work," she murmured. "Right? It didn't work!"

"I guess not," he whispered, but he wasn't so sure. He almost wished she'd lost control right here, where he could hold her and keep her safe. Then, at least, he'd know what the Night Bird had done to her.

The song drifted to an end and left them in silence. They didn't move. He could feel her holding on to him, and in the darkness of the hillside, she was soft and warm. Her body relaxed, as if a storm had passed. She had a faint smell of perfume in his arms. Finally, she let go and stared at him, just inches away. Her face was filled with yearning and confusion.

"Do you think I'm really okay?" she asked.

"I hope so. Let's get you to the hospital and make sure."

"Frost, don't let anything happen to me," Lucy said, taking his hand.

"I won't," he told her. "Don't worry, I won't."

37

Pam dressed to make sure everyone was looking at her. She wore a knee-length bodycon dress in a bold orange color, with black buttons making an S from her neck to her hips. Her blond hair framed her face and hung in layers halfway down her back. Her lipstick was baby pink. She wore a tiny crooked smile, as if the world were a joke and she knew the punch line.

For Frankie, staring at Pam was like looking at a mirror that transformed her into a younger, more erotic version of herself. She felt jealous of Pam, and Pam felt jealous of her. The war never ended.

She sat down opposite Pam at the Zingari window table. Virgil, whose dark eyes looked hungover, swooped in with iced tea, and Pam already had a martini in front of her. Her sister pointedly studied her phone without looking up. Frankie ordered a prosciutto pizza for lunch.

"So all this time, you knew," Frankie said after the silence had gone on too long.

Her sister didn't stop texting. "That Daddy took a dive? Yes."

"And it doesn't bother you?"

Pam put down the phone and laced her long fingers together. Her fingernails matched her dress. "What part do you mean, Sis? The part where our father kills himself? Or the part where my delicate flower of a sister can't handle it and decides to forget the whole thing?"

Frankie thought, *Missile launched.* She wanted to fire back in kind, but she didn't even remember enough to explain herself. She didn't know why she'd felt the need to wipe away what she saw. She'd always thought of herself as strong, but maybe Pam was right. Maybe Frankie was afraid of feeling anything. Love. Hate. Desire. Grief.

God knows Pam would never let emotion get in the way of doing what she wanted.

"You've been playing with me, haven't you?" Frankie asked.

"What do you mean?"

"The things you've said about Dad lately. It was a game to you. You wanted to see if I remembered anything."

Pam sipped her martini and shrugged. "I've always wondered if your shrink biz is just a big scam. Can you really change someone's memory? Or if you poke and prod, does it all come rushing back?"

"It doesn't work like that."

Virgil returned to the table. He put a caprese salad in front of Pam and glanced between the sisters. "If you're going to have a girl fight, ladies, at least give me time to sell tickets."

"No fight," Pam said with a cool stare at Frankie. "She knows I'd win."

"I'm sure you would," Frankie replied.

Pam examined the bags under Virgil's eyes and the limp swoop in his lavish hair. "Bad night, V? You look all hangdog."

"When I look like this, it was a *good* night," Virgil replied.

Pam smirked. Frankie waited until they had the table to themselves again. She didn't know why she wanted to torture herself with the details when it was too late to change anything.

"When did Jason tell you?" Frankie asked. "Before or after?"

"Before. He thought I should know what you were going to do. Not that I had a say in it. You do what's best for Frankie. You always have."

Frankie's lips pressed tighter together, and she didn't reply. Pam leaned across the table and whispered, "Why, does it piss you off that Jason told me? At least someone in the family cares enough to include me."

"That's a cheap shot," Frankie replied.

"Really? You've been MIA for the past year. You're off in Frankie world, and some of us are back here in the real world."

"That's rich, coming from you. You've never lived a day in the real world."

"At least I don't run away from it," Pam snapped.

Frankie's brow furrowed as she felt the emptiness in her brain again, the place where something was missing that she couldn't get back. Now that it was gone, she wanted to remember.

Virgil set Frankie's pizza in front of her. He'd overheard most of their conversation. "Tickets, ladies. Remember, tickets."

"Not now, Virgil, please," Frankie murmured.

"You're right, a thousand apologies to both of you. Write it off to last night's party." Virgil leaned down and whispered in Frankie's ear. "Truly, darling, I'm sorry to intrude. You know I can't stop myself. With everything going on, though, I thought you should know. Somebody outside the restaurant is watching you."

Frankie's eyes shot to the window.

Todd Ferris stood on Post Street. His eyes had the same intense, faraway sadness they always did. As if, in his young life, he'd already given up on the future. She could see him mouthing three words.

It happened again.

She persuaded Todd to go with her to her Union Square office by promising no notes and no recordings. He refused to go into her treatment room, and she struggled even to get him to sit down. He paced repeatedly on his long legs, twisting his navy wool cap between his fingers.

"The last thing I remember is Monday night," he murmured in his low voice, making her struggle to hear him. "I had a tech job over at the planetarium. I help them with their videography sometimes. The job went late. But that's it. The next thing I knew, I was waking up on the street. In *Dogpatch* again. The other side of the city."

"Where in Dogpatch?" Frankie asked.

He shook his head. "I don't know. One of the abandoned buildings around there. I hiked a couple blocks and caught a bus."

"Has it been the same place every time?" she asked.

"No. The same area, but not the same place."

"Could you find the areas again?"

"Maybe. When I woke up, I wasn't thinking straight. I just wanted to get the hell away from there."

"What else do you remember?" she asked.

"There was another girl," Todd said.

"Did you recognize her?"

"No."

"Was it the same white room again?"

"Yes."

"Anything else?" Frankie asked.

Todd stopped in the middle of her office. "A knife."

"What?"

"I have this image of a knife," Todd said. "I don't know why or what it means, but I can't get it out of my head."

He sat down in the chair opposite Frankie and grabbed hold of the edge of her desk with both hands. "What's happening to me, Dr. Stein? Don't tell me you don't know."

Frankie tried to concentrate. Todd's memory of the knife disturbed her. She thought about the smart young college student who lived two doors down from Darren Newman. Merrilyn Somers, singer, gamer, techie. She was a sweet girl who wound up dead on her apartment bed, stabbed seven times with a knife.

"Dr. Stein?" Todd said again, when Frankie didn't answer. His honey voice was almost a whisper. "Do you know what it's like when something terrible happens to you? You relive it over and over. It won't go away. It starts to take over your whole life."

"Yes, I know."

That was why patients came to her. To wipe those memories clean like chalk from a blackboard.

"I can't keep waking up with these nightmares in my head," Todd said. "I don't know who I am anymore. I have to do something about it."

She didn't like what she heard in his voice or saw in his eyes. "Exactly what are you saying, Todd?"

"I'm going crazy," he told her. "I'd rather die than go on feeling like this. I have to make it stop."

"If you want to do something, talk to the police. Tell them your story."

Todd bolted out of the chair. His voice got louder. "Are you kidding? Do you want them to arrest me? Don't you get it? I've been doing terrible things to these women. *I'm* the Night Bird."

"That's not the only explanation," Frankie replied.

"Come on, Dr. Stein, nothing else makes sense! You know it, too. You just want me to turn myself in. You can't do it yourself, so you want me to go to the police and admit everything. Hell, maybe I should, but that wouldn't get rid of the nightmares. Don't you get it? I'm scared of what's going on in my own mind."

Frankie got out of her chair and came around the desk. She put both hands on Todd's shoulders. "What I'm saying is, it's possible that someone is manipulating you. He wants you to believe that you're guilty."

Todd's eyes narrowed with suspicion. "What are you talking about?"

Frankie switched on the video player in her office. She didn't need to go far to find what she wanted. She froze the screen on the image that Todd had taken in the bathroom of the bar.

"Do you recognize this video?"

He cocked his head. "Sure, it's mine."

"What about that man?"

Todd stared at Darren Newman. He took two steps closer to the screen without saying anything. He *shouldn't* have recognized Newman. The man should have been one of thousands of strangers who passed in and out of a person's life in a few seconds. But seeing him, Todd couldn't let go. He inched closer to the television. Newman's face held him with the power of a magnet.

"Who is he?" Todd murmured.

"Do you recognize him?" Frankie repeated.

"What's his *name*?"

She hesitated. "His name is Darren Newman. Have you seen him before?"

"No, I've never seen him," Todd said, "but I *know* him. Why do I know him?"

"He's been in the news. Last year, a lot of people thought he was guilty of murder."

"You think it's him, don't you?" Todd said. "You think he's the one who's been doing this to these women. And to me."

"It's possible."

"It's more than possible, isn't it? That's why he's in my video. He's been stalking me. Why don't I remember him?"

"He may be using drugs and hypnosis to change your memory," Frankie said.

Todd spun around. His face was black. "Like you do."

"Yes," she acknowledged. "Like I do."

He loomed over her, and for a moment, she was afraid of what he would do. She saw a man who was about to lose control, who would lash out at anyone in front of him. Then Todd spun away from her and charged toward her office door.

"Todd, where you are you going?" she asked.

"I'm going to kill him," he said.

38

"How's the girl?" Lieutenant Jess Salceda asked Frost.

She sucked on her cigarette. The two of them stood outside the police headquarters building in Mission Bay near the water. Giants fans swarmed the street, heading to an afternoon game at the water-front stadium two blocks away. The parking lot across the street smelled of popcorn, hot dogs, and beer. Hip-hop music blared from portable speakers. The afternoon was cloudy and cold, with rain storms on the way, but that didn't stop the tailgaters.

"She's at the hospital," Frost told her. "I'm heading over there to take her home. The docs found traces of barbiturates in her system."

"Any sexual assault?" Jess asked.

"No."

"Well, that's good."

"What about the Malibu?" Frost asked her. "What's the report on the car? Did we find any evidence?"

"Oh, yeah, lots," Jess replied. "Prints, DNA. But I bet it all traces back to the car's owner, not our guy."

She leaned back against the building's concrete wall as she smoked. She was short—at least six inches shorter than Frost—but tough and strong for her size-ten uniform. In her early forties, she wore her hair short, with dyed brown-and-gold streaks and bangs hanging down to her eyes. She had a slightly hooked nose and a round copper face that didn't smile often. She was usually angry. Angry about crime. Angry about poverty. Angry about men who treated women like punching bags. And she wasn't quiet about the things in the city that she didn't like. Her mouth regularly got her in trouble with the captains and commanders, but the street cops and investigators all knew she was fearless, and they respected her blue blood. She'd been a cop since she was eighteen, just like her father had been a cop since he was eighteen.

"So what's this guy doing?" Jess asked him. "What's his plan?"

"I don't know."

"You said the song had no effect on the girl, right? Not like the others?"

Frost nodded. "Right. This guy took her and drugged her, but I can't figure out his next move. Whatever he did to Lucy isn't the same as the other women, and that's what worries me. I'd like to keep a cop on her 24-7 for now."

Jess eyed him from behind her spiky bangs. "Lucy?"

"Yeah."

She knew him well enough to read him. "Do you have some kind of personal thing with her?"

Frost didn't answer immediately. He watched the fans parading toward the stadium. "Not in the way you mean."

Jess squinted at the sky, where darker clouds massed. "Stay objective, Frost."

"Don't worry, nothing's going to happen with her. It's not that kind of relationship. At least not for me."

"Well, I'm in no position to give you lectures about who to get involved with."

He knew she was pissed at him, but it wasn't just about the case.

Frost and Jess had a complicated relationship, and it had been that way since they met. Jess wasn't anyone's idea of drop-dead gorgeous, but she had heat, and Frost felt it. They'd known each other since before he was a cop. Jess Salceda had been the homicide inspector on Katie's murder. She'd encouraged him to join the force because she saw something in how he looked at the world that she thought the police needed. When he did, she mentored him, sometimes ahead of older cops who didn't like the special treatment he got. They thought there was something between them, and they weren't entirely wrong.

Last spring, when Jess was splitting from her husband—a captain in special operations—she and Frost got drunk together and spent all night in bed in an airport motel. The next morning, they woke up to their mistake and swore off it, which lasted a month. Then they found themselves back at the same motel for another one-night stand.

Since then, they'd been sober with each other. Neither one of them wanted a relationship, but like alcoholics, they knew how good a drink could taste.

"I got a call from someone I was hoping I'd never have to talk to again," Lieutenant Jess Salceda told Frost.

"Let me guess. Darren Newman."

"Bingo," Jess said.

"What'd Newman say?" Frost asked.

"He said you broke into his house, harassed him at gunpoint, and couldn't take your eyes off his girlfriend's tits."

"That's not totally inaccurate," Frost admitted.

Jess snickered. "He wants me to keep you out of his face, or he's going to sue the department."

"Yeah?"

"Yeah, so stay *in* his face," Jess snapped. "Do you think he's the one doing this? Do you think he's the Night Bird?"

"I don't know. The puzzle pieces fit, but we don't have a shred of real evidence against him yet."

"Yeah, he's clever," Jess said.

"Herb still thinks he killed Merrilyn Somers."

Jess had half a cigarette left, but she crushed it under her boot. "Yeah, Herb and his crew were all over me about Newman from the get-go. They put me in touch with other women who'd been involved with him. Guy was a nightmare. Abuse, assault, stalking, harassment. He always skated thanks to his parents. But the stories these women told me? Wow. One girl stood him up on a date because her boss made her work late. She came home and found all of her tropical fish pinned to her bedroom wall with a nail gun. Nice, huh? I mean, we're talking about a guy with zero soul. There's nothing inside."

"And yet he keeps hooking up with new girlfriends. I met one of them last night. She knows all about his past, but she doesn't care."

"What can I tell you, Frost? Biology's a bitch. I get it. I spent hours with Newman, and I knew what kind of a psycho he was. Doesn't mean I was immune to his sex appeal."

Frost knew she was right, but he didn't pretend to understand.

"What about the Somers murder?" he asked.

"That case really got to me," Jess said, shaking her head. "Here's this pretty young black girl from Reno. Religious. Choir singer. Engaged to her high school sweetheart. Smart as a whip, already lining up jobs after college. Every kid should be like her, you know? And then some bastard rapes her and kills her in her apartment. That shit makes me crazy."

"I know."

"Herb's right," Jess told him. "Newman did it. I *know* he did it. And you know what? I don't think Merrilyn was his first."

"There were others?"

"Yeah, I did some digging. When Newman was eighteen years old, living near Green Bay, a college girl was found stabbed in a local park. Case was never solved. Three years later, there was a murder in Boulder, while Newman was going to school there. The dead girl had a class with Newman the previous semester, but he was never on their radar.

A local sex offender got drunk and hung himself, and the police found the girl's panties in his house. That was as good as a confession, but if you ask me, Newman was already figuring out how to cover his tracks. He likes using fall guys."

"And then came Merrilyn?" Frost asked.

"Yeah, he was all over Merrilyn from the day she moved in. She told him she was engaged, but he wasn't going to let that stop him."

"Except the DNA pointed to somebody else."

"Yeah, DNA don't lie, right? But this time it did."

"How?"

"Hell if I know," Jess said, shaking her head. "I tried to figure out a way to prove that Newman planted the evidence. There was nothing. Leon Willis's attorney knew he didn't stand a chance with a jury, so he took a plea. Chief made me go and *apologize* to Newman, and all the time, the guy was laughing at me because we both knew he killed her. Not only that, but he must have planned it, too. At first, I figured it was a crime of passion, but the DNA matching Willis? No, he knew what he was going to do for weeks. Same thing was probably true in Wisconsin and Colorado. He's smart. Merrilyn Somers didn't stand a chance."

"And we haven't been able to touch the guy," Frost said.

"That's right. I don't like it. If Newman is the Night Bird, he's still laughing at us. It's time to take this guy down."

Frost took Lucy upstairs to check that her apartment was safe. She'd been excited to see him when he came to pick her up at the hospital, but by the time they were alone at her place, a shadow had replaced her smile. She sat on the bed and ran a hand over the dress she'd planned to wear to meet him at Alembic. Her knee bounced nervously. He knew the look of someone who had something important to say but was scared to say it.

"I'm sorry about last night," she murmured.

"Don't be."

"I shouldn't have run. It was stupid."

"You were scared," Frost said. "I get it."

She got off the bed and stood in front of him. When she tilted her chin, their eyes met. He watched her swallow hard. "I guess you know that I like you. I've been pretty obvious about it."

"I like you, too," he said. "You're sweet, and you're special."

She shook her head. "I never think of myself that way."

"Well, you should. You don't have to conquer the world to be a special person. You have a good heart. I knew that as soon as I met you."

Lucy gave him a sad smile. "We're talking about different things, though, huh? You don't like me the way I like you."

"If you mean romantically, then no. I'm sorry. I should have said something before now. I really do like you, Lucy. Being with you brings back a lot of memories for me. Memories of my sister."

"Oh."

"I know that's not what you want to hear, but for me, it's something really important."

"Well, I never had a brother, so I don't know what that's like. I bet you were a good one to Katie."

"We were very close when we weren't driving each other crazy," he told her, smiling.

"Is that why you look upset?" she asked. "Are you remembering Katie?"

"No, I'm upset because I'm worried about you. I want to make sure you stay safe."

"I'm fine!" she assured him with a false lightness in her voice. She made a muscle with her bicep and giggled. "See? Me too strong for Night Bird."

"This guy isn't a joke, Lucy."

"I know."

"I wish you'd talk to Dr. Stein. Or another psychiatrist."

"*No.* The last thing I want is someone else messing around in my head. Really, I'm okay."

Frost thought she was trying to convince herself. He didn't believe that she was fine, or that the Night Bird had failed, even if he didn't know what had happened to her. He also knew that Lucy's confidence was an act. Deep down, she was terrified.

He took her hand and led her to the apartment window. He pointed at a squad car parked outside on Haight behind his Suburban.

"That car's not going anywhere," Frost told her. "You're going to have protection 24-7 until we find this guy."

"You don't have to do that," Lucy told him.

"Yes, we do. If you want to go anywhere, talk to the cop in the car first, and she'll go with you. Frankly, I'd feel better if you stayed home. And don't put on any music or watch television, okay? I don't want you taking any chances."

Lucy stared at the floor and looked overwhelmed.

"Do you remember anything more from your missing day?" he asked her. "Did anything else come back to you?"

She shook her head, but her lip trembled. "I don't think so."

"You don't think so? That sounds like you do remember something. What is it?"

"I have this odd memory in my head. It's a bridge. It's nowhere I've ever been, but I remember it. I feel it. I'm in the middle of this awful gorge, and I can barely hold on. I would do anything to make it go away. I would die to make it stop."

Her eyes filled with tears.

"This is what he does, Lucy," Frost murmured. "He plays on your fears. He exploits the things that terrify you. Just tell yourself that it wasn't real. It was an illusion."

"How can I *remember* something that wasn't real?" Lucy asked. "Because it feels like it actually happened. It's in my head. If you asked me to swear on the Bible, I'd tell you that I've been on that bridge."

"You can't trust your memory," Frost said. "Memories lie. Even the good ones don't always tell the truth."

"I just want this to be over."

"Soon. It will be over soon."

She reached her arms out to embrace him, but at that moment, he heard his phone ringing in his pocket. He checked his caller ID and saw Francesca Stein's name. He glanced at Lucy, who gave him a broken smile and waved him away. He stood up and answered the call. "Dr. Stein?"

"Hello, Inspector."

The cool maturity in the psychiatrist's voice was such a contrast to the youth and innocence of Lucy Hagen. They were two very different women. He also noticed something strange. Lucy clapped her hands over her ears to block out the sound of Dr. Stein's voice through his phone.

"How are you feeling today?" he asked Frankie. "Are you okay? You had me worried last night."

"I'm fine, but I need to see you," she replied. "The patient I've been protecting is a man named Todd Ferris. We need to find him right away."

39

"That's Darren Newman's house," Frankie told Frost.

The detective put down his binoculars, which were trained on a Victorian house on Oak Street, opposite the narrow strip of Panhandle Park. The house looked like one of the painted ladies snipped out of a postcard of Alamo Square. It was narrow, with a paisley design on its green-and-lilac trim and red steps leading up to the door. The roof featured a single gable with a bay window in the middle.

The park's century-old eucalyptus trees towered over their heads and scattered dagger-shaped leaves across the green grass. It was early evening, and the dark clouds had turned to mist, making their faces damp. More rain was coming.

"Newman's at home," Frost said. "I can see him inside."

"I haven't seen Todd, but I'm sure he's going to show up here sooner or later."

"And he said he would kill Newman?" Frost asked.

"He did. That's the only reason I can tell you about any of this, Inspector. Todd is on the brink. I don't know what he'll do. Although honestly, I'm more worried that Darren will do something to *him* when he realizes that Todd has figured out what's going on."

Moisture from the drizzle gave a wet shine to Frost's hair and beard. He shifted the binoculars to the parked cars on Oak Street. He panned along the sidewalk and the park's dense trees, but the spitting rain had driven everyone away. They were alone.

"No one else is watching the house," he said.

"I saw Todd's face. He was serious. He'll be here."

They waited silently. Traffic came and went behind them, kicking up spray. Frankie kept her eyes on the old Victorian, but in the wet and cold, her mind drifted to the cliffs of Point Reyes. When she thought about that last weekend with her father, she could see him clearly now, broken body below her on the rocks. Face looking up at her. Blood.

She could hear her own voice, too. *"Stop!"*

But nothing else. Her memory was a blank space.

She found herself resenting what Jason had done, even if she'd asked him to do it. She'd been there to witness her father's last moments, and now that walk on the trail had been stripped from her brain.

This is what you do to everyone else, her mind whispered.

She'd never understood what her patients experienced when they lay on her chaise and stared at the images she'd made for them and responded to her subliminal suggestions. She'd never known what it felt like, afterward, to have part of your past stolen away. This was her chance to look through the other end of the microscope. She didn't like what she saw.

"Are you okay?"

She realized Frost was staring at her, his forehead wrinkled with concern.

"Yes, I'm fine. I'm not going to have another seizure, if that's what you're worried about."

"You looked far away," Frost said, "and not in a happy place."

Frankie shivered in the rain. "I'm questioning things. Some days I wonder if I've done more harm than good in my life."

Frost's eyes were curious, but he didn't push her for details. She was grateful for that. He went back to his binoculars.

"Newman's getting a call," he told her. And then a minute later, "Come on, he's on the move."

Frost led her across the wet grass back to his Suburban, which was parked on Fell Street. Across the park, Frankie could see the door sliding up on the garage of Darren's Victorian house. His red Lexus inched down the driveway, and when the traffic was clear, he backed onto Oak Street. The one-way street headed east, away from them, and Darren made an immediate right. His car disappeared.

Frost accelerated toward the point of the Panhandle and cruised through the yellow light into a left turn. Sutro Tower loomed on the hillside ahead of them. He sped to the next block and did another left to lay chase, but almost immediately, he hissed, "Get down!"

Darren's Lexus sped toward them, no more than half a block away. Frankie slid as far as she could below the dash, and Frost dropped his visor to block his face. The two vehicles whipped by each other in opposite directions. Frost eyed his mirror, and Frankie took a quick look backward over the seat. She saw the Lexus make a right turn. Frost did a U-turn and followed.

They spotted Darren's Lexus three cars ahead of them.

"He's heading into Golden Gate Park," Frost said.

They pursued Darren down a boulevard lined with trees and wide lawns on the north side of the park. A handful of bicyclists and joggers braved the rain on the trails beside them. The sky felt low, painted in angry charcoal. On their right, they passed the Conservatory of Flowers, surrounded by palm trees and gardens. Farther on, they saw the tower of the de Young museum.

Traffic thinned. The Lexus turned onto a small road leading deep into the center of the park, and Frost lingered to give the other vehicle space, then turned behind him. Dense trees soon enveloped them on both sides.

"He's heading for Stow Lake," Frost said. "Maybe he's looking for the White Lady."

"Ghost stories, Inspector? From you?"

"At night, the lake trail can make you believe almost anything," Frost said. "I've been there."

Ahead of them, the road split. Darren followed the lake's northeastern border. It was as if they'd left the city completely behind them. Under the trees and the gray sky, the evening felt like night. Emerald water opened up on their right. The forested slope of Strawberry Hill rose from the middle of the lake. It was a steep climb to the top, with sweeping views of the city and a peek-a-boo glimpse of the spires of the Golden Gate Bridge.

Darren's Lexus disappeared, but he couldn't go far on the one-way street. Frost inched along the lake road in his wake. They followed a horseshoe bend to the southern shore, where the shoulder sloped upward above them, and the water disappeared through a mass of heavy brush. Gnarled trees lined the shoulders, deepening the darkness with their tall crowns.

When they wound around the next curve, they saw Darren's Lexus parked on the side of the road. The car was empty. Darren was already gone. Frost backed up until the Lexus was out of sight, and then he pulled his Suburban into the dirt and turned off the engine. They both got out. Rain pattered on the tree leaves above them. It was quiet, far from the city noise.

Frost walked toward Darren's car, and Frankie followed. The loneliness of the park made her uneasy. When they reached the Lexus, Frost checked inside, but Darren had left nothing behind.

"He wasn't dressed for jogging," Frankie said. "So where is he?"

"He got a call. He may be meeting someone."

Together, they climbed the slope to a lakeside hiking path. Stow Lake's ribbon of lazy green water hugged the trail. Frost stopped to listen, but they heard no footsteps on the gravel, just rain tapping on leaves. She'd been here on summer weekends, when the lake felt as peaceful as Chopin piano music. But not now. Now the dark water under the storm felt ominous.

"White Lady, White Lady, I have your baby," Frost murmured. "Do you know the legend? Apparently, the ghost is searching for a child who drowned in the lake. If she asks you if you've seen her baby, she'll haunt you if you say yes, and she'll kill you if you say no. So you're basically screwed either way."

"I don't believe in ghosts," Frankie replied.

"It's worth believing in something," Frost said.

He moved cautiously on the gravel trail. Frankie stayed beside him. The lake was on their right, and not thirty feet away, on the other side of the water, a dirt trail mirrored their path at the base of Strawberry Hill. The slope rose sharply through a tangle of tree roots and vines.

"Where did he go?" Frankie asked, too loudly.

Frost held out an arm to stop her and put a finger to his lips. Then he pointed. Just ahead, through the lace of tree branches, she spotted a stone arch bridge crossing the water to Strawberry Hill. A man, almost in silhouette, stood on the bridge. It wasn't Darren Newman. Frankie recognized the man's lanky frame and the wool cap on his head.

"That's Todd Ferris," she whispered to Frost.

The detective brought the binoculars to his eyes and aimed them at the man on the bridge.

"He has a gun," Frost said.

40

"Get back to the car," Frost told Dr. Stein. "I've got backup on the way. Just stay inside."

He didn't give her time to protest; he simply shoved his keys and binoculars into her hands. He left her standing on the gravel trail and took off running between low-hanging branches of the evergreens. By the time he reached the base of the stone bridge, Todd Ferris had vanished.

Frost drew his own gun. Slowly, he did a 360-degree turn. The trees and the gray sky buried the park in shadows, offering plenty of hiding places. He didn't see Darren Newman, and he didn't see Todd Ferris. The rain sharpened, hammering his face, and he had to wipe his eyes to see. When he listened, he heard footsteps on Strawberry Hill.

Crouching, he jogged across the shallow arch of the bridge. Ripples dotted the water where the lake widened. On the other side of the bridge, a narrow dirt trail stretched along the base of the hill, and the four-hundred-foot slope climbed sharply in front of him into a jungle of trees. He saw footprints in the mud. Running. Heading west. Clouds of rain blew into Frost's face as he followed.

Fifty yards away, the footprints stopped. He saw furrows in the slope where someone had scrambled up the hill, clawing at the ground with hands and feet. Above him, he saw a moving shadow on the next terrace of the trail. He couldn't see who it was.

Frost stayed beside the lake and found a switchback leading uphill from the water. He climbed on a soft trail of pine needles. Footing was treacherous on the wet slope, making him struggle to keep his balance. The storm closed in on him, as if the White Lady were unhappy with trespassers. Through the trees, lightning split across the sky, and a rolling, rumbling clap of thunder followed. A shower of leaves blew from the trees with the next gust of wind. Then another crack shot through the rain.

This one came from a gun.

Frost dove off the trail behind a thick redwood tree clinging to the slope. He didn't know where the shot had come from, or how close it was. High above him, someone shouted. Two voices, back and forth. He squinted uphill, but it was too dark to see anyone. With his gun in his hand, he ran. As he did, another shot echoed across the hilltop.

Strawberry Hill leveled out at its summit into a patch of sawdust and picnic benches nestled inside the grove of trees. Where the land opened up, rain sheeted down to the wet ground, bringing a heavy scent of eucalyptus and pine. He crept onto the top of the hill and swung back and forth. The storm brought the forest to life. The evergreens around him were like tall black soldiers, and he glimpsed the dark panorama of the city through a web of branches. He took each step slowly. The wet ground sank under his feet.

"Darren Newman!" he shouted. "Todd Ferris! This is the police. I want to see both of you in the open with your hands up."

The drumming of rain overwhelmed his voice, but he knew they could hear him. No one broke from the trees.

Frost stayed on the fringe of the hilltop and made a circle around the summit. Where a massive tree had been cut down, he caught a glimpse of the bay, but the eastern hills were invisible under the clouds. Blurry lights sprang up in the neighborhoods below him. His clothes were soaked. He was cold. He could barely see. With each footstep, he stopped and listened, trying to find a human noise hiding behind the roar of the downpour. If they were still here, the two men were silent, huddled in the protection of the woods.

It took him five minutes to circle the summit and arrive back where he started. He worried that he'd been lured here as a ruse and that both men had slipped back down to Stow Lake on one of the other trails. He holstered his gun. He slid his phone from his pocket to call Dr. Stein.

When he turned his back for a split second, he felt a rush of movement behind him.

Frost reached for his gun and spun around, but the back of his skull erupted into a fire of pain. His eyes burst with light and went black, and he sank to his knees and then pitched into the mud. Through the roaring in his ears, he heard shouting and pounding steps, but the noise went wildly up and down. He tried to stand. Dizziness screwed through his head like a spike, and he collapsed again. When he opened his eyes, the world was upside down.

Somewhere, far away, he heard another gunshot.

He crawled toward the slope. Mud and leaves covered his face, and lights exploded behind his eyes like pinpoint fireworks. His fingernails scraped at the bark of a redwood tree, and he used the tree trunk to pull himself to a standing position. He leaned against it, feeling the world spin as it righted itself. He could hear the two men on the hillside below him. They were getting away.

Frost pushed off from the tree and took a step down. His brain felt sucked up into the cyclone. He opened his mouth to say something, but he couldn't say anything at all. Rain trickled down his back, but it wasn't rain. He tasted metallic wetness on his fingers, and it was blood.

He felt himself falling sideways, with no way to stop it; he fell, hit the slope, and rolled. His body slid, spun, slammed against tree roots, and the hill carried him shoulder over shoulder to the dirt of the next trail fifty feet below him.

He landed hard, and he passed out.

Lucy sat by the window with a mug of tea. She leaned her head against the cold glass and watched the rain sweep through the street. A MUNI bus plowed down Haight like a ship slicing through ocean waves. Three teenage girls splashed through puddles on the sidewalk. Lights had come on in the other apartment buildings, and she could see people inside.

She felt anxious, as if she'd walked into a room and couldn't remember why she'd come here. She had something important to do, but she had no idea what it was. She'd felt that way all day, and the rain didn't help.

She was depressed about Frost rejecting her. He would have been the perfect man for a rainy night like this. He was funny and serious, mature and playful, handsome and boy next door. That was exactly what she'd always wanted and what she'd thought she would never find. She'd let herself hope there might be something between them, so it hurt to find out that he was looking for a sister, not a girlfriend. She still wanted him. It was easy to imagine him kissing her and making love to her, even if it was never going to happen.

Where was her life going? Nowhere.

Seven years on her own in San Francisco, and she still felt like a visitor here. The city overwhelmed her. There was too much of everything, and she found herself carried along, not choosing where to go. She wasn't like Frost. Or Brynn.

Growing up in Modesto, she couldn't wait to get out to the big world. Her parents lived in a boring suburb where girls became teachers and married guys who worked in banks or insurance companies. She'd wanted to escape all of that, but now it didn't sound so bad.

There was a lot of sunshine in Modesto. There were no bridges.

She sipped her tea and thought again, *I have something to do.* What?

Lucy peered down at the street below her window. The police car was still there, hammered by the rain. She'd met the officer inside, a woman about her own age named Violet Harris. Two hours earlier, Officer Harris had walked with her to the corner to get take-out coffee, and Lucy had bought her an almond–white chocolate scone. They talked about Macy's and makeup, which was a strange conversation to have with a cop. When Lucy went back upstairs, Officer Harris told her to stop by the car if she needed anything. She'd be on duty until midnight, and then someone else would take over.

"I'll have to use the back door to the alley," Lucy murmured to herself.

She sat up sharply, almost spilling her tea. She had no idea why she'd said that or where the thought had come from. It just popped into her head.

Lucy got up and paced, unable to shake her restless, anxious feeling. Nothing felt right. Time barely moved. She didn't want to put on music. She didn't want to eat, because she wasn't hungry. She turned on the television, despite Frost's warning, but five minutes later, she turned it off. She wished he would come back, but she knew it might be hours before she saw him again. And even if he did come back, it wouldn't be the same. It wouldn't be what she wanted.

"This is stupid," she told herself.

She reheated her tea and took it to the window to watch the black clouds slouch across the sky. The downpour sounded like fingernails tapping on the glass.

Luuuucy.

She spun around, stifling a scream. The mug slipped from her fingers and spilled. She'd heard a voice, but no one was there. The apartment was empty. She was alone in the silence. And yet the voice was in her head, as crystal clear as if someone were standing next to her.

Lucy grabbed her phone and dialed. She wanted to talk to Frost, and she was disappointed when the call went to his voice mail.

"Hey, it's me," she said, leaving him a message. "I'd love to talk to you. Will you be able to come by later? Or I could come to your place. Don't worry, everything's fine."

She hung up. Then, almost immediately, she called him again.

"Actually, no, everything's not fine. Something's wrong. I don't know what it is. Call me as soon as you can, okay?"

Lucy put down her phone and went to get paper towels to sop up the spilled tea. Before she got there, her phone started ringing, and she sprinted back to scoop it up and answer it on the second ring. "Wow, that was fast," she told him. "I'm so glad you called back. I really needed to hear your voice."

But it wasn't Frost.

At first, there was a long stretch of eerie quiet.

Then the music began.

She heard a flourish of drums and guitar and the whine of a synthesized keyboard. The monster beat started in her ear and wormed into her brain. Her jaw went slack. Her breathing got faster. She didn't want to look down, but she had no choice, and when she did, she saw the gorge below her and felt the sway of the rope bridge. Her body was paralyzed. She couldn't move.

"Luuuucy," the Night Bird whispered into the phone. *"Luuuucy."*

"Please . . . no . . . please . . . don't do this . . ."

The song thumped its rhythm over and over. The synthesizer drowned out the storm and the wind. Spasms rippled through her muscles. She didn't see her apartment anymore. Her world was a thousand feet of air, descending past stone cliffs to an icy glacial river.

"Listen to me, do you want to be free?"

"Yes . . . yes . . . what do you want?"

"It's up to you, you know what to do."

Tears streamed down Lucy's face. She listened to the music. She felt the bridge go back and forth, bucking with the gusts. She wanted to fly, to die, to go anywhere, to do anything, if only she could make it stop.

"It's up to you, you know what to do."

He said it again. And again.

"You know what to do. You know what to do. You know what to do."

Calmly, Lucy hung up the phone. Yes, she knew what to do. She walked to her closet and collected her raincoat and umbrella. She gathered up her purse from the dinette table.

Go out the back, she remembered.

She marched to the door of her apartment and opened it, but she paused as she stared into the dusty hallway. Her work wasn't done. Not yet. She wasn't ready to leave. There was one more thing.

Leaving the door ajar, Lucy turned around and went to the kitchen.

She opened the middle drawer, extracted a carving knife with a ten-inch blade, and slid it inside her purse.

41

Frankie waited as long as she could.

Five minutes passed. Lightning lit up the trees, and thunder followed, reverberating under the ground. Frost didn't come back. The backup he'd requested didn't arrive.

Sitting alone in the car, she heard a distant noise. It was almost part of the air. Moments later, she heard it a second time. She opened the door, letting in the rain, and leaned out to listen. Whatever the noise was, it was gone now, and it didn't happen again. She pulled the door shut. Her impatience grew. She called Frost's phone number, but there was no answer.

Ten minutes passed.

He should have been back by now.

Frankie climbed out of the truck into the driving rain. The street was empty. Trees bent, waving their branches at her. She continued past the bend in the road and saw that Darren Newman's Lexus was gone. It had left recently; there was still a dry patch where the car had been parked. She squinted into the storm but couldn't see taillights.

"Frost!" she shouted. Her voice sounded muffled, and she shouted again, as loud as she could. "Frost!"

She hiked up the shoulder to the gravel trail beside Stow Lake. The first thing she saw, sopping wet and lying in the mud, was a wool cap.

It was Todd's.

Six feet away, in the middle of the path, was a gun.

"Frost!" she screamed again, but he didn't answer. A finger of worry crept up her spine.

She started running into the wind. At the stone arch bridge, she crossed over the water to Strawberry Hill. Her hair was plastered to her skin, and she wiped rain from her eyes. The mud grabbed at her shoes. She followed overlapping footprints next to the lake, with leaves and pine needles blowing into her face. Where the path curved, she found a cross trail leading sharply uphill.

There she saw a ghost.

It wasn't the White Lady. A man rose in darkness from the ground, barely visible against the forest. It was Frost. His skin was pale. Dirt matted his hair and clothes. He moved slowly, cupping the back of his skull with one hand. His other hand was striped with blood. He navigated one step downward, and Frankie rushed to his side and let him ease his weight against her with an arm around his waist. They struggled to the lakeside trail.

"Did you see them?" he asked.

Frankie shook her head. "No. Darren's car is gone. I think he has Todd Ferris with him. I saw a gun on the trail."

"One of them jumped me," Frost said. "I don't know which one. He hit me from behind. Did the backup get here?"

"Not yet."

She checked the back of his head. Rain had washed away most of the blood, but she found swelling near the back of his ear, and when she grazed the area with her fingers, he winced with pain.

"Let's get you to a hospital. They'll need to check for concussion."

"I'm okay."

"Did you pass out?"

"A couple seconds, no more."

"You're not okay," Frankie said.

She helped him along the path and across the stone bridge. The rain showed no signs of stopping. They retrieved the gun from the trail, and then Frankie helped Frost into the passenger seat of the Suburban. She went around the other side and got behind the wheel, but before she could start the engine, red lights flared ahead and behind, lighting up the park and the downpour. Silently, without sirens, four police cars surrounded her like phantoms. A dark-blue sedan joined them and pulled adjacent to the window, close enough that Frankie couldn't open the door. She saw a severe, heavyset Hispanic woman climb out of the sedan.

"That's my lieutenant," Frost said. "Jess Salceda."

"I know her," Frankie murmured. "From last year."

Frost lowered the passenger window. The lieutenant leaned inside, dripping rain. Her eyes acknowledged Frankie, but there was no love lost between them. Frankie knew that Salceda blamed her for Darren Newman. Then and now.

"Did you pass Newman's car on the way in?" Frost asked.

"No."

"We need a BOLO. He has a hostage with him."

Salceda passed on the details to another officer, but she didn't move from the Suburban. Her eyes shot coldly to Frankie and then back to Frost. "Lucy Hagen is gone," she said.

"*What?*"

"Violet checked on her. The apartment is empty. I'm sorry, Frost, but I wanted you to know. We've put out a report on her, but right now, the best thing we can do is find Newman. Chances are, if we find him, we find Lucy."

Salceda marched back to her sedan. Frankie watched Frost stare through the windshield. His face was black with shadows. He didn't even roll up the window. Rain swept inside. The red lights of the police cars made the water shine like blood.

"Frost?" she said.

He didn't answer.

"Are you okay?"

He still said nothing.

And then, making her jump, her phone rang. She didn't recognize the number, but she knew who it was.

"Oh my God, what do I do?" she asked.

His voice was calm. "Answer it. Put it on speaker."

She clicked open the speakerphone. "Hello?"

She heard breathing on the end of the phone and the noise of city traffic. He was in a car. She said again, "Hello?"

A singsong voice, as bitter as the wind, chanted to her.

"Fran-kie . . . Fran-kie."

She tried to answer, but she couldn't make her mouth form any words.

"Fran-kie . . ."

Chills wracked her wet body. She hissed into the phone. "Stop this, you sick son of a bitch. Stop playing this game."

He didn't answer; he simply breathed. And then he said with an odd, childish giggle, *"Game's almost done . . . game's almost done."*

Frost gestured for the phone, but Frankie clutched it tightly in her hand. "What else do you want from me? Leave my patients alone. Leave me alone. Don't you know you've already destroyed me? What more is there?"

The Night Bird didn't answer. Laughter bubbled out of his throat.

Frankie felt her self-control bleeding away. "For God's sake, why are you doing this? Why?"

The laughter faded to silence, and when he spoke again, his voice was low and cruel.

"You know why . . . to watch you die."

Frost peeled the phone out of Frankie's fingers and barked into it. "This is Frost Easton. Stop the car, and tell us where you are."

He listened to the dead air.

"You don't have anywhere to run. Where are you? Where's Lucy?"

The Night Bird finally whispered back. *"Luuuucy . . . Luuuucy . . . where are you . . . Luuuucy . . ."*

Frankie watched Frost close his eyes and try to control himself. "What did you do to her?"

"Luuuucy . . ."

He slapped the phone shut and pushed it back into her hand.

"Drive," he told Frankie. "We need to hurry."

"Drive where?"

"You said Todd woke up in Dogpatch. We'll start there."

"Frost, what do you think he's doing?"

He turned to face her. She could almost hear the pound of the detective's heartbeat. "I don't know what this game is all about, but Lucy's in the middle of it. And so are you."

42

Frost guided Dr. Stein up and down the streets of the bayside area south of the ballpark known as Dogpatch.

The neighborhood was a study in contradictions. Million-dollar lofts looked out on warehouses. Trendy restaurants sprang up next to boarded-up buildings. At midnight, in the midst of the driving rain, the hip neighborhood was mostly empty. The headlights of a dozen squad cars crisscrossed the streets, searching the ruins near the water. Flashlights swept through the weeds and parking lots underneath the concrete jungle of the elevated 280 freeway.

Two hours had passed, but the hunt had turned up no evidence of Darren Newman's Lexus or the torture chamber of the Night Bird. Frost's mood was dark, and his head throbbed with intermittent shocks of pain.

The windshield wipers ran back and forth, pushing away rain. They drove past a long, low building with windowless metal walls, and Frost gestured for Frankie to stop. He got out into the rain and shined his light around the grounds. He saw metal storage sheds painted over with graffiti. The beam lit up the columns of the freeway ramp beyond the industrial yard, and trucks kicked spray over the side of the highway as they passed overhead. There were no signs of life.

He got back inside, and they inched down the street, checking each vehicle parked on both sides.

"It's late," he said finally. "I can get someone to take you home."

"No. You heard him. He wants to see me die. If you're out here looking for him, I want to be here, too."

He didn't try to dissuade her. He knew she was stubborn. Another stretch of silence lingered between them.

"Do you mind if I ask you a question?" he said.

Stein shrugged. "Go ahead."

"Why did you say you're not sure if you've done more harm than good in your life?" he asked.

She gripped the steering wheel tightly. Her eyes closed briefly and then opened again. The rain drowned out any other sounds around them.

"Oh, there are about a thousand answers to that," she replied. And then a moment later, she added, "I'm an arrogant human being."

"There are worse flaws."

"Well, it can be fatal in a scientist. All this time, I thought I knew what I was doing, and the people who opposed me were simply misguided. Now I wonder if I was just a child pushing buttons on a computer I didn't really understand."

"People aren't computers," he pointed out.

"Maybe it would be better if we were. Then we'd know the right answers. It's ironic, really. We build machines that remember everything, but our own brains are like the world's most disorganized storage units. We put memories away and never see them again, or if we find them, they don't look anything like we thought they did. I thought I was bringing order to all this chaos, but maybe I was just making it worse."

He was trying to think of something to say when Dr. Stein stopped the car.

"Storage units," she murmured.

"What?"

"I'm so sorry. I'm a fool. Here I am complaining about memory, and I forgot something important. I followed Darren that night when he went across the bay, but before he did, he stopped at a storage unit here in Dogpatch. I couldn't see what he kept inside—"

"Where is it?" Frost interrupted her.

"At the end of Twenty-Second Street near the bay."

"Let's go. I'll have Jess and a squad car meet us."

"Do you think it means something?"

"I think a man who owns multiple buildings in this area doesn't need a separate storage unit unless he has something to hide."

Stein accelerated his Suburban through the rain. They headed east toward the water, and once they crossed the main artery at Third, they found themselves in a deserted commercial area leading toward the piers. Frankie drove until it looked like the road was ending, and then she turned again, where the street was barely wider than the SUV. She continued to the gates of a self-storage complex, and she stopped.

"It's here," she said.

Frost got out. The storm lashed his face. He walked up to the locked gates of the storage complex and found a bell to alert the security guard. Behind him, he saw the flashing lights of a police car racing to join them. Jess's sedan followed.

The guard, who wore a hooded raincoat to stay dry, didn't protest when he saw their badges. He slid the gates open for them. Like a mini parade, Frankie drove them through the gates, and Jess and the squad car entered behind them. She navigated the maze and stopped in front of a green trailer with a metal door. All of the other trailers had white doors, but here, the door had been painted green to match the rest of the unit. Frost wondered why.

"You saw Darren Newman go inside this storage unit?" he asked Frankie. "You're sure it was this one?"

"I'm sure."

Frost got out. Jess was waiting for him. They checked the door, which was secured with a heavy padlock. The rain on the metal roofs around them sounded like nails being hammered into wood. Jess wiped her face and had to shout to let Frost hear her.

"What do you think is inside?" she called.

"Lucy Hagen," Frost replied. "I hope."

Jess stared at his wet face, reading his eyes. Her round face showed no reluctance to break inside the compartment. She gestured at the squad car, and when a burly cop got out of the door, Jess put her arms over her head and banged the heels of her palms together. The cop retrieved a large bolt cutter from the trunk of his car, and he used it to make two cuts in the lock's shackle, as easily as if he were slicing butter. The lock fell to the ground, and the door was open.

Frost hesitated. Part of him didn't want to see what was inside. He slipped gloves over his hands, then bent down and threw the door open on its tracks with a loud jolt. The small interior space was dark, and he groped for a light switch. When he found it, two overhead fluorescent bars blinked to life.

He couldn't hide his disappointment.

No one was there.

The storage unit was no more than ten feet by twenty feet in size. The metal walls were painted bright yellow. Packing crates lined the walls and took up most of the floor. Frost saw an oak desk on the back wall, with a mirror hung above it. The interior had an odd, heavy smell of tea, and when he pushed aside the lid on the nearest crate, he saw bulk Chinese tea stored inside.

He saw Frankie in the doorway. She didn't cross the threshold. "Are you sure Darren came in here?" he asked. "There are a lot of units around this place. Maybe you got it wrong."

"This is the one, Frost."

He opened another crate and found more tea. He dug down as far as his arm would reach, but he found sealed plastic bags of tea all the way to the bottom. When he withdrew his arm, his wet skin smelled of cinnamon and cherry. The same was true of the next crate. And the next.

"Man likes his tea," Jess said. Then she eyed the depth of the crates. "Hang on. Hand me those bolt cutters."

The uniformed officer handed the bolt cutters to the lieutenant, and Jess shoved them inside the nearest crate as deep as they would go. She marked the point on the handle of the cutters with her thumb and then pulled out the bolt cutters and measured the length of the crate on the outside.

"There's a six-inch difference. The crates have a false floor."

Frost overturned the crate and dumped the tea on the floor. Using the blade end of the bolt cutters, he made a sharp downward thrust to the base of the crate, splitting through the wood. He repeated the motion until he'd made a jagged hole in the floor of the crate, and then he reached through the hole. He found dozens of vacuum-sealed bags under his fingers, and he pulled one out.

Six plastic bottles were locked inside the sterile bag.

"Oxycodone," Jess said, reading the labels. "Newman is smuggling prescription pain pills."

Frost looked around at the storage unit, as if it held more answers. He didn't think this place was just about pills. "Did Newman load or unload anything when he came here?" he asked Frankie.

"Not that I saw. He went inside, stayed for fifteen minutes or so, and then came out."

"So what was he doing here?" Frost asked.

No one in the room answered. Frost went to the desk at the back of the storage unit and sat down in the chair in front of it. He stared into the mirror reflecting his face. That was odd, too. A mirror. He wondered why Darren Newman felt the need to look at his reflection.

Then he thought, *He wants to see if anyone comes inside behind him.*

Frost studied the desktop, which had almost nothing on it, other than a bright lamp, a letter opener, and a magnifying glass. He opened the drawers and found billing orders and invoices. All of it was for tea. It still told him nothing about Lucy.

"What was Newman doing here?" he asked aloud again.

He opened the deepest drawer of the desk, which contained a series of vertical files. He scooped the entire set of files out with his hand and stared at the bottom of the desk drawer.

"Fool me once," he said.

Using the letter opener, Frost pried at the wood panel on the bottom of the drawer, and it came up easily. Immediately underneath the panel was a manila envelope. He retrieved the envelope, opened the flap, and dumped the contents across the surface of the desk.

Behind him, Jess sucked in her breath.

"That son of a bitch," Frost said.

43

Photographs.

The envelope contained dozens of photographs. Frost picked up each picture and laid them out in rows, taking up the entire surface of the desk. He spotted at least five different women among the faces. He didn't recognize any of them, but Jess leaned over his shoulder and jabbed one of the photos with her fingernail.

"That's Merrilyn Somers," she said.

Newman had at least thirty photographs of his former neighbor. He'd stalked her everywhere she went. On campus at SF State, at a library computer, singing in a church choir, drinking coffee with friends on Market Street. The zoom lens he'd used captured every detail of her body and face in intimate, uncomfortable detail. Frost could see the brightness in Merrilyn's distinctive blue eyes and the pencil-thin lines of her eyebrows, the curves of her hips in frayed jeans, and the ebony shine of her long, straight hair.

She was magnetic. And she'd attracted the wrong man.

There were more pictures of Merrilyn. After. She lay on her bed, naked. Her blue eyes were fixed, staring in death. Mouth open. Blood stained her body like red paint where the knife had violated her.

Newman had recorded the murder in the same horrifying detail he'd used to stalk her.

"Do you know the other women, Jess?" Frost asked.

She didn't answer immediately. Her eyes couldn't let go of the photographs.

"That one there, I think that's the girl in Green Bay who was killed when Newman was eighteen. And this other one, that's his classmate at college in Boulder. I don't know the rest." She leaned closer to the array of pictures. "Wait, no, I know that girl, too. She's local. A prostitute. She disappeared nine months ago, and a couple of the other street girls reported her missing. We never found her."

"She doesn't fit the pattern," Frost said. "There are pictures of her after the murder, but not before. And he hid the body, rather than let us find her, like the others. I wonder why."

"I know why," Frankie murmured.

Frost turned around. Dr. Stein had crept up behind them. Her lips were pressed together in horror as she stared at the photos laid out on the desk. Rain dripped from her hair to the metal floor like music.

"He made a joke about it," she said. "He talked about using a hooker to get a sperm sample from Leon Willis. And about how he would have had to get rid of the hooker if he did that."

"And you didn't think that information was worth sharing with the police?" Jess asked acidly. Her brown bangs fell in front of her eyes.

"He put it in a speculative context, not as a confession. It was all 'what if.' There wasn't enough to break privilege. Even though my gut told me that he was telling the truth."

Jess pounded out of the storage unit with loud, heavy footsteps. Frost knew she didn't cover her anger well.

"There wasn't anything I could do," Frankie said to Frost. "I'm sorry."

"What else do you see in these photographs?" he asked her. "What do they tell you? I need a read on this man, Frankie. I need to know what he's really doing."

"Well, for one thing, it's pretty obvious why he stopped here that night," Frankie told him.

"Why?"

"He was going to Berkeley to have sex with Simona. He stopped here first to look at the pictures."

Frost was puzzled, and then he understood. "My God. This is what turns him on."

"Yes."

"What else? Get inside this guy's head."

He knew that was the last place she wanted to be, but she bent over his shoulder, until she could make out every detail in the collection of photographs. Then she turned around and studied the rest of the storage unit. The crates. The yellow walls. The tea and the pill bottles. The rain pouring across the open doorway.

"Something's wrong," she said.

"What?"

"I don't know."

"You wrote that down on the note I found in your office, too. Something's wrong. What did you mean by that?"

"Just that I can't make all the pieces of the puzzle fit. I mean, most of them do, but there's one piece that feels like it comes from a different puzzle. I'm sorry, I know that's not helpful."

"Right now, I don't care what doesn't fit," Frost told her. "What *does* fit?"

Frankie hesitated. "The knife."

"What do you mean?"

"He's consistent. Newman uses a knife on these women."

"So?"

"Todd talked about seeing a knife. He remembered seeing a knife the last time he was taken."

"The last time," Frost said. "You mean, when the Night Bird took Lucy?"

"Yes. I'm sorry."

"What does that mean?" Frost asked.

"I'm not sure, Frost, but he says the game's almost done, and now there's a knife in the mix. He always uses a knife. It tells me we need to find Lucy soon. Before something happens to her."

Frost got out of the chair. He took a long, hard look at the women pictured on the desk. Their faces. Their smiles. And then their bodies, riddled by knife wounds. He had a brief, grotesque image of Lucy in the same position. He thought about Darren Newman standing over her with a camera. After. His anger consumed him, and he felt powerless.

Then Jess walked back inside the storage unit through the waterfall of rain.

"Let's go," she said to him. "I've got a forensics team on the way, and the boy outside will keep this place secure until they get here."

"Go where?" Frost said.

"The Night Bird just turned his phone back on," Jess told him. "We got a ping."

The GPS signal took them to one of the neighborhood's ruined industrial sites. It was a three-story building, stretching the length of a football field. The walls were red brick, mottled by decades of salt water carried off the bay. Round arched windows lined the wall facing the street. The ground-floor glass had been replaced by heavy plywood, and above it, the windows were pockmarked with cracks and bullet holes. A barbed wire fence surrounded the entire property.

They parked a block away. Lightning lit up the night sky in streaks above the angled roof. Frost could feel the thunder under the street. He left Frankie behind in the Suburban, and he joined Jess and half a dozen other officers as they converged on the shell of the building.

"He knows we're coming," Jess reminded them.

Their flashlight beams led the way through the rain. They followed the fence along the exterior of the building, and when they reached the back corner, they found a section of netting that had been cut away, opening up a way inside. One by one, they pushed through the gap in the wire. The building wall was in front of them, and the plywood blocking the first window had been splintered with an ax, which lay on the sidewalk.

"Welcome to the party," Frost murmured.

Jess went inside first. Frost followed.

The stone floor was a minefield of debris. His light passed over rusted tools, jagged chunks of mortar fallen from the ceiling, and garbage left behind by squatters who'd broken in over the years. Concrete support columns with peeling white paint made a row of soldiers from one end of the building to the other. The wind whistled like a ghost through broken windows. Standing pools of black water reflected the glow of the flashlight. He smelled mold and dampness in the shut-up space. It was cold.

Jess sent two officers along each of the perpendicular walls. She and Frost picked their way through rubble toward the center of the building. Each step dislodged rats, who squeaked and scurried. Rain squeezed through the ceiling. Drip. Drip. Drip. They didn't hear anyone else inside the ruins.

Ahead of them, open stone steps led toward the building's second floor.

"There's a light up there," Jess murmured.

Frost saw it, too. The light went on and off, throwing moving shadows above them. Jess took a step toward the stairs, but she didn't have her flashlight aimed at her feet. Frost did, and he saw something in her path half-concealed by a grease-covered towel. It was gray metal, and it had teeth. He shouted for her to stop, and Jess put her foot down short of the towel, but the toe of her boot kicked the device forward. A metal bang rocked the space as the iron mouth snapped shut.

"A bear trap," Frost said. "That was meant for us."

Jess hissed into her radio. "Everybody, *watch your step*. We've got booby traps in here." And then to Frost, "This is a setup. We're getting out."

"You go. I'll check the second floor."

"Frost, he's not here. He lured us inside to make us targets."

"Lucy might be up those stairs," Frost snapped.

"I'm ordering you *out*."

Frost shook his head. "No way, Jess. I'll leave when I know the place is empty."

He stepped over the bear trap and marched toward the stairs, using his flashlight to sweep the floor as he did. Behind him, he heard Jess exhale with a loud sigh. She barked into the radio again. "Hold your positions. Do. Not. Move."

Jess followed him.

On the stairs, his flashlight lit up dust and broken glass. He saw glints of gold. The stairs were lined with long brass tacks, all of them pointing upward. He took the steps one at a time, knocking the tacks aside with the side of his boot as he went. They tumbled downward.

"Watch out, Jess," he murmured.

"I see them."

The light above them got brighter. The shadows got larger, dancing on the stairs. He saw an electric lantern hanging from the ceiling on a hook. The wind through the holes in the wall made the lantern swing back and forth, like a man dangling at the end of a hangman's rope.

At the top of the steps, Frost found the front half of a rat, severed from the rest of its body. Two feet away, the rat's back half spilled blood over the claws of another bear trap.

Jess caught up to him and saw it, too. "This guy is nuts."

"Not nuts. Angry."

They cast their lights around the building. The glass in the arched windows was mostly gone here, letting in sheets of rain. Thunder boomed like an earthquake over their heads. Dust and paint flecked from the ceiling. As the thunder quieted, he heard another kind of muffled thunder, louder and closer. A strange, snickering scrape joined the chorus, like fingernails on chalkboard. Something was alive in here. Jess heard it, too, and they both turned their flashlights toward the ceiling and flinched.

Sagging water pipes hung from the mortar. Lining the pipes, thousands of seagulls squeezed together, causing a rumbling noise with the shifting and rubbing of their wings. Their claws restlessly scratched on the metal pipes. As the light hit them, dozens flew toward the open windows in panic, and others spread their wings wide and screeched, their cries amplified into screams between the building walls.

"You a Hitchcock fan, Frost?" Jess asked.

"Not anymore."

"This guy's not here. Let's go. These birds look hungry."

"Wait," Frost said.

He stopped and listened. Fighting with the cacophony of the gulls, he heard music close by. It started as low as a whisper and grew steadily louder. The song was sweet, but to him it was sickening.

It was "Nightingale."

He swept his flashlight around the building again but saw nothing. The song came from in front of him. He headed toward the far wall, ducking gulls that swooped past his face. Slick guano covered the floor. At the wall, a rounded gap for a missing window looked out on a deserted parking lot and the street below them. A heavy plank had been nailed diagonally across the space to prevent someone from falling out. He moved his light along the floor and found a cell phone lying on the floor near a glistening pool of rainwater. The phone's ringtone continued to sing.

"Nightingale."

Over and over. The phone was ringing.

Jess came up beside him. "Nothing we can do but answer it."

Frost bent down and snatched up the phone. He answered the call, but he didn't say anything at all. He waited.

"*You took the bait,*" the Night Bird chanted, "*but now you're too late.*"

And then another song began. It wasn't Carole King. This song was hard rock, played so loudly that Frost had to wrench the phone away from his ear. He put it on speaker, and he and Jess listened to a synthesizer thumping out a chorus. No words. Just the beat. It annoyed the birds, who screeched in protest, and their cries became deafening.

"What the hell is that song?" Frost asked. "I know it."

"This guy has a nasty sense of humor," Jess replied. "It's the Edgar Winter Group. The song is 'Frankenstein.'"

Frost didn't get the joke at first, but then he did. *"Frankie."*

He splashed through the water to the giant window and looked down at the street. He could see his SUV parked at the end of the block. As he watched, the driver's door flew open.

Francesca Stein climbed out, slammed the door shut, and ran.

44

Frankie thought to herself again, *Something's wrong.*

She felt as if she were in a strange bubble inside the SUV. Streaks of rain covered up the windows so that she couldn't see the street, and all she could hear was the hypnotic drumming of the storm on the hood. Her wet clothes felt cold, and she sat and shivered. She kept the doors locked.

She turned the key in the ignition and ran the windshield wipers long enough to see through the glass. Down the street, the police disappeared inside the building through a hole in the fence. She was on her own, and all she had to do was wait, but waiting wasn't something she did well. She didn't like the idea of putting her life in anyone else's hands.

She adjusted the mirror and looked at her own reflection. Her wet hair ran down her forehead and face like snakes. Shadows brought out the bones of her face. Her dark eyes stared back like the eyes of a stranger. She wished she could see behind them. For all the time she spent in the minds of other people, she didn't really know herself.

Something's wrong.

What?

Her phone pinged with an e-mail, making her jump. She saw the glow of the screen on the seat next to her. He was still with her. Still stalking her. She didn't want to pick it up, but she had no choice. She checked the e-mail, and the return address was the same as it had been in the beginning.

The Night Bird was writing to her again.

It all comes down to this.

He was right. One way or another, this all ended now. She leaned forward to watch the silhouette of the ruins a block away, and somehow she knew it was all a ruse. The white room wasn't inside that building. Neither was the Night Bird. Neither was Lucy Hagen. He'd lured the police there, because in the end, this came down to the two of them and no one else.

She waited impatiently, knowing another e-mail would follow soon. Seconds passed, and her phone pinged again.

She's waiting for you.

Lucy Hagen was in his hands. Another patient. Another death. More blood. She didn't know how much more loss her conscience could stand. She could see their faces in her brain. Monica Farr. Brynn Lansing. Christie Parke. She could even see the face of Merrilyn Somers in the photographs that Frost had laid out on Darren Newman's desk. Merrilyn Somers, alive, and Merrilyn Somers, dead. Frankie could have stopped him, but she'd let Darren fool her, the way he fooled everyone else in his life. He'd seduced her mind and almost seduced her body, too.

It ended now. Tonight.

He e-mailed her again. Another ping.

You're the only one who can save her.

She knew she should alert Frost. She could get out of the car and scream for the police. End the ruse; get them out of the ruins. Her voice would bring them running. They could save her, but they couldn't save Lucy Hagen. And it would start all over again with someone else. She wasn't going to let that happen.

She finally sent an e-mail back.

I'm right here. You know where I am.

Frankie held her phone in her hand, and she waited for him to reply. The silence went on and on. No e-mail. Nothing. It was a slow torture, as if he wanted her to suffer in anticipation.

Finally, her phone vibrated. She sucked in her breath, realizing that he was making a video call this time. He wanted to *see* her, and he wanted her to see him, too. That was part of the game. She wished she could throw the phone out of the car into the rain, but she held it up in front of her face and steeled herself as she answered the call.

There he was.

The mask.

Everyone else had seen it before, but not her. Frost. Todd. Lucy. They'd described it to her and shown her pictures, but the reality was a thousand times worse. Close up. Filling the entire screen. The plastic was deathly white, drained of all color. Candy-red lips grinned at her, a huge grin, stretching from the point of the chin to the high false cheekbones. His teeth looked like gold railroad tracks. The eyeholes were rimmed in silver, and where the eyes should have been was the gleaming black mesh of an insect's eyes. Dreadlocks dripped down the mask in braids of fake hair.

The mask spoke to her.

"Fran-kie . . . Fran-kie."

She knew he could see her, and she wasn't going to give him the satisfaction of letting him see how terrified she was. She made her own face into a pale mask. Her lips curled with contempt. "Where's Lucy?"

"Wanna see . . . wanna see?"

"Show me."

Like a page turning, the camera reversed. Frankie couldn't help herself. She cried out in anguish at what she saw. The screen blazed with whiteness, as if the luminous ivory paint on the walls could blind her. Everything was white—walls, floor, and ceiling. In the midst of it, she saw Lucy Hagen. Tears, like rain, streamed down the young woman's cheeks. The huge whites of her eyes matched the walls. Frankie knew she was drugged. Hypnotized. So far into a trance that she stood on the surface of another planet. It was the look that her patients had when she was working with them to change their memories, but this was the dark side. This was everything she'd ever tried to do in life turned against her.

Lucy had both hands wrapped around the black handle of a knife. Its silvery blade was almost a foot long, its razor point facing downward. Her arms were outstretched from her body. Every muscle trembled. She stared into the camera, her glassy eyes helpless.

"Help me," she called, with the whimper of a child. "Save me."

Then she screamed, so loudly that Frankie jerked back in her seat.

"Stop me!"

Frankie could barely hold the phone in her hand. She wanted to run to Lucy and gather her up in her arms. "Let her go," she shouted into the phone. "Let her go. Take me. I'm the one you want!"

The camera reversed, and the mask came back, grinning at her with its red lips. Behind the mask, the Night Bird laughed. His laughter bubbled up from his throat and filled the SUV, getting louder. She could still hear Lucy in the white room. "Save me, save me, save me."

"Where are you?" Frankie yelled into the phone. "I'll come to you. I'll let you do whatever you want. Let Lucy go!"

He kept laughing.

The call ended, and the screen went black. The Night Bird was gone.

"No!" Frankie shouted. "Tell me where you are!"

She waited. Her breaths were short and fast. Her fists tightened the way they would around the man's throat. "Come on, come on, come on," she murmured, knowing he wasn't done with her, waiting for the next e-mail.

Ping.

She whipped her fingers across the screen.

You have five minutes.

Frankie punched back her reply in capital letters.

WHERE ARE YOU?

The seconds ticked. One, two, three, four. She rolled down the window, and rain poured inside. Where did he want her to go? What did he want her to see? She leaned out and looked up and down the street. She was alone.

Ping.

Another e-mail.

Only you can save her.

"I know that!" she shouted out the window. "Don't you think I know that? Tell me where you are!"

Her fingers trembled as she typed a message.

I will come to you. Please. I will do whatever you want.

One minute of her five minutes was gone. Frankie cried; sobs wracked her chest. That was what he wanted. To torture her. And this was how he did it. Not by laying hands on her body, not by feeding drugs into her brain. He made her sit in the truck, impotent and desperate. He let the time go by, until there was no time for her to stop what came next. To pry the knife out of Lucy's hands.

Ping.

She read the e-mail through her tears.

Look up.

Frankie pushed her head out of the window of the SUV and craned her neck to stare at the cloud-layered sky. It was night. Lightning flashed. Silver curtains of rain descended.

"What am I supposed to see?" she shouted.

But then she saw it.

She was across the street from a four-story white stone building. It looked like a government palace airlifted out of Washington DC. Columns divided the rows of windows. A balcony jutted out from one window, as if Evita might stand there, waving to adoring crowds. But this building, like everything also around her, was abandoned. Dirt marred the white stone. The windows were covered over. Everything was dark.

No, she realized as she looked closer. Not everything.

Where she'd seen nothing before, now a pinpoint light blinked on the top floor. It flashed behind the center window, on, off, on, off. A message. That's where he was.

That's where she had to go.

She threw open the door of the car.

Frankie climbed out, slammed the door shut, and ran.

Frost climbed into the open window frame. He braced himself against the walls on either side and delivered a kick to the diagonal plank that was nailed across the space. The first kick splintered the wood, and the second dislodged it from the side of the building and sent it spiraling to the ground. Behind him, Jess shouted, but Frost simply took a step forward and jumped.

The ground didn't look far from the second-floor window, but it felt far as he dropped. He picked up speed and landed on his feet with an impact that shuddered through his spine. One leg crumpled under him, and he collapsed to the ground, which was a rocky slope of dirt and weeds. He got up and half limped, half ran toward the locked gates.

Jess yelled from the window. "What the hell are you doing?"

Frost pointed at the white building on the far side of the street, where Francesca Stein was disappearing inside. "There!"

He reached the property gates, which were eight feet high but free of barbed wire. He dug his shoes into the mesh and climbed. His fingers slipped on the wet netting, and spasms shot up and down his legs. He reached the top, wobbled, and basically let his body fall to the street on the other side.

"Frankie!" he shouted, but she was already out of sight.

He dragged himself toward the building's main door at the street corner. A block away, he heard police officers sprinting to catch up with him. He limped up the outside stairs to a boarded door, which flapped open and closed as the wind blew. He wrenched it open and saw elegant marble steps in front of him, making a spiral toward the upper floors. Concrete dust littered the stone. Picture frames hung askew on the walls.

Heels tapped over his head, climbing the stairs.

"Frankie!" he called again. "Stop!"

She stopped, but not because he'd called to her. She stopped because at that moment, a guttural scream filled the entire stairwell. It came from speakers; it came from everywhere. High above him, and right beside him, he heard a man's wail, throaty and terrible, begging for mercy that never came. It began, cut off, and began again, and died away into the gasp of someone laboring to breathe. It was a scream he'd never heard in his life, but there was no mistaking what it was.

It was a scream of death.

45

Frankie heard the scream. She froze halfway between the second and third floors of the building. The agony of it made her cover her ears. She fell against the railing and couldn't take another step. The sound pushed through to her brain, no matter how much she tried to keep it out. If you came to the end of the road and saw the devil standing in front of you, that would be the howl of despair baying from your throat.

She wanted to turn back, but a woman's voice rose over the scream. It was Lucy. "No, no, make it stop!"

Frankie shook off her fear and bolted up the last few steps. She found herself in a long hallway, with closed doors stretching the length of the building. The noise came from everywhere; she didn't know which door to choose. She tried the first one, and it was locked. They were all locked. She went from door to door, shouting Lucy's name.

Halfway down the hall, she found an open door, and she burst inside.

Her heart stopped.

Whiteness overwhelmed her. What she'd seen on her phone didn't compare to the dazzling shock of white above, below, and around her. She had to stop to adjust to the brightness. It made her want to shield her eyes, as if she were looking into the sun. White room. White lights. Every window covered in white.

The room was large, at least a hundred feet from end to end. The ceiling was low. Video projectors—all white—had been mounted in intervals around the entire room. The walls were screens; the ceiling was a screen; the floor was a screen. She realized in an instant that this was a room that could be turned into anything. Any scene out of the pit of your imagination. Any dream come to life. It was a room where all your deepest fears could come true.

There were three people in the torture chamber.

In the corner, twenty feet away from her, was Todd Ferris. He was alive. He sat on the floor, knees pulled up to his chest. He had his fingers laced together, his hands against his chin, as if he were praying. As she ran into the room, his head swiveled, and he stared directly at her, but he didn't act as if he recognized her. His winsome face looked dazed. His eyes were wide, unblinking circles of disbelief. She thought he was drugged. Like Lucy.

Lucy Hagen stood in the center of the room. Her mouth hung open. Her breathing was loud, as if she couldn't drag air into her lungs fast enough. Her legs were slightly apart, and Frankie could see them trembling. She had the pretty face that Frankie remembered, but the face didn't even belong to Lucy anymore. She looked like someone else entirely. Someone who'd been thrown onto an island alone.

One of Lucy's arms hung limply at her side. The other held the long-bladed knife. Her elbow was cocked, and Lucy clenched the black handle as if it were part of her body.

The blade of the knife wasn't silver anymore.

It was soaked in blood.

Lucy stood over the body of a man. He was the third person in the room. He lay back, draped across a chaise that was an exact match for the one in Frankie's office. This *was* her office, taken to a violent extreme. The man's arms and legs sprawled off the chair; his fingers and shoes grazed the floor. The gruesome, grinning mask half covered his face.

It was Darren Newman. She recognized the wild, bright colors of his clothes. He wore a bright-yellow dress shirt, but the yellow was dyed crimson where he'd been stabbed multiple times. His chest heaved. Blood seeped from his body onto the white chair and onto the white floor, dotting it with red beads. He was on his last, gagging breaths. Bile spat from his lips. His skin grayed as oxygen fled.

The Night Bird was dead. He'd lost the last game, and yet the game went on.

"Lucy," Frankie murmured. "It's okay. I'm here. You're safe."

Lucy saw her, but she didn't really *see* her. She stared down at Darren's body with a crazed disbelief.

Frankie walked across the room, moving closer to her step by step. "There's nothing to be afraid of now, Lucy. Put the knife down. Let me help you."

"No," Lucy whimpered. "No, please. Don't make me."

She got closer. And closer.

"Lucy, it's Dr. Stein. You are Lucy Hagen. Do you remember? You're okay. You went through a terrible thing, but now you're okay."

Lucy kept the knife poised in her hand. Then, slowly, horribly, she put it to her throat. Frankie walked faster, holding up her hands. They were only twenty feet apart now.

"Put it down, Lucy," Frankie told her softly. "Just kneel down and lay the knife on the floor. Nothing will happen to you."

Lucy sobbed inconsolably. "No, no, just go away. Don't come any closer. I don't want to do this."

"I know you don't, and you don't have to."

"No, you don't understand."

Frankie heard thunder on the stairs of the building. Voices shouted. Frost was almost here, and he wasn't alone. In seconds, the police would storm into the room. They'd have guns. And Lucy still had the knife pressed against her trachea. She had it pressed so hard that Frankie could see blood seeping from her skin around the edge of the blade. If she pushed any more, she'd sever her own throat.

Calm. All Frankie could focus on was calmness. She wanted Lucy's entire world to be calm.

She took another step. And another. She made her way around the far side of the chair where Darren's body lay. She wanted to draw Lucy away from the horror at her feet, and as Frankie walked, Lucy turned. She followed every step that Frankie made. It was just the two of them now, confronting each other. Lucy held the knife. Frankie held her hands up.

They were ten feet apart.

"Lucy, it's me. Do you recognize me? Do you remember me? I'm here to help you. I know you're afraid, but believe me, it's *over*. It's done. No one will hurt you anymore."

"Stay away from me."

Lucy's hand shook. She could barely hold the handle now. The knife twitched at her skin.

"Lucy, it's Dr. Stein. Give me the knife. You don't want to hurt yourself. I know you want everything to go away, but you don't have to do this. It's already over. You're already safe. Take the knife away from your throat, okay? Just let your fingers loosen, and it will fall to the ground, and it won't hurt you or anyone ever again. Okay? Listen to my voice, Lucy. Don't pay attention to anything else. The only thing you hear is the sound of my voice."

Lucy was hypnotized, but Frankie tried to take over, to break in, to snatch her away from the Night Bird. She held Lucy's eyes and didn't blink. She kept the same cadence in her words, as lulling as an ocean wave.

"My voice, Lucy. Listen to my voice."

The thunder drew closer. Footsteps pounded outside the door. She heard Frost calling now, shouting from the hallway. He called Lucy's name, but Lucy didn't hear him. She was trapped in another world, and she couldn't escape.

Frankie wanted to shout for them to stop, to stay away, to leave her alone, but she couldn't break the connection with Lucy. She didn't know what would happen when the police came in. She didn't know what the chaos would do to the girl's brain. The knife was still in her hand. It was just a small motion away from cutting her open.

"That's all you have to do, Lucy. You don't have to do anything else at all. Just listen to my voice."

Frankie took another step. Just one step. And then the hell began.

She heard a metallic click below her as she triggered some kind of electronic switch under the floor tiles. Lucy heard it, too, and terror consumed her face, as if she knew what that click meant. What it would bring. What it would do to her. The Night Bird was dead, but he still controlled the game.

Hard, loud rock music filled the room. Frankie knew the song and knew it was a sick joke. She'd been teased about it all her life.

"Frankenstein."

The entire room transformed around her. The cameras awakened automatically, and ultra-high-definition images swept the space. The white walls, white floor, and white ceiling mutated into a landscape so real that she felt as if she'd been lifted out of San Francisco and carried thousands of miles away. Cold air blew from hidden vents. The temperature dropped like a stone.

They were in the mountains, as high as God. Craggy pinnacles rose on every side toward a gray sky. Snow clung to furrows in the rock. Far below, hundreds of feet below, a glacier crawled between the hills, calving icebergs into a ribbon of sea-foam-green water. Between two peaks, a perilous footbridge sagged into the arms of the air, hanging on the thinnest of wires.

Lucy stood on that bridge, frozen with fear.

Frankie shouted. "Lucy, *it's not real.*"

But to Lucy, it was real. She was there. On the bridge. Living her nightmare.

"You!" Lucy screamed, her voice rising over the music. She stared directly at Frankie and knew exactly who she was. She'd been waiting for Francesca Stein. She'd been programmed for this exact moment. *"You did this to me!"*

"Close your eyes, Lucy. Close your eyes. We'll make it go away. Together."

The Night Bird's singsong voice chanted from overhead speakers. *"Luuuucy . . . Luuuucy."*

"Don't listen to him," Frankie called to her. "You're safe. Just close your eyes. He can't hurt you anymore."

"The knife is the key . . . set yourself free."

"No, Lucy. Close your eyes. None of this is real."

From the doorway in the corner, the police stampeded into the room. Frost. Jess Salceda. Four uniformed officers. They saw the body and the blood; they saw the knife in Lucy's hand; they drew their guns. Chaos descended. Shouts rang out. The music throbbed.

Everything began to spin out of control.

That was just what he wanted.

"You did this to me!" Lucy screamed again at Frankie. She stared down at the bridge under her feet, which looked as if it would give way when she took a single step. She swept the knife away from her throat and brandished it like a weapon with her arm held high. *"I'M GOING TO KILL YOU!"*

46

Frost saw the gun in Jess's hand, pointed at Lucy's chest. "Jess, don't shoot. Don't shoot. All of you, back off."

He knew none of them would stand down. If it had been a stranger standing there, not Lucy, his own gun would have been in his hand. They wouldn't let her out of their gunsights. Not while Lucy held the knife. Not while she was threatening Frankie. Not while there was a stabbed body in the middle of the room.

"Put down the knife right now!" Jess barked.

Lucy didn't hear her. Her eyes were locked on Frankie. Her hand quivered around the knife.

For a long, fragile moment, nobody moved. Frost sized up the room. He saw Todd Ferris in the corner, watching the events unfold from behind fixed eyes. He saw Darren Newman sprawled on the chair, his chest a sea of red. Newman wasn't moving or breathing.

Frost looked down. He felt as if he were standing on a glass platform suspended from the mountaintops, with the winter landscape below his feet. Frigid air rolled over his skin. If it felt real to him, he knew how it felt to Lucy, locked inside her trance. Lucy, with her fear of bridges.

He gestured to one of the officers. "There must be a control panel in one of the other rooms. Get out of here and find a way to shut off this damn music and turn off the cameras."

The officer glanced at Jess, who nodded. He holstered his weapon and retreated from the room.

Frost took a step toward Lucy, but Frankie lifted a hand to stop him. She shook her head, but she kept her eyes on Lucy. "Don't do it, Frost," she called. "Anything could set her off."

"Lucy," Frost called, trying to cast his voice above the pounding music. "Lucy, it's Frost."

"She can't hear you," Frankie said.

He didn't care. He needed to reach her. The guns were still trained on her heart. "Lucy, come on, let's get out of here. Shack wants to see you. You can stay at my place tonight. We can watch the city lights through the window. We can just sit there. You and me. Talking. What do you think?"

Somewhere inside her head, he knew that she had to hear him, but nothing he said reached her.

"Lucy," he pleaded again.

He thought he saw a glimmer of hesitation in her face, but then the Night Bird's voice interrupted from the speakers. The awful, singsong cadence rose over the music. It was too late. He watched Lucy's mind breaking into glass pieces.

"Can you fly? Can you fly? Will you die? Will you die?"

"Stop it," Frost hissed under his breath. "Stop it, stop it, stop it."

"It's up to you, you know what to do."

High on the imaginary bridge, Lucy shook her head back and forth, over and over. "No, don't make me. Please don't make me."

"It's up to you, you know what to do."

"Oh no. Oh no, no, no, no, no, no."

"You know what to do. You know what to do."

"I can't. I can't. No, please . . . please . . ."

"The knife is the key . . . set yourself free. The knife is the key . . ."

"Put it down," Jess called again, her low voice a warning. She knew they were running out of time. "Put the knife down right now, Ms. Hagen. Nobody wants to hurt you."

"*Luuuucy . . . the knife is the key, set yourself free.*"

Then everything happened at once.

Lucy screamed like a war cry. She pushed off her feet and charged at Frankie. Lucy was on her before the police could take action, and with the two women locked in a knot, no one could shoot. Lucy stabbed with the knife; Frankie held her arm back. They twisted, circled, and stumbled, battling hand to hand. Frankie was taller and stronger, but Lucy had a fever of adrenaline.

Frost ran. He needed to get to them now, while there was no clean shot. It wasn't far, not far at all; he could cross the distance in five seconds, but he didn't have time.

Five seconds was too long.

Lucy charged into Frankie's body, and Frankie lost her balance and tumbled backward. Frankie had nothing to break her fall, and her head cracked against the stone floor. Lucy leaped.

Three seconds, two seconds, it was still too long.

Frankie couldn't fight back, couldn't lift her splayed arms. All she could do was stare helplessly at the girl kneeling over her. Lucy clasped both hands around the black handle and hoisted the knife high over her head. Frankie's chest was below her, skin and bone and heart. Defenseless.

One second was all Lucy needed to swing the knife downward and bury it in Frankie's body, but one second was too long. One second was all Frost needed to reach Lucy and pull her away, but one second was too long.

Lucy was still there in that frozen moment, knife over her head, poised to strike.

In that second, the music went off. The screens went blank. The room fell silent. The mountains, the glacier, and the bridge disappeared. Lucy blinked, as if waking up from a dream.

Jess fired.

47

The first bullet struck Lucy in the muscles of her right shoulder. Her hand froze; the knife slipped out of her fingers and clattered to the floor. A second officer fired in the same instant. His bullet hit Lucy in the side, under her rib cage, penetrating kidney and bowel and exiting out her back and slamming into the wall.

The third officer fired and missed her head by less than an inch, but the damage was done.

She was on her knees when Frost reached her. Her eyes blinked in confusion. He eased her onto her back, and he took off his jacket and propped it under her head. He found the wound in her side and kept pressure on it to stanch the bleeding.

Lucy stared at him. "Frost?"

"I'm right here, Lucy."

"Did you get me off the bridge?"

"Yeah," he told her, giving her a smile he didn't feel. "Yeah, you're safe now. Nothing to worry about. No bridges."

"I can't move," she murmured. "It happens like that sometimes. The fear overwhelms me, and I get paralyzed. Don't worry, though, it always goes away. I'll be fine."

"You'll be fine," Frost said.

She closed her eyes. Time passed slowly as he waited for the paramedics, and all he could do was stare at her face and watch her steady breathing. Warm blood pushed between his fingers. He didn't know how many minutes had gone by when he felt a hand graze his shoulder. It was Frankie.

"Let me take over, Frost," she told him. "I'm a doctor, remember?"

"Are you okay?"

"I'm fine. I want to help."

He let her trade places with him. He got up from the floor, but he didn't go far. He stood with his arms folded tightly across his chest. The pain at the base of his neck had become needles pressing everywhere into his skull. As he waited, Jess came up next to him, close enough that her shoulder brushed his arm. They stood silently for a few seconds.

"You know I didn't have a choice," she said.

Frost didn't answer. She was right, but he couldn't bring himself to say it. Not yet. He didn't blame her. If anything, he blamed himself. History was full of bad moments that should have gone differently.

"None of this is your fault, either," Jess told him.

He still said nothing. He didn't want her to think he was being deliberately cold, but he had nothing to give. Jess got the message, and she left him alone. He watched Frankie, who looked up from Lucy and gave him a reassuring smile. It was a smile without the distance he usually felt from her.

"She'll make it," Frankie told him. "These wounds aren't fatal."

Not the bullet wounds, Frost thought. He didn't know about the wounds inside. It was cruel enough to torture a person's body, but it was even worse to torture someone's mind. There was no surgery for that. No gauze pads to press against the blood, no stitches. He began to understand the temptation of manipulating someone's memory to make the past go away. He wondered if, given the choice, Lucy would want to forget everything. Erase the last week of her life that began on the bridge with Brynn. Forget the Night Bird.

Forget Frost, too.

Then he stared at the stark white walls and thought, *This is what a blank slate looks like. This is the emptiness that's left when your memory is gone.* It didn't seem any better than the alternative.

Finally, finally, he heard sirens drawing closer.

The police officer who drove Frankie home loved to chat. She wasn't in a mood to talk, but that didn't bother him.

His name was Harmon Krug. He was one of the largest human beings that Frankie had ever met, with a chest so deep that he had trouble turning the steering wheel. He was bald, with no neck and hands that resembled baseball gloves. He slouched in his seat to avoid grazing the roof of the car with his head.

"So you're a shrink, huh?" Harmon asked, in a voice that had its own amplifier. "Messing around in people's heads, that's gotta be weird. Most of the people I meet, I don't think you'd want to take a good look under the hood, know what I mean?"

Frankie didn't answer. She closed her eyes and leaned against the cold window of the squad car, but Harmon didn't take the hint.

"I guess everybody's a freak about something. Hell, it's San Fran. People say we got more than our fair share of the weirds, right? I've got a brother who lives in North Dakota. Him and his family come out here, and they watch the pride parade, and they can't believe it. Of course, then he calls on Christmas, and he tells me they're eating *lutefisk*. You ever had lutefisk? Soak fish in lye until it's some kind of jelly? No, thanks, that's weirder than anything you'll find in the Castro District."

Frankie couldn't help but laugh. It felt good to let go of some of the stress of the past week.

"I suppose you deal with phobias and stuff," he said.

"Sometimes."

"Spiders, snakes, germs, all those?"

"All those," she said.

"Sidewalk cracks," Harmon said. "Are there really people who can't walk on sidewalk cracks? What's that about?"

Frankie sighed. "Phobias aren't rational, Harmon."

"Yeah, but sidewalk cracks?"

"Usually, it's a question of association," she explained. "Maybe you're a child who used to hide in your closet when your father came home drunk and violent. Later on in life, you find yourself experiencing intense claustrophobia. You can't be in a room where the door is closed. To your brain, those places take you right back to that closet when you were a kid."

Harmon pursed his big lips. "Huh."

Outside the squad car, they passed Union Square. She could see her office building and the dark windows on the top floor where she had her practice. A parade of patient faces passed through her mind. Not just the recent stories—Monica, Brynn, Christie, Lucy—but many of the people who had been in pain, with fears taking over their lives and making it almost impossible for them to function. She told herself that she'd helped them. She wanted to believe that, but she wasn't sure anymore.

"Almost home," Harmon said. "You're going to get wet."

The rain kept on, sheeting across the windshield of the squad car. Rivers ran through the street gutters.

"That's okay."

"Hell, we need the rain, right? All these years of drought, and we're finally getting some payback. My brother talks about the snow they get in Williston. Two, three feet at a time. No, thanks. His kids love it, though. My brother sends me pics of them out in the yard building snowmen and snow forts."

Frankie smiled at the thought of kids playing in the snow. And then, strangely, her heart raced. A heaviness weighed on her chest, and she found it difficult to breathe. It was as if she were buried in cold, white snow.

Harmon stopped at her condo on O'Farrell. A torrent separated her from the doorway of the building, but she didn't care. She needed to get inside.

"This the place?" he asked.

"This is it. Thank you for the ride, Harmon."

Frankie climbed out into the deserted street. It was very late. The police officer waited while she swiped her key card to enter the building, and then the squad car peeled away. Her heels tapped on the tile floor of the foyer, but she could hardly put one foot in front of the other. She realized how bone tired she was, but this was more than exhaustion. Her heartbeat drummed in her ears, louder and louder. Dizziness rolled over her like a wave, and she put one hand on the building wall to steady herself.

The elevator arrived, and she crossed paths with a stranger. He gave her a charming smile, which looked like the smile of a man who'd gotten lucky tonight. He was still dressed for work, with his suit coat slung over his shoulder and his crisp white dress shirt unbuttoned at the collar. Frankie got in the elevator. As the doors closed, she watched the man in the white shirt head for the street.

All she could see was his white, white shirt.

All she could feel was the heaviness of snow.

The elevator climbed.

As it reached the top floor, she watched the doors open, and then she watched them close. She rode the elevator all the way back down to the lobby, and still she couldn't move. The doors started to close again, but she blocked them with her hand, and she got out. She stood, alone, dripping, on the stone floor. She was utterly unsure what to do.

She had the same uneasy sensation that had drifted like a fog around her brain for days. *Something's wrong.*

But now she knew what it was.

48

Frost slouched in an uncomfortable chair in the hospital cafeteria, with his legs stretched out and a cup of coffee cradled in his hands. He had a vending machine hot dog on the table in front of him. It tasted like sawdust. The overhead lights had been turned down, leaving him in shadow. The restaurant was empty overnight, except for a maintenance man pushing a wet mop around the floor.

He saw Jess in the doorway. The lieutenant went to the vending machines and bought herself a package of mini donuts dusted with sugar. She joined Frost and sat on the other side of the wide table from him. She ripped open the package and popped a donut into her mouth, then licked the sticky tips of her fingers. She was small and heavy, but she had a fierce charisma.

They sat across from each other in silence. Frost finished his hot dog. Jess ate her donuts. He found himself staring into his coffee cup, rather than at her, but Jess stared directly at him and waited. Sooner or later, she knew he'd talk to her.

Eventually, he met her eyes. They knew each other well. You couldn't look at someone the same way after you'd seen them naked. It was like taking off a superhero's mask. He and Jess didn't love each other, and there were days when they didn't even like each other. They were oil and water, but it didn't matter. They would always be connected, more than most cops, more than most friends.

"You doing okay?" he asked her.

He knew he wasn't the only one who was struggling. Jess had pulled the trigger tonight. No cop did that without going through hell. It didn't matter who was on the other end of the bullet. Frost had never faced that split-second choice, or the consequences that came with it.

"Not really," she replied.

"I know you had to do it, Jess. If you didn't, Dr. Stein would have taken a knife in her chest. Lucy wasn't Lucy."

"I know that, too, but it doesn't mean I'm not going to see the girl's face when I close my eyes. She was an innocent kid, and she was a friend of yours. I'm sorry, Frost."

It took a lot for Jess to say that, and they both knew it. Jess locked up her emotions behind her badge. She had only one philosophy on the job. You do what you have to do. You make the tough choices, because no one else will.

"You talk to the doctors?" she asked.

Frost nodded. "The outlook is good, but the surgery will take several more hours."

"Keep me posted."

"I will. Her parents are on the way. I'm waiting for them."

"You want me to talk to them?" Jess asked.

"No, I'd like to do it."

"Whatever you want." She studied him up and down. "You look like you could use a doctor yourself. They should run a CT or an MRI on that thick head of yours."

Frost smiled. "Yeah. Soon."

Jess got up from the chair. She headed for the door, and his eyes followed her until she was gone. They'd said what they needed to say to each other. They'd had disagreements over the years, but they always made peace.

He lingered in the cafeteria. His headache was back, and he popped more Advil. He thought about Lucy, on the operating table, and he pictured the faces of the women in the photographs in Darren Newman's storage locker. Victims. *Lock it down,* Jess would tell him, but he felt a wave of anger at the world. That was how he'd felt when Katie died, too.

"Frost?"

He looked up in surprise. Francesca Stein was in front of him. He hadn't even heard her as she walked across the cafeteria floor.

"Dr. Stein," he said, dropping into her formal name again. She wore the same clothes she'd worn all evening. She hadn't been home. "I thought I asked an officer to take you back to your place."

"You did. I needed to see you."

He gestured at the chair that Jess had left pulled out, and Frankie sat down. She laced her long fingers together and looked uncomfortable. It was a strange look for a woman who always seemed in control of things around her.

He could read the trouble in her eyes.

"What's bothering you, Frankie?"

"I wanted to talk to you about something. I think—well, I think there's a problem."

"What kind of problem?"

She leaned back in the chair and put her palms flat on the table. Her fingers were slim and long. Even when she was wet and upset, she had a precision about every motion she made.

"Do you remember what Darren Newman was wearing tonight?" she asked.

"Orange shirt, black pants, some kind of psychedelic tie."

"That's right."

Frankie didn't say anything more. Her lips were pressed together.

"Is that supposed to mean something to me?" Frost asked her.

"I'm not sure."

Frost smiled. "Look, it's been a long night for you. Maybe you should get some sleep. We can talk things over tomorrow."

"No. I don't think this can wait. Tell me something, do you have any police officers searching Darren's house?"

"Near the Panhandle? Yes, there's a team there now."

"Are you able to reach them?" Frankie asked.

"Sure. What is it you're concerned about?"

"I was hoping they could text you a picture of Darren's living room and bedroom."

Frost cocked his head. "Why?"

"I'll explain when I see it. I could be completely wrong about all of this, but I want to be sure."

She was upset enough that he was willing to indulge her. He called the head of the forensics team and put in a request for photos from inside Newman's house. Less than ninety seconds later, his phone began to chime, and he downloaded a series of pictures of the house from multiple rooms and multiple angles. He handed his phone to Frankie, who scrolled through the photos. The more she did, the more her face darkened.

Finally, she handed him his phone again.

"Well?" Frost asked. "Do we have a problem?"

"Yes."

"Okay. What is it?"

She breathed in and out, and then she said, "When Darren first came to me, he told me a story from his childhood. He grew up in a rural area not far from Green Bay. He was an only child. When he was seven years old, he built a snow fort for himself during a Thanksgiving Day blizzard. The fort collapsed on him. He nearly suffocated and died before anyone realized what had happened. A lot of the stories he told me in therapy were lies, but that one was true. His mother showed me a newspaper article about it."

Frost shrugged. "Must have been scary for a kid, but I hope you're not saying it excuses the monster he became."

"No. No, that's not it at all. Do you know what leukophobia is?"

"I don't."

"It's a pathological aversion to the color white," Frankie said.

"That's a real thing?"

"Yes. And it can be triggered by exactly the kind of experience that Darren went through as a child. The color white becomes a symbol in the brain of the near-death experience he went through in the snow. That was all he could see as he tried to breathe. Nothing but whiteness. So the color brings back the terror."

"You think Darren Newman suffered from leukophobia?" Frost asked.

"He never talked to me about it, and I didn't catch it at the time, but yes, I think so. I never saw him wear anything except brightly colored shirts. His car? Candy red. And remember his storage locker? The door was painted green. All the other lockers had white doors, but Darren's door was green."

"That seems like a stretch," Frost said.

Frankie grabbed his phone and put it on the table in front of him. She used her finger to swipe through the photos. "These pictures were all taken inside Newman's house. Look at the walls. There's not a white wall anywhere in the house. It's either wallpaper or bright pastels. Look, you can see, even the *ceilings* aren't white. Who does that?"

Frost studied the photos. "Okay, let's assume you're right about Newman's condition. What does that mean? Why is it important?"

But he already knew what she was going to say.

"The torture chamber," Frankie told him. "*It was all white.* Don't you see? If Darren had leukophobia, he would never have painted that room white. He would never even have been able to walk inside that room. He couldn't make it past the doorway. It's impossible."

"Maybe Newman worked through his leukophobia after he saw you. It's been a year."

"No. Not based on his house. Not based on how he dressed."

Frost frowned. "You saw the pictures inside that storage locker. You know what kind of man Newman was. He wasn't an innocent victim."

"I'm not saying Darren wasn't a murderer and a sociopath, but I'm telling you what I know as a psychiatrist, Frost. If that was the room used to manipulate those women, then Darren didn't do it. He *couldn't* have done it. A man with leukophobia going into that room is as likely as Lucy Hagen voluntarily climbing the span of the Bay Bridge."

"Frankie, he was *there*," Frost pointed out. "He was wearing the mask. Lucy killed him. We both heard it happen."

Frankie shook her head. "Did we? I'm not sure about that. Maybe that's what we're supposed to think. I came into the room and saw Lucy holding a knife. Darren was dying. And Todd Ferris was just sitting in the corner, watching the whole thing. *He* could have been the one who stabbed Darren."

"Todd was drugged," Frost said.

"Are you sure? Did you run a blood test? What if *Darren* was drugged? What if *Todd* won the fight in Golden Gate Park? Todd could have called me and then put the mask on Darren while I was running into the building. He had time to stab Darren himself, put the knife in Lucy's hands, and sit down and wait for us. He would have been there to see Lucy attack me. To watch me die, just like he promised."

Frost thought about it. He replayed the timing in his head and thought about the white room as he ran inside. Frankie was right. It could all have happened that way.

"Why?" Frost asked. "Why would he do all that?"

"I don't know why, but I think Todd played me from the beginning," Frankie said. "He came to me because he wanted to understand my methods. He bugged my phone to find his targets. He told me the truth about himself, and I was too arrogant to believe him, but this has been *his* twisted scheme all along. It wasn't Darren at all. Todd Ferris is the Night Bird."

49

"Ferris is a ghost," Jess said.

The three of them stood in an empty hospital room. Frost, Frankie, and Jess. Todd had checked in for observation hours earlier, under the watch of one of the uniformed officers. He'd pretended to sleep, and when the officer at his door took two minutes to go to the restroom, he'd made a silent escape. The cop hadn't even realized that Todd was gone until Frost came looking for him.

"What does that mean?" Frankie asked. "A ghost?"

"It means there's no such person," Jess replied. "There's no one by that name in any of the state databases. The address in Pacifica that he used with you is a fake. Todd Ferris doesn't exist."

"You were right about the drugs, too," Frost added. "The hospital tested a blood sample. Todd—or whatever his name really is—had no drugs in his system. The whole thing was an act."

Frankie thought about the young man who had first come into her office. She'd sized him up as shy. Overwhelmed by the world. His eyes had a childlike dreaminess, and his stories of bullying made her feel sorry for him. She'd only caught a glimpse, every now and then, of anger. Now she realized that anger overrode every other emotion in his life, and he'd kept it carefully hidden from her.

But anger about what?

"What else did he tell you about himself?" Frost asked.

Frankie shook her head. "Does it matter? I don't know what to believe anymore. It sounds like everything he told me was a lie."

"People who lie often tuck in kernels of truth," Frost said. "Sometimes they do it unconsciously, because the truth is so familiar to them. Other times it's a taunt. Or they may find it's easier to build a fake story on top of something that's real."

She tried to remember what Todd had told her. Then and now. "He said he did freelance tech work. He mentioned some kind of tech start-up near SF State that was like an Uber for computer support. He worked for them."

"We'll check it out," Frost said. "He was a tech wizard, no doubt about that. He built an elaborate setup inside that room, and he had to have a lot of experience to pull off something like that. It must have taken him weeks of planning."

"What else?" Jess asked her. "The Night Bird is still out there, Dr. Stein, and you're our only link to him."

Frankie shook her head. "I'm sorry, I don't remember much. It was months ago."

"Why did he come to you in the first place?" she asked.

"He said he'd been bullied as a child by one of his cousins. He had a boss whose treatment at work was bringing the memories back."

"Do you think any of that was true?" Frost asked.

"Knowing what I know about him now? No. If I had to guess, he used someone else's story and pretended that it was his own. He wanted to get into my treatment room. He wanted to see exactly how I worked with people's memories. The whole thing was a way to spy on me."

"He learned his lessons," Frost said.

Yes, that was true. Todd was smart. He'd figured out exactly how to lead her down the path he wanted her to follow. How to make her play his game move by move. The unexpected meetings outside the office, designed to startle her and keep her off balance. The fake horror of his memories of torture, perfectly timed with the deaths of Brynn Lansing and Christie Parke. He fed her the clues, and she put them together.

"Todd was the one who led me to Darren Newman in the first place," Frankie recalled. "He knew I'd recognize Darren in the videos he gave me. I saw him in that men's room in the bar, and I leaped to the conclusion that Darren was stalking Todd. Which was exactly what he wanted me to believe. I never dreamed that it was the other way around. Todd was stalking Darren. He probably bumped into Darren and stole the button off his sport coat, too. So you could find it, and I could see Darren wearing the coat with the missing button. He covered all the bases."

Jess said, "Videos?"

Frost jumped in at the same time. "Todd gave you videos of places he's been over the past few weeks. This guy likes to play games. I doubt that anything you saw was in there by accident."

"Did you recognize specific places in these videos?" Jess asked. "Did he film anything in or near his apartment? Or places he'd worked?"

Frankie was tired, and her mind was slow. She'd watched the videos from Todd Ferris in a marathon fueled by wine, in the midst of an argument with Jason and her usual sparring matches with Pam. Most of what she'd seen was a blur. Restaurants. Bars. Parks. Street scenes.

"There was a choir," she said.

Jess cocked her head. "What?"

"He took video at some kind of student choral competition. It was in a performing space. I thought it was a little strange. It didn't fit with the other places he'd visited."

"Did you recognize the space?" Frost asked.

She shook her head. "No, I'd never been there."

"What else?" Jess asked.

Frankie tried to think. "A diner. He went there several times. I saw it at least three or four times in the videos on different nights."

"Nights?"

"Yes, he always went there at night. Late. One of the videos showed a clock, and the time was like two in the morning. I figured he was going there after his tech jobs."

"So it's a twenty-four-hour diner," Frost said. "Any idea where it was located?"

Frankie thought back. She'd seen the greasy spoon in the videos. He'd *wanted* her to see it. He'd *wanted* her to remember it. "Red upholstery," she said, with her eyes closed. "The guy behind the counter had a big, full beard and a lot of piercings. It was near Market, and there was a gas station and a bus stop across the street."

"I know where it is," Frost said.

"Is that a taxi driver flashback?" Jess asked him.

"Exactly right. I had a lot of four-in-the-morning meals there when I was driving. It's Orphan Andy's in the Castro." He held out a hand to Frankie. "I could go for some hotcakes. How about you?"

The diner was located on Seventeenth between a funky card shop and a tattoo parlor. The time of the night didn't matter. It was crowded. They found two seats together at the counter, under a Tiffany-style overhead lamp. Frost ordered banana hotcakes, and Frankie, who realized she was starving, ordered stuffed French toast. She watched Frost study the diner with a mixture of nostalgia and curiosity.

"It hasn't changed at all," he said. "I don't see Woody, though. I wonder if he still works here. Woody's the guy with the beard. You can't miss him."

She thought that Frost looked completely at home here. He knew what to say, whom to look at, what to order, what jokes to make. He had a way of fitting in wherever he was, and she admired that about him. She didn't move well outside her own comfort zone. That was why she usually went to the same places over and over.

Frost called over the man behind the counter, who didn't look older than nineteen. Frankie described Todd, but the waiter didn't recognize him, and she wasn't surprised. Todd blended into the background. You could stand next to him for an hour and not remember what he looked like.

"So now what?" she asked Frost.

"Now we eat," he said.

Somehow, in the midst of chaos, he knew how to be normal. He acted as if nothing strange were going on, and maybe, to him, that was true.

Their meals came fast. She ate all her French toast, which was stuffed with cream cheese and spiced apples and gave her a sugar high. Frost had three cups of coffee in the time they spent at the counter. Watching him, she remembered what she'd thought when she first met him at Zingari. He was smart. Handsome, with that off-kilter smile and eyes that wouldn't let go. Young, but with maturity in his face. She felt no raw attraction to him, and she didn't think he felt any attraction to her, but she found herself enjoying being around him. Maybe because he was outside her comfort zone.

Talking to Frost at a diner in the middle of the night, she forgot about Todd Ferris for a few brief minutes.

But the Night Bird was still alive.

"Excuse me," said a female voice behind her.

Frankie turned and found a young woman hovering by her chair at the counter. She could sense Frost's tension at the interruption. His eyes shot around the diner. Anything new, anything unexpected, was a threat.

The woman had shock-red curly hair and freckled skin. She wore a big smile with slightly crooked teeth. Her cheeks had a rosy flush, and alcohol wafted from her breath.

"Are you Frankie?" she asked.

"Yes."

"A guy outside asked me to give you this."

She extended an envelope in her hand. Frankie could see her own name written in black ink on the outside.

"Where's this guy?" Frost asked immediately, but he didn't wait for the answer. He bolted to the street. Frankie could see him on the sidewalk, scanning the late-night pedestrians in both directions. He ran across the MUNI tracks to the gas station, but he was too late. Todd was already gone.

Frankie stared at the envelope in her hand. She didn't open it. The woman with the red hair left to take a seat halfway down the counter, and she flirted loudly with the waiter. Five minutes later, Frost came back and took his seat again. His hair was mussed and wet, and he looked frustrated.

"I couldn't find him."

Frankie pushed aside the dirty plates and put the envelope down on the counter. "Should I open it?"

"That's what he wants," Frost said.

She hesitated and then tore open the flap. A greeting card was inside, but as she extracted it from the envelope, something loose fluttered to the ground. Frost bent down and retrieved it and held it up for both of them by pinching the corner with his fingers. It was a photograph, four inches by five inches.

"A choir," Frankie said with a question in her voice.

The picture showed the members of a student choir. It had to be a high school singing group, based on the ages of the kids.

"Is this the same choir, the same space, that you saw in Todd's video?" Frost asked.

She shook her head. "No."

"What about the kids? Do you recognize any of them?"

Frankie looked closely at the photograph. The group shot made the faces small, so it was hard to pick out the details. Kids all looked the same in student photos. Same smiles. Same hair. Same school uniform. Then her eyes focused on a tall boy in the back row. She recognized the feminine line of his jaw and the faraway expression. None of that had changed in the years since the picture was taken.

"That's Todd," she said, pointing with her finger.

"Are you sure?"

"Yes."

She focused so tightly on him that she didn't immediately pay attention to the pretty black girl next to Todd. Then, when she did, she couldn't take her eyes off her. The face was familiar. Not someone she knew. Not even someone she'd seen. But she recognized that same high school smile from other photographs.

"Oh my God," she murmured. "That's Merrilyn Somers."

Frost leaned closer and swore. He flipped the picture and saw what was written on the back. "The Nightingales. Reno."

"They sang together in choir," Frankie murmured.

Frost shook his head. "I'm guessing it's a lot more than that. Jess said Merrilyn was engaged to a boy from her high school. Look at the two of them. They're two kids in love."

Frankie felt a sickness all the way into her heart. "Darren murdered his fiancée. No wonder Todd did all this. He must have been insane with grief. He wanted revenge against Darren in the worst way."

"Not just Darren," Frost reminded her softly. "Against you."

Frankie remembered the card in the envelope. She slid it into her hand. The cover showed a watercolor painting of the California coast, with waves tumbling onto sand and bluffs looming over the strip of beach. She opened the card and saw one sentence written inside.

"Frankie?" Frost asked.

She couldn't tell him anything. She couldn't form the words.

"Frankie, what does it say?"

She felt as if her world had come full circle. Everything that had gone wrong in her life lay inside that card in one sentence. One sentence, burning her eyes. One sentence, meant only for her. Todd knew the truth. Todd knew everything that she'd forgotten.

Don't you want to know what happened to your father?

50

She knew where to find Todd. She knew he would be there, in the morning, waiting for her.

The rain had passed away overnight, leaving the early daylight clear and cold. Under her feet, the ground was soft. Far below her, waves thundered against the cliffs, casting up angry white spray and eating into the headlands bit by bit with each season. As she passed in and out of the trees, wind hurtled across the trail. It slapped her face until her cheeks were raw and shoved her so hard with its gusts that she could barely walk.

Her father had taken this same trail. He'd never come back.

Frankie shoved her hands deep into her jacket pockets. She was alone, but she wasn't really alone. Frost talked to her through the microphone secreted in her ear, under the protection of her fleece ear warmers.

"Any sign of him?"

"No," she murmured.

"Sorry, you're breaking up. The wind is causing interference."

"No," she repeated. "I don't see him."

Todd could be anywhere. He had miles of empty parkland in which to hide. She'd already hiked for an hour after sunrise, waiting for him to confront her, but if he was here, he was watching her silently. Even so, it was only a matter of time before he stepped from the shelter of a tree and blocked the trail.

"You don't have to do this," Frost told her again. He'd been urging her not to go to Point Reyes all night.

"Yes, I do."

Frost didn't say anything more. He and Jess were half a mile behind her on the trail. Another team of officers, dressed like ordinary hikers, scouted the land to the north. A police helicopter waited on an open hillside two miles away for an order to lift off. The trailheads had been closed; the overnight campgrounds had been evacuated. The police were laying a trap, but Todd knew perfectly well that they were coming for him.

Todd was his real name. Todd Farley, not Todd Ferris. Until last summer, he'd worked for a video production company in Reno. He was three years older than Merrilyn Somers, but the two of them had dated since she was in eighth grade. They'd sung together in the Nightingales choir at their local high school. They'd gotten engaged the summer after Todd graduated from college. They were in love the way only young people can be in love, with no dark clouds hanging over their future.

Until Darren Newman.

Todd had stayed at his job in Reno while Merrilyn went to SF State. He drove over the Sierra Nevada mountains one weekend a month to see her. They had everything planned. Money. Jobs. Children. According to their friends, Todd knew he had something special in Merrilyn. He counted the days until her graduation. He lived and died for her.

Until Darren Newman.

After Merrilyn's murder, anger filled him up. He raged against Newman. He raged against Frankie. He raged against the police who'd let it happen. Weeks later, with no note or warning, Todd disappeared from Reno. His friends and family had no idea where he went. They only knew that something had broken inside Todd's soul. He was officially a missing person, according to the Reno police, and the expectation in his hometown was that he'd gone off to a remote spot in the mountains and killed himself, because he couldn't live without Merrilyn.

But that wasn't the truth.

He'd gone to San Francisco. Todd Farley had become Todd Ferris. The Night Bird was born.

"He might not come," Frost said in her ear.

Frankie shook her head, although no one was around to see her. "He'll be here."

She struggled against the wind up the coastal trail, following the path along the jagged inlets of the headlands. Low brush clung to the cliff side twenty feet away, where the sharp wall dropped off to a ribbon of beach. Waterfalls spilled down the rocks. Huge stones made islands in the surf. Overhead, the cloudless sky stretched in a swath of azure until it met the midnight blue of the Pacific at the horizon.

Just like it had been on January 1.

She tried to remember, but all she saw in her mind was her father below her, dead eyes staring back where he'd fallen. Everything else—how they got there, what she said, what she did—was blank. Jason knew, but Jason was lying. She didn't believe him; she didn't think her father had killed himself. Something else happened. And Todd knew what it was.

He'd listened through the spy software on her phone as Frankie's memory was wiped away, like a wave erasing footprints on the sand. She had to know what he'd heard.

The trail dipped. The scrub brush of the flatlands disappeared briefly as she sank into a nest of trees. When she climbed out of it, she could see the path hugging the cliffs, with all the low vegetation shivering in the wind.

There he was.

She didn't know where he'd come from, but now he was directly ahead of her, no more than fifty yards away. His back was to her. He faced the water.

"I see him," Frankie murmured.

"Say again. You're breaking up."

"I see him."

Todd had tramped away from the trail through the brush to the fragile clifftop. Bits of wet dirt trickled away under his feet toward the beach. Blooms of California poppies dotted the land around him like orange drips of paint. He wore no coat, just a gray sweatshirt and jeans. His thinning hair blew back over his forehead. His eyes looked out into the distance of the ocean, but he knew she was there.

"Where is he?"

"At the cliff."

"Stay away from him. Let us take it from here."

"No, I can't do that," she said.

In her ear, Frost swore. She knew he was running, but they were far behind her. Frost, Jess, the police officers, the helicopters, all were minutes away. For now, she and Todd had the cliff to themselves.

She left the path and pushed through the sandy soil. The wind nearly lifted her body from the ground. The waves and the gales screamed. So did the white-and-black gulls, hovering gracefully on the currents of air beyond the cliff, as if to taunt those who couldn't fly.

Todd's head swiveled as she approached him. He stared at her with his dreamy eyes, but now she could see what was behind those eyes. Loss. Tragedy. Madness. And more than anything else, anger. Fury at the world. Fury at her.

"Fran-kie," he chanted, using the Night Bird's voice. *"Fran-kie."*

She felt an instant chill. She was conscious of the long drop beside her. In both directions, up and down the coast, she saw no one at all.

"I know who you are," she told him, raising her voice to be heard over the wind.

He shook his head. When he spoke, he used his own voice again, and she had to come closer to hear him. They were near enough that he could have sent her off the cliff with a swipe of his hand. "You don't have any idea who I am."

"You're Todd Farley. You were in love with Merrilyn Somers. I'm sorry. Really, Todd. I hate what you've done, but I'm sorry, too. I know you lost someone you loved. I know the pain you must have felt."

"Todd Farley is who I *was*," he replied. "That's not who I am anymore. I'm someone different."

She wondered if Frost could hear him talking, or if the wind drowned Todd's soft voice.

"Merrilyn would hate that," Frankie said.

"Don't pretend that you understand me, and don't you dare mention her name. *You* made me what I am now. You. Darren Newman. And the worthless police who couldn't even put him behind bars. All of you—you're the ones to blame. You can crucify me if you want, but everyone who died is because of you. You're the guilty ones."

"I'm not saying I'm innocent," she told him. "I made a mistake about Darren Newman."

"Well, we all have to pay for our mistakes," Todd said. He stared along the length of the headlands in both directions. "I imagine we have about five minutes before the police get here?"

She didn't try to lie. "Yes, they're coming. You can't get away."

"I don't care about getting away."

"I figured that," she said.

"Are they listening to us?"

Frankie nodded. "Yes."

"You know how easy it would be to throw you from this cliff, right?" he said.

"Frankie, get away. Run. Right now. Run."

She heard Frost in her ear, but she didn't move. "Is that what you want?"

Todd turned and faced the ocean again. "I told you that I wanted to watch you die, but it was supposed to be one of your patients who plunged in the knife. I thought you would appreciate the irony, having your methods turned against you. Just like I did with those other women. First I wanted to destroy you. Your career. Your reputation. And then I wanted to watch that girl kill you right in front of me. One more second, and she would have done it."

"And Darren Newman?"

Todd moved as swiftly as a cat. He spun toward her and slid both arms under hers and locked her torso against his chest. She fought, but she couldn't move. His face was an inch away. He bent to her ear and whispered in a voice that dripped malevolence. "That was all *me*. Do you really think I'd come this far and let anyone else put a blade down through that monster's flesh and bone? Do you think I wouldn't take my revenge on him myself? That I wouldn't feel his heart slice open under my hand? That I wouldn't be there to do to him what he did to Merrilyn?"

Todd let go, and she stumbled backward, taking a step away from him. She was breathing hard. She had her chance now. She could turn and run. But they both knew she wouldn't do that.

"That's not why you're here, is it, Frankie?" Todd asked.

"No."

"No, you have to know the truth. You'd risk my killing you to find out what you forgot. To get your memory back. Imagine that, *Dr. Frankenstein*. You play your little mind games with everyone else, as if there are no consequences to having part of your soul erased like a defective silicon chip. Well, now you know what it's really like, don't you?"

"Yes," she spat at him through clenched teeth.

"Tell me what you want to know. Ask me."

"What happened to my father?" Frankie asked.

"What do you think happened to him?"

She closed her eyes. The wind roared. She reached for something, anything, any fragment of reality. "He killed himself," she said.

"You know that's not true. Is that what your husband wants you to believe? You know it's a lie."

"What happened to him?" she asked again.

"You already know," Todd told her. "Somewhere deep inside, you know. That's why you wanted to forget it, but you can't, can you?"

"Tell me," she repeated.

"Your father was *murdered*," Todd told her. "He didn't fall. He didn't jump. He was pushed."

Frost stopped running. Jess stopped two steps ahead of him and looked back. "What is it? What did you hear?"

He shook his head. "Nothing. The wind keeps cutting out the mic."

She didn't believe him. "What the hell is going on out there, Frost?"

He ignored her and barked into the microphone of his headset. "*Frankie.* I know you can hear me. Get away from him right now. We're coming in from both sides. We'll have a chopper and sharpshooter overhead in seconds, but we need you out of there."

He listened. The microphone on the other end was still live. He heard Frankie through the static, but she wasn't listening to him. She was caught up in the story that Todd was telling her. It didn't matter whether it was true.

"Did I . . . ?" she murmured.

Frost shouted. "Frankie, he's lying to you. Get out of there! He's playing games with your head, and then he's going to kill you."

She didn't answer. She was under his spell.

Frost took off running again. Jess tried to keep up with him, but he was younger and faster, and adrenaline drove him forward. He widened the gap between the two of them. His shoes slipped and splashed through mud. He bolted through pockets of trees and then emerged into the full fury of the wind in his face. A slight slope rose on the hillside in front of him, and when he reached the summit, he could see the headlands spread out like a panorama.

They were there. Frankie and Todd. Two hundred yards away, down the winding path, inches from the unstable rocks of the cliff face.

Far beyond them, he saw the rest of his team running southward, trying to close the gap.

Over his head, he heard the throb of the police helicopter.

"Frankie," he shouted again. *"Run."*

"Did *I* do it?" Frankie asked, her mind flooded with confusion. "Was it me? Did I kill him?"

"Is that so hard to believe?" Todd said. "A daughter killing her father? A father who never loved her for even a minute of his life?"

"I wouldn't do something like that. Never."

"Are you sure?" Todd taunted her. "Come on, Frankie. You know what happened. You were right here. *Remember.*"

Her fists clenched. She heard voices in her head. Her father's voice, bloodless, demanding, accusing.

Question. Is it acceptable to pursue your own selfish satisfaction when it causes risk to someone else?

Question. So it's okay to risk another's life or happiness simply because you *really want something?*

And then one more. The worst one.

Question. Are you and Jason still sleeping together?

That bastard. How dare he ask something like that. As if he knew that the answer was no.

Or was it just a dream?

Frankie closed her eyes. She no longer knew what was real and what wasn't. "I don't remember anything from that weekend."

"I think you do," Todd badgered her. He was relentless, not letting go. "I heard your husband try to drive the memory out of your brain in your office, but you resisted him. You didn't want to forget what happened. He tried over and over, but the truth kept squirming back in."

"No," she whispered, trying to convince herself. "There's nothing left."

"Do you know what Jason did while you were under hypnosis? While he was trying to erase your past? He asked you about Darren Newman. He was obsessed with the two of you."

"What?"

"He made you tell him everything that happened between you and Darren," Todd said. "It was sickening, Frankie."

"There was nothing between us. I never had sex with Darren."

"Are you sure? Or do you think Jason erased that memory, too?"

"I *didn't*," she repeated, trying to convince herself. She was sure it was the truth, but suddenly, she didn't know. She didn't know *anything*. Reality slipped out of her grasp.

"You told Jason all about it, Frankie. He made you go through every detail. Every position. Every place you did it. You told him everything."

"No, those were fantasies—"

"Were they? Or did Jason simply make you think that? Did your father know what you did? Did he know that you slept with Darren Newman? Did he confront you? Is that why you pushed him off the cliff?"

"I didn't do that. I didn't. I never would."

"Then what really happened, Frankie? *Tell me.*"

"I don't know!"

"Of course you do. You remember. Think. You were so smooth when you lied to the rangers. They believed your story. They believed that your father went off on the trail by himself, and he fell. But that's a lie. You were here on the cliff with him. You know what happened. You saw everything."

"It's all blank," she said. "I don't remember anything."

"A daughter killing her father," Todd repeated. "A father who never loved her for even a minute of his life."

"That's not true. He loved me."

"Did he? Did he really love you? Well, what about *her*?"

Frankie blinked. "What?"

"What about your *sister*, Frankie? Did he love her? She was always a disappointment to him, wasn't she? Always a failure."

"What are you saying—"

"You're not the only one who lied to the rangers. Your sister lied, too. You both covered it up."

"Pam wasn't there," Frankie said.

Todd smiled at her. "Of course she was."

Frankie heard a roaring in her head. It got louder and louder. Somewhere, distantly, someone shouted. It was Frost, but she heard other shouts in her memory, too. An argument. Voices raised. Over her head, she heard the beat-beat-beat of a helicopter drawing closer, but she also heard her own voice, months earlier, screaming.

She could see them on the cliff. The two of them. Her father and her sister.

"Stop!"

She screamed it again in the here and now. Out loud. Over and over. She shouted exactly what she'd shouted at Pam. "Stop, stop, stop, what are you doing, stop!"

Todd grabbed her wrists. "Pam didn't stop, did she?"

"Oh my God."

Frost was close to the two of them. He was almost here, sprinting, calling to her. He was steps away. She could hear him in her ear, and she could hear him on the trail: "Run, get away, get away!"

Todd took Frankie's wrists and slapped them against his own chest. He had them locked tightly in his grasp, and she couldn't wriggle free. "It was just like this, wasn't it? Remember? Pam and your father were right by the edge. Right like we are now. You saw them."

Frankie heard it in her head. In her memory. Her own voice.

Pam, stop! Don't!

"You know what happened next," Todd said. "You saw what she did to him. I'm not going to let you forget. I want you to remember everything. I want you to die with the truth."

Frankie saw it in her head. The memories came back. It was a blur, and the blur became a sketch, and the sketch became a painting, and the painting became a photograph. Pam was on the cliff's edge. So was her father. They were arguing. Screaming. She didn't understand it. She'd heard it get bad between them before, but never like that. And then—

"Say it," Todd hissed.

Frankie felt Todd drag her toward the cliff. "She pushed him."

Frost stopped on the trail and drew his gun, but he had no shot. Frankie and Todd were too close together, doing battle over a few inches of ragged ground where the headland fell away toward the beach.

Overhead, the police helicopter hovered, insanely loud, wobbling in the wind toward a soft landing in the field. A sharpshooter balanced near the door, but he had no shot, either. The chopper would be on the ground in thirty seconds, but by then, it would all be over, one way or another. From the north, three other police officers sprinted toward them, but they were nearly a football field away.

Todd had Frankie by the wrists, their arms locked in a tug-of-war. She fought him step by step, digging her shoes into the mud, but the sodden earth sank into ruts under her feet. The wind shoved their bodies back and forth. Their struggle kicked up dirt that flew into the air. Below them, the ocean raged against the beach, and the rocks waited at the base of the cliff, black and sharp.

Frost holstered his gun. The land sloped downward, and he sprinted the last twenty feet separating him from Frankie and Todd. The fall loomed beside him, sucking him closer. His shoes trampled over slick green vines that dripped over the edge. He ran fast, too fast to stop.

Ahead of him, Frankie's legs buckled. Todd yanked backward, but he lost his grip on one of Frankie's wrists. Her arm came free, and she spun, leaning away from the cliff. The sudden shift in weight forced Todd to take two staggering steps forward, but he still had Frankie's other wrist in a death grip, and she had no leverage to fight back anymore. He braced himself, and he jerked her toward him. Frankie's body flew. Her eyes grew wide, and her mouth opened in a silent scream.

It was now or never.

Frost leaped with his arms outstretched. He landed full against Frankie and wrapped himself tightly around her. She toppled backward. The impact ripped her out of Todd's grasp. Frost drove her hard to the wet ground under him and instinctively rolled right, once, twice, three times. They were clear of the edge, both on their backs.

Frost reached for his gun again, but he didn't need it.

Six feet away, Todd struggled for balance. His body yawed, pushed and pulled by the wind. He danced on the edge, but he smiled, his eyes staring upward at the blue sky, his arms slowly spreading wide. One heel spilled over the edge. He was losing, and he knew it, and he didn't care.

"Close your eyes," Frost told Frankie, but she didn't.

As they watched, Todd caved backward, releasing himself into the arms of the air. His body made an *X*. Gravity took him. He flew and fell like a bird with a broken wing, and he disappeared down to the rocks without a sound. It didn't matter whether it was a cliff or a bridge. Five seconds was all it took to end a life.

Frankie scrambled out of his arms and ran to the edge. He had the wildest thought that she might throw herself after him, but instead, she simply stared down at the broken body below her. Her mouth hung open. Her eyes never blinked. He tugged gently at her shoulder, because the soft fringe of the cliff wasn't safe, but he couldn't drag her away.

Frost wondered whose body she really saw down there.

The Night Bird. Or her father.

51

She pushed him.

The truth made sense to Frankie now. She knew what she'd seen on the cliffs and why she'd been desperate to forget it.

Pam was there. Pam killed their father. It was no accident; it was no suicide. It was murder.

Frankie waited at a remote table at Zingari. She checked the time over and over, but she knew they would both be here sooner or later. She watched the windows and the street. Her stomach twisted with nervous foreboding, because she wasn't sure how she would react when she saw the two of them.

Her husband. Her sister.

The restaurant throbbed with the mellow sounds of jazz. Piano. Saxophone. Bass. A soloist in a black dress sang a siren song about love in the streets of Paris. People talked, and knives clattered. The smell of mussels and garlic wafted like a cloud as Virgil carried steaming plates through the restaurant. He looked like Adonis, with his mane of blond hair and his pressed black uniform.

Then the door opened, and there they were.

Pam glided through the crowd, her shoulders squared, her long legs on display. She owned the room, the way she always did, and her cornflower dress popped, like a glint of sky on a gray day. Jason trailed behind her. The angles of his face in the shadows made him look like a skeleton.

They slid into the two chairs across from Frankie. Virgil was right there to serve them, and Pam blew him a kiss. She looked utterly unconcerned, without a care in the world. Jason, by contrast, was a man in a cage.

"Champagne, V," Pam said lightly. "A bottle."

"Expensive?"

"Is there another kind?" she asked.

Virgil grinned and disappeared. Pam noted sparkling water in Frankie's glass with a frown. "No wine?"

"No."

"Well, if you're good, you can share my champagne."

"I don't want anything from you," Frankie snapped.

Pam leaned across the table with an exaggerated sigh. "Oh, for God's sake. I'm sure all of this was horrible for you. I'm not saying it wasn't. But you're here, and you're alive. That's worth celebrating. Or are you just disappointed that the police didn't arrest me?"

"Frost texted me. He said they let you go."

Her sister rolled her eyes. "Of course they let me go! Jason and I spent hours telling them the story over and over. Nothing this sadist told you was true. I mean, come on, you don't really believe it, do you? He wanted to torture you. He wanted to play with your head. But there's no mystery, Frankie. Dad fell. Or he jumped, I don't know, we were too far away to be sure. That's what we told the park rangers back then because that's exactly what happened. End of story."

"I'm remembering things, Pam. It's all coming back to me."

"I don't know what you think you're remembering, but it didn't happen that way. You of all people should know you can't trust your memory. Especially not after you choose to wipe it clean."

"Why would I want to forget any of this in the first place, Pam?" Frankie asked her. "Why would I want to forget that you were there, too?"

Pam shook her head. "Because you couldn't deal with it! I can't blame you for that. It was awful. We watched our father die. I'd forget it, too, if I could, but I decided one of us had to live with it. I figured one day you might change your mind and want to remember what really happened."

She was very, very good. She was as smooth as Darren Newman. And as immoral.

Virgil brought a bottle of Veuve Clicquot Brut, popped it, and poured one bubbling glass for Pam. He tipped the bottle at Frankie, who shook her head. Jason did the same. Pam drank one glass before Virgil left, and he poured another one for her. The crystal reflected the pale blue of her nail polish.

"Damn, that's good," Pam said.

Frankie stared at Jason, who was silent, with his jaw as hard as stone. His dark face was haunted; he knew that she'd figured it out. All of it. The truth, not the cover story. She wanted to see guilt in his face, but his arrogance told her that he didn't really care. Things had already gone too far, and he was immune to her cold eyes. She was angry at him, but she didn't feel blameless herself. She'd always let her patients come first. She'd shut him out time after time. And there had been something, real or not, between her and Darren Newman.

"Do you have anything to say?" she asked him.

This time, just for a moment, he looked at her. An understanding passed between them. Welcome to the end of days.

"I never wanted this to happen."

He was deliberately vague. Maybe he was apologizing, and maybe he was just blaming her. It didn't matter. They both knew it was coming, and they both knew it was over. Seven years together had left them strangers. She couldn't even feel sad about what she was losing. The only thing she felt was emptiness at what had been done to her.

"Leave us alone," Frankie told him.

He reached out toward her hand, but he drew it back without touching her. He didn't need to say that once he left, he was gone for good. He got up and walked away from the table without a word, and then it was just the two of them. Two sisters. Connected by blood. Pam sipped her champagne, displaying no more than idle curiosity about what came next.

"You must think I'm stupid," Frankie told her. "I suppose I have been stupid. I missed all the signs. Or maybe I just didn't want to see them."

"Signs?" Pam asked with mock innocence.

"Don't pretend. We're way past that, Pam. I knew you resented me, but I never knew how deep it went. Or how far you would go."

"Is that all you have? Paranoia? Insults? You're boring me, Sis."

Frankie didn't stop. She simply went on. "I've been wondering all day what this was really about. Why you did it. I mean, I know you hated Dad, but even for you—to kill him? To push him off a cliff? The sister I know would laugh, or swear at him, but she'd never lose control. No, there had to be something else. Something that drove *you* over the edge."

"I'm not going to sit here and listen to this nonsense," Pam said, but she made no attempt to leave.

"Don't worry. I'm not wearing a wire. This is just us. You and me."

"Well, how sweet."

"I really couldn't figure it out," Frankie said, "but then I remembered something you said. You reminded me that all of those New Year's weekend discussions were just an excuse for Dad to tell you what you were doing wrong with your life. And you're right. He did that all the time. Why would this year be any different? The thing is, I've been remembering his infuriating questions for days. They were about *risk* this year. About my doing something terrible that put someone else in jeopardy. I didn't understand, because I kept thinking I was the only one there. What did I do that he disapproved of? Who was I putting at risk? But it wasn't me. He wasn't asking me any of those questions. It was *you*."

Virgil came to the table again and poured more champagne. Frankie waited. Bitterness brewed in Pam's eyes, but she smiled as if nothing were wrong.

"Question," Frankie said when they were alone again. "Is it acceptable to pursue your own selfish satisfaction when it causes risk to someone else?"

"Go screw yourself, Sister."

"Question," Frankie said. "So it's okay to risk another's life or happiness simply because *you* really want something?"

Pam's pretty face was a mask of hatred. She lifted her champagne glass. "Is that all? Are you done?"

"No, there was another question," Frankie went on. "Back then, I couldn't be sure I heard it right. I figured I was wrong. He couldn't have said something like that, not to you. But I wasn't wrong, was I? I heard exactly what he asked you."

"Oh? And what was that?"

"Question," Frankie interrogated her, leaning across the table and grabbing Pam's wrist. *"Are you and Jason still sleeping together?"*

Pam hesitated only a moment, then freed herself and took another drink of champagne. She spoke without a hint of shame in her voice. She was nonchalant. Casual. As if they were talking about the weather.

"Yes."

Frankie closed her eyes. She'd known what the answer would be, but she still had to wait for the breath to come back into her chest. "How long?"

Pam shrugged. "Since last fall. And don't climb on your moral high horse with me. I know about you and Darren Newman."

"Nothing happened between us. I never touched him."

"No? You just fantasized about him. A murderer. A rapist. Do you feel good about yourself?"

"Shut up," Frankie snapped.

"Face it, you wanted Darren more than your own husband."

"Do you think that gives you the right to sleep with him?"

"I don't ask you for permission for anything I do," Pam retorted.

"My God, what a heartless bitch you are. Are you in love with him?"

"Oh, please."

"Is he in love with you?"

"Grow up, Frankie. Why are you so concerned about love? Did you have a different father than I did? Neither one of us knows what love is."

"So why did you do it? Spite? Revenge?"

"Don't flatter yourself," Pam said. "Yes, I'll admit, I loved the idea of humiliating you. Every time I heard another of your success stories, I wanted to say, 'Oh, really? Well, I'm sleeping with your husband.' But I don't overanalyze everything, Frankie, not like you. I wanted it. He wanted it. So it happened."

"Dad found out?"

Pam sighed. "Yes, our interfering father. He saw me and Jason outside the building when he came to visit. We were kissing. This was right before Christmas. Of course, he was full of righteous indignation. He swore to me that he would tell you about the affair if I didn't stop. When we were hiking that morning by the ocean, he wouldn't let it go. He kept lecturing me about ruining my sister's life. I didn't care about that, to be honest, but he said he would cut me out of his will, too, and I knew he was serious. I wasn't going to let that happen."

Frankie could see them on the cliff's edge. Arguing.

She could see Pam's hands on his chest.

She could see him fall.

"You saw us," Pam went on. "You'd gotten ahead of us, but you turned back while we were arguing, and you saw us. I begged you to forget it. I said it was an accident, that I got angry over all those years of emotional abuse, that I didn't know what the hell I was doing. You believed me. You may be a psychiatrist, but you fell for my poor, poor pitiful me act. So you asked Jason to wipe it all away."

Frankie stood up from the table. Her legs barely supported her, but she didn't want her sister to see her trembling.

"I want you out," Frankie told Pam. "You have twenty-four hours to get everything out of my place. Take Jason with you. I never want to see either of you again."

Pam raised her glass in a toast and picked up a menu. "Whatever you say."

Frankie wanted to do something. Slap her. Hit her. Throw the champagne in her face. But she didn't. She stalked from the restaurant onto the street, and when she was on her own, beyond the view of the windows, she finally broke down. Tears welled up and poured from her eyes. She fell against the wall and beat her fists against the stone. People stopped and offered help, and she waved them away. She wailed, even though she didn't even know what she was crying for. In the end, she felt nothing. She was dead inside.

A text tone sounded on her phone. She wondered if it was Jason. Or Pam. What could they say to her now?

Instead, it was from Frost Easton.

```
I'm here.
```

Frankie composed herself. She wiped her face as best she could and hugged herself against the chill as she headed toward Union Square. It was dark. The lights of the city didn't lift her heart. The shadows felt ominous, and the mounds of the homeless under blankets in the door-ways depressed her. Right now, she wanted to be anywhere but here. She wanted to leave the city and never look back.

She found Frost waiting for her on a bench in the park. It was their prearranged meeting place. He could read her face, and he seemed to understand that her world was falling to the ground brick by brick. She liked his empathy. She liked the worry that she saw in his eyes.

"That didn't take long," Frost said.

"No, it didn't."

They were silent for a while. He knew she needed time. Frankie felt another tear slip from her eye, and she quickly wiped it away.

"Did she say anything?" Frost asked finally. "Did she admit it?"

Frankie took a breath, deciding what to tell him. She had to choose whether to acknowledge to the world what her sister had said. What she'd done. And why.

"No, she didn't," Frankie said.

"She stuck to her story? Even with you?"

"I'm sorry, Frost. She didn't say a word."

He pursed his lips and studied her face as if she were wearing a mask. She didn't think he believed her, but he seemed to understand there were places she couldn't go. She owed Pam nothing, but still she couldn't do it. She couldn't turn her in.

"I think she's guilty, but I can't prove anything without a confession," Frost told her. "Your father is dead, and your memory—"

"Is gone," Frankie said. "I understand. She's going to get away with it. There's nothing I can do about that."

It was the end. The journey stopped here.

"So how are you?" Frost asked.

Frankie stared at the park. She'd spent so many days here. Day after day that melded into years. "Free," she said. "And alone. I've cut the cord with both of them. Permanently."

"I can't blame you for that, but maybe with time, you'll feel differently."

She shook her head. "No, I don't think so. There are some things that you can never forget. And yes, I hear the irony of that, coming from me."

Frost stood up from the bench. "Well, I have to go see Lucy."

"I know she won't want to see me, but if I can help—"

"I'll make the offer."

He began to walk away, but she called after him. "I haven't had a chance to talk to you alone before now, Frost. I wanted to thank you."

"For what?"

"For saving my life on the cliff," she said.

He came back and sat down next to her. "I'm glad I was there."

"A small part of me wishes you'd been too late."

"I don't believe that," he said.

"I said it was a small part. I'm just feeling sorry for myself. And I'm a little scared, too. I'm used to having my future planned out, and now I don't know what I'm going to do."

Frost smiled. "Planning is overrated."

"Not for me. I'm my father's daughter. Tell me something, have you ever been to Copenhagen?"

His face furrowed with confusion. "No. Why?"

"I've had a standing offer for a couple years at a university in Copenhagen. To teach."

"And now you're thinking about it?" he asked.

"I don't know what I'm thinking about," she admitted. "I only know that I can't continue my life the way it was. I won't put any more lies in people's heads. Never again."

"That doesn't mean you have to run away. You can help people *live* with their past instead of changing it. Is that so bad?"

"No. You're right, it's not so bad."

He stood up again, but he put a hand on her shoulder. "I guess you've earned a change if you want one. Teaching in Copenhagen would be a change, but for what it's worth, I hope you stay."

"Really? Why is that?"

"Because San Francisco deserves the best," Frost said. "We already have the best views, the best food, the best anything. We need the best people, too."

She smiled. "That's very sweet of you."

"It's the truth, Frankie."

He headed across the park, and she watched him go. She realized that he had something that she didn't. Frost Easton was grounded. He knew who he was and where he was, and she couldn't say the same about herself anymore.

Frankie didn't move from the bench. For the first time in a long time, she had nowhere to go and nothing to do. Her life was a white room. She felt like one of her patients who came out of her treatments and suddenly had an emptiness in their brain where something horrible had been. They'd faced their fears, but they always asked her what to do next.

She told them: the hardest part is to start over by building something new.

52

Frost found Lucy awake in her hospital bed.

Her parents sat on either side, each holding one of her hands like protective parents. They didn't look happy to see him. He was the one who'd put their girl in jeopardy. He was a symbol of everything perilous about the city. Here she was, wounded twice, hooked to an IV, skin almost white. They shot him daggers and wished he would go away.

"It's okay," Lucy told her parents when they lingered and refused to leave. Her voice was weak but firm. "Go get some coffee or something. I want to talk to Frost."

They stood up reluctantly, as if nothing good could happen if they left her alone with him.

"Ten minutes," her father said. "No more."

They passed Frost without shaking hands. Lucy's mother closed the door behind them. The room was warm, and the silence was punctuated by the electronic blips that tracked Lucy's heart rate, oxygen, and blood pressure. Frost had a big box in his arms, and he sat down in a chair beside her bed with the box in his lap.

Lucy gave him a puzzled smile. "Flowers?"

"A secret visitor," Frost said. He put his index finger over his lips. "Shhh."

He undid one of the flaps on the box, and a black-and-white head popped over the side.

"Shack!" Lucy exclaimed happily. The cat looked happy to see her, too. He squeaked with excitement.

Frost scooped him out of the box. He held the cat close to Lucy's face, and Shack licked her cheek with his sandpaper tongue, making her giggle. She rubbed his head and scratched under his chin and nuzzled him with her nose. He could hear Shack's loud purr. He let her fuss over him silently for several minutes, and then he slipped the cat back inside the box.

They stared at each other, and it was awkward between them. He didn't know how to measure the water that had gone under the bridge.

"Hey," he said.

"Hey, you. Thanks for coming. Thanks for bringing Shack. You both cheer me up."

"You're going to be fine," Frost said.

"That's what they tell me. It's going to take a while, I guess. Inside and out."

"Yeah."

More silence took over. Shack scratched at the box.

"You didn't do it, Lucy," Frost told her. "I wasn't sure if you'd heard. It wasn't you. You didn't hurt anyone."

"I know. My parents talked to your lieutenant. She said Dr. Stein gave a statement. The guy admitted it."

Frost nodded. "Do you remember anything?"

"No. It's like I lost everything from the last couple days. I guess that's good, huh? The last thing I remember—"

He waited.

"The last thing I remember is you and me," she said. "On the hillside. You holding me. You made me feel safe."

"I'm glad."

"I'm not sure I'll ever feel that way again. Not here. Not after everything that's happened."

"Lucy—" he began, but she jumped in to stop him. She had more to say.

"So I'm moving back to Modesto when I get out of here. My parents think I should live with them for a while. You know, while I get back on my feet. I figured it was a pretty good idea. I thought you should know."

"Yeah, I get it," Frost said. "If that's what you want."

"I've thought about it a lot. I'm not made for the city, like you."

"Well, the city will miss you. So will Shack. So will I."

"Yeah, me, too. It's pretty far away, but there are no bridges out there. I need some time without any bridges, you know?"

"I know."

There wasn't much more to say than that. He'd come here to say good-bye, and she'd already done that for him. He stood up and put the box on the floor. He took her hand and squeezed it, and she squeezed back, and then he bent down and kissed her lightly on the lips. She closed her eyes, as if she were trying to memorize how it felt. He stroked her hair and kissed her forehead, too.

"Bye, Lucy."

"Bye."

He carried Shack's box out of the room. Lucy's parents were there, and they looked relieved to see him go.

Outside the hospital, Frost drove through the darkness back to his Russian Hill house. The hill always felt like it was on top of the world, as if he could roll a marble down and watch it bounce all the way to the bay. He was tired, and he felt something he hadn't felt in a long time. He was lonely. He was often alone, but rarely lonely. But tonight was one of those nights. When he stared at the house, it felt big and empty, not like home at all.

He carried Shack inside, but when he opened the door, he smelled the spicy aroma of chicken parmigiana, and he heard male voices from the living room. He wasn't alone anymore. He had family.

His brother was there.

Herb was there, too.

"Sierra Nevada?" Herb called, hoisting a wet bottle from a cooler on the floor.

"You read my mind," Frost said. He was suddenly wide awake.

His brother stood up and grabbed bowls of hummus and olives. "Dinner will be ready in a few minutes," Duane said. "Come on, let's sit outside."

The three of them headed for the patio. Herb brought the cooler. Shack jumped on the glass table and closed his eyes against the breeze. Down the hill, San Francisco spread out in a million lights below them, and fog clung to the distance. They clinked bottles, they drank, and Herb began telling old stories from his days in the Summer of Love. Soon they forgot all about dinner, and they hung around on the wrought-iron chairs with their feet propped on the railing, laughing and getting very loud until the night was mostly gone.

FROM THE AUTHOR

Thanks for reading my newest thriller.

You can write to me with your feedback at brian@bfreemanbooks.com. I love to get e-mails from readers around the world. Visit my website at www.bfreemanbooks.com to join my mailing list, get book club discussion questions, read bonus content, and find out more about my books.

You can "like" my official fan page on Facebook at www.facebook.com/bfreemanfans or follow me on Twitter or Instagram using the handle bfreemanbooks. For a look at the fun side of the author's life, you can also "like" the Facebook page of my wife, Marcia, at www.facebook.com/theauthorswife.

Finally, if you enjoy my books, please post your reviews online at Goodreads, Amazon, and other sites for book lovers—and spread the word to your reader friends. Thanks!

ACKNOWLEDGMENTS

Getting a book in your hands requires a lot of work from many talented people.

It's been a privilege to work with the entire team at Thomas & Mercer on *The Night Bird*. Jacque Ben-Zekry did an amazing job leading the project, from the earliest editorial concepts through all the design and marketing plans. Charlotte Herscher provided great insights on editorial issues. Kjersti Egerdahl and Alan Turkus were instrumental in bringing the book to Thomas & Mercer. I'm grateful to all of them for all their faith, support, and effort on my behalf—and to the whole Thomas & Mercer staff for getting behind this book.

My agent, Deborah Schneider, makes all of this possible on the business side, along with her terrific team—Cathy, Victoria, and Penelope.

When I finish the first draft of a novel, I get feedback from advance readers before the book goes to my publishers. My wife, Marcia, is the best (and toughest) editor an author could hope for. A big thanks to her and to Ann Sullivan for their helpful and thoughtful feedback on the draft of *The Night Bird*.

Of course, Marcia is not only my first editor, but more importantly, she has been my best friend and partner for more than three decades. She gets the first two words in every book, and she always will.

On a sad note, I lost my dad while I was in the midst of writing *The Night Bird*. For ninety years, he had the secret of life figured out: smile and laugh often, cherish your spouse, turn strangers into friends, and devote yourself to the things that make you happy and proud. He may not be with me now, but I'm still learning from him every day. I miss you, Dad.

ABOUT THE AUTHOR

Photo by Martin Hoffsten

Brian Freeman is a bestselling author of psychological thrillers, including the Jonathan Stride and Cab Bolton series. His works have been sold in forty-six countries and translated into twenty languages. His book *Spilled Blood* was named Best Hardcover Novel in the International Thriller Writers Awards, and *The Burying Place* was a finalist for the same honor. His debut thriller, *Immoral*, won the Macavity Award and was a finalist for the Edgar, Dagger, Anthony, and Barry awards for Best First Novel. It was also chosen as International Book of the Month by book clubs around the world. His novels *Season of Fear* and *The Bone House* were both finalists for the Audie Award in the thriller/suspense category.

Brian lives in Minnesota with his wife, Marcia. For more information on the author and his work, visit www.bfreemanbooks.com.